# Also by Stephanie Alves

## Standalone

Love Me or Hate Me

## Campus Games Series

Never Have I Ever (Book #1)
Spin The Bottle (Book #2)
Would You Rather (Book #3)

For all the girls who just want to be loved, spoiled, and treated like a princess.

# WOULD YOU

# RATHER

CAMPUS GAMES BOOK #3

STEPHANIE ALVES

This book contains detailed sexual content, graphic
language and some other heavy topics.
You can see the full list of content warnings on my website
here: stephaniealvesauthor.com

Happy Reading!

# Playlist

WOULD YOU RATHER - Stephanie Alves

**HRS & HRS** - Muni Long ♥

**NEEDY** - Ariana Grande ♥

**THAT'S YOU** - Lucky Daye ♥

**SNOOZE** - Sza ♥

**DIE FOR YOU** - The Weeknd ♥

**I'M YOURS** - Isabel LaRosa ♥

**SAFETY NET** - Ariana Grande ft Ty Dolla $ign ♥

**HOTEL** - Montell Fish ♥

**EVERYTHING** - Kehlani ♥

**MAKE YOU MINE** - Giveon ♥

**WORTH IT** - Raye ♥

**DO I WANNA KNOW?** - Arctic Monkeys ♥

**ALL I NEED** - Lloyd ♥

**PROPOSTA** - Matheus Caettano, Pedro Stone, DJ Cash ♥

# 1

Lights go out

## Madeline

"Popcorn or Ice cream?"

"Death."

My roommate, Gabi, laughs on the other end, and I squeeze my phone in my hand. "That bad?" she asks.

"It bit," I reply, adjusting the phone onto my shoulder so I can open the door. I haven't even left the building yet, and I'm already dying to go home. I just want to crawl into bed and forget all about this day. "They didn't even look at me."

*Thanks for coming in.*

The fake smiles plastered on their faces were the last thing I saw before I left with another rejection and the only thing I'd see in my nightmares.

I've heard those four words so many times that I might as well get it tattooed on me. Day after day, audition after audition, it always ends in the same way.

A smile, a thanks, and a big, fat rejection.

"Maybe my parents are right," I mumble, pushing through another door. My eyes briefly drift to the staircase where a group of people are descending. I shake my head, knowing there's no way I'm tackling twelve flights of stairs in heels.

Her gasp rings so loud that, despite the rough day I've had, I can't help but let out a laugh. She's nothing if not a drama queen. "Madeline Davis." I lift my brows at the use of my full name. *Oh boy*. "You did not just say that," she replies, and I can practically visualize her disapproving headshake.

"This is my third audition this week, Gabi. I can't keep going through this. It always ends the same way."

"Not with that attitude," Gabi retorts. She clears her throat and continues, "Repeat after me. I am smart."

I roll my eyes, letting out a sigh. She does this sometimes— makes me repeat positive affirmations, and as much as I love her for it, I don't feel very positive at the moment. "Gabi—"

"I am smart," she repeats.

I let out a breath, knowing she won't drop it. "I am smart," I parrot back to her.

"I am talented."

My lips press together. I like to think I am. I've loved acting ever since I was a child, and my sister and I used to put on little productions for our parents. I watched movies constantly, kept posters, and even studied scripts. But if I was talented, wouldn't I have landed an audition by now? Even a small one? "I am talented," I recite, having a hard time believing the words coming out of my mouth.

"I am more important than a stupid audition," Gabi says, making me smile.

"I am more important than a stupid audition," I repeat.

"And my best friend Gabi should kick their asses for not hiring me."

They didn't exactly *not* hire me, but with the way they hardly paid attention, I know I don't have a chance in hell at a callback. I let out a laugh all the same, passing a few people on this floor. Where the hell is this damn elevator?

2

"And my best friend Gabi should kick their stuffy asses for not even looking at me when I was pouring my heart and soul into a stinking perfume commercial."

Her laugh radiates through the phone. "That's my girl. I like the improvising."

"Thanks for that," I tell her, feeling a little better than I did a few minutes ago. "I can't wait to go home. Where are you?"

"I'm heading out of class right now," she says and then lets out a yelp. "Oh fuck."

"What?"

"It's raining." I shift my gaze to the windows, seeing the rain hitting the glass. "Hard."

"Great." I sigh, frustration building as I wonder how this day can get any worse. Not only did I not get the audition, but now I'm going to ruin my meticulously styled hair and carefully chosen outfit. "How far are you?" I ask her.

"I sh... home..."

"Ugh, you're breaking up," I sigh, knowing the bad signal will make it even harder to get a cab.

"I should be home in five," she says again, her voice sounding slightly breathless, most likely from her running from the rain. "Want me to put on 'Step Up' when you get here?"

I can't help but smirk. "That's your favorite movie, not mine."

"Come on," she says. "Channing Tatum can turn any bad day around."

I scrunch my nose in disagreement as I round the corner, and I spot the elevator. Finally. "Not really my type."

She lets out another dramatic gasp. "Blasphemy!"

I shake my head, my lips curling in a smile. "Fine," I relent. "I'll be there in ten. Hopefully."

3

"Kay," she says, letting out a grunt. "Fuck, I'm drenched."

"Take a cab," I instruct her, not wanting her to get sick.

"No point," she says. "I'm nearly home."

"So stubborn," I mutter, shaking my head. "Make sure you take a shower when you get home. You're going to be freezing."

"Fine, *Mom*." Her little remark makes me laugh. "But you didn't answer my question. Popcorn or ice cream?" she asks again. "Death isn't an option, I'm afraid."

A scoff escapes my lips. "Popcorn."

"Good choice."

She hangs up the call, and I shove my phone back into my bag, heading into the elevator. It's empty, and I let out a breath of relief. Fewer stops means I'll get out of here quicker.

Gabi was right. I am more important than a stupid audition. If they don't want me to be the face of their perfume ad, which probably smells like cheap granny flowers anyway, then I don't want any part of it, either.

This shouldn't affect my career choice or make me question my talent. My parents might not be on board with the idea of me becoming an actress, but I'm not giving up. Not until it all crashes and burns, and I know I gave it my all.

The doors start to close, but before they do, a deep voice shouts. "Wait up." I peek out of the elevator and place my foot between the doors, stopping them from closing. I look down at my white heels, a smudge mark on the side. Fuck, I'm going to have to clean those.

The doors open again, and a guy jogs into the elevator, blowing out a breath once he's inside. He runs a hand through his wavy brown hair and glances at me. "Thank you," he breathes out.

I let my eyes travel down his face, his stubbly beard catching my attention more than I'd like to admit. There's something about a beard that's so damn attractive, even if it's a stubble like his. I press my lips together in a smile and face forward, staring at my reflection in the elevator doors.

I stand there, quietly observing as the guy leans against the wall, his arms crossed. Our eyes connect in the reflection of the elevator doors, his gaze fixed on me. I watch as his eyes roam over my form before he releases a sigh, staring back at his own reflection.

I look away and focus on getting out of here. I might have joked about Gabi's movie choice of the night, but maybe a cheesy rom-com and a big bowl of buttery popcorn are exactly what I need to help me forget about how my dreams are slowly slipping through my fingertips.

Ten more minutes, I think to myself. Ten more minutes, and I'll be able to relax.

And that's when the elevator stops, and the lights go out.

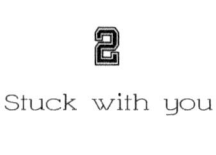

# 2

Stuck with you

## *Lucas*

What was he thinking?

That asshole better have a good excuse for why he decided that trying to take a shower on his own was a good idea. He's heard the doctor's orders, and even though he might have joked, I never once thought he might do this.

He knows it was stupid as fuck, and now it's landed him in hospital.

My phone rings in my pocket, and I let out a curse when I see Ana's name on the screen. My agent is good at her job, one of the best, but when I see her text, my jaw ticks with annoyance.

Ana:

> We weren't finished. That isn't a
> way to leave a meeting. Be a little
> more professional next time.

Professional? How the fuck could I stay another second in that room when I got a call from the hospital? I couldn't. Didn't even care what they were saying. It's all the same shit, anyway.

*We need something different. Something new.*

*People are bored, Lucas. Our current strategy is no longer working.*

*You don't want to be irrelevant, do you?*

Fuck that. I didn't even want to be part of that perfume commercial. I couldn't stay in that room a second longer, hearing how everything I worked so hard for was no longer good enough. That *I'm* no longer good enough. As soon as I got that call, her voice drowned out, and I raced out of there.

James has been my best friend for the better part of my life, so leaving to check up on him was a no-brainer. I just hope they didn't call my mom. That poor woman would jump over hoops to be at the hospital.

Heavy pelts hit the glass, and I turn my head to see rain pouring down over the city, droplets hitting the glass. "Great," I mutter with a sigh. This will make it ten times harder to find a cab.

I stuff my phone in my pocket, ignoring the rush of texts my agent keeps sending, and lift my head just in time to see the elevator doors about to close. "Wait up," I call out to whoever is inside.

A slim, white heel props itself between the doors, opening them back up. My eyes drift up to see a girl standing there, with her foot in front of her. She moves back when she sees me about to enter, and I let out a breath, jogging inside. "Thank you," I tell her. She presses her lips together in a smile and faces forward, staring at her reflection. Or is she looking at me?

She didn't seem to know who I was, or maybe she was faking. It's not the first time someone's tried to get my attention that way. I've been in the eyes of the public for so long that it doesn't surprise me. People are fake. They lie and cheat and do whatever they need to for fame and money.

7

I lean against the back of the elevator and cross my arms, looking at her. I let my eyes drift down her body, taking in her outfit. It's the middle of the day, during a rainstorm, and this girl is in a dress. A mid-length, dark red dress that brings out the warm brown tones of her deep skin color.

I rub my chin, and I feel my lips turning up in a smirk. Really hope she's not a crazed fan or, worse, a pap. Lord knows it's not the first time I got tricked by the paparazzi before, ambushing me when I least expect it. They have no limits when it comes to taking pictures to get the story they want to tell, even if it isn't true.

I glance up at her again, meeting her eyes in her reflection. She isn't looking at me, though. She's just staring back at herself. Does she really not know who I am, or is she just playing me? I hope it's the former. It's kind of relaxing.

Of course, that's before the lights go out and the elevator grinds to a halt.

"What the hell?" I step forward, trying not to panic as the whole room fills with complete darkness. There was probably a blackout because of the rain, I'm sure it will start moving again in no time.

But the girl next to me doesn't seem to think the same. Her panicked voice startles me. "No," she cries out, banging on the doors. I blink, trying to adjust my eyes to the dark, but it's no use. "No," she yells again. Oh hell, what a way to stay calm.

"Hey," I try to coax her, approaching wherever she is. It's only me and her in this dingy elevator, and she might think I'm a murderer or something. And by the sound of her screaming, she'd be able to convince anyone of it. "Calm down. Everything's going to be fine."

"Don't tell me to calm down!" she shouts back.

My eyebrows raise. "I'm just trying to help you," I tell her. "These things have generators. You don't need to panic. It's probably going to kick in anytime now."

"How do you know that?" she asks, her voice cracking. "What if it doesn't?" I hear her sniffling and then drop to the floor.

I let out a sigh, feeling a little bad. It's a shitty situation to be in, especially with a stranger. I pull my phone out of my pocket and turn on the flash. "We'll have to make do with what we've got until it comes back on," I tell her, trying to adjust my eyes to the dark room with only the flash as an aid. I spot a small figure curled up in a ball on the ground, her face buried in her hands.

I lift myself off the ground and point the flash to the wall, looking for the emergency phone. My fingers reach for it, pressing it and waiting for someone to pick up. It rings, and rings, and rings. "Hello?" I call into the intercom, but there's no response.

"I can't do this again," the girl says to herself. "Not again." She cries out again, and as much as I want to comfort her and help her out, I don't fucking know what to do.

"You're seriously not helping." I turn around, pointing the flash to her. "We have some light for now, and the power will come back on soon. Just relax."

"Relax?" she repeats, lifting her head to look at me. Tears stream down her scowling face. "How can I relax when I'm stuck in an elevator twelve stories from the ground with a stranger."

I narrow my eyes at her. "The first rule of these things is to remain calm, and you're not doing that. You panicking is not helping, so please, just stop crying. I'm trying to help us here."

"What are you doing to help?" she asks. "Have you called someone yet?"

I glare down at her. "Yes. The intercoms don't work."

"No," she says, shaking her head. "I mean on your phone."

Fuck. My brows furrow. Why didn't I think of that? "I was just about to," I lie, searching for my mom's name. The line beeps a few times, and then the call ends. "Fuck. No signal. The blackout must have interfered with the power lines."

The girl starts crying again, and I turn around, the sight of her crying and shaking her head in absolute agony. It stabs at my chest, so I let out a sigh and crouch down to her level. "Hey," I say, approaching her. "What's your name?" I reach out my hand and place it on her arm.

Oh fuck. Wrong move. She sucks in a breath and flinches away from me. "Don't touch me." Her voice cracks, and I take a step back from her.

"Okay, okay." I hold my hands up. "I'm not going to touch you, okay? Just open your eyes and look at me. Can you do that?"

She shakes her head and squeezes her eyes even tighter. Her breathing has become erratic as small hiccups escape her. Jesus, I need to calm her down.

"What's your name?" I ask her again, using a gentler tone this time. She doesn't reply; she just keeps crying. "My name's Lucas. What's yours?"

She looks up at me, her eyes glassy as tears stream down her face. At least it's a start. "Mad-e-line." It comes out choppy and mixed with hiccups, but at least she said it.

I give her a smile, wanting to make her feel comfortable and, most importantly—calm. "That's a nice name," I tell her.

10

"Okay, Madeline. I need you to breathe for me. Can you do that?"

She narrows her eyes. "Why are you speaking to me like a child?"

I press my lips together in amusement. This girl is not easy to work with, is she? "Hey, you're making jokes."

She lets out a breath, but it still sounds choppy. I shake my head. "Breathe, Madeline," I tell her. I inhale deeply, wanting her to do the same. "Come on. Just breathe."

She glances at me and imitates me by inhaling deeply and then lets out a breath. I drop to my ass, sitting back against the wall, and run my hand through my hair. Fuck my life. I need to be at the hospital right now.

"Are you scared of heights or something?" I ask her.

She shakes her head. Huh. I wonder why she's freaking out then. I don't have much time to think about it because the lights turn back on, making my eyes widen.

"Hey." I glance toward her, seeing more of her now that we're not in the dark. "See? I told you it would come back on soon."

When the elevator starts moving, I grin, lifting myself off the floor. She doesn't move, though, still in the same position, and I hear her soft cries. Fuck, I've never been good with tears, and hers are like a shot through the heart.

The elevator dings when we reach the ground floor, and the doors open up. "Oh, thank goodness." I lift my eyes to see an older woman letting out a breath. She clutches her jacket and shakes her head. "I tried getting help. I saw the elevator was stuck."

"Thank you," I tell the woman, noting the repair guy beside her.

11

She smiles back, but then a frown appears as her eyes drop to the ground, where Madeline is still sitting. "Is she okay?" the lady asks.

Fuck knows. "She's fine," I reply, heading back into the elevator. "Madeline," I call out for her. "The doors are open now. You're all good."

She doesn't move from the spot on the floor, and my brows furrow. Murmurs sound behind me, and I glance outside to see more people gathering around, trying to look inside. Shit. This is not good. If someone recognizes me, the paparazzi won't stop, and this girl doesn't deserve that.

I clench my jaw and lean closer to her. "Madeline," I whisper, careful not to touch her again. "You need to get up."

It's like she doesn't hear me. She makes no effort to move, and the crowd gathering is getting bigger by the second. I blow out a breath, taking matters into my own hands.

Positioning my hands below her, I lift her off the ground and pick her up in my arms. She gasps, wrapping her arms around my neck so she doesn't fall. *Finally.* A damn reaction from her. Her eyes widen when she looks up at me and I carry her out of the elevator and head outside. People murmur and talk behind me, but I honestly don't give a fuck. Fat chance I'll ever see them again anyway.

"What are you doing?" she asks when I push through the doors, the rain falling on us. She starts to kick her feet, but at least she's not screaming.

"I'm getting you out of here." I narrow my eyes at her. "Stop kicking your feet." The rain falls on us harder, coating us from head to toe, and she kicks her feet harder. "Stop that," I tell her. "Someone's going to think I've kidnapped you."

"Then put me down."

I stare down at her, noting her face drenched from the rain, her narrowed eyes, her full lips in a scowl, and I breathe harshly.

*This fucking woman.*

The sound of a loud flash of a camera makes my head snap to my side, and I curse when I see paparazzi surrounding me. "Fuck."

I drop her to the ground, and she lets out a yelp from the fast movement. But before she can say anything, I take hold of her hand and run toward the hotel a few feet nearby, where they can't follow us inside.

I push through the revolving doors and rush inside, letting go of her hand as soon as we're safe from the rain and the cameras.

I glance behind, trying to see if any of them snuck in, but when I don't see anyone, I run a hand down my face and blow out a breath. I can't wait to see what the press will say about that. More rumors, no doubt. They don't care about the truth. They just want drama so they can fill their pockets at the expense of others.

"Excuse me," a feminine voice gets my attention from behind me. I turn to face her and blink to take in her appearance. It's the first time I've seen her properly since it was dark in the elevator. So now, as she stands in front of me, with her hand propped on her hip, I take her in.

She's drenched from the rain, her hair flat against her head, a row of curls popping around her face. Her makeup is a little smudged, and her long dress is now stuck to her body, not leaving anything to the imagination.

Her nipples are little pebbles pressed against the silky material, and I force myself to look away. Fuck, she's pretty as hell.

Except she's scowling at me. "Yes?" I ask her like I wasn't just checking her out.

"Am I free to leave, or do you want to hold me captive a little longer?"

My eyebrows raise, and although I should be offended by her interpretation of my help as some form of captivity, I can't help but find it amusing. I press my lips together to hide my smirk. "A thank you would be nice."

She blinks. "For what, exactly?"

I shrug. "Helping you in there. Getting you away from the paparazzi."

She narrows her eyes at me. "The paparazzi?" she asks. "Why would they care about me?"

I smile at her, liking the fact that she doesn't know who I am. "Just say thank you. Is it really that hard for you?"

She looks to the side, pressing her lips together. "Thanks," she mumbles.

I cross my arms, smirking at her. "I don't know." I shake my head at her. "Didn't really seem like you meant it."

She turns her head to look at me, and her gaze is filled with anger as she glares at me. "Are you serious?"

"Very."

She lets out an aggravated sigh. "Thank you," she says. "For helping me… in there."

"Better," I say, nodding. "You should work on that." When she narrows her eyes, I chuckle. "You're welcome."

"So I can go?"

I hold out my hand to the front door, glancing outside to see if the paparazzi are still there. I don't see them, and hopefully, they forget what she looks like, or else she's going to be hit with a thousand different questions about me and us and whatever else they ask.

She walks past me and heads toward the exit. "Nice to meet you," I call out to her.

She looks behind her shoulder at me and scrunches her brows. "Can't say the same." She turns around, pushes open the revolving doors, and steps outside.

I run my hands over my mouth. Any other girl would be dying to spend time with me, but she couldn't run away from me any faster if she tried.

My phone buzzes in my pocket, and I pull it out with a smile on my face, but when I see my mom's text, my smile drops.

Mãe:

> On the way to the hospital.
> Where are you?

"Shit. James."

# 3

The plot thickens

## *Lucas*

I don't know what I expected to find when I push through the doors, but it definitely wasn't this.

James is sitting in bed, laughing at the TV like nothing happened.

"Are you crazy?" I ask him once I walk inside the cold hospital room.

He glances to the side for a second, spotting me there, and then turns his head back to the TV. "You're wet."

I glare at him, approaching where he's sat up, propped up by about five pillows, no doubt placed there by my mom. "Thanks for stating the obvious." I grab a towel from his bathroom and dry my hair. "I'm serious," I tell him, sitting at the edge of the bed. "You could have been hurt."

He shrugs, and I watch as his jaw clenches. "I just wanted to take a shower. What's the big deal?"

I let out a sigh, noting how he seems off. "You need help for that, James." Which is exactly why I hired the live-in nurse since he refused to move in with me or my mom. I hate seeing him like this. He was always the one who pushed me to do stuff. He would dare me to climb trees when I was too scared to do so, or he would sneak into my room late at night, knowing I was too chicken shit to go to his. He was the wild one in our friendship, and now he's in the hospital without the feeling of his legs.

It fucking kills me.

"I don't want help," he says, his tone growing agitated. "I can do it myself."

"No, you can't." I shake my head. "I thought you were doing better."

"I am," he says with a shrug.

My eyes narrow. "This isn't doing better. You were supposed to talk this shit out with someone. The hero mentality, or whatever the fuck this is, isn't helping you. You went through some rough shit, and it's changed your life, but you need to learn how to deal with it."

"I told you I'm fine," he snaps. "I don't want to talk to a therapist. What the fuck am I supposed to talk about?" he asks, his shoulders slumping. "How I'm a fucking orphan? How, after I finally started healing after my dad died, I lost my mom, too? How the same car crash that killed her took away my ability to do shit like a normal fucking human?" He shakes his head, letting out a scoff. "Fuck that."

My chest burns with every word he says, and I squeeze my eyes closed. We both lost our dads at a young age, and while we both had our mothers growing up, and I had my sister, I still have them. James doesn't have his mom anymore. But he has us. He will always have us.

"Don't say that," I tell him. "You are normal, and you're going to walk again, James." He injured his spinal cord in the accident, and while the possibility of him being able to walk again isn't crazy high, it isn't impossible either.

He lets out a scoff, not believing a word I'm saying. "You guys should just leave me. I'm a fucking burden."

17

I twist to face him. "No, you're not." His head shakes, and the pain in my chest intensifies. How could he ever think that? "You're our family, and we show up for family. You aren't getting rid of us, no matter how hard you try."

His injury isn't final. With rehabilitation and physical therapy, he could walk again, and I'm holding onto that grain of hope so fucking hard.

He blinks and swallows harshly. I can't even begin to understand what he's going through and how he's feeling, but fuck, the least I can do is let him know we're not going anywhere. We're here for him. Always.

"Jeez," he says, letting out a strained laugh before he turns to face the tv again. "No need to cry."

My shoulders drop, and I breathe out a laugh. James always manages to deflect from the hard stuff with jokes, wanting everything to be shits and giggles all the time. "You're an asshole." I bump my shoulder against his. "You're my best friend, and I'm worried about you." I narrow my eyes at him. "Also, I'm not crying."

He squints at me. "I swear I saw a tear."

I let out a laugh, loving how easy it is with him. This guy is more my brother than my best friend. "Nah. You wish." He laughs, too, and I glance back at him. "You sure you're alright?"

He rolls his eyes. "Yes. I'm fine. I have like ten nurses drooling over me all the time. Not to mention your mother."

I groan, remembering how my mom raced here. She gets really worried about him, and I hate seeing her like that. "Where is she?" I ask him.

"Probably down at the cafeteria." He shrugs. "She mentioned something about soup."

I chuckle, shaking my head. My mom's way of expressing her love revolves around food. If something's wrong, she cooks. If we're feeling sad, she feeds us, and even when we're happy, she celebrates with food.

"I could have been here sooner if it wasn't for that girl," I mumble to myself.

That grabs his attention. His head whips to the side, and his brows arch. "What girl?" he asks, his tone carrying a hint of intrigue.

I can't help but let out a grunt. "There was this girl in the elevator with me. The rain messed with the power, and it stopped working, and the lights went out. She freaked out."

"Fuck, really?"

I nod. "She was crying the whole time, yelling at me while I was trying to help." I shake my head, remembering her snide remarks. "And then, when the lights finally came back on, she wouldn't get up. It was like she couldn't hear me, so I picked her up and dragged her out of there."

"The plot thickens," he says with a grin.

I nudge him again. James is a slut for gossip of any kind. "Yeah, well, the paps were after us and even managed to take some pictures of us, so I rushed us to a hotel, and then we parted ways."

"That's it? All of that and nothing?" he asks. "Not even a kiss or a number exchange?"

"Since when am I that guy?" I ask, glaring at him.

"True." He snorts out a laugh. "You're a prude."

I let out a laugh. "I am not a prude. I just don't go for random girls, especially rude ones who drive me crazy when I'm trying to help her."

"Was she a crazy fan or something?"

I shake my head. "Not an ounce of recognition," I smirk. "I kind of liked it, to be honest. You know, until she yelled at me."

He laughs. "I would have loved to be a fly on the wall," he muses, leaning back against the pillows.

"Of course you would."

The door opens, and a male nurse comes in, checking his chart while I watch as James plainly checks him out—his eyes drifting to his figure with intrigue. The nurse smiles at him. "How you feeling?" he asks James. "That was a hard fall."

James sits up and shrugs. "I have a hard body. Nothing can hurt me."

The nurse laughs. "Well, that's good." He walks out a minute later, and James tracks his movement until he leaves.

"You're flirting with your nurse?" I ask him, when we're alone again.

He whistles. "Did you see him?"

I let out a laugh. "Did you forget I'm not into guys?"

He sighs like it's a disappointment. "Your loss."

"How about you focus on your own health before anything else?"

His lips lift in a grin. "Hey, I can still have fun. My dick still works."

I grimace. That's definitely more than I wanted to know about my best friend. "That's wonderful information. Happy for you, bro."

He laughs, facing the TV again. "Tell me more about this girl."

# 4

Taking chances

## Madeline

I need coffee.

Desperately.

I had the worst night ever, having spent most of the night tossing and turning, unable to shake off what happened yesterday. And eventually, which they always do, the unsettling memories of high school crept back, haunting me, hanging over my head like a dark shadow.

I always end up back there, in that damned closet. Five feet of space that haunts my every thought.

My feet drag as I attempt to keep my eyes open long enough until I can get some caffeine. I'd take it in an IV if possible. When I lift my eyes and spot Gabi leaning against the wall, staring down at her phone, I relax a little, knowing that I'm almost there.

I met Gabriella freshman year, so it's been a little over two years since we were paired as roommates, and become friends ever since. But that girl has too much energy. Like a puppy or a kid hooked on candy.

So when I see her look up at me with a grin on her face, my eyes narrow in suspicion. "What's going on?" I ask her when she stands in front of the door, blocking me from my caffeinated happiness.

A smirk breaks out on her face as she holds her phone out to me. "Anything you want to tell me?"

I grab her phone and glance down at the screen, my eyes widening when I see the mention of my name. I quickly swipe, scrolling down to see what the hell is going on.

*Lucas Silva has a new girlfriend!*

"What?" I practically yell.

Scrolling down further, I spot a picture of me, or more accurately, of Lucas holding me in his arms like a baby. We're drenched from the rain, my hair a complete mess stuck to my face, and my eyes are widened in shock.

I can still feel the way my stomach dropped when he picked me up in that elevator. I didn't even realize the doors had opened. I was stuck, thinking back to the darkness, the hours I spent alone with no one else to talk to. So when I finally came to, I was more than a little shocked that I was halfway up in the air, in the arms of a stranger.

Little did I know it would end up all over the internet.

I scroll down again and scan the article, my head shaking in bewilderment the more I read. Lines and lines of absolute lies about how I'm his secret girlfriend, and we're finally announcing our relationship. Who the hell is this guy?

My brows furrow as I keep reading. A picture of him shows up, and my eyes linger on it. I remember thinking he was attractive yesterday, but this picture is another level.

"When did this happen?" Gabi asks. "And why didn't I know about it?"

"It didn't," I say, keeping my eyes on the screen. "I only met him yesterday."

"Wait, so you don't know who he is?" she asks.

I lift my head and sigh. "No, I don't. This is all bullshit," I tell her, giving her phone back before pushing the doors open to the café.

"Woah," she says, trailing behind me. "I'm going to need more information. How did you meet? Where did you meet? Why's he holding you? Did you kiss? Is he single? Did you get his number?"

"Gabi," I cut her off. "I'm running on two hours of sleep. Let me have my fix first, and then I'll be more inclined to answer those questions."

"Oh my god. Something happened, didn't it?"

I turn to face her and lift my eyebrows. "Do you even know me?"

She scoffs, shaking her head. "Right."

"What can I get you?" I lift my eyes to see a warm smile from the barista in front of me.

"I'll have a medium brewed coffee with two pumps of vanilla syrup and a hint of caramel drizzle, please," I tell her, pulling out my wallet.

"Coming right up," she says before heading into the back.

"So this guy," Gabi asks, moving out of the way while I wait for my drink. "He just picked you up?"

"We're still talking about that?"

"C'mon," she says, giving me a smirk. "This is huge."

My shoulders lift in a shrug. "It's nothing. I don't even know the guy. It all happened so fast."

"Where did you meet, though?" she asks, furrowing her brows. "How did you end up in his arms?"

The door opens, and I spot Leila and Rosalie walking in, my other two best friends whom I also met freshman year. Leila's phone is in her hand, and I already know what's coming.

23

"When were you going to tell me about this?" she asks, her brows lifted.

"Not you, too," I groan.

She shakes her head. "You're dating one of my best friends and weren't going to tell me?"

"Best friend?" I ask. "Since when?"

"Yeah," Rosalie adds. "Since when?" I smirk when I see Rosie narrowing her eyes at her best friend since high school.

"You know Lucas," Leila says to Rosie. "You met him like three times."

"Not as your best friend," she replies, crossing her arms in a huff.

Leila chuckles. "I said *one* of my best friends. Your position is safe, don't worry."

"Wait." I shake my head, trying to understand. It's too damn early for this. "How do you know Lucas?"

"We met when I was a younger, doing commercial modeling," she says. "How do *you* know him?"

"He's a model?" I ask her.

"Madi." She shakes her head. "He's a very well-known model. He's been on billboards, and he's been the face of clothing brands, underwear brands, even perfumes."

"Perfumes?" I repeat, narrowing my eyes. Bastard stole my spot in that audition, didn't he?

"That's not important," she says. "Question is, why is there a picture of you two, and why are people saying you're dating?"

"She says she only met him yesterday," Gabi tells her. "Doesn't even know the guy."

"Then how did you end up in his arms?" Rosalie asks, flicking her blonde hair behind her shoulder.

"I asked her that," Gabi says. "Still hasn't given me a response." They all turn to me, seeking for answers I can't give them. I still don't quite understand what the hell happened yesterday and why it's all over the internet.

"Medium brew, two pumps of vanilla."

My head snaps to the left, seeing my drink on the counter. "Oh, thank God." I grab the drink and quickly pay. My eyes close when I take a sip, and my shoulders slump, feeling the caffeine travel down my veins. I might be a little addicted, but hey, at least it's legal. When I look up, all three of the girls are staring back at me, waiting for an answer.

I let out a sigh and head to the nearest table, taking a seat. "It's a long story," I tell them, waiting for them to sit. I take a sip of my coffee and blow out a breath before I continue. "The elevator broke down yesterday because of the blackout."

"Fuck," Leila says, her lime green eyes softening. "Are you okay?"

I nod. "I'm fine, I was just…" I shake my head, not wanting to relive it, or anything else for that matter.

"Why didn't you tell me this yesterday?" Gabi asks, with a frown on her face.

I shrug. "I just didn't want to talk about it. It all happened so fast. One minute, it was dark. The next, he was picking me up, and people were taking pictures."

"The paparazzi go crazy over Lucas," Leila says, shaking her head. "I'm lucky people don't care about me as much." She lets out a laugh. "It's insane with him, especially when he was still living in New York."

Leila's been modeling since she was a child, doing small commercial shoots before she bloomed out into plus-size modeling once she graduated. She manages to attend college as

25

well as do some jobs here and there, but something tells me the same can't be said for Lucas. I only had a small dose of what it could be like for him yesterday.

"And now he's not?" I ask her.

She shakes her head. "He moved back to be close to his family. I'm actually surprised that you don't know who he is."

I groan. "I'd rather keep it that way," I say, taking a sip of my coffee. "He was an ass."

"What?" Leila asks with a laugh. "Lucas is one of the kindest people I've met."

I shrug. "Maybe with you, but he kept yelling at me the whole time." I shake my head, remembering how he was being a pain about me being freaked out. "I mean, come on, who doesn't freak out when an elevator stops?" I ask with a huff, swallowing harshly.

My phone buzzes, and I snap myself out of thinking about what went down yesterday and grab my phone. My eyes widen when I see the first line of the email and I quickly open it.

"Oh my god," I gasp, my eyes scanning down the email.

"What?" the girls ask.

I lift my head with a grin. "I just got an email from an agent. Someone called Ana Parker at Merge Media wants to meet with me."

"You're serious?" Gabi asks.

I nod, reading over the email again. "She said she had an interesting opportunity for me and would love to schedule a meeting."

"That's huge," Leila says.

"Do you think it's from yesterday's audition?" Gabi asks.

I scoff, shaking my head. "No way. That audition tanked."

"Maybe it was from another audition?" Rosie asks.

I shrug, my smile too big to contain. My heart starts to beat with anticipation and something similar to hope. "Maybe," I say. "But I'm excited for what this could mean," I admit, feeling a little better after the whole fiasco with Lucas Silva.

"I'm so fucking happy for you right now," Gabi says, reaching over to pull me in for a hug.

I shake my head, unable to say any words. How long have I been waiting for an opportunity like this? For someone to see my potential and want to hire me?

Way too long.

## 5

We need her

*Lucas*

"This was your idea!"

She lifts an eyebrow at my tone, and I drop my shoulders, wiping a hand down my face. "It's just not working anymore," she says. "We need a change."

Fuck. My. Life.

"It's worked until now," I tell her. I didn't want to do it, but a few years ago, my agent suggested that playing up the idea of being seen with a new girl every night would help spread my name out into the press, and in turn, it would help get more jobs. And while I hate to admit this, it did work. My name was on the news more often. I got hired by bigger companies, and she got a chunky paycheck from it. And as for me… well, my family are fed and have a roof over their heads.

"I know it's hard to hear, Lucas, but It's getting old," she says with a shrug. "We need to change your image."

I blow out a breath, aggravated with her. *We need to change your image.* Why can't I just be… me? Why do I have to have an image and pretend to be someone I'm not? I'm tired of it. Having to play a part, having bullshit news spread about me knowing I can't do a single thing about it. "So what do you suggest we do now?"

Someone knocks on the door, and my agent, Ana, smiles, glancing behind me. "I might have an idea," she says, gesturing at whoever just knocked on the door.

The door opens and I hear heels hit the floor. "Excuse me, is this Ana's office?"

"Perfect timing," Ana says, nodding. "Come in."

My brows furrow as I turn around to see who the hell is here. But when I see her standing at the door, my face falls. She notices me at the same time as I do, and the previous smile she had on drops, too, a scowl replacing it.

I turn back to my agent and furrow my brows. "What the hell is she doing here?"

"You two remember each other, right?" Ana asks.

I scoff, leaning back in my chair. "Hardly."

"I was supposed to have a meeting with Ana?" the girl asks. Fuck, what's her name? I know it started with an M.

"Why don't you have a seat," Ana tells her, gesturing to the empty chair beside me.

What the hell is going on? I furrow my brows at her, but she just looks back at the girl, waiting for her to sit down on the chair beside me. The metal legs scrape against the floor as she tries to put more distance between us. I let out a scoff. The feeling's mutual, *princesa.*

I glance toward her, my eyes drifting to her outfit. Last time she was in a short little dress, but this time she's in a dark grey suit with a black blouse, and some heels, of course.

Fuck, she looks good.

I quickly snap my head away, my jaw clenching in annoyance for even thinking it. She might be smoking hot, but if she's here, then that can only mean one thing. She's here for fame.

I knew it was too good to be true. I really thought the girl didn't know me back in the elevator, that she didn't want anything from me.

I guess I was wrong.

"Can you just get on with it?" I ask Ana, wanting to get the fuck out of here. "The quicker you tell me why she's here, the quicker I can say no."

The girl narrows her eyes at me. "I was told I had a meeting about an opportunity," she says, turning to face Ana. "What does that have to do with him?"

I let out a laugh. "Listen, Mandy—"

"Madeline," she corrects.

Madeline. Of course. I remember thinking it was a pretty name, that it suited her. "Right. Well, the thing is, I'm sure the opportunity that Ana was talking about has *everything* to do with me. And I bet you already know that."

Her brows furrow deeper. "What are you talking about?"

I shake my head. Ana always does this. Sets me up with girls so the paparazzi can take a few quick pictures and post their usual bullshit. I never get photographed with the same girl twice, though, so I'm really fucking confused about why this girl is here. We already made front page news with that picture of us from last week.

"Why don't I clear some things up," Ana says, intertwining her hands in front of her. "I'm Lucas' agent. I help him with booking him gigs, and—"

"I'm sure she knows what an agent is," I say dryly. "Can you just get on with it?"

Ana pins her interlocked hands in front of her. "I'm sure both of you are aware of the press going around with your names."

More than fucking aware. My mom saw those pictures. She's always chastising me for going along with this stupid plan, thinking I'm only doing this to get more fame. Couldn't give a fuck about that. I just care about making money so that my mom doesn't have to kill herself working two jobs anymore. It's the whole reason why I started modeling in the first place.

"And I'm sure you guys are wondering why we asked you both to come here today," she continues.

I sure as fuck am.

"The picture of you guys last week blew up. And the comments…" She shakes her head. "They're immense. People loved seeing you two together, specifically the story that the paparazzi decided to spin."

How she's my secret girlfriend. Yeah, fucking right.

"I have a proposition for you two." Ana eyes me, and I know where she's going with this before she even opens her mouth.

"No."

Madeline looks at me with a frown, and Ana sighs, shaking her head. "Lucas—"

"No," I repeat. "I am not having a fake relationship with her. No fucking way."

"What?" Madeline asks, her eyes wide in shock as her head snaps to look at Ana.

Ana has mentioned this before. She told me people enter fake relationships for publicity all the time. But when she saw the reactions people had with random girls I got photographed with, she figured the single player who sleeps with a new girl every night would be way more beneficial, so that's what we went with. But now she tells me she wants to 'change my image' and brings in the girl who the press is claiming is my

31

secret girlfriend. I should have known where this was going when she first walked in.

Ana glances at me. "Have you checked the comments?"

"You know I haven't." Rule number one. Never check the comments. Whether they're good or not, I just don't do it.

"Then I suggest you do," she says, turning her monitor to us. On the screen is the picture from that day. I've seen this picture hundreds of times without wanting to, but I never really *looked* at it. My gaze drifts to Madeline, who's holding onto me for dear life, her red, long nails clawing at my neck. Her mouth is parted in an O as she looks up at me in shock. She has her head pressed against my chest, and I'm looking down at her with my brows furrowed. Fuck. We actually look like a real couple.

I glance down at the comments. They're all about how cute we look and how happy they are for us.

I almost laugh. People believe anything.

"They aren't commenting the usual stuff. They think you've changed," Ana tells me, making my eyes lift to hers. "They think you've settled down. That you're dating."

"Dating?" Madeline asks, sounding like she's been offended. "That was the first time we met."

"You're right," she says. "But they don't know that. They've never seen Lucas act so intimately with anyone before, so it's natural for them to just take what the press publishes as facts when the picture backs it up."

She's spewing a load of bullshit. Other people might believe it, but I know it's not true. I shake my head. "No," I tell her. "I'm not fucking doing it."

"I've already had interest from the press. Photoshoots, interviews. People want to see more of you two," Ana tells me.

"And I really think I can get more gigs for you if we keep this up."

Madeline's brows furrow. "People are that interested in his love life?"

My agent breathes out a laugh. "You'd be surprised what people care about when it comes to celebrities."

Madeline's head snaps to face me. "Celebrity?" she asks.

"I'm not a celebrity," I assure her. "And it doesn't matter anyway," I say with a shrug before turning to look at Ana. "Because I'm not doing it."

Ana shakes her head. "I'm at a loss here, Lucas. I've had a hard time finding you work. And we've been talking a lot about switching your image up," she reminds me. "I really think this is the way to go if you just—"

I don't even wait for her to finish that sentence. I shake my head, interrupting her. "You'll have to find something else because I'm not doing it." I turn to face Madeline, seeing her brows knitted together. "You'd be up for this?" I ask her, anticipating her response.

She crosses her arms. "Of course not. I'm not dating you, real or otherwise."

Well fuck. I smile, glancing at my agent. "Well, you heard her. It's a no-go."

Ana faces Madeline with a serious look on her face. "This could be beneficial for you, too," she tells her. I grind my teeth. She's good at persuading people to do what she wants. I would know. It's how she got me to agree to this whole thing in the first place. She got me right where she wanted me, using all of my weaknesses against me, and I folded like a lawn chair, pure putty in her hands. And now it's biting me in the ass.

"What do you mean?" Madeline asks with intrigue in her tone.

Oh great. She's already falling for it.

"You want to be an actress, right?" Ana asks her. "Well, this would be great publicity. You can get your name out there and make people notice you. You might not know who Lucas is, but a lot of people do."

Madeline's eyes widen and I squeeze my eyes shut, cursing under my breath. Of course, she's just another actress wanting fame. She's a damn good one, too, almost had me convinced she was different.

She'll say yes, and I'll have to spend a few weeks with this girl acting like I'm in love with her when it's the furthest thing from the truth. I'll lie to everyone I know, and when this is all said and done, she'll have the fame, she'll move on and get to do what she wants, and I'll be stuck doing the same old thing until I'm old and fucking gray.

"You're saying that pretending to be in a relationship with him would help me land an audition?" she asks.

Ana smiles at her. "Honey, it could make you a star. Do you know how many girls wish they were in your position right now? Lucas is one of New York's biggest models. They love him. And if they see you with him, then they'll love you too. This could be the stepping stone to finally landing a role in the movie business. Isn't that what you want?"

I glance at Madeline, and for an actress, she's not hiding her emotions very well. They're all over her face. She's fucking thinking about it. I can tell in the way she chews on her bottom lip, staring into space, her brows knitted together. Shit. I've got to end this now. No way are we going to be able to be around each other for a day, never mind however long they want this to go on for.

I sit up in my chair. "What about the hate comments?"

Madeline turns to face me, her eyes widening. "Hate comments?" she asks.

"Yeah," I say with a shrug. "You'll get attention, that's for sure, but not all of it will be good. You'll get hate comments just for being with me. Do you know how many girls want to date me? They won't like seeing you with me. They love that I'm single, that I have a new girl in my bed every night." Everything I'm telling her is true. People are like that, but little do they know it's all a fucking lie. "They think it could be them one day. But if I have a girlfriend?" I shake my head. "They know that can't happen anymore. They're going to hate you, Madeline."

Hey eyes widen in shock, and I almost smile. I might not like the girl, but I don't want to see her get hurt by those comments. They're fucking brutal, and if it helps me scare her off from going along with this ruse, then all the better.

But of course, Ana interrupts again. "Don't let him scare you," she tells her. "Yes, there might be some negative comments here and there, but people are already interested in the two of you together. This will be big," she says before looking at me. "For both of you."

"No," I repeat. "I'm not doing it. I'm not letting another girl you bribe take advantage of me again. No fucking way."

"Excuse me?" Madeline replies, her eyes flashing with frustration, her tone sharp as knives. "I'm not taking advantage of you. I don't even know who you are, except that you're an asshole. And besides, I don't want to do this either." She turns

35

to face Ana. "I want to make it on my own. I don't need your help or his," she says, glancing back to me.

"Good," I say, my jaw clenching. "I don't need your help anyway."

"Great."

"Fantastic."

She lets out a frustrated groan and lifts herself off the chair, heading to the door. I look back at her to see she's got her arms crossed, facing my agent. "If you have a real opportunity, then you can call me. If not, then don't bother me again." Her eyes slide to mine, and I feel the chill from her gaze a mile away. "I'm going to make it even without your help."

She turns around and walks out, the door slamming behind her. The silence in the room is deafening while Ana stares back at me with disappointment.

"Great," Ana says, shaking her head. "The one plan we had. Gone."

"You'll come up with something else." I shuffle in my chair, my body growing hot with irritation.

She pins me with a glare. "You pay me for a reason, Lucas."

"Yeah, I pay you to make sure things run smoothly. I pay you to find me gigs, to make me reach more people, not to pimp me out."

She shakes her head, sighing disapprovingly. "We need her, Lucas."

My skin starts to itch. I don't want to need anyone. I can do it myself. It's how I've done it ever since I've started this. "We don't. I don't want to do this."

"Well, what do you suggest we do? If you don't change things, you won't get any jobs. This business is so much more than looking good. You need to keep people interested. They're getting tired of the same old stuff. This is gold. This will work. Believe it or not, I'm only trying to help you, Lucas. I don't want you to be washed up."

My jaw aches from grinding my teeth. Fuck. I reach up, brushing my hair back, tugging at the strands as I do. I can't stop getting Jobs. Adrianna needs braces. James' hospital bill is going to cost more than I have saved up. And my mom... she'll go back to working.

How did I let things get so fucked up? I run a hand down my face. I hate what I'm about to say, but... "Fine," I relent, gritting out the words, hating how I'm going to have to resort to more schemes. Will this be my life forever? "I'll do it."

Ana laughs. "You're kidding, right? After you just scared her off."

Shit. I guess I did. I made her walk out of that door, and now I'm eating my words. "We don't need her. We can find someone else," I suggest. "Like you said, there are hundreds of girls that would love this position."

Ana shakes her head. "That won't work," she says. "We can't have you holding some girl one day and claiming another as your girlfriend the next. They'll see right through it."

Of fucking course. "So what do we do?"

She gestures to the door. "You need to get her to agree."

"You're joking."

"No, Lucas. I'm not. We had the perfect plan, and you messed it up. You need to talk her into it," she says. "We need her." Her eyes narrow at those last two words and I slump back in my chair.

Yeah.

We do.

# 6

It would be agony

## *Madeline*

"Hey, wait up."

I freeze, my eyes widening when I hear his voice. My head leisurely turns around, and my pulse starts to pick up when I see Connor Ellis running toward me.

I swallow down, my heart racing the closer he gets, and when he reaches me, he blows out a breath and grins at me. Damn, he has a nice smile, perfect white teeth, good lips. Shit. Am I staring at his mouth?

"Hey," he says, sounding a little out of breath.

"Hi," I reply.

He gestures behind him with his thumb. "I called you back there, didn't you hear me?"

He did? I was, too, in my own head, thinking about what went down at the meeting yesterday. I thought I was finally getting my chance, but instead, they want to use me to make Lucas even more famous. "No," I tell him. "I didn't. Sorry." My fingers clutch my bag hanging off my shoulders.

"That's okay," he says, flashing me a smile. "I was wondering… a bunch of the guys are going over to Murphy's later, and I was just thinking if maybe…," he shrugs. "You'd like to come?"

Is he asking me out on a date? My lips part in shock as I stare back at his face, unable to think straight. Sure, I might have a teeny, tiny crush on Connor, but it only exists in my mind, where I know it can't turn into anything more. "Um." I fiddle with the strap of my bag. "No, I don't think so."

His brows furrow. "Oh, ok. No worries." The corner of his lips turns up in a small smile, and he starts to step back. "I'll see you in class?"

I nod. "Of course."

He presses his lips together in a smile and turns around. As soon as I see that he's gone, I blow out a breath. I hate how I get shy when I'm around him. I shouldn't be attracted to him, even if it's in the confines of my brain, and I shouldn't want to go to the bar with him tonight. Nothing good will come of it. I promised myself I wouldn't let myself get distracted by boys again. And I intend to keep that promise. I won't lose myself to another guy ever again.

I shake my head and turn around. I don't have time to go to a bar anyway. I have to study, maybe even watch a movie with Gabi. But when I lift my head, my face drops. "You've got to be kidding me."

His brows lift, and I have to admit he's got good eyebrows. It's something I notice in guys, whether or not they take care of themselves. And Lucas seems to tick all the boxes. Groomed facial hair, trimmed nails, hygienic. I guess it comes with the territory of being a model with an ego as big as his bank account. It's second nature for him to look good.

"Pleasure as always," he says, stepping off the wall. He gestures with his chin behind me. "Was that your boyfriend?" he asks.

My brows furrow. "Connor?" I ask. "No, he's not my boyfriend." Not that it's any of his business. "What are you? Some kind of stalker?"

He lets out a chuckle, but it's laced with anything but humor. "Believe me," he says, running a hand down his face. "I wish I didn't have to chase after you."

"Then why are you here?" I ask him.

"Ana's offer," he says, taking his hands out of his pockets and crossing them over his chest. "You need to accept it."

My eyebrows shoot up. "You're joking."

His jaw ticks, and he shakes his head. "I wish I was. But I'm not."

I let out a bitter laugh. "After you told me every reason under the sun, why I shouldn't?" This guy makes my blood boil. Of course, the one time I thought my acting career was going somewhere, he had to come in and crash my dreams. I knew it was too good to be true.

"I needed you to drop it. I didn't want to go along with that stupid plan," he says.

I cock my head. "And now you do?"

He lets out a sigh, his eyes drifting closed. "I wouldn't ask if I didn't need you."

My eyes widen when I see his frown. "You...need me?" I repeat.

He glares at me. "Don't make me repeat it, okay? Listen, it won't be that bad." His shoulders lift in a shrug. "It would just be some pictures here and there. I'm sure that it won't be for too long, and then we can both go our separate ways, and you can..." He waves his hand. "Go into acting or whatever it is you want, and I..." He shrugs again with a subtle shake of his head. "I just really need your help."

40

I let out a laugh. The nerve of this guy asking me for help when he did everything he could to scare me off. "Why would I do that?"

He narrows his eyes. "Listen, I know you're not my biggest fan. Trust me, right now, I feel the same. But this wouldn't just be about me. Ana was right. This could help you, too."

My pulse starts to race. I hate the idea of this guy knowing my weak spots and holding something over me. "I don't need your help," I tell him, crossing my arms. "I can do it on my own."

He tilts his head. "Yeah?" he asks. "And how's that worked out for you so far?"

Asshole. I press my lips together, trying to calm myself down. God, I hate him. "And you?" I ask him. "You're here begging for my help. Doesn't seem like it's going well for you either."

He scoffs. "I wouldn't say I'm begging. Merely asking for something that would be beneficial for both of us."

"And you need me?" I ask him. "You can't find anyone else to play your girlfriend?"

He shakes his head, visibly annoyed. "Tried that," he says. "Ana said it wouldn't work."

I know I shouldn't be. But I'm honestly a little relieved that I'm the only option. I feel my hope brewing up again, but I need to make sure this guy isn't just going to crash it down again. "Why do you need help anyway?" I ask him. "Aren't you rich or something?"

He narrows his eyes, his jaw clenching. "You don't know everything," he says. "You don't know me or what my life is like, so don't act like you do. Just tell me, are you going to help me or not?"

I want to. I do. But having this guy hold my future in the palm of his hands, having the power to shut it down, makes me wary about accepting it. "Not." I turn from him and walk away. My heart is racing, and I honestly don't know if that was the right decision or not.

I hear him scoff from behind me. "I knew you'd say that." My shoulders slump and I stop walking, looking at him from over my shoulder. "I thought you'd look past who you think I am and realize that this could help you, too. More than it could ever help me. But of course, you'd say no to spite me." He shakes his head. "I knew this would be a waste of time." He starts to walk away, and my stomach churns. Fuck. If he walks away, that's it. I would lose this opportunity for good.

"Wait," I tell him, turning back around. He stops in place and faces me. I let out a sigh. "How long would this be for?" I ask him.

His face lights up, his small smirk making my eyes drift to his lips. *Snap out of it.* He shrugs. "I'm not sure, but I don't think it would be for too long. I know you would hate spending more time with me than necessary." His lips twitch in a smile.

"It would be agony," I agree.

He nods. "The worst."

I catch myself smiling and quickly drop it, letting out a sigh. "Can we really pull this off?"

He takes a step closer. "I think we can. We're both adults. I'm sure we'll be able to deal with whatever it is we have to do." He squints, staring at me. "So, is that a yes?" he asks.

"No," I say, watching as he frowns, and I'm quick to amend. "It's a maybe."

He lets out a breath. "That's all I need. Here," he says, pulling out his phone from his pocket. "Let me give you my number. Take your time and think about it. Don't make any rash decisions because of a shitty first impression you had of me. Think of everything it will do for you." He glances up at me and smiles. "And when you're ready to say yes, give me a call."

I laugh. "You're certain I'm going to say yes?"

He shrugs. "It's worth a try."

I roll my eyes and tell him my number. Once he saves it, he pockets his phone and smirks. "I'll be waiting for your call," he says before he turns around and walks away.

He hasn't even gotten out of my eyesight yet, and I already know, without a doubt.

I'm going to say yes.

# 7

Only if necessary

## Madeline

"I'm glad you changed your mind." Ana rounds her desk, dropping into her chair. The smile she gives me is warm and welcoming, and I remind myself I'm only doing this because of everything she said it could do for me.

The biggest reason why I caved and said yes to the offer, however, was hearing Lucas say he needed me. I like that. Feeling needed. I don't think I've ever felt like I was needed before. So now I'm here, agreeing to pretend to be his girlfriend.

The door opens behind me, and my head snaps to see Lucas walking inside. I haven't seen him since last week, and obviously, I knew I'd see him again, but I forgot he looks like *that*. Tall and handsome, his wavy hair framing his face perfectly. The way his black t-shirt fits around his biceps makes my eyes drift to them, a few tattoos peeking out, and I force myself to look away, glancing at the coffees in his hand.

I raise my eyebrow, hope lingering within me. Maybe this thing with Lucas won't be so bad after all. Especially if he brings me coffee every morning.

But when he approaches Ana and hands one over to her, I quickly realize my mistake and slump back in my chair.

"Did you want one?" he asks, eyeing me. "I'm sorry. I didn't know your order."

I run my tongue over my teeth, needing some caffeine – desperately. "No. It's fine," I say.

"So now that you're both here," Ana says, taking a sip of her coffee. "We can get started."

Lucas sits on the chair beside me and leans back, taking a sip of the other coffee. "So, what do we need to do? Take some pictures and stuff?"

Ana nods. "A little more than that."

"Like what?" I ask, confused about how this works.

"Well, you need to act like a couple for starters," she says, gesturing to the large space between our chairs. "So this is not a good start."

My eyes lock with Lucas', and I swallow visibly, but he lets out a sigh, reaching over to place his hands on the back of my chair and dragging it closer until my chair touches his. "Got it." I try not to think of his arm still hanging over the back of my chair or the fact that we're now so close that I could move just an inch, and my leg would touch his. "What else?" he asks.

She purses her lips, scanning her desk until she finds and slides over two sheets of paper. One for me and one for Lucas. I glance down at the papers, skimming them briefly. "Before we get into the details, I'm going to need you both to sign this."

"A non-disclosure agreement?" I ask, my brows knitted together. "Is this really necessary?" I don't know what I expected, but I kind of thought we'd just take a few more pictures and then announce our break-up, and that would be it. But there's a lot more to this agreement than I realized.

"Yes," she says, her face unwavering. "I need to make sure there will be no scandals." Her eyes narrow slightly on us, adding, "I know you two have some… animosity between you, but this is important to both your career." I glance down, reading through the contract. It's times like these when I wish I were interested in law because I don't have a clue what any of this is. "Which is why you need to sign so that we make sure we're all safe."

I lift my head up, my brows furrowed. Safe? "If anyone finds out this is fake," she continues, seeing my expression. "It will ruin both of your reputations and legitimacy." Her glance balances between us both. "Can you do that?"

My eyes drift down to the paper again, and when they lock on the fine for breaking it, they nearly pop out of my sockets. "A hundred thousand dollars fine?" I ask, my tone raising about three octaves.

"It's for your safety, too," Ana tells me. "This goes both ways. This arrangement has to stay between us and no one else. Got it?"

Lucas lets out a sigh, reaching over Ana's desk to grab a pen. He quickly flips the pages, signs his name, and slides the contract back to her. "What else?" he asks.

I glance over the document once again, trying to see if any red flags pop out at me, but none so far, so I follow his lead, grabbing the pen and signing my name over the bold black line.

"Great," Ana says, collecting the documents. "We'll start simple. Something to get the press talking." Her brows lift, a smile on her lips. "How about a walk?"

"A walk?" I ask, taking out my planner from my bag. Lucas eyes me for a second, but he turns back around with a shake of his head.

She nods. "Roam the city, get people used to seeing you as a couple, and get them talking to you. Maybe get some coffee, or an ice cream, or a stroll in the park. As long as the paparazzi can photograph you."

"That seems easy enough." My shoulders relax as I write down the details.

"Well, obviously, there needs to be some form of PDA," Ana continues. My head snaps up, my muscles tensing up all over again.

"PDA?" I ask her, licking my dry lips, feeling my hands start to get clammy. "Like what, exactly?"

She lifts her shoulder. "Whatever you're comfortable with," she says. "Holding hands, maybe a kiss. Whatever you guys want. We need to make it clear that you two are dating and not just friends. Feed into the story the press is spinning. We want to keep people talking about you."

My pulse starts to race, and scratch that. Yep, my hands are definitely clammy. I drop my pen onto my planner, discreetly trying to wipe my hands on my pants. "A kiss?" I ask her, swallowing the words down like they don't belong in my throat. "Is that necessary, or can we do without?"

Lucas lets out a scoff, and I turn my head to look at him, seeing him shake his head. "Are you not attracted to me or something?" he asks. As much as I hate to admit it, being attracted to him isn't the problem. And therein lies the problem. "You know," he continues when I don't answer. "Most girls would die for a chance to kiss me."

I narrow my eyes at him. "You're right," I say with a bite. "Death is a much better outcome than kissing you."

His chest shakes with a laugh. "No kissing. Got it." He lifts his brow at me. "Anything else, *princesa*?" he says in that smooth Brazilian accent of his. My lips part, and my eyes widen at the use of the nickname, which I have no doubt – from his cocky smirk – he means as an insult.

I am not a princess. I just have boundaries. I snap my mouth closed and turn to face Ana, trying to ignore Lucas, who is still grinning at me. "What else?" I ask her, reaching for my pen.

She smirks, giving a subtle shake of her head. "I can tell you guys are going to be trouble." She glances down at her monitor and then lifts her head. "The paparazzi will be there," she informs us. "Make sure you don't look at them. Better yet, just pretend they're not there. Take the day to get to know each other," she says, tilting her head at us, a smile on her lips. "You'll be spending quite some time together after all."

I make the mistake of glancing toward Lucas to find him already grinning at me. He chuckles, shooting me a wink. "Can't wait."

I roll my eyes. Kill me now.

A knock hits the door, and Ana lifts her head, ushering whoever is at the door in. "Mr. Daniels is waiting for you downstairs," she says.

"Of course." Ana lifts herself from her desk and glances at us. "I'll be right back." Her head cocks to the side. "Try not to kill each other." She rounds her desk and heads out of the room, and I realize I'm left here with the one person who makes my blood boil.

Lucas swivels his head to glance at me, his brows furrowing. "What are you writing in there?"

"None of your business." A shadow looms over me as I jot down the time, date, and a few extra details. I lift my head, seeing Lucas looking down at my planner, a playful grin on his lips. "Well, *girlfriend*," he teases, making my eyes narrow. "Look like you're excited for our first date." He grins

48

mischievously, clearly finding the situation amusing, as opposed to me.

"Don't call me that," I tell him. "And I'm not excited. I just want to be prepared."

He lets out a laugh, sitting back in his chair. "A little too prepared if you ask me. Remember to smile? Really?" he asks, arching a brow.

My eyes narrow at the fact that he managed to read my planner. "You've been doing this for a lot longer than I have."

He laughs again, shaking his head. "Don't worry, I'll remind you to smile." With that, he flashes me a grin, making my eyes drift down to his lips.

I rip my eyes away from his mouth, tucking my planner back into my bag. "If we're going to do this, then we need to set some rules."

He sighs, wiping a hand down his face. "Of course we do."

I arch an eyebrow. "Do you have a problem with that?" I ask him. "I'm not sure what you were expecting to happen. I'm not going to sleep with you."

His eyes widen. "What?" He questions, a laugh escaping his lips. "You don't need to worry about that. That's definitely not going to happen."

"Good," I say, squaring my shoulders. "And no kissing either."

The corner of his mouth twitches. "You said that already," he says. "Even though I think it's stupid," he admits, with a shake of his head. "Who's going to believe we're dating if we don't kiss?" His brow lifts, enquiring, but he continues before I can respond.

"You were in my arms, Madeline. I held you against my chest while your arms were wrapped around my neck. Your eyes were locked on mine, looking up at me like someone in love." As he speaks, flashes of the pictures of us I've seen repeatedly come rushing back. I pull my bottom lip between my teeth at the memory. "How are we going to go from that to being five feet apart?" he asks, frowning. "You need to know how suspicious that will be."

He's right. I know he is. We need to do whatever is necessary to make this work. But the thought of someone's lips on mine for the first time in years makes my heart beat so fast I swear I stop breathing. I can't do it. I don't want to do it. "No kissing," I repeat firmly. "But you can do anything else."

A smug grin dances on his lips. "Anything?" he asks with an arched brow. My mind spirals out of control, thinking of what *anything* could entail.

"Within our boundaries," I clarify.

His lips curve into a smile. "So I can hold your hand?" he questions teasingly.

"Sure," I reply, attempting to keep my composure even though the thought of it makes my skin break out into a sweat.

"I can…" His eyes trail over my face. "Kiss your cheek?"

I feel my heartbeat in my throat, just from picturing it, but I nod against my better judgment.

His hand reaches out, running the back of his hand down my arm slowly. His eyes track his movements, and my skin breaks out into goosebumps from the featherlight touch of his skin on mine. It seems to go on forever until he reaches my wrists and glances up at me. "I can touch you?" he murmurs, his voice dipped in a deep, husky tone.

I swallow harshly and let out a breath. "Only if necessary."

He pulls back, a smirk on his lips. "Interesting," he muses to himself. "Any more rules?"

50

My mind goes blank for a second, but then I breathe out a laugh. "I'd say we can't fall in love, but that won't be a problem for us."

He laughs, shaking his head. "It definitely won't for me," he says, squinting at me. "What about you? Are you sure you can handle that?"

I scoff. "I'm sure I'll be able to manage it."

"Are you sure?" he asks, teasingly. "I could swear I saw some love hearts in your eyes earlier."

"You're delusional," I drawl, rolling my eyes. "Consider any hypothetical hearts crushed."

He laughs a little, rubbing his chin. "Good." His shoulders square, and he glances back at me. "I have one rule," he says, making my eyes widen.

"What is it?" I ask.

"For however long we're doing this," he starts, gesturing between us, "I don't think we should date other people." My brows lift, but he continues. "I don't know your life or if you're seeing anyone right now." I almost scoff. "But, while we're in this arrangement, we should cut off things with anyone else. In case someone finds out, and we get exposed."

He seems serious, and although I want to laugh at the idea, I don't. "Fine," I say, turning my head when the doors open, and Ana walks in, narrowing her eyes at us.

"Everything good in here?" she asks us, her eyes shifting from me to Lucas.

Lucas flashes me a cocky grin. "Perfect."

## 8

Just go with it

# Lucas

"You need to relax."

Her head whips back to face me, and she narrows her eyes. I wonder if there will ever be a day when I see a smile from this girl. I doubt it. "I'm trying," she says, glancing behind her shoulder once again.

God damn it. She's going to blow it.

"Come on," I gesture to the small café ahead of us. "Let's grab a coffee." She's lucky they're not here yet. At least I don't see them. We're supposed to act like a happy couple, but Madeline here is making that a little hard to do.

She shakes her head. "I've had two already."

My eyes widen as I stare back at her. "It's ten thirty."

She shrugs, letting out an aggravated sigh. "I was nervous and had the worst night's sleep. I needed it."

I let out a laugh, shaking my head. "That explains it."

"Explains what?" she asks, her brows knitted together.

"Why you're so jumpy," I clarify, nudging my shoulder against hers. She rolls her eyes, but I can see a hint of a smile on there.

"I am not jumpy," she says as she glances to the left and right.

"Are you sure about that?" My tone is filled with humor, but she doesn't even catch it because she's still looking around. Fuck, I need to distract her. "If not coffee, then what should we do for our first date?"

I get the reaction I was looking for when she narrows her brown eyes at me. "This is not a date."

*That's it. Just keep looking at me.* If I can manage to get her mind off the paparazzi, maybe she won't give us away. "I don't know about that," I joke. "Looks like a date to me."

Her nose scrunches as she shakes her head. "This would be the last place I would go on for a date," she says.

"Yeah?" I ask her, rubbing a hand over my chin. "Then what would you prefer? What's your dream first date?" She glances at me, blinking, and I let out a laugh. "Come on, I know girls think about this. Trust me, I've heard my sister talk about it enough."

She smiles a little. "You have a sister?"

I nod. "She just turned thirteen and is already wiser than I'll ever be." Too smart for her own good, that little shit.

Madeline smirks. "It's not hard to do," she quips.

I narrow my eyes at her. "Stop trying to insult me and answer the question."

Her grin settles when she breathes out a sigh. She's quiet while we walk, but then I see her lips curve downwards. "I don't know," she finally says.

"Are you afraid you'll tell me and then want me to recreate it?" I tease.

She lets out a scoff. "Never in a million years."

Yeah, I'm starting to see that she means that, which is good. Other girls Ana hired might have wanted to date or more

53

specifically, sleep with me, but I know I don't have to worry about that with Madeline.

Would I like to settle down one day? Sure, the idea seems nice, but I just don't know if it will ever happen. But even if I wanted to, I'm not ready to date. I have people I need to take care of that need my undivided attention. There's none left to go to anyone else.

"You want some ice cream?" I ask her, gesturing to the small ice cream truck ahead. The ice cream truck looking like something out of the fifties, tattered, and its paint chipping off. She doesn't answer, but keeps walking, which I'll take as a yes. "What flavor do you want?" I ask her.

She cocks her head at me. "You're going to order something weird, aren't you?"

"What's your idea of weird?"

She scans my face, finally letting out a small breath, almost sounding like an actual laugh. "You just look like the type that orders mint ice cream."

How the hell? "Hey, don't knock it 'till you try it," I tell her, watching as she grimaces.

"I knew it. How can you like that flavor? It tastes of toothpaste."

My chest shakes with a laugh. "I don't get why everyone says that. It doesn't taste of toothpaste." Seriously? What is it with the mint ice cream hate?

"What else should I know about you?" she asks. "Any dead bodies? Crazy ex-girlfriends? Maybe a scandal?"

"Nothing," I say, heading toward the older lady in the truck. She smiles when we approach her, like I'm one of few customers, and it caves my chest in. "I'm perfectly normal."

"You know I could just look you up, and I'd know everything I needed to know about you."

I shake my head. "I'd rather you didn't."

"So you do have a dark past?"

"No," I affirm. "I just don't want you to see the lies the press spread about me."

She's quiet for a moment, but then she lets out a breath. "I guess I'm one of them now, right? A lie."

My brows knit together, hating how that sounds.

"What can I get for you today?" I turn my head to the lady smiling down at us from inside her truck.

"Mint chocolate chip, please." I catch the way Madeline grimaces at my order.

"Cherry deluxe. Thank you," Madeline says, flashing her a smile I've never seen directed at me. It's a good thing, really. Because fuck, it's a nice smile.

I shake my head with a laugh. "Seriously?" I ask her. "You gave me a hard time about choosing mint, and you pick cherry?" I breathe out a laugh. "That's got to be the worst flavor."

"Don't judge my ice cream preference," she says, shooting me a glare.

I let out a laugh, pulling out my wallet to pay for the ice cream, leaving a hefty tip that she gasps at. She's got to be older than my mom, and she's on her feet all day in a small ass truck. The least I could do was make her day.

I shoot her a smile, thanking her for the ice cream before we head to the park. It's quiet today, being a Monday. Not a lot of people around, which is good if this is going to work. I'm not sure how Madeline would react to fans coming up to us, asking for pictures, or wanting to talk.

But when I turn my gaze to hers, she's frowning at me. "You didn't have to do that," she says.

"Do what?"

"Pay for me," she elaborates. "I can pay for myself."

"I know that," I say, furrowing my brows. "It wasn't a big deal." I didn't even think twice about it, but I'm not about to argue about a five-dollar ice cream.

"I don't want to owe you," she says, holding out her ice cream.

What the fuck?

"Owe me?" I repeat, letting out a laugh, but when I see the serious look on her face, I realize she isn't joking. "Madeline, you don't owe me anything," I assure her. I watch as her scowl dissipates, her eyes softening. I swear they get bigger the more she looks at me. "Not now or ever. If I ever decide to do something for you, no matter what it is, I don't expect anything back."

Honestly, I know we're not the best of friends, and we got off on the wrong foot, but come on, does she really think I'd do that?

She's still staring at me, her big brown eyes glancing up as her lips are twisted in a frown. They're not red this time, and I've got to say, I kind of miss it. She glances down at her ice cream once again, and I let out a sigh. "Just eat the damn ice cream woman," I tell her, shaking my head. "It's melting."

The corner of her mouth lifts before her tongue swipes out, swirling around the tip of the ice cream, sucking it into her mouth.

Fuck.

I rip my gaze away from her, finishing off my dessert at a rate that will probably give me brain freeze, but I need to focus on something else other than the thoughts roaming around my head.

What the fuck am I doing staring at her mouth? I shouldn't do that. I don't even like the girl. She's a pain in my ass, annoying as hell, and makes being around me seem like a chore. I reluctantly turn around, looking at her again.

She glances up at me, her brows furrowed. "What?" she asks, wiping at the corner of her mouth. "Do I have something on my face?"

I shake my head, but when something flashes behind her, my head snaps up, spotting a camera. Wait, no, two cameras. And where there's two, there's more somewhere. I watch as one of the guys talks to the other, shaking his head. Fuck, they're not buying it.

Before I can talk myself out of it, I grab Madeline by her waist and pull her flush to me. Her lips part open as she lets out a gasp, placing her hand flat against my chest. "What are you doing?" she asks, scowling at me.

*Saving your ass, that's what.* "Just go with it," I murmur, trying not to look up at them.

"We agreed only necessary touching," she says like she's offended I'm actually touching her right now.

I narrow my eyes down at her. "Believe me, this is necessary."

"How so?" she asks, arching an eyebrow. I let out a sigh, and my hand moves half an inch across her back, making her stiffen under my touch. Jesus, this girl really does not like me touching her.

"The paps are here," I tell her.

Wrong fucking move.

57

"What?" Her head twists in every direction, trying to seek them out.

"Jesus." My hand reaches up to cup her face. "Stop that. you're going to blow our cover."

Our eyes meet for a second, and she lets out a harsh breath. "We're not detectives, you know."

"Good thing we're not." I cock my head at her. "If we were, you would have gotten us fired. Or killed." My eyes glance up, noticing the camera flashing at us.

I rub my thumb over her cheek, hearing her suck in a breath, her eyes widening. "What are you doing?" she whispers.

"I can see them," I tell her, feeling her soft skin under my fingers as I brush her hair behind her ear. "They're not buying it. We have to make it believable."

"You're ruining my silk press," she whispers, narrowing her eyes at me.

I glare down at her. "My hands are dry."

"I can feel your clammy hands," she murmurs.

I let out a laugh, finding it amusing how stubborn this woman is, but it isn't until her lips part that I realize how close we are. My eyes instinctively drop to them, and I let myself picture it. Kissing her. Tasting her. I know exactly what she would taste of right now. Rich, sweet cherries. What would it be like?

But when I see the rapid movement of her chest, I know that will never happen.

I let out a sigh, dropping my shoulders. "You don't have to be nervous. I'm not going to kiss you," I assure her. "You said that was off limits, and I listen, okay?"

She stares up at me for a while but then nods, licking her lips. I rub my thumb over her cheek again. "We need to give them something, though," I tell her, scanning her eyes for any sort of discomfort. We need to make it interesting enough that people talk about it, about us. But I also need to keep it within Madeline's rules.

"My cheek," she whispers. I nod, leaning in, and press my lips to her left cheek, her warm skin heating my lips from the touch.

The subtle sound of her throat as she swallows, prompts me to pull back and meet her eyes. I can see how nervous she is, and I don't want her to be. "You see? That wasn't too bad," I tease.

Her shoulders relax, and she lets out a scoff. "Well, I didn't burst into flames from touching you, if that's what you mean."

A laugh escapes me. It's astounding how she goes right back to hating me so quickly when she was shaking in my arms less than a minute ago. "Who would have guessed an actress was bad under pressure."

She frowns, and I instantly want to kick myself for saying it. "I'm normally better than that. I was just worried they'd see through it."

"I get it," I assure her. "I was just joking. You don't need to prove anything to me, Madeline. It can be scary to be under observation constantly." I do a quick glance, trying to see if the paparazzi are still following us, but I can't see them. "This was fun, though," I tell her as we walk ahead. "I can see why you want to be an actress."

"Yeah," she says, with a small smile as she looks down at her half-eaten ice cream cone. "It's been my dream for so long. I don't know what I'll do if it doesn't happen."

"You don't know it won't," I tell her, even though I've never seen this girl act before. "You're still young. It could happen. Are you a drama major?"

She laughs, shaking her head. "I wish," she says, scrunching her nose. "I study political science."

"Parents idea?" I guess.

She nods, finishing off her ice cream. "I can't really blame them. They just wanted me to have a stable career, not worry about money." Her shoulders lift in a shrug. "They're both lawyers, so they assumed I would want to be as well." Her eyes lift to mine. "I don't."

"I got that," I say with a laugh.

"They paid for my tuition as long as I chose a bachelor's degree," she continues. "I guess in a way I wanted to please them, but I know they're still holding out hope that I'll go to law school once I graduate." She shakes her head. "But I hate it. I have no interest in the subject."

"Have you told them that?" I ask her.

"No way. I don't want to disappoint them," she admits with a slight frown. "I'll let them think I'm following in their footsteps, and in the meantime, I'll do whatever I can to try and make my dreams come true."

I admire how determined she is to get what she wants. She isn't scared to go after it, even when she knows it might not lead her where she wants it to. I wish I had that gumption. "So, what made you want to be an actress?" I ask.

"Cinderella," she admits, glancing at me from the side. "I know it's cliché, but I was obsessed with Disney movies as a kid. Especially Cinderella."

"Pftt. Cinderella?" I shake my head. "Aladdin is the best Disney movie by far."

A laugh escapes her. "That's just one of many things we disagree on," she says, flicking her long brown hair behind her shoulder when the wind blows it into her face. I let my eyes wander down her body, taking in the little blue and white dress she has on.

"I guess I knew then and there I wanted to do that." Her voice snaps me out of whatever the hell I was doing, and I blink.

"Be rescued by a prince?" I taunt.

She glares at me. "Be the one behind the screen, not in front of it." She cocks her head as she looks at me. "What made you want to be a model?"

I shrug. "I'll let you know when I find it."

"Something must have made you want to choose this career," she says, and I don't miss the way her eyes drop down to my figure as she gives me a once over.

I press my lips together in an attempt to hide my smile, and when her eyes meet mine again, I can't help it. "Did you just check me out?" I ask her, unable to keep my grin at bay.

Her eyes widen. "Believe me, I very much didn't."

"Liar," I whisper, leaning down. "I think you did."

She rolls her eyes, pushing at my chest. "I knew you had a big ego. Was that it?" she asks, with a smirk. "You just loved seeing pictures of yourself?

My laugh settles, and I decide to be honest. "It was the money."

She shakes her head. "Of course it was. So you didn't have a passion for it, like Leila?"

I blink, my brows furrowing. "You know Leila?"

"I probably should have mentioned that before. She's one of my best friends," she explains. "When she saw the picture of us, she freaked out a little."

I let out a laugh, picturing Leila wondering what the hell I was doing holding her friend. "Yeah, my mom did too. Did you tell her?" I ask. "About…" I gesture between us.

She shakes her head. "I told her the headlines were a lie, but that was before we agreed to the whole…" she drifts off, glancing around. Right. We probably shouldn't be talking about how we're faking a relationship in public. "But once she sees these pictures…" She shrugs, sighing. "I'll have to lie, right?"

Well, shit. I already told my family and James, but I nod anyway. "It was stated in the NDA."

She frowns a little, and I get it. I hate lying, especially to my family. "No," I tell her. Her head snaps up, looking confused, and I continue. "To answer your previous question, I don't have a passion for it. It's just something that paid the bills, and it's the only thing I'm good at so…"

"That can't be true."

I lift my shoulder. "This is all I have to offer," I admit. "I didn't go to college or do anything interesting other than this." Her frown deepens, but I shake it off. "It's fine," I assure her. "It got me where I needed to be."

"So you don't have a dream? Something you'd love to do if you could?"

I don't have time for dreams. Dreams get me nowhere, they don't pay the bills, and they're a complete waste of time. "Nope," I tell her, even though I get a flash of my sketchbook in my mind. "Nothing."

"That's sad," she admits.

Yeah, well. My phone buzzes in my pocket, and I pull it out, reading the text Ana sent.

Ana:

> We got it.

"Is that Ana?" Madeline asks.

I nod, placing my phone back in my pocket. "Yeah, she said we got it." I let out a sigh when I realize this is finally done. We can both leave and go our separate ways. There's no reason for us to hang out together, not when we don't need to.

"We make a pretty good team," I tell her, flashing her a smirk.

She rolls her eyes. "When you don't piss me off," she says, but then her eyes crinkle in thought. "It wasn't as bad as I thought, though."

No. It really wasn't.

# 9

Stake your bet

# *Madeline*

"Pay up!"

I wake up with a thud when Gabi jumps on top of my bed, startling me. A groan escapes me when I peel an eye open, seeing her grin down at me like a puppy. "What time is it?" I reach for my phone on my nightstand and almost choke when I see it's 6 am.

"You're crazy," I grumble, pulling my covers over my head. "Let me sleep."

"Nope." She pulls the covers off my face. "We made a deal. You lost."

"What the hell are you talking about?" I mumble into my pillow.

"We made a bet, remember?" I reluctantly open my eyes, seeing a grin spread across her face as she shakes a bottle of red hair dye in my face.

"I have no idea what you're talking about. I didn't make any bets."

She lets out a laugh. "Oh yes, you did. You said, and I quote, 'I will never get a boyfriend, and if I do, I'll dye my hair red, and I'll do anything my best friend Gabi wants for a week.'"

I narrow my eyes at her. "I definitely didn't say that."

She sighs. "Okay, well, I added that last part, but the rest is true. You were so confident that you would never date again," she says with a head tilt. "And we both knew that was bullshit." The red hair dye is shoved in front of my face again. "So it's time to pay up."

"Did I miss the part where I'm dating?"

She smirks. "You're trying to deny it," she says, tutting at me. "You little cheater."

"Deny what?" I ask her, wiping my eyes, knowing I'll never be able to get back to sleep now.

She shakes her head, a smile on her face, and pulls out her phone, holding it out to me. A picture of Lucas and me at the park a few days ago is front and center on the screen, with the headline saying, 'The hottest celebrity couple debuts their relationship'. Well, then, seems like it worked.

"Shit."

"Yeah, shit," she says, pocketing her phone. "I thought you said you didn't even know him." She narrows her eyes at me. "And now you're suddenly dating? How the hell did this happen?" She shakes her head. "You know what, I don't care. You lost," she says. "I can't wait to see you with red hair."

*That is not happening.* "I did not lose. I said the day I fall in love will be the day I dye my hair red. That hasn't – and will not – happen."

She squints at me and then drops her shoulders. "Fine," she says, sitting on the edge of my bed. "But it won't take long. You're already halfway there."

I choke on my laughter. "I'm nowhere near close. Believe me, you're going to be getting a tattoo of my choice before that ever happens." If *and when* Gabi undoubtedly falls in love first,

I'll be picking out a tattoo for her. And I can't wait for that to happen.

She narrows her eyes at me. "When did you see him again?" she asks. "Why didn't you tell me? Is it serious? Is he nice? Is he—"

Gabriella doesn't have time to finish her sentence because both Leila and Rosie open the door and come inside. "You're dating Lucas?" Leila asks.

I groan again. "Seriously? Can't I get some sleep here?" I fall back onto my pillow and squeeze my eyes shut. When I lift my head, they're all staring at me, waiting for answers. "How do you even know about it?"

"Gabi called us," she says.

I look over to the traitor in question, who simply shrugs. "It's a big deal," she says. "I never thought this day would happen." She pretends to sniff and wipe a tear. *Such a drama queen.* "My baby is growing up."

I pick up my pillow and hit her on the arm with it. She lets out a laugh, and Rosie sits down beside me. "I know I'm not one to say anything since I kept Grayson a secret from you guys, but why didn't you tell us? Didn't you know it would be all over the internet?" she asks.

I did. I knew, and I should have prepared for this moment, but the thought of lying to them gives me hives. I pull my bottom lip between my teeth. "I... forgot?"

They all narrow their eyes at me, and Leila shakes her head. "Okay, what's going on?" she asks. "Last week, you told us you didn't know him, and now you're apparently dating? Besides, the Lucas I know doesn't date, at least not seriously."

I frown, thinking of all the girls that came before me, getting photographed with him. I'm no different. I'm now one of those girls. "It's complicated," I tell her, not wanting to lie but also not wanting to go broke from this NDA.

"What's going on?" Leila asks again. "If anyone understands 'complicated,' it's us."

Shit. God, I hate lying. "I... can't say."

That makes them even more suspicious, and I inwardly curse at myself for signing that NDA. This is the hardest thing in my life. I don't keep secrets from them. They know everything there is to know about me. Even what happened with Daniel.

"Are you okay?" Leila asks, her tone sounding worried. "Is there something going on?"

"Whatever it is, you can tell us," Rosalie says.

"Who's ass do we need to beat?" Gabi asks.

I let out a laugh, shaking my head. I love these girls so much. I can't lie. Not to them. I sigh, and the words just come tumbling out. "It's not real."

"What?" they all ask, clearly confused.

"It's fake," I admit with a shrug. "That meeting I had with an agent last week? It was Lucas' agent. She said people were loving the picture of us and the idea of us as a couple, and his agent suggested we continue the ruse. Pretend to date." I look at the girls, who all seem confused, and shake my head. "She said this would be good for me, for both of us. That it would get us publicity and make my name known."

Leila nods. "Yeah, it'll definitely do that. Lucas is well known and loved, and with you being photographed with him... people will start to notice you, for sure."

"So this is all fake?" Gabi asks, looking down at the picture again. "None of it is real?"

"Definitely not," I confirm. "We're not even kissing in this picture. He was warning me about the paparazzi, that's it." I glance down at the picture on her phone. It really does look like we're kissing. "Trust me, the last thing I would want is to be in a relationship, less of all him."

"You still don't like him, huh?" Leila asks.

"He just knows how to get on my nerves. At first, he scared me off taking the deal, and then he chased me down, begging me to take it. I don't like that he has the power to decide what I do."

Leila shakes her head. "Everyone loves Lucas. I don't understand how you don't like him."

"So you've said," I tell her with a sigh, wishing I could just go back to sleep. "But we just don't get along."

"How's that going to work?" Gabi asks. "You're going to have to spend time with him, right?"

"I'm sure it won't be for long. Just some public outings here and there, and then he'll get what he needs."

"And you?" Rosie asks. "What do you get from this?"

I shrug. "Hopefully, this will get me some recognition and help me land an audition. Nepotism is alive and thriving after all."

She chuckles. "Don't I know it." Rosie's family is very well off, so while she prefers slumming it with us, her family could get her anywhere she wants.

My phone buzzes on my nightstand, and I reach out to grab it, seeing a text from Lucas. My brows furrow when I open it.

Lucas:

Did you get Ana's email?

What email? I quickly check, going through my emails, and there it is. The next part of this plan. I scan the details, and when Lucas' name flashes at the top again, I let out a groan.

Lucas:

> Are you ready for this?

Ready? Does he think I'm incompetent or something? Ok, sure, I might have panicked at the park. But I had never done that before. Of course, I'd be on edge.

Madeline:

> What the hell are you doing up at this time?

Lucas:

> Some of us wake up early.

I groan, burying my head in my hands.

"Is that Lucas?" Leila asks.

I lift my head and nod. "We have a photoshoot next week to announce our relationship," I tell her.

When my phone rings, my eyes widen, and the girls all look at me. I glance at the screen, see Lucas' name, and shake my head. "Why the hell is he calling me?"

"Answer it," Gabi says.

I shake my head. "You guys can't speak," I tell them while the phone rings. "I signed an NDA. If I tell anyone, I pay a hundred thousand dollars."

"Fuck," Gabi says, her eyes widened. "That's a lot of money."

"I know."

"Don't worry," Leila says. "We won't say a word."

Rosie pretends to zip up her lips, so I let out a sigh and answer the call, bringing it to my ear. "Why are you calling me at six am?" I ask him.

He lets out a laugh. "Let me guess, you're not a morning person?"

"Not when you're calling."

"Put it on speaker," Gabi whispers.

I pull my phone away and put it on speaker so the girls hear.

"Charmer as always," Lucas says. The girls all listen intently. "So, are you ready?" he asks.

"For what?"

"The photoshoot," he clarifies. "I know you've never done one before, and I wanted to check in on you. I would hate for you to embarrass yourself or anything."

I press my lips, glancing at Leila to prove to her that her 'friend' manages to get on every one of my nerves.

"Don't worry," I reply. "It's just a photoshoot. You do it. How hard can it be?"

He laughs, and the sound radiates through the room. It's smooth and husky, and I hate it. "Very hard, *princesa*." The girls widen their eyes at the term, and I look away, my cheeks feeling hot.

"I'm sure I'll be fine."

"We'll see about that," he says. "The photo shoot is at ten. Don't be late."

I let out a scoff. "I'm never late."

"Are you sure?" he says. "It would be very unprofessional for the crew to have to wait for you."

"Trust me," I say, my eyes narrowing. "I'll be the first one there."

He chuckles again. "Can't wait. I'm heading into the gym now. But if you change your mind and decide to ask for my help for the photo shoot, I'll expect a please."

"I don't need your help," I reassure him. "I have class in a few hours, and as fun as this was, I'm going to hang up and go back to sleep."

He hums. "Night. Dream of me." I can picture the stupid grin on his face, and I resist the urge to groan.

"That would be a nightmare," I say into the phone before I hang up.

"Well," Gabi says. "That was… interesting."

"He calls you princess?" Rosie asks, smiling.

She's so sweet it hurts. I mean, her boyfriend calls her *angel*. "Hate to break it to you, but he doesn't use that in a good way." Lucas' term is laced with sarcasm, reminding me that he thinks I'm a princess who gets everything my way.

"Lucas was right, though," Leila says. "Photoshoots can be hard for someone who's never done them."

I know that. I was just trying to get under his skin like he has mine, but the thought of asking him for help is not an option. I give Leila my sweetest smile and flutter my eyelashes at her. "Help me?"

She laughs. "Of course I will."

I let out a breath. I'm going to show up at that photoshoot and prove to Lucas that I don't need his help, nor will I ever beg for it.

He's going to eat his words, and I can't fucking wait.

71

# 10

Picture perfect

*Madeline*

"You're late."

Lucas startles when he hears my voice and glances down at his watch. When he lifts his head, his glare stabs through me. "It's ten thirty-five."

"And we were supposed to be at the studio at ten thirty," I remind him.

He shakes his head with a laugh, holding two cups of coffee in his hands. "Well, excuse me, your highness. I was doing something."

"What were you doing?" I ask.

He smiles at me, but it's laced with the complete opposite of kindness. "None of your business."

I place my hand on my hips. "Must have been really important to show up late to the photoshoot you hounded me about."

He lifts his shoulder in a shrug. "Yeah, it was." He leans closer, a smirk on his lips. "Was that all, or do you want to interrogate me some more?"

I lift my head to meet his gaze, and a nervous gulp escapes me. "That's all."

His smirk widens briefly, but then his brows furrow as he inhales deeply. "What's that smell?" he asks, his voice deepening as his eyes lock with mine.

My eyes narrow in confusion. "My perfume?"

He lets out a deep groan, his eyes falling closed as he pulls back and walks away, heading into the dressing rooms.

Figures. He doesn't like my perfume. Good thing I didn't wear it for him. I let out a sigh, glancing around. The room is crowded, with clusters of people, deep in conversation, cameras and lights everywhere, and a sudden rush of nerves washes over me.

I feel so out of place. I hardly know anyone, and I'm not entirely sure what I'm supposed to be doing. Leila did her best to walk me through some things when I asked for her help, but the reality of being here is completely different.

"Hey," I turn my head to see Ana approaching with a cup of coffee in her hands. "You look like you need this."

I gratefully take the coffee from her, offering a smile. "Yes, thank you." I take a sip, and it's perfect – not too sweet, but still strong. I hum in satisfaction, savoring the coffee. "Wow. You nailed it."

She chuckles, lifting a shoulder in a shrug. When she looks down at my outfit, her eyes widen. "You look amazing. Did you get into hair and makeup already?" she asks.

"No, I actually wasn't sure if I should come dressed up."

She nods. "I get it, you're new to this, but you didn't. We have people for that," she says, pointing at a blonde woman currently putting makeup on Lucas. "That's Lexi. She's our makeup artist around here." She gestures to the older lady currently sorting a rack of clothes. "And that's Cynthia. She takes care of the outfits," she says before she glances down at my clothes again. "But you clearly don't need it."

I let out a laugh. "Thank you." I pride myself on my outfits. Not only is one of my best friends an amazing designer, but my older sister, Nia, used to be obsessed with clothes. My heart aches at the thought of her, thinking of what she'd say if she saw me here. It's been four years since the accident, and I still miss her. So much.

"So," I say, trying to move on before I start crying. "Where do I go?"

"We need to wait for Lucas to finish up, but I'm sure he'll help you out."

I groan, shaking my head. "I'd rather not ask for his help." I take a sip of my coffee, glancing back to where Lucas is, smiling and laughing with his makeup artist.

She laughs. "You guys didn't get along at the park?" she asks. "Those pictures seemed to say the opposite."

I shrug, smirking at her. "I'm a good actress." But I don't want to admit that most of that was because of Lucas. If not for him, I'm sure we would have been called out on our fake relationship by now.

"Well, in that case, I'll help you," she says. "You see that guy?" She points to who I assume is the photographer since he's behind the camera. I nod. "That's Jack. He's our photographer. He's been in this business for years, you're in good hands, I promise."

"Good to know."

"You'll both stand over there," she points to the backdrop. "And Jack will take it from there," she says, giving me a smile. "You're gorgeous. He'll have no issues with you. You guys will look perfect together."

Her words make my stomach cramp a little, but when Lucas shows up and gestures to the backdrop, I stop thinking of what Ana said and square my shoulders. I will not let him see me weak. Not again.

"You ready to do this?" he asks.

"Of course."

Lucas walks in front of me, and I follow his lead. My nerves start to kick in, but I tell myself this is what I wanted. Sure, none of this is real, but I can pretend I'm playing a part, which I technically am.

Lucas glances down at me, when we approach our mark and narrows his eyes. "You asked for help, didn't you?"

"What?" I ask, furrowing my brows. "What are you talking about?"

"Come on," he says with a laugh. "There's no way you could just walk in here and go with the flow. I bet you asked Leila to draw a map and give you point-by-point directions on what to do."

His grin infuriates me, and I narrow my eyes at him. "I did not," I lie.

"I don't buy it," he says. "I bet you even asked Ana for help. All because you didn't want to ask me."

I give him a shrug, not bothering to deny it. "Well, you said I would need to beg, so I had to work around that."

His smirk makes me shiver as his gaze drops to my body, and he shakes his head. "It's a shame. It would do you some good saying please."

I narrow my eyes at him. "Never."

He hums, leaning down to whisper against my ear. "So you're not nervous right now?" he asks. My heart races as I shake my head. But he just chuckles, the vibrations making my

75

skin erupt into goosebumps. "I'll help you out if you say please."

"I told you," I say, my voice sounding breathy and rough. I clear my throat and shake my head. "I don't need your help."

"Please," he whispers, even closer now. "That's all I need to hear, and I'll help you out."

"I'm good." I face forward and try to ignore the way his scent travels up my nose. He smells *so* good. *God, I hate him.* He moves back into place, and when he does, I get another whiff of his scent. I don't even think he's wearing cologne, it just smells, clean and... manly. I haven't smelled something like that in a long time.

He lets out a heavy sigh, and with a shake of his head murmurs, "*Por que uma garota tão bonita como ela me deixa louco?*"

I blink, staring up at him. "What did you just say?"

He glares at me. "I said you're a stubborn pain in my ass," he says, placing his hands in his pockets. His head snaps back into place as he stands in a pose, ready for the cameras.

Okay, so I might be stubborn and have lied about being ready. I'm definitely not. I don't have a fucking clue on what to do, so I smile at the camera and hope this is good enough.

It's not.

I gather that when the photographer squints at me, not liking what he sees.

"Still don't want my help?" Lucas whispers, still facing forward.

"I..." I sigh, squeezing my eyes closed. The quicker we do this, the quicker I'll get to leave. "Please," I grit out.

His head snaps to face me, and he grins. "Repeat that for me."

God, this man really knows how to push my buttons. I exhale harshly. "Please," I repeat, not daring to look at him.

His dark chuckle makes me shiver as his hand encloses around my elbow and turns me to face him. "Models and actresses are very similar, Madeline," he says. "They both have to act for whatever it is we're doing. Whether it's a perfume commercial or a clothing line, we become someone else. We become the product, not a person."

I blink up at him. "So you're saying I'm a product?" I raise my brows at him.

He shakes his head. "Pain in my ass," he murmurs. "Here," he says, pulling me closer to him. "Follow my lead." He drags his hands down my arms and twists me around so I'm facing the camera, but this time he moves an inch closer and looks down at me. I instinctively look up at him, and he smiles. "Good," he whispers as the cameras start to click. "Just relax."

I let out a breath, my lips parting, and I do what he said.

"Great," the photographer calls out, more clicking going off. "Perfect. Now move a bit closer."

Lucas shuffles an inch closer until his arms brush against mine. I stiffen and try to move away again. He groans and leans down until he's close to my ear and whispers, "You're making this harder than it needs to be."

His husky voice makes my skin flush, and I force myself to breathe, looking up at him. "You're too close to me."

He pulls back with a frown on his face. "Necessary touching," he says. "This is a press release of our relationship. We can't be five feet apart." He scans my eyes. "You just need to act like a doting girlfriend for a few minutes, and then we can go home." He narrows his eyes. "Can you do that for me?"

"I doubt it," I murmur, glancing at the photographer who's getting impatient.

His hand snakes around my waist as he pulls me flush to him and I gasp, staring up at him. "That's it," he says. "Keep looking at me." His other hand curls up under my chin and lifts my head. Our eyes meet, and my heart starts to beat as more flashes go off. Lucas gives me a sultry look, and I drink it in, admiring his face. Ugh. Why does he have to be so hot?

"Yes. Beautiful," the photographer says. "You guys look amazing."

Lucas' dark brown eyes remain on mine, and my skin starts to burn, feeling hot and sweaty. It's the lights. It has to be.

"You guys look great," Jake says again as more flashes go off. The sounds of the camera make me zone out a little, and I let myself wonder what these pictures will look like. I'm wearing a long, red dress that compliments my warm, brown skin tone and my deep, red lipstick perfectly. Lucas is wearing a black button-down with jeans. His hair is perfectly styled, the messy brown curls falling strategically onto his face, and I let myself see how other people will see us.

We look like a couple.

"Perfect," Jake says as he steps out from behind the camera. "Now can we get a kiss from the beautiful couple?"

My eyes widen at his request because despite how the outside world perceives us, we are not a couple. We are nothing. This is fake. And there is no way I am going to kiss him.

Lucas notes my reaction and frowns, because he knows there is no way I'm going to let him kiss me, and he promised he wouldn't. It's one of my rules.

But what if he changes his mind? What if he just tells me to suck it up for the picture and to just go with it? It's just one stupid kiss. We both know it doesn't mean anything, but... I can't do it.

The last time I had someone's lips on mine, it ended in a nightmare, and I can't think of anyone else ever kissing me. I don't want to.

I step back from him and his hands drop as he lets out a breath. He forces a laugh and turns to face Jake, running a hand over his chin. "We'd prefer to do that alone," he says.

My heartbeat settles as I let out an exhale. Thank god he's keeping his promise.

"We need something for the pictures," the photographer says. "Come on. Just give us a kiss and we'll be on our way."

Lucas looks at me again and I know he can see the panic in my eyes as he reaches out to me. "Relax," he tells me. "I'm not going to kiss you. Just... close your eyes." I look up at him and part my lips. What is he going to do? He must see the question in my eyes because he leans in again. "Just trust me."

I let my eyes fall closed and my heart races twice as fast now. I can't see anything. But I can feel. I feel his hand run over my face as he cups my neck, his thumb resting on my cheek. I feel his breath hit my neck as he leans into me, closer than we ever have been before. I feel his heart beating just as fast as mine when his chest presses up against my arm.

Clicks go off in the distance as Jake takes the pictures and I let myself melt into him, knowing that Jake still got the picture he wanted without us having to kiss.

"Beautiful," Jake says again as the clicks stop. I snap my eyes open and see Lucas staring down at me, only an inch away. "We got it," he says.

Lucas removes his hand from my neck and we untangle ourselves from each other. He furrows his brows as he looks at me. "You panicked," he says. "I told you that we would only do whatever you're comfortable with. I told you we wouldn't kiss if you didn't want to. Did you not believe me?" he asks.

Honestly? I knew he would keep his promise. He kept it when we were at the park, and he hasn't given me an inkling of taking what he wants without asking me, but... it's all I'm used to from men, or one man in particular. Why should I believe any different? "I don't really know you," I say with a shrug.

He raises his brows. "Then maybe we should change that."

# 11

I love balls

*Lucas*

"Your mom's going to make me fat," James groans, shoving a half-eaten sandwich in his mouth.

I glare down at him, spotting another two sandwiches on his plate. Where the hell does he put it all? "Then stop eating."

He shakes his head, humming with his mouth full. "Can't," he mumbles. "Too good."

Yeah, my mom's an amazing cook. One of the things I missed most about home when I was living in New York, was my mom's home-cooked meals. Since I've moved back, there isn't a single Sunday that I don't spend at my mom's house for family dinner.

"She's just worried about you," I tell him. "Food is how she shows she cares."

He sighs, gulping when he finishes off the sandwich. "I'm fine," he says. "Don't know how many times I have to tell you guys that."

I hate when he does that. Acts like everything's fine when it was one of the worst things that could happen to someone. "It wasn't that long ago, James." It's only been a few months since the accident, and the funeral. It's a lot to deal with.

He shrugs. "It's not like it hasn't happened before."

He lost his dad a few years ago, right around the time my dad passed away. I was a fucking mess when I lost my dad, so I can't even begin to imagine how James must be feeling now that both of his parents are gone.

"You want to talk about it?" I ask him. He might not want to talk to therapists about it, but maybe he wants to talk to me about it.

He lets out a laugh, furrowing his brows at me. "Since when have we ever done that?"

We're not the talking kind. More the 'let's forget about it and move on', but maybe it's not such a terrible idea. "We could start," I tell him.

He scoffs. "I'd rather not. You get this ugly face when you cry."

I nudge him on the shoulder. "Fuck you."

He laughs, and everything is back to normal. He's been my best friend for most of my life, and we've been through too much together. It sucks that this happened to him. But you'd never know he was unhappy with how he's always smiling.

The door creaks open, and then a knock hits. My mom peeks in before opening the door and gives James a smile. "Hey, honey," she says. James might as well be her other son at this point. She reaches over and fluffs the pillows behind his back. "How was the sandwich?" she asks.

He left the hospital last week and moved into my old bedroom, which is why I was a little late for the photoshoot. He was living alone, but after what happened, we all thought it would be best if he moved in with my mom. That way, he has someone taking care of him.

"Good, mama Silva." He grins at her. He's called her that ever since I've known him. It makes me laugh every time. "Was there bacon in there this time?"

My mom nods. "I picked it up for you this morning."

"What about me?" I ask her, even though I'm not a big fan of bacon. "I'm hungry too." I ate an hour ago, but I'm not going to lie, I'm feeling a little left out.

"Nossa," she says in Portuguese. "Tem sopa na geladeira." *There's soup in the fridge.*

Well then. Guess we know who's the favorite.

James grins. He loves receiving the attention from my mom. "Don't know what she said, but she's right."

I scoff. "Asshole." My mom shifts his legs, placing a blanket on them. I let out a sigh. "He's fine, mom." But she shakes her head.

She loves taking care of people. I guess she's been doing it for so long it's all she knows. "Are you comfortable? Do you need anything else?" she asks him.

"Yeah," James says, grinning like an idiot. "Some good di—"

"Dinner," I interrupt before he gives my mother a heart attack.

We've known James was gay since he announced he had a crush on Justin Timberlake one day when we were watching the Music Awards. But even though my mom might not have an issue with it, that doesn't mean she can handle hearing the gory details.

"He was just saying he can't wait to have your meatballs."

"Yeah," James scoffs. "I love balls."

I wipe a hand down my face. I should have seen that coming. She smiles at him, completely oblivious. "Then I'll go get dinner ready." She fluffs the pillows once more before she heads out of the room.

"Dude," I say, smacking him on the arm, once she leaves.

"What?" He laughs. "She asked."

I shake my head, a laugh escaping me. "You're going to get your ass whooped by her someday."

A mischievous grin creeps on his face as he leans back on the bed. "You would know about tough women, huh? How's it going with that girl... what's her name?"

"Madeline."

"That's right. Madeline. So, are things better?"

I blow out a breath. "Define better."

His chest shakes with laughter. "I guess not then. What happened at the photoshoot?"

A heavy sigh escapes me when I turn to face him. "Why do you always have to bring her up?" I ask him. I mean, come on. She's already invaded my work life, but now my personal life too?

"Because it's fun watching you trip over your words whenever you talk about her," he admits, grinning down at me like an idiot.

"What are you talking about?" I ask, my brows knitting together. "I do not."

His shoulder lifts in a shrug. "I haven't seen you this interested in a girl before, that's all."

"I'm not interested in her," I say, glaring at him. "I'm just around her. All the damn time." It's seriously impossible to get rid of her. She's everywhere. At my work, on the internet, in my fucking head. Everywhere.

"And it's driving you crazy," he guesses.

I blow out a breath. "Insane."

He laughs, shaking his head. "I don't get why she affects you so much."

I don't fucking know either. I shrug, wiping a hand down my face. "Since I met her she has made it very fucking clear that she doesn't like me, and there's nothing I can do to change that," I admit, my shoulders slumping.

I don't even know why I care. It's not like I like her either, but I just don't get her. Every girl I've met has always been interested in me, whether it's in sleeping with me, or for fame, they've wanted something from me. But this girl... "She just knows how to irritate me," I say. "It's a fucking gift."

He's quiet for a while but then he hums. "You two looked pretty cozy in the pictures together."

Yeah, we fucking do. I don't even know how it happens, but every single picture we've taken together looks like we're about to rip each other's clothes off. Those photographers are good at their jobs because the truth couldn't be any more different.

"I was just doing my job. And so was she. She's an actress," I remind him.

He snickers. "She can't be that good of an actress."

I rub my chin, my beard rubbing against my fingers. "Trust me, she is." Those pictures have everyone fooled, me included. When it comes down to it, she lets herself melt, looking at me in a way that's so intoxicating I seem to forget there's anyone around. Those brown eyes burn into mine, her plump lips parting as she looks up at me. She's like a completely different person when the cameras are on us. But once they go away, and it's just the two of us, the spell breaks, and she does everything to remind me that none of it is real.

The door opens again, but this time my sister comes in. She's so tall and looks just like my dad. Long brown hair, tanned skin, big, hazel eyes. "Hey froggy," I say, amusement crossing my face when she narrows her eyes at the term. She might hate it, but it's stuck ever since she freaked out from a frog on her head when she was six. It was the funniest shit me and James had seen.

"I saw your girlfriend," she says.

God damn it. I let out an aggravated sigh. "What did I tell you about looking at that stuff?" She's too damn young, and the internet is ruthless. I don't want her seeing those damn headlines about all the different girls in my bed. My family knows it's not true, but that doesn't mean I want her exposed to that shit.

"You told me not to look," she explains, which tells me she's just a little shit who does everything I tell her not to.

"And you did anyway?" I ask, already knowing the answer.

She drops down on the edge of the bed and lifts her shoulder. "It was different this time. Those pictures weren't like the other ones."

No, they weren't. Madeline is completely different from all those other girls Ana hired. But I know where Adrianna is going with this, and I have to shut it down. "It's not different," I remind her. "She's just some girl my agent hired, froggy."

Her brows furrow. "So you're not dating her?" she asks with a frown.

"No, Adri."

Her expression deflates a little. "She was pretty though," she says, peering up at me. "Even Mom said so."

Yeah, I've heard it myself. My mom told me how beautiful she thinks Madeline is whenever she sees the pictures of us together.

"Yeah," James says, nodding with a grin. "She was."

I turn my attention to him and narrow my eyes. "Need I remind you, you like boys?"

"Men," he corrects. "Besides, I can still see beauty. And she's pretty."

"Like *really* pretty," Adriana emphasizes, her eyes widening.

I flick her on her forehead. "Then you date her."

She pulls back, rubbing her forehead, but then she narrows her eyes at me. "You don't agree?" she asks. "You don't think she's pretty?"

*She's fucking gorgeous.*

I wipe a hand down my mouth, thinking back to the photoshoot. She had that red lipstick on again, matching her long, floor-length dress. And that fucking perfume. It's been a week and I can still smell it everywhere I go. It's ingrained in my mind and I hate it. Hate that she smells so sweet when she's anything but.

"Doesn't matter what I think. It's not real, froggy. Don't get your hopes up again."

"You mean like with Leila?" she asks.

Exactly like that. Leila has been one of my best friends since I started modeling, and while she's beautiful, she's more like my sister than anything else. But Adriana fell in love with Leila. She looked up to her and wanted to be like her, and when she got bullied in school for being bigger than other girls, she turned to Leila knowing she had the same experience.

I'm so grateful for everything Leila has done for my sister, and for being one of my best friends. But Froggy, here, was already planning our marriage in her head, thinking that we'd eventually date, and when that didn't happen, she was very upset.

"If her boyfriend ever heard about you wanting us together, he'd break my legs." Dude is tall as fuck. I'm a tall guy, but he has to be at least 6'5". Not to mention he's buff, and would undoubtedly kick my ass if he even thought I had an inkling of interest in Leila.

I get it though. I'd be jealous too if my girlfriend was best friends with some other guy. I don't blame him for being possessive over her.

"Hmm," she says, her eyes shining with mischief. "Maybe I'll tell him then."

*Little shit.* I breathe out a laugh. "You've been spending too much time with Leila."

She sticks her tongue out at me before she walks out of the room.

"Jesus," James says with a laugh. "You're surrounded by hard-headed women. Wouldn't want to be you," he says.

I shrug, a smile playing on my lips. "I don't mind it."

# 12

## What was my rule?

# *Madeline*

My professor is a dick.

Like seriously, the biggest asshole on Campus. It's well-known that he's a drag. He takes class way too seriously, not to mention he's misogynistic as well as old-fashioned. One of those professors who goes on and on about how technology is ruining the youth and how this generation is doomed.

So, when he asks a question, I don't even have to look to know who he's going to pick. Hint: It's never a girl.

He chooses a guy in the fourth row – shocker – and sits on the edge of his desk, waiting for him to answer. "The primary purpose of a constitution in a democratic political system is to establish the fundamental framework of government, allocate powers and to protect individual rights."

Professor Harrison nods, tapping his pen against his white beard. "Very good."

"Of course, they never follow it," the guy continues, making the room erupt in laughter. I chuckle along.

"Okay," Professor Harrison says, getting irritated. "Settle down, or I'll have to ask you to leave."

The room quietens, and I stare at my laptop, counting down the seconds until class ends. My attention shifts when I hear hushed murmurs and the name Lucas thrown in there. My head snaps up, and I see two girls sneaking glances at me, whispering to each other.

I swallow, trying to look away. I didn't even think of what would happen once people found out about me and Lucas. Sure, I wanted recognition, I wanted to be in the public eye, and hopefully land a part in a movie, but this… I'm not ready for this.

"A constitution plays a pivotal role in shaping the course of a nation's governance. The extent to which politicians adhere to the constitution can be a complex matter, and while many choose not to follow it," he looks pointedly at the guy who made the joke, "political science seeks to unravel these complexities."

*Bore.*

Sometimes, I wonder what would happen if I just… left. Being in college is fun, and of course, I want an education, but do I want one in a subject as dull as this? And for what? To give it all up when I finally graduate? To go to law school, even though it pains me to think of living life as a lawyer? I want to make my parents happy. I do. I don't want to disappoint them. Especially after my sister died, and I'm all they have left.

Nia had just been accepted into Harvard when she died. A few months before she moved into campus, a drunk driver hit the back of her car, leaving her dead on the side of the road while they drove off.

I was only fifteen at the time, and sometimes it feels like my parents tried to replace her with me. I'd been adopted at a very young age. And while I never felt like I wasn't part of the family, our dynamic shifted after Nia died. It seemed like my parents wanted my life to go the way Nia's was supposed to.

I didn't feel like me anymore. I felt like a replacement. And I yearned to make the only parents I had known to see *me,* so I tried everything to be the perfect child. But nothing I did worked. Which led me straight into the arms of someone I never should have gotten close to.

When Professor Harrison dismisses the class, I blow out a breath, relieved I can finally get out of here, and I pack my bags, getting up from my seat.

I rush toward the exit before people crowd the area, but I don't get far before I feel a tap on my shoulder. I hesitantly turn around, seeing the girls from before. "You're Madeline, right?" the blonde one asks.

I nod, clutching the strap of my bag. "Yeah, I am."

"You're dating Lucas Silva?" her friend asks.

"Um…" I squeeze the strap of my bag tighter, wanting the ground to open up and swallow me whole. I was not at all prepared for this. I wonder if it's what Lucas goes through every day. He's probably used to girls throwing themselves at him, wanting pictures, and throwing out marriage proposals, but I am not. "Yes," I say, feeling my throat tighten.

The blonde one furrows her brows, dipping her eyes, giving me a once over. "That's cool," she says before they both walk off.

I blow out a breath, hoping I won't have to do that too often. Lying is not my forte, and the thought of having to lie to strangers with a smile on my face is agony. I head out of class, pushing open the door before the fresh air hits my face. Fuck, it's cold. I shiver, pulling my jacket closed.

"Madi." I turn my head to look behind my shoulder and see Connor a few feet behind, shooting me a smile. "Hey," he says, approaching me. "Harrison is such an old fart."

I let out a chuckle. Glad I'm not the only one who thinks so. "Yeah, he takes that class so seriously."

He sighs. "That joke was pretty lame, though."

I kind of thought it was funny. I nod, anyway.

"So, um," he says, rubbing the back of his neck. "I was wondering if you wanted to hang out later?"

My heart race spikes, and I clutch my bag tighter against my side. "Um…"

God, what is wrong with me? This guy is attractive, and he's actually nice. Most guys are assholes, or if you're Lucas, a hot model who complains about my perfume and drives me crazy. If I say yes, just give in and tell him I'd love to hang out with him. What's the worst thing that could happen?

*He could be like Daniel.*

Connor shrugs, dropping his hand. "I just figured since you're smart, I could use a study partner."

He wants to *study*. Of course.

"Yeah," I tell him, giving him a smile. "That sounds great."

"Yeah?" his voice jumps an octave, sounding surprised as he lifts his brows. "Well, great. Does tomorrow work?"

I nod. "Tomorrow's great."

"Cool." He grins again, pulling out his phone. "What's your number?" he asks. "That way, you can send me your address."

"Oh, um, sure." Crap. I didn't think of that. Gabi won't be home until later, so it would just be us. Alone. In my apartment. It'll be fine, right? We're just studying. I take my phone out of my bag and we exchange numbers.

"I'll see you tomorrow," he says, pocketing his phone.

"Okay." The more I think of this, the more I'm regretting it.

I watch as he walks away, heading toward the gym building. Of course, he works out. Someone who looks like that definitely works out.

"Who was that?"

I flinch at the voice and spin around, spotting Lucas leaning against the wall, his arms crossed as he looks at me with furrowed brows.

"Jesus," I breathe out. "You scared me."

"Apologies," he drawls. "Who was that?"

"Who?" I feign ignorance as I keep walking. He steps off the wall and trails behind me.

"Boyfriend?" he asks with a bite. "Need I remind you, you already have one of those."

My eyes widen as I stop in place and turn around, face to face with him. "Excuse me?"

"You heard me."

I let out a humorless laugh. "Okay, first of all, I am your *fake* girlfriend."

"Semantics."

I shake my head. "And second of all, what are you doing here?"

"I was coming to see Leila, but then you and your *boyfriend* came out together, and it caught my attention."

He says the word with so much venom that it rubs me the wrong way. "He's not my boyfriend. He's just a guy from my class."

His frown deepens. "Was that the same guy I saw you talking to the other day?"

"Yeah," I say with a shrug. "So what?"

His eyes darken as he shakes his head. "What was my rule, Madeline?"

I lift my shoulder. "I don't know, I don't listen to you."

He laughs, taking a step closer. "You're such a brat," he says, making my stomach plummet. "I specifically said there will be no dating other people while this thing between us is happening."

I cross my arms. "I am not dating him," I repeat. "He just wants to study."

He scoffs, running a hand through his hair. "I think he wants to study your bedroom."

"Unbelievable." I let out a bitter laugh, dropping my arms. "It's none of your business."

"Are you kidding?" he says, narrowing his eyes. "This is definitely my business. Everything to do with you is my business, especially if you're going out with guys when you're supposed to be my girlfriend. Did you forget that one slip-up could make this all come crashing down?"

My brows furrow, but before I can say anything, he continues. "One mistake, one date, one kiss, and news could spread that you're cheating." My eyes widen. "Or that this was all fake. This isn't just about me, Madeline. This is about you, too. Is that what you want?"

Of course not. "You don't have to worry about that," I tell him. "There won't be any dates, and I told you I don't kiss."

His eyebrows shoot up. "I thought that was just with me?"

I press my lips together and look to the side. "No, it's not."

He's quiet for a moment. "Is there a reason?"

"None that concerns you."

He lets out a heavy exhale, his shoulders dropping. "I know you don't like me, and since the first time we met, you've made me out to be the bad guy, no matter what I do."

I glance up at him, seeing his brows tugged. "It was one hell of a first impression," I tell him, not wanting to admit that I hate that he saw me that way. *Weak.*

"I'm serious, Madeline," he says. "You might want to get back at me or whatever, but you need to be more careful. You can't be sloppy, not when it comes to this. It's going to be embarrassing if you're on the cover with me one day and in some other guy's bed the next."

My eyes narrow. Who the hell does he think I am? "You don't have to worry about that. It won't happen."

"It better not," he says, glaring down at me. "When's the study date?"

I squint in confusion. "Why do you care?"

"So I can be there," he says with a lift of his shoulder.

A humorless laugh leaves my lips. He's out of his mind. "You're not serious."

"What's the big deal?" he asks, humor coating his tone. "Hiding something?"

"No."

Lucas nods knowingly, a smirk on the corner of his mouth. "Then I'm tagging along."

"You're not even a student here," I say, placing my hand on my hip. "How do I explain why you're there?"

He gives a slight, resigned shrug. "You can tell him we're going on a date after."

My eyes narrow as suspicion creeps in. "I know what you're doing."

"Yeah?" he asks with a cocky grin on his lips. "And what's that?"

I can't help but roll my eyes in disbelief at his amused tone. "You think if you're there, then nothing will happen."

His brows lift, and he runs a hand over his chin. "Then what are you so afraid of?" he asks. "If you say this isn't a date and nothing will happen, then you won't mind if I come along, will you?"

Asshole. He knows exactly how to play me. If I say I don't want him there, then he'll assume something is going on with Connor. I have no choice but to let him come. My stomach settles when I think of Lucas there. It won't be me and Connor alone anymore, and for some reason, I actually prefer it. "Fine," I huff. "It's tomorrow at my place."

"Great. Send me the address."

I let out an audible sigh of frustration as I turn around and start to walk away when I hear his voice. "See you tomorrow, Madeline."

# 13

Study date

*Lucas*

Madeline's frown is the first thing I see when she opens the door. Most people wouldn't like that, they'd be offended or even feel hurt by it.

But when she does it, I just smile instead. I wonder if she thought I was bluffing on the whole crashing her date thing. There is no way I'd let her be alone with him. I've only seen that guy twice, but he does not want to study. He wants *her*.

And much to Madeline's dismay, I can't let that happen. When she signed the NDA, she agreed to the rules, including the ones that weren't on the contract, which means no other guys.

"You seem glad to see me," I joke, my eyes drifting to the curls on her head. It's the first time I've seen her with curly hair, and fuck, she looks good. Too bad she's a pain in my ass.

"Delighted," she drawls, opening her door and allowing me to enter.

I glance around, noting that there isn't a single speck of dirt. Every inch of this place seems to have been freshly cleaned from the floors to the tables to the cabinets. "Nice place."

Her head snaps to the left, those eyes widening at me. "Was that… a compliment?"

I let out a laugh, running my hand through my hair. "I am capable of those, you know?"

She hums, disagreeing. "Really? I wouldn't know."

I snicker, rubbing a thumb over my lip. *If only she could hear my thoughts.* "Maybe because you're ripping my head off every chance you get."

She lets out a sigh, heading into the kitchen when the microwave beeps. She pulls out a bag of freshly made popcorn.

"You made food?" I ask her.

She looks at me from behind her shoulder. "I wouldn't really consider popcorn food," she says, ripping open the bag, the steam filling the apartment.

She really likes this guy.

I don't know why that bothers me.

Maybe because she's been hellbent on hating me since that first shitty interaction, or that she never gives me the time of day when we're together. But why does this guy get this Madeline? The one who smiles and cooks for him, and can't wait to see him. And I get...

"Are you sure you want to stay?" she asks.

That.

"Are you trying to kick me out?" I ask her, raising a brow.

She shakes her head, filling the bowl with the popcorn. "I'm not kicking you out. I'm giving you an out. It's probably going to be boring," she says with a lift of her shoulders as she places the bowl on the table. "I know you want to make sure nothing happens, and I can honestly tell you nothing will."

I don't buy that for a second. She seems way too excited for someone about to study. No one likes studying that much, especially on a subject they hate.

I let my eyes drift down her outfit. Tight-fitting jeans and a long sleeve brown top clinging to her. Who dresses like that to study? Someone trying to impress a guy, that's who.

I pull out a chair and take a seat, watching how her eyes narrow when I do. "I'm good here."

"Seriously?" she asks, placing her hand on her hip. My eyes linger on her curvy figure, slim in the waist and full in the hips. There is no way this guy will be able to keep his hands off her.

"Very."

Her eyes narrow in a squint. "You don't trust me when I tell you nothing's going to happen?" she asks.

I think back to the photoshoot when she was a nervous wreck, panicking when she thought I was going to kiss her. It pained me to think she was so afraid I'd cross her boundaries when I had given her my word. She doesn't trust me. Why should I trust her?

"Trust is a two-way street," I tell her, stretching my arms over the chair beside me. "When you learn to trust me, I'll do the same."

She purses her lips before heading to the sink, where the window is wide open, the air hitting her skin and her hair. Is she in fucking slow motion? I blink, begging myself to remember all of times she's driven me crazy. "You're going to get sick," I tell her, gesturing to the open window.

She raises an eyebrow. "I'll be fine," she says, turning back around to finish off cleaning the counters.

I turn my head and grab a few chips she laid out on a plate before bringing them to my mouth, letting out a laugh when I see all of the snacks on the table. "Look at you," I say, shaking my head at her. "You're wearing jeans and heels to study, you have food out for this guy, cleaned the place, and you honestly want me to believe nothing's going to happen?" I let out a strained laugh when she comes back to the table. "I'm not a fool, Madeline."

"I wouldn't do that to you," she says, glancing down at me. "We made a deal."

I want to believe that, but the way she's fidgeting over the idea of this guy coming over doesn't ease my suspicions.

When a knock hits the door, and her eyes widen, I see how nervous she is. Her eyes drift to me, and I'm guessing she would rather I not be here, but I don't care about what she wants right now. She lets out a sigh and heads toward the door, but not without fluffing out her curls before she opens the door.

What is it with her and always having to look perfect?

She opens the door with a smile, and he smiles back. I don't like that at all.

I rub my jaw, watching how they interact. How she smiles and laughs with him, a little shy – something she never is with me – and how he eats it up, laughing with her.

But as soon as he walks inside and sees me, the laughter stops.

I lift my eyebrows and give him a wave, trying not to find his reaction amusing as fuck, but it's hilarious. He definitely didn't expect to see anyone here, let alone a guy.

"Connor, this is Lucas," Madeline tells her little crush.

"Her boyfriend," I finish for her. Yeah, this dude did not like that, and neither does Madeline. I can tell by the way she's narrowing her eyes at me.

Sorry, *princesa*, but I'm not letting you ruin this for me, for both of us. When this is all over, she can giggle with him all she wants, but in the meantime, the only guy she'll be seen with is me.

He turns his head to Madeline and scans her face. "Oh," he says. "Sorry, I didn't realize." I wonder what they talk about. Do they flirt? Has she told him she's single?

Madeline shakes her head. "It's fine," she says. "I should have told you."

Yeah, she should have.

Connor is even more confused as he looks at Madeline again. "Is he in our class?" he asks her. "I don't think I've seen him before."

"No, I'm not," I say, leaning over to grab some popcorn before stuffing it in my mouth. "Came to pick up my girl for a date, and she'd told me you two were studying together."

Madeline gives him a warm smile. *Hate that.* "He wanted to stay," she tells him.

I munch away, my eyebrows lifting when he turns to face me. "Is that a problem?" I ask him.

He swallows, shaking his head. "No, I guess not." I can see how much he wanted to be alone with her. That sucks… for him.

He takes a seat and glances up at Madeline, her eyes dropping to the empty seat beside him. *Absolutely fucking not.* "Come here," I say, pushing out the chair beside me.

She looks up at me with wide eyes and squares her shoulders, but the asshole in front of me speaks up. "Um… I actually forgot my books. Mind if I share yours?"

He came to study without any books? I almost scoff. Is she really buying this? "I'm sure you'll manage," I drawl, glancing up at Madeline. "Now, come and sit beside me." I let out a sigh. "I miss you, *amorzinho*." I push my lips into a pout, loving how she narrows her eyes. God, it's fun to fuck with her. Even more fun to watch Connor swallow at the term of endearment.

But when she walks around the table and drops into the seat beside me, I break out into a smile, unable to stop it from spreading across my face. Connor frowns as he stares at the snacks in front of him. Yeah, tough luck, buddy.

"You're an asshole," Madeline whispers low enough, only I can hear as she tries to shuffle away from me.

I grin, grabbing the back of her chair and pulling her until she's pressed up against me. She gasps a little, but I don't even give her time to think before I stretch my arm around the back of her chair. "Much better," I murmur, loving how her crush is blanching every second he spends in front of us. "I love having you next to me, *meu coração*."

Madeline faces forward, avoiding my eyes. I don't even know if she knows what it means, I can tell by the way she's fidgeting that it got to her. She places her textbooks on the table, along with a small planner filled with color-coded sections and sticky notes on the edges. She places a blue and a black pen perpendicular to each other on the table, adjusting their position. Jesus. This girl isn't just organized. She's meticulous.

My eyes widen when I scan her planner, noticing every little detail she has marked down. I lean down close to her ear. "You plan your meals?" I whisper. She ignores me as she keeps flipping through her planner until she reaches today's date.

I chuckle, lifting my head, but when I see Connor's eyes locked on her, my smile disappears, my jaw tightening in its place. I fucking hate how he looks at her. He can't keep his eyes off her, and she's completely oblivious to it, her eyes locked on her planner as she writes away.

His eyes lock with mine for a second when he notices I caught him looking at her, and he looks away, grabbing a handful of chips before shoving it in his mouth.

She might have told me she doesn't date or kiss, but one thing is clear. It won't stop him. He wants her. I can see it plain as day.

But there's one big problem.

Fake or not, Madeline is mine, at least until our deal is over. And this guy isn't going to make her fuck me over, no matter how much she's crushing on him.

If I have to crash every one of their 'study dates,' then so fucking be it.

# 14

21 questions

## *Madeline*

An hour later, Connor leaves my apartment, and when the door clicks shut behind him, I let out a deep breath. But when I turn around, Lucas is watching me, his jaw clenched, clearly frustrated. The fear of being alone with Connor had my mind racing so much that I didn't consider the fact that once he left, I'd be left alone with Lucas instead.

"You like him," he says, lifting an eyebrow.

"I don't know what you're talking about." I make my way to the table to pack up my books, trying to ignore Lucas behind me.

He lets out a scoff, trailing behind me as I head to my bedroom to stow away my books. "You can deny it all you want, *princesa*." I turn around, finding him leaning against my door frame, his arms folded tightly across his chest. "But I've just witnessed you blushing and giggling for him for the past hour."

I hate when he uses that nickname. I hate the way it's filled with mockery, and I definitely hate how my pulse races it whenever he says it. "You're crazy," I say, pushing past him to pick up the half-empty bowls.

I barely touched the food, as did Connor. Lucas, however, kept himself busy eating snacks while I attempted to study with

Connor. Of course, I couldn't focus when I had Lucas' arm pressed against me, calling me every Portuguese nickname under the sun. And even though I might not have known what they all meant, they served their purpose, making sure Connor got the idea that we were dating.

He leans against the countertops, watching as I dump the bowls in the sink. "If I hadn't been here, would you have kissed him?"

My head snaps to him. "What?"

"You heard me," he says, his lips pressed into a thin line. "You swore up and down that nothing would happen, but would it have if I hadn't been here?"

I let out a bitter laugh, turning on the faucet. "You can't be serious. We were *studying*."

"He didn't bring any books, Madeline," he says, his tone sharp. "How do you not see that guy is into you?"

Fine, it was a little weird that he didn't bring any books when it was his idea to study, but I quickly brushed it off. Connor's friendly, sure, and he always smiles, but is Lucas right? Is he actually into me? I don't know how I feel about that. I mean, sure, I find him attractive, but that doesn't mean anything. Hell, I find Lucas attractive, and I don't *like* him.

He lets out a scoff. "You're happy about it, aren't you?" I don't even get a chance to say anything because he continues. "You act like my touch would make you detonate, but I don't think you'd mind if it were him." He shakes his head, his lips dropping into a frown. "What did I do that was so bad, Madeline?"

I swallow, turning my head away from him. He's touched me so many times. His hand around my waist, his hands on my face, his breath an inch away from my skin, and all I could do

105

was drink it in. But thinking about Connor doing the same? I hate the idea.

"I know we didn't have the best first impression," he says, a sigh leaving his lips. "I just thought… I thought you were using me," he admits, making my eyes widen when I look up at him. "I thought you orchestrated it all in the elevator to make sure we were seen together, and I guess… I resented you for it."

That's why he was such an ass in the beginning? "I wouldn't do that," I tell him, my brows knitting together.

"I know that now," he says with a nod. "I've just had enough experiences like that to think any differently." He shrugs. "You don't have to like me, but maybe you can act like you don't want to stick pins in your eyes rather than being around me? Maybe frown less?" He tilts his head, a smirk on his face. "You know it causes wrinkles, right?"

I squint at him. "Are you giving me beauty advice?"

He lets out a chuckle, a smile dancing on his lips, and shakes his head. "Nah. You don't need it." My heart races uncontrollably. "I'm just asking for us to work together, at least until this is over. Once we're done, you can turn the other way and never talk to me again." He shrugs dismissively, but for some reason, the mere idea of that happening knots my stomach.

"But until then, I need you to trust me," he says, taking a step closer to me. "I need you to believe me when I say your rules are always going to be a priority." His voice has gone deeper, and I swallow, my throat feeling constricted. "I won't kiss you, and I'll only touch you when it's necessary." His eyes scan my face, landing on my lips, just for a second, but I feel the burn of his gaze all the same. "But I need you to stop dating,

106

drop any other crushes, and just focus on us." His face is right in front of me, and I have to strain my neck to look up at him. God, he's tall. "Can you do that for me?" he asks in a whisper.

"I don't date," I manage to get out, swallowing when his brows knit together. "I've told you that before."

His lips lift the tiniest bit, and then he pulls back. "Good."

Good? What the hell does that mean? I shake away the thought and turn on the faucet, washing up the dishes.

"So you don't date," Lucas says, reaching over to grab a cloth before he grabs the clean bowl from my hands, drying it off. *God, why is that so hot?* "Are you into hookups then? Maybe with guys like Connor?"

I glance at him, glaring. "I don't do that either."

He's quiet for a second, and that second seems to drag on forever, especially since his eyes are laser-focused on me. "Is that why you're always moody, then?" He grins, grabbing another dish before drying it. "You just need to get laid?" he jokes.

I let out a scoff, shaking my head. "I don't need a guy to make me feel good."

His dark chuckle makes my skin grow hot, my stomach churning at the sound. "Are you telling me you know how to get yourself off?"

My cheeks heat as I finish off the dishes and turn away from him. "Can we stop talking about this?"

"You're embarrassed," he says, throwing the dish towel on the rack. "It's cute."

"I am not embarrassed," I lie, reaching for the bag of chips before I place it back in the cabinet. My eyes scan my apartment, looking around for something to do. Cleaning is my stress relief, but I already did that this morning, so now... there's nothing to clean.

"You definitely are," Lucas says, humor coating his tone. "This is fun. Tell me more."

I roll my eyes, turning to face him. "You're irritating."

He smirks, drops down to the couch and stretches his legs onto the coffee table. "And you've just become a lot more intriguing."

"Because I choose not to indulge in casual sex?" I scoff. "Yeah, that must be a shock for someone who's seen with a different girl every night."

His eyes narrow. "You looked me up." He says it as a statement, not a question.

"No," I tell him. "But Leila might have filled me in."

He laughs, shaking his head. "I can't believe she still believes that crap." He wipes a hand down his face and exhales, looking at me. "I don't either," he says. "Indulge in casual sex."

I scoff. "Right."

"I'm serious." When I glance at him, his shoulders lift in a shrug, and he gives me a smirk. "Cross my heart," he says, gesturing over his chest in an X motion. "The last girl I slept with was over a year ago."

I squint at him. "You really expect me to believe that?"

"Believe what you want," he says. "I'm just telling you the truth."

Huh.

I drop down onto the armchair, facing him, and smile. "Guess who just became interesting too."

He shakes his head. "I've always been interesting," he says with a grin. "You're just too hard-headed to see it."

My eyes roll at his cockiness, but a smile plays on my lips, and I realize… I'm actually having a good time with Lucas. "So we have something in common," I say. "Doesn't mean we have to hold hands and skip."

"God no, I wouldn't go that far," he jokes. "But we can get to know each other better."

My eyes narrow, wearingly. "So, what do you suggest?"

"21 questions?" he asks. "That way, you don't have to tell me your entire life story, but we actually know stuff about each other. After all, you are supposed to be my girlfriend."

"Okay," I agree, knowing it would be hard to convince someone we were dating if we didn't know anything about each other. "Question number one. Where are you from?"

He leans back into the couch and adjusts his position, rubbing his chin. I try not to ogle his chest when his t-shirt clings to his muscles, and I try not to think of what his beard would feel like against my skin, but it's really hard to do so. God, what is wrong with me? I clear my throat and bring my attention back to his face.

"I was born and raised here," he says. "I moved away to New York a few years ago for my career, but I decided to move back to Pennsylvania."

"Why?" I ask.

He tuts, shaking his head. "It's my turn," he points out. "Question number two. Where are you from?"

"Born and raised in Colorado," I tell him. "Moved here for college, never been anywhere else." I paste a smile and say, "Question number three. Why did you move back?"

He lets out a laugh, but then it drops when he sighs. "My best friend had an accident," he says, swallowing hard. "A few months ago, he was in a terrible car crash, and while he

109

survived, he injured his spine, lost mobility in his legs, and um…" He scratches at his beard. "His mom died, so me and my family are all he has now."

My stomach plummets, my brain flooding with memories of Nia. How I felt after the car crash that took her from me. I was so lost without her, but at least I still had my family. Even if their attention stopped, they were still *there*. I can't imagine not having anyone. "Shit. I'm so sorry."

He shrugs, but I can see his face dropping. "He's okay," he says. "He's doing physical therapy, and he's slowly learning to walk again." He nods, more to himself. "But when I heard the news, there was nothing that could keep me in New York."

I see the sadness in his face, and I feel it in my heart, in my bones. "I lost my sister in high school," I tell him, blinking away the tears building in my eyes. "It was raining pretty hard, and she… um." I shake my head, unable to finish the story.

"Fuck." His face drops. "Madeline, I'm sorry. If I had known…"

I shake my head, wiping away the tears. "Don't be, I was the one who asked."

He shakes his head. "I can't imagine losing my sister," he says, his brows furrowing. "My dad passed away when she was only two. She didn't even get to know him."

His jaw clenches when he looks at me, and my chest aches at the thought of growing up without my dad. Sure, my birth parents might have given up on me, but I love my mom and dad so much. I can't imagine life without them.

"She's been more like my daughter than my sister," Lucas continues. "I've watched her grow up. I watched her become her own person and the thought of something happening to her…" A heavy breath leaves his lips. "It would fucking kill me."

"It sounds like you're a good big brother."

A soft chuckle escapes him. "I try," he admits. "I really fucking do, but there are some things that I can't help her with."

"What do you mean?"

He sighs, shaking his head. "My sister has always been bigger than other girls, even as a little kid, and she… she was having some problems with bullying." My heart aches for her, for every little girl who grows up to hate their bodies. "I couldn't do shit," he admits with a shrug. "They were twelve-year-old girls. What could I do?" His jaw tightens. "Adrianna wouldn't talk to me, she would just shut herself in her room for hours, and it broke my fucking heart knowing those girls were hurting my sister."

"That's so awful. Is she ok now?" I ask, worried for Lucas' sister. I saw the toll it took on Leila growing up with constant negative comments about her body and the way she treated herself like she wasn't worthy of love just because she lived in a bigger body. I'm so glad she found Aiden, who's completely obsessed with her. She deserves it.

"Luckily, yes. But it was all thanks to Leila." He shakes his head. "I honestly think she saved her, Mads." My throat swells at the nickname. "If she hadn't talked to Leila, I genuinely think…" He shakes his head, not wanting to finish the conversation. His eyes drop, and his lips part as he lets out a shaky exhale. I can see how much this is hurting him.

I blink away the wetness in my eyes and sit back on the armchair. "My turn," I say, wanting him to forget about what might have happened if Leila hadn't been there for his sister.

He runs a hand through his hair. "Hit me."

I look to the side wondering what to ask him, when the biggest question roaming through my mind hits me. "Question number four. Why don't you date?" I ask him.

He narrows his eyes at me. "Seriously?"

I shrug. "I'm just trying to get to know you better."

He chuckles, shaking his head. "I don't trust easy," he admits, blowing out a breath. "And being in this line of work, the girls I meet only want one thing."

"Sex?" I guess.

"Well, that, yes, but mostly they want fame." He shrugs. "They want to be seen with me, be my date to an event, or get their picture taken with me because if they do… they become someone, they get a piece of my fame."

I bite my bottom lip, wondering how often it had to happen for him to write off every girl as being after his fame. "So that's what you thought of me?" I ask him. "The day we met?"

"You were a pain in my ass that day." He laughs. "But I genuinely thought you were panicking, and I was trying to help you. But then, when I saw the headlines and when I saw you again in Ana's office, I was certain you had used me and that I fell for it."

My brows furrow, trying to imagine not being able to trust anyone. He was so cold that first meeting, but I had cracked it up to him just being an asshole who thought he was better than everyone else. "I didn't even know who you were," I tell him, wanting him to know I'm not the kind of girl who uses people. "I just thought you were a bossy asshole." He chuckles. "And honestly, I was too preoccupied with being stuck in a giant metal box twenty feet in the air with a stranger who was yelling at me."

He scoffs. "I was not yelling."

I narrow my eyes. "You definitely were."

"Next question," he says.

I let out a laugh. "Deflecting from admitting the truth, I see."

"Question number five," he says, grinning. "When was your first kiss?"

"You're joking." I glare at him.

"Hey," he says with a playful smile. "I'm just trying to get to know you better." He throws my words back in my face, and I narrow my eyes at him.

"And knowing about my first kiss will do that?"

He shrugs. "You never know. It could have been a memorable kiss."

I sigh, looking to the side when I think of my first kiss. "Sixteen," I tell him.

"Late bloomer," he teases.

I was too damn young and stupid, but I just press my lips together and ask, "Why, when was yours?"

"I was seven. It was with this girl I went to school with. I had seen my parents kiss, so when I was saying goodbye to her, I smashed my lips against her face and kissed her instead."

I chuckle, imagining little Lucas running around kissing people as a goodbye. "As adorable as that sounds, that isn't a real kiss."

"Hey." He frowns. "It was real to me."

"I doubt the girl thinks so."

He sighs, tilting his head. "Fine. I guess my first real kiss was with this girl in middle school. I was…" He squints, deep in thought. "Twelve, I think."

My eyes widen. "Oh my god, you were just a baby."

"She didn't think so," he says with a grin. "Who was yours with? Boyfriend?"

I hate thinking of him as my boyfriend. I don't want to think of him at all, but I won't get far if I avoid the question, so I just nod. "Yeah. It was on my sixteenth birthday, actually." I think back to that day, only a few months after Nia had died, and I let myself get distracted by him.

"Happy sweet sixteen," he jokes. "Question number six. What's your dream date?"

The question caught me off guard, and I let out a laugh. "Seriously? Again?"

"Hey," he says with a shrug. "How am I supposed to know what my girlfriend likes if I don't even know her favorite date?"

"Fake girlfriend," I reiterate, narrowing my eyes.

His smirk makes a shiver run down my body. I hate when he does that, and I hate how attractive he is when he does it. "Answer the question, Madeline."

A sigh escapes me as I shake my head. "I told you I don't think about that stuff," I tell him.

"Why not?" he asks, rubbing his chin.

"I don't know," I admit, pulling my bottom lip between my teeth. "I guess I just know it will never happen, so I try not to get my hopes up."

"So, you've never been in love?" he asks.

"No," I admit to both him and myself. What I had with Daniel was everything *but* love. "And I don't think I ever will."

His brows shoot up. "Seriously?" he asks.

I lift my shoulder in a shrug. "It's just not for me," I tell him, seeing his brows drop into a frown.

"Why not?"

*I don't want to get hurt again.* "Just isn't," I say, not wanting to go into it, and I clear my throat. "Question number seven."

114

His eyes turn to me, waiting for my question. I smile when I ask, "What's your dream date?"

He returns my grin. "You trying to ask me out?"

"Of course, your ego would think that." He chuckles, and I hate to admit I like that sound. "Just answer my question."

He tuts, shaking my head. "Sorry, only my future girlfriend gets to know that."

My eyebrows lift. "Seriously?"

"Of course," he says with a shrug. "I can't tell you all my secrets. You might fall for me."

"Careful," I say, narrowing my eyes at him. "Your head might not fit through the door on your way out."

He laughs again, settling into the couch. "Question number eight."

I stop him with a raise of my hand. "You didn't answer my question, why should I?"

He smirks, running his thumb over his bottom lip. "You're dying to know what I like, huh?"

I roll my eyes. "I take it back. I don't care anymore."

"You little liar," he says with a laugh. "My answer isn't going to be some elaborate date I had planned since I was five, Madeline." My eyes drift to his, and he breathes out a sigh when I look at him. "The truth is, I've never had a girlfriend." My eyes widen at his admission. "I don't have the slightest clue what I would do if I ever did get one."

"What about all the girls before me?" I ask him.

He smirks sheepishly. "You should know the answer to that. They were all hired by Ana. A kiss here, a picture there, and I'd never see them again."

"Never?" I ask, my brows knitting together.

"Never," he repeats. "You're the first girl I've dated."

115

My throat closes with that information, and I force myself to swallow. "But it's not real."

"Regardless," he says with a shrug. "Real or not, hate me or don't. This is the first relationship I've had."

Silence bounces between us at his confession until he leans forward and flashes me a smile. "Can I ask my question now?" I nod, unable to form any words, and he settles back into the couch. "Have you had any luck with auditions?" he asks.

I frown. "Not yet, why do you ask?"

He shrugs. "This deal was about the both of us. I want to make sure you're getting something out of it, too."

It's only been a few weeks since we started doing this, so I don't expect to be hired already, but it would be nice to know that it's going somewhere. "I haven't even had time to apply for auditions. School takes up ninety percent of my time," I tell him. "And the other ten percent has been taken up by you."

His brows bunch together, but before he can say anything, our phones go off at the same time. He reaches into his pocket and I reach for mine on the table.

Ana:

CelebCentral Tonight
Interview Thursday 10:00am

I look up, and Lucas' eyes meet mine. "Ana?" he asks.

My brows furrow as I grab my planner from the table and open it up, letting out a sigh. "I have class."

"But you'll be there, right?" he asks, narrowing his eyes. "CelebCentral is one of the biggest media outlets."

"I'll be there," I assure him, jotting down the information. "I guess I'll just have to skip that day."

The door opens and Gabi walks in, singing to herself with her earbuds in. When she looks up and sees us, she pulls one out of her ear, her eyes widening. "Oh shit, sorry." She looks toward me. "I didn't know you had anyone over."

"It's ok," Lucas says, lifting himself off the couch. "I was just leaving." He gives Gabi a smile.

"You don't have to leave because of me," she tells him, a smile on her lips. My eyes narrow at her. What the hell is she doing? "If you want to hang out with your *girlfriend*, then go ahead."

Lucas glances at me, and I force my face to remain still. Gabi knows we aren't dating, whereas Lucas is under the impression that Gabi thinks we're dating, which makes this whole situation a little complicated.

"No," Lucas says, shaking his head and ripping his gaze away from mine. "It's late, I uh…" He rubs at the back of his neck. "I should get going." He nods toward me and heads toward the door.

"Aren't you going to give her a kiss goodbye?" Gabi's voice stops him, and I narrow my eyes at her, but she just grins.

Lucas turns around, and his eyes lock with mine. I watch his throat move as he swallows, and then, his lips lift in a smirk as he heads back toward me. "Of course," he murmurs, grabbing my face in his hands, and leans down until our lips are a few inches apart. "How could I forget?"

"What are doing?" I whisper, my eyes widening.

He just smirks, leaning in closer. "Necessary," he says before he leans in and presses his lips against my cheek, a couple of inches away from my lips.

One second. Merely one second that his lips were on my skin, but it still felt like an eternity. My chest rises and falls as I breathe hard, trying to keep some control, but when he pulls back, his hand still on my face and grins, my core grows hot, need pulsing through me.

"See you next Thursday, *girlfriend*." Then he narrows his eyes and whispers, "And don't be late."

"I won't."

# 15

In sickness and
in health

*Lucas*

She's late.

I can't believe this. After hounding me about being late to the photoshoot and assuring me she would be there on time, here I am, at her apartment, knocking on her damn door.

She still hasn't answered, and my body breaks out into a sweat. Where the hell is she? I've called her, and it goes straight to voicemail. I've texted her, and she hasn't replied. I've been knocking on her door for the past five minutes, and no answer.

I bang on her door once again, reaching for my phone with the other hand to check on the time. Five minutes until the interview is supposed to start, and she's nowhere to be found.

"Madeline," I shout again, knocking harder. "Where the hell are you?" I run a hand through my hair, cursing when my phone buzzes, Ana's name on the screen. I quickly hang up the call and stuff my phone back in my pocket. I can't deal with her right now, not until I find Madeline. I can't exactly show up girlfriend-less, which means I need her. Wherever the hell she is.

"Madeline," I call out, knocking again. "Are you in there?"

My shoulders drop in relief when I hear mumbles from behind the door. Thank fuck. I don't know what the hell she's been doing or why she's late, but at least now I know she's alive.

But as soon as the door opens, and I see her face, I quickly retract my statement. She might be alive, but holy fuck, she looks halfway to death. Her sunken eyes are squinting, trying her hardest to open them.

"Jesus," I exhale. "What the hell happened to you?"

"What are you doing here?" she asks, her brows furrowed as she tries to open her eyes wider.

As charming as ever, I see.

I let out a sigh, not wanting to argue. "You're late," I point out, trying not to convey how pissed I am. I trusted her. She assured me she'd be there, and she's not.

She blinks, shaking her head. "Late?" she asks, her face contorting as if the word tastes bitter in her mouth.

"For the interview?" I remind her. "The CelebCentral interview we had planned to announce our relationship and how I've settled down. Blah, blah, blah," I trail off, waving my hand.

Her eyes widen immediately as she covers her mouth with her hand. "Oh shit!" She turns around, rushing inside her apartment, closing her bedroom door once she's inside.

I blink, staring into her apartment. Does she want me to wait inside? I walk into her apartment and close the door before sitting down on the armchair as I hear her mumbling to herself in her room.

She wasn't just late. She forgot. The girl who writes down what she's going to eat for the week just simply forgot?

Something falls to the ground, catching my attention, and I snap my head toward the sound coming from inside her bedroom. "Are you ok in there?" I ask her, a little worried.

"Yes," she snaps, a little harsher than needed. "I'm fine. Just... wait for a second while I get changed."

I scoff, shaking my head. "It's not like I can show up without you." I doubt it's going to take a second. I've seen what that girl wears, how she always seems to have her makeup and hair done to perfection. She doesn't rush anything, and based on the warzone going on in her bedroom, I can guess I'm going to have to wait a lot more than just a second.

I glance down at my phone, ignoring the hundreds of calls from Ana, and notice the time. We're clearly not going to make it.

Ten minutes and a bunch of curse words later, Madeline's door opens, and she walks out, looking as beautiful as ever, with her usual gorgeous outfit, this time, a little pink dress on her body and her makeup done. But something about her is... off. She doesn't look the same; she looks completely defeated.

I rub my chin, my brows knitting together as I look up at her. "Are you sure you're okay?" I ask her.

She glances down at her outfit with a frown. "Do you have a problem with what I'm wearing?"

I shake my head. "No, that's not—"

But when she sneezes, my eyebrows furrow, and I lift myself off the chair, heading toward her. I place the back of my hand on her forehead. She tries to step back as soon as my hand touches her, but she's too late. I already felt her skin. She's burning up. "You're sick," I say, realization dawning on me.

"What?" she says, sniffling. "Of course, I'm not sick. You're crazy." She shivers, trying to push past me. "We're going to be late. We need to go."

We're way past late, but I don't mention that to her. If she thinks I'm going to let her go like this, she's dead wrong.

"Madeline." I reach out to grab her wrist. Her eyes fall to my hand wrapped around her, and I quickly drop my hand, remembering how she doesn't like when I touch her. "You're not going anywhere."

"What are you talking about?" She shakes her head. "The interview is today. Can we still make it? How long does it take to get there?"

*A long fucking time.* "Madeline, you're not going anywhere," I repeat. "Not like this."

"Like what? I'm fine." The way she coughs tells me she definitely is not fine. "You're being ridiculous."

"Ridiculous for looking out for you?" I tilt my head at her. "It's okay to admit you're sick, you know?"

"I am not sick." She frowns before sneezing again. "I'm perfectly fine."

"Yeah," I scoff. "Real convincing."

"I am not sick," she repeats, her face hardening. "I don't *get* sick."

I let out a laugh, thinking it's a joke, but from the hardened look on her face, I can tell she genuinely means it. "What the hell are you talking about? Everyone gets sick."

She shakes her head. "Not me. Now, can we go?"

My hand wraps around her waist, halting her when she tries to move past me again. Why the hell is she so adamant about this? "You are so stubborn," I grit out, feeling her body heat up. She's shivering, and it takes everything in me not to wrap my arms around her. "You're not going anywhere but to bed."

Her chest is an inch away from mine and her eyes drop with exhaustion. "But…" She shakes her head. "We can't miss this. You said it's important."

*Not as important as this.* "It's been cancelled," I tell her, holding on to her when I feel her body melt into mine. God, she must be exhausted.

"It is?" she asks, peering up at me beneath her lashes.

I nod. "Yep." At least, *It's about to be.* "Come on." I attempt to straighten her body enough so she's able to walk before I grab her hand in mine. She doesn't even try to push me away. That's how I know she's too out of it to argue.

Pushing open her bedroom door, I find her bed all crumpled up, her clothes scattered everywhere. My brows furrow at the mess, and I turn to her. "Are you sure this is your room?" I joke.

She sighs, closing her eyes. "I was in a rush, okay?" She coughs again, shivering as her hand sweats in mine, and she looks downright exhausted. I let go of her hand, heading toward her bed to pick up the pile of clothes and place it on the empty chair in the corner of her room. She drops to her bed, and reaches down to take off her heels.

I watch her fiddle with the straps for a second too long before I get down on my knees and place her foot on my leg. "What are you doing?" she asks.

"Helping you out." I pull at the straps until the first shoe comes off, clanking to the ground.

"I can do it myself," she says, reaching for her other shoe.

My chest shakes with a low chuckle. "You're so stubborn. Always fighting me, even when I'm just trying to do something nice for you." My hand wraps around her other ankle, working the straps off.

"Why?" she asks. "There's no one around."

*I'm well aware.*

123

My head lifts once both of her shoes are off, and I watch her swallow as she looks at me. Fuck, she looks so frail as she sniffles, shivering while her skin burns against mine. I lift off my knees, pulling off her covers. "Get in," I tell her.

She doesn't even talk back. She just slides into bed, letting out a relieved sigh when I pull the covers back up. "I'm not sick," she reiterates. "I'm just… tired," she says with a yawn.

"Yeah," I let out a snicker. "I know. Just rest."

I look down at her, buried in the covers, making little noises as she adjusts herself to get comfortable. I can't take my eyes off her as I watch her cuddle the comforter. Reluctantly, I rip my gaze off her before I head out of her bedroom.

Opening up her bathroom door, I grab one of her face towels and run it under the hot water, soaking the material before I wring it out.

When I walk back into her room, I spot her on the bed, her eyes closed as she buries herself in bed. I watch with a smile until she cracks an eye open, glancing right at me. "Are you just going to stand there and stare at me while I sleep?"

I let out a laugh. "I can leave if you want me to." I don't want to leave her here when she's like this, but if she tells me to go…

"No," she says, closing her eyes again. "Stay. Please." It's stupid how much that one word makes me smile.

I press my lips together to stop my grin. "I'm not going anywhere," I tell her, sitting at the edge of the bed. "Lie back." I place the warm towel on her forehead. "Is it too hot?" I ask when she lets out a whimper at the contact.

She shakes her head, her eyes fluttering closed. "It's perfect," she whispers. "It's just… humiliating," she admits, her brows furrowing.

I adjust the cloth on her forehead. "There's nothing humiliating about needing help once in a while, Madeline."

Her eyes crack open, and she purses her lips together like she's going to say something, but instead, she closes her eyes again, falling into a deep sleep. It isn't long until she's snoring. I smile to myself when I hear it, glancing down at her. My chest aches, and I have the urge to trail my fingers over her face. I keep myself in check, balling my hands into a fist before I do just that.

My phone buzzes in my pocket, the sound blaring compared to the quiet snores coming from Madeline, and I rip my gaze away from her and run a hand through my hair. I reach for my phone and let out a sharp exhale when I see all of the missed calls from Ana.

My eyes find Madeline once again, seeing she's fast asleep, and I ease myself out of her room, making sure not to wake her up before I call Ana.

She picks up immediately. "Where the hell are you?" she yells. "You were supposed to be here thirty minutes ago."

"Yeah," I sigh. "There's been a problem."

"A problem?" she asks. "What kind of problem? Don't tell me it's because of Madeline. We thought she'd be professional, not cause trouble."

My brows tug together. I don't like how she's talking about Madeline at all. "No, actually," I interrupt. "It was me."

"You?"

"Yes. I uh…" My hand reaches behind my neck, tugging at the strands there. Shit, what do I say? "I have some family problems right now, and I just couldn't make it."

"Unbelievable." She scoffs. "Do you know how hard I had to work to get this interview for you? You know you won't be relevant forever, Lucas. I'm trying to help you. I'm trying to make sure your career doesn't fall down the drain. Do you want to lose everything?"

My jaw clenches, and every muscle in my body feels tight. I know what's on the line. It's all I ever think about. "Listen. I've got to go. Rebook it for another day, or don't. I don't give a shit. Right now, I have something more important to do."

I don't even wait for a reply, hanging up before I shove my phone in my pocket. Yes, this interview was important. It was CelebCentral Media, for fucks sake. They're huge. But I'm not about to let Madeline go out there when she isn't feeling or looking her best. She was struggling to keep her eyes open, her body breaking out into shivers in my fucking arms. I'm not putting her through that. No fucking way.

I open her door again, and walk inside, seeing her still sleeping. I head to the chair where all of her clothes are crumpled up and start folding. The last thing Madeline needs is to wake up to a mess. Knowing her, she'd probably pass out at the sight.

"Lucas?" My head snaps to where she's lying in bed, shuffling in the sheets. Her tone is sweet and hushed, completely the opposite of what she normally sounds like.

My heart fucking melts. "Yes, Madeline?"

"You stayed?" She says it more as a question like she can't believe I stayed.

"Yeah," I tell her, approaching her. Her eyes are still closed, and I look down at her, swallowing hard. "I told you I would."

Her brows knit together when she sighs. "I thought you'd leave," she whispers. "I know you don't like me. You didn't have to do any of this." Her voice trails off into a murmur. "Why didn't you leave?"

I stare down at her, my brows furrowing and an ache in my chest that I don't quite understand. "I'm not a bad guy, Mads," I tell her, wondering if she's fallen back asleep. "When we met... I was going through a hard time, and I guess I still am. But none of that is because of you," I admit more to myself than to her. I might have resented her a bit for being forced into this situation when everything around me is crumbling, but if I'm honest with myself...

I hear her soft snores again, and I know she's fallen back asleep.

I sigh, running a hand down my face and looking down at her face. "You're the only good thing that's been happening to me lately."

# 16

Sketches and soulmates

## Madeline

I don't expect anyone to be in my room.

Least of all a strange figure that I can't make out in the dark. My pulse races, and I quickly lift myself up, and do what any sane person would do. I throw a pillow at it, letting out a scream.

"What the hell?" the voice says, groaning when the pillow hits him in the chest.

Wait. I know that voice. "Lucas?" I ask, trying to adjust my eyes to the dark. Thankfully the lights turn on, and I let out a breath when I see Lucas' face scowling at me, liquid dripping down his clothes.

"Who else?" he asks. "Why the hell did you just throw a pillow at me?"

"I thought you were an intruder," I tell him, slumping back down into bed when I feel my body give up on me. But I know exactly who I thought it was in my head. And the thought made my stomach churn. "I was defending myself," I admit, pulling the covers over my body again.

He shoots me a glare, placing down a bowl on my nightstand. "With a pillow?"

"It was the only thing I had next to me." My eyes drift down to his shirt, which is sopping wet with a big, ugly stain. Great, now I feel bad. I let out a sigh. "Take off your shirt."

He freezes, turning to face me with wide eyes. "What?" He swallows.

Heat travels to my cheek when the implication dawns on me, and I shake my head. "To wash it," I explain, pulling back the covers and… oh fuck, it's cold. My body breaks out into a shiver when I feel the cold air hit my skin.

"Stop that. Get your ass back into bed," he tells me, covering me with the blankets again. God, that feels so nice. "You're going to get worse."

"But your shirt—"

"Is fine," he finishes, staring down at me. "You're not."

"I am." My teeth chatter as I bury myself back in bed. "It's just cold in here, that's all," I say, glancing at him.

"Right. That must be it." Sarcasm drips from him as he picks up the bowl from my nightstand and hands it to me. "Here," he says, placing the hot bowl in my hands. "Eat this."

"But your shirt is—"

"Oh, for crying out loud." He steps back and pulls his hoodie over his head. My eyes widen for a second, and they drift down to where a slither of his stomach is exposed when the black t-shirt he has on underneath lifts, showing the chiseled cut of his abs. Five, six, seven… do they ever end? "Are you happy now?" My eyes snap back to his face and I feel my face heating from the realization that I was ogling him. "I'll take care of it when I get home." He sits beside me on the bed, glancing down at the bowl. "Now eat."

I follow his gaze, looking down at the bowl in my hands. "Chicken soup?"

"Yeah," he says, scooching closer to me. "Or as my mom calls it, *Canja de galinha*. My mom used to make it for me and my sister whenever we got sick. It always made me feel better, I thought it might do the same for you."

I roll my eyes. "But I'm not—"

"If you deny being sick one more time..." He shakes his head. "What is it with you and wanting to be perfect all of the damn time?" he asks. "Hair never out of place, makeup always on, nails done, outfit perfectly matched." A harsh breath escapes his lips. "Doesn't it get exhausting?"

I press my lips together, frowning at the accusation. I guess it's just something I've been doing for so long, it's become like second nature to me. "I don't look perfect right now." I'm guessing I look like a mess. My hair feels heavy and tight, my skin is clammy, and my body... ugh, I don't even want to think of what I look like.

But you'd never know with the way Lucas is looking at me. His jaw clenches as he scans my face, landing on my eyes. "You're pretty damn close."

My heart beats faster, and I force myself to look down at the soup. I pick up the spoon and dig in, the small pieces of pasta and chicken floating around in the broth as I bring it to my mouth. Damn, it's so good. I glance up at him, seeing him look at me, and I think back to what he said.

"I don't have any memories before I was adopted," I tell him, watching as his forehead creases with a frown. "I don't remember my birth parents, not even a flash of a memory. All I've ever known are my parents." I sigh. "I look just like my mom," I say with a laugh. "I know that's not possible, but it's true. I have her hair, her nose, even her lips. I didn't even know I was adopted until they told me."

I shake my head, my nose tingling with the urge to cry. "I was young when they told me, but after that, everything changed for me." I lift my shoulder in a shrug. "Once I knew that my birth parents had given me away and didn't want me anymore, I thought the same thing would happen with them," I admit. "I tried my hardest to be the perfect daughter. I guess I didn't want to give them a reason not to want me either." I blink away the wetness building in my eyes, letting out a strained laugh. "I don't even know why I care that my birth parents didn't want me when I have an amazing family. They chose me, they wanted me, but…"

"It still hurts," he guesses.

I nod, pressing my lips together to keep myself from crying. "Yeah, it really fucking does."

He's quiet for a minute, and then he shakes his head. "Your birth parents are fucking idiots." Our eyes lock, and I'm sunken into his gaze, his golden brown eyes flickering. "I met you a month ago, and I hate the thought of letting you go once this ends."

My body breaks out into shivers again, but it's not the cold weather or my fever. It's the way he looks at me. It's the words he's saying and how it affects me. And I hate it. I hate that I don't hate it. I look down at the bowl again, swallowing the lump in my throat. "What are you doing here?" I ask, having another spoonful. "It's late." I don't even know how long I slept, but the dark sky gives me an inkling that it's been a long time.

He tilts his head. "You don't remember asking me to stay?"

My brows tug together. "I did?"

"Madeline." He smirks. "You practically begged me to."

My mouth gapes open. "I did not."

He shakes his head, a cocky grin on his lips. "I'm pretty sure I heard a *please* in there somewhere."

I shake my head, having another spoonful. "You're so annoying."

"And you're allergic to common decency," he says with a laugh. "You realize you haven't even said thank you for the soup yet?"

I glance down, seeing it's already half gone. It was delicious, and my body warms at the thought of Lucas doing that for me. "Thank you," I mumble.

"Holy shit," he says with a laugh. "You have manners."

I narrow my eyes at him. "You want me to take it back?"

His chest shakes with a chuckle as he settles into the bed beside me. "You're welcome, Mads."

I blink, glancing up at him. "You called me Mads."

"Yeah," he says, running a hand over his chin. "I guess I did. Is that okay?"

I nod, a smile slipping on my lips. "Nia used to call me that."

"Your sister?" he guesses.

I nod again. "Yeah. She actually named me," I tell him. "When my parents adopted me, they were set on the name Amelia, but my sister hated it, demanding I be called Madeline." I let out a laugh, thinking back to when she told me that story. To every memory I had of her. Of us.

"She sounds amazing," he says, giving me a sad smile.

"Yeah," I agree. "She was."

"Good taste, too. Madeline suits you way better." He grins, and it makes me feel a sense of familiarity. I haven't spoken about Nia in a while, and I like it. I miss it. I miss her.

132

I let out a laugh, bringing another spoonful to my mouth. "You must have been bored out of your mind, though, while I was asleep."

He shrugs, leaning back against my headboard. "I kept myself busy."

"With what?"

A smirk slides on his lips as he leans closer to me. "Hearing you snore, for one."

My body grows hot as I narrow my eyes at him. "I do not snore." Do I?

His laugh makes my stomach flutter, and I don't know what to make of it. "Oh, trust me, you do, but don't worry, it's cute."

*Cute?* "So what did you do?" I ask him.

"Is that another question?"

"Question number nine," I say with narrowed eyes. "What did you do while I was asleep?"

His laugh settles as he gestures with his head to my nightstand, where a folded piece of paper lies. My brows furrow as I reach out and unfold it, staring down at the rough sketches on the paper.

"You draw?" I ask him, enamored by the strokes, creating a beautiful piece. I swallow hard, looking down at my face on the paper.

"Sometimes," he says, his voice hushed. "Whenever I have time, or I'm stressed. It's a way for me to escape sometimes, I guess."

I lift my head, and when his eyes lock with mine, my heart starts to beat out of my chest. "It's amazing," I tell him, his smirk making the knocking against my chest even harder. "Why me?"

He blows out a breath at my question, running a hand through his hair before he shrugs. "I like to draw beautiful things," he mumbles. "Whether that's buildings or people, it eases my mind a little."

His words repeat themselves over and over in my head until I blurt out, "You think I'm beautiful?"

A light scoff escapes his lips as he glances at me, a small smile on his lips. "Of course you're beautiful, but you already know that. You don't need validation, not from me or anyone else."

I turn away, feeling my cheeks flush with heat, and stare down at the drawing of me, looking at all of the intricate details. "So when you said you had nothing else to offer," I start, glancing back up at him. "That was a lie."

He huffs out a laugh, shaking his head. "Not really," he says. "I meant what I said. Modeling is the only thing that brings me money."

"There are more important things than money, Lucas."

"You're right." He nods. "Like making sure my family is taken care of. That's important."

My shoulders drop, knowing he's right. "But you could still do something you love and make money," I offer. "You said you like to draw buildings?" I raise an eyebrow, and he smirks when he catches on.

"Are you going to talk about how much potential I have and that I could be an architect?"

My nose scrunches as I shake my head. "I would never compliment you that much," I joke, my chest feeling light when he laughs along. "But... yeah."

His laugh settles as he sighs. "I thought about it," he admits. "Back when I was in high school, a few teachers told me I was good, and I did think about it."

"But…?"

With a shrug, he shakes his head. "But it wasn't meant to be," he says, a frown forming on his lips. "I was making money by then, and my mom could finally rest. She worked non-stop after my dad died, and I could tell it was killing her. I couldn't risk it all for some *dream*. I just had to accept that it was never going to happen."

I frown, thinking about how Lucas had to give up his dream in exchange for stability. Will I have to do that someday? I hope not.

"Question number ten," he says, crossing his arms, his elbows touching mine in the process. I shoot him a look, but he just shrugs. "Hey, you started it. Besides, I still have things I want to know."

"Fine," I say, leaning back against the headboard. "What do you want to know?"

His thumb runs over his bottom lip while he scans me from head to toe. "What do you see in Connor?"

"You're serious?" I ask with a glare. "This again?"

"I just want to know what you see in him," he says with a dismissive shrug, but nothing about the tone of his voice says he's dismissive about this.

I let out a sigh. "I like his smile, I guess. It's the first thing about him that caught my attention. He smiles with his whole chest, and I like that. I like how happy he is."

"So that's it?" he asks. "You like him because he's happy?" He puts so much emphasis on the last word it makes me rethink everything.

"I guess so." My brows furrow, and the conviction behind my words isn't there.

"Happy is overrated," he says with a scoff.

"You don't want to be happy?" I ask him.

His shoulders lift in a shrug. "I do. Of course, I do. I just meant that happiness is fleeting. It's here one minute, and the next... gone." His face is hardened, and I wonder if he's thinking of his dad or what his friend went through. "It doesn't last forever."

"Neither does beauty," I retort. "But isn't that the leading factor in why people get together?"

He rubs his chin. "I guess. But beauty can last forever if you love someone. Even when they get old, gray, and saggy, their beauty doesn't fade with age in the eyes of that person. It grows."

His eyes fix on mine, and the thought is nice. Forever beauty. Someone loving you through everything. But if it's anything like what I had with Daniel. I don't want it.

"Question number eleven. Is that what you want, then?" I ask. "Are you looking for a soulmate?"

He sighs, tipping his head back. "I don't know," he admits. "I don't even know if I believe in soulmates. While I love the thought, I don't know if it even exists. Or if it just doesn't exist for me."

My brows furrow. "Why not?"

He shrugs, glancing my way. "I can't see myself getting lost in someone like that, where they're the only thing that matters, my whole world," he admits. "Besides, the only girls I 'date' are hired by Ana." He smirks. "Can't exactly start a loving relationship like that, can I?"

*You never know.* The words are on the tip of my tongue, but I shove them back down. He's had other fake dates. And there will be more after me.

"Do you?" he asks, snapping me out of whatever the hell those thoughts were. "Believe in soulmates and all that stuff?"

My face falls into a frown. "I don't know," I admit. "I'd like to think there are some people who find their true match, that give their other half everything they want, like love letters and a room full of flowers, but… I don't think I'll ever find that."

"Is that what you want?" he asks, with a tilt of his head. "Love letters and a room full of flowers."

I let out a sigh. "It wouldn't be the worst thing in the world, but if I have to get into a relationship for that to happen, then I'll pass."

He lets out a laugh. "Guess we have more in common than we thought," he muses.

Yeah. I guess so.

Although this is the closest I've gotten to an actual boyfriend since I was sixteen, and if I'm being completely honest with myself… it's not so bad. Sure, we have to pretend while we're in public and do photoshoots and interviews, but—

"Shit." My head snaps to Lucas. "The interview."

"Don't worry about it," he says. "I told you I'd handle it."

I narrow my eyes. "You said it got canceled."

"Oh, well." His cheeks start to turn pink, and… is he blushing? "I might have…lied."

I frown. "Why would you do that?"

He sighs, running a hand through his hair. "You were sick, Madeline." I open my mouth to protest, but he stops me. "Don't even try to deny it. We both know it. You were holding onto me, you know that? You hate when I touch you, and you were grabbing onto me, for fucks sake." He shakes his head. "I couldn't let you go out like that. No way in hell."

My cheeks start to warm, and I want to tell him I don't hate when he touches me. Not at all. Instead, I look up at him sheepishly and flash him a smile. "Thank you."

"It was no big deal," he says with a shrug. "We can do the interview another time."

"Was Ana mad?" I ask.

He shakes his head. "It's fine, Madeline. You're allowed to be sick, and you're allowed to admit it. As opposed to what you think, you don't have to be perfect. No one's expecting that of you. We just want you to be... *you*."

A smile spreads across my face, and I'm surprised to find it's because of Lucas. "Thank you," I repeat. "For everything. I know I was a pain, but—"

"You're welcome." He smiles, and our eyes lock. I don't think I realized how close we were to each other, but his shoulders are pressed against mine, and I can see his chest rising as he breathes, and his lips... they're right there.

I wonder, only just for a second, what it would feel like. Would he like it? *Would I like it?* Would he push me away or let me explore? But I don't get another second to think about it because the door bursts open, and Gabi walks in.

Lucas and I break apart just as she tumbles onto my bed, and I squeeze my eyes closed, letting out a harsh breath. What the hell was I thinking? It's this stupid sickness. It has to be.

"Oh hey," Gabi mumbles, her eyes widening when she spots Lucas in the corner of my room. "You again." Her slurred speech makes my brows pinch together. Is she drunk?

"Yeah," he says, giving her a tight-lipped smile.

"Hi," I brush back her hair from her face, and she grins up at me. "Were you at a party?"

She nods with a grin. "It was fun." She mumbles the words, but then her eyes drop, and a heavy sigh escapes her. "I miss him."

My brows furrow as she kicks off her shoes. Oh god, not the shoes in my bedroom. "Who?" I ask her.

She falls back onto my bed, her eyes drifting closed. "My best friend," she mumbles.

"I thought I was your best friend," I joke, trying to make sure she doesn't fall asleep.

"You are," she drifts off, her voice turning into a whisper. "But he's…"

The words die on her lips as she starts to breathe heavily, falling into a deep sleep. I let out a laugh, lifting my head to see Lucas standing at my door.

He runs a hand through his hair and presses his lips together. "I um… I should go," he gestures to the door with his thumb. "Are you going to be okay?" he asks, glancing down at Gabi.

I nod, even though something weird happens in my chest at the thought of him leaving. "Yeah, I'll be fine." I lick my lips, glancing up at him. "Thanks again. I know I'm hard to be around." My eyebrows knit together. "Not everyone would stay to look after someone they don't like."

He turns his body to face me, brows furrowed. "You're not hard to be around at all, Madeline. You just have to let someone in." My lips part at his words and he gives me a smile. "I'll see you," he says before he leaves my room. I hear the front door close, and I know he's gone.

"Madi?"

I glance down at Gabi. "Yeah, it's me. Want to go to bed now?" I ask her.

She nods, eyes cracking open. "You had that interview today, right? How was it?"

"I didn't go, I um... I was sick." The words taste funny in my mouth. I don't get sick. I make sure of it. I take care of my body, I take so many damn vitamins, and I've even started drinking those green smoothies Leila likes so much.

Gabi's eyes widen. "Are you okay?" she says, lifting herself off the bed. "Do you need anything? Do you want me to make you some soup?"

I laugh, shaking my head. "No," I tell her. "I'm good, Lucas made me some." Good thing, too, because this girl has never cooked a day in her life. The kitchen would likely catch on fire.

"Come on," I tell her. "You need to sleep." Especially because Gabi has two modes when she drinks. Party animal and dead asleep. And she's, without a doubt, heading toward the latter right now.

She manages to drag herself out of my bed, and walks out of my room, mumbling to herself. When the door closes, I shuffle back beneath the covers and close my eyes, attempting to fall back asleep. But the same seven words repeat themselves over and over in my head.

*You just have to let someone in.*

# 17

Is it safe?

## Madeline

I'm sick.

There, I admit it.

I felt awful yesterday, and this morning, it seems to be worse. I can't stop coughing, sneezing, and wishing there was more of that chicken soup. It hasn't even been a whole twenty-four hours since I last saw Lucas, and I'm already wondering when I'll see him next.

The sound of my phone ringing on my nightstand startles me, and my heart races. Is that him? But when I see the name on the screen, my shoulders drop in disappointment.

"Hi, Mom," I say into the phone.

"Darling. You sound terrible."

I laugh. "Thanks." A cough forces itself out of my throat, making my face twist in pain. "I'm just a little sick."

She lets out a sigh. "If you weren't so far away, I would come over to help you."

I had a great childhood. My parents and I were always close, especially when I was a kid, and my dad used to give me piggyback rides everywhere we went. I will always be grateful for them for giving me the family and life I wouldn't have if they never chose me that day.

But then Nia died. And the bond I felt with them was gone. They became more distant, and even though I had never felt like that before, I stopped feeling like their daughter. I felt like I was in the way, like they had lost their real daughter, and I was all that was left.

It's a horrible thought to have because they have always loved me, but I always tried so hard to be the perfect daughter for them. Nia gave them trouble sometimes, sneaking off with guys and being late for curfew, but she was their daughter. She was allowed to do that.

I, however, did everything possible not to give them any trouble. But once Nia died, it felt like nothing I did was good enough, like I wasn't good enough. I feel like a piece of our relationship died the day she did.

"I'm okay, Mom, I promise." I pull the covers higher, my body freezing cold. "How's dad?"

"Good, you know your father. Busy with work." And for good reason. My parents worked hard for what they got, resulting in them being the first generation of their family to go to college.

"What about you?" she asks. "Studying hard, I assume?"

*When am I not?* Part of me wants to tell her about the deal I have with Lucas, but if she knew that I was trying to pursue acting again, I know she would disapprove. I get it, she doesn't think it's a stable career, but am I going to have to hide this from her forever?

Even if this thing with Lucas doesn't bring anything, I'm not going to stop. Being an actress is all I have ever wanted, and the thought of giving up that dream crushes my heart. Would my parents really be that disappointed with me if I ended up doing something completely different from what they envisioned for me, or more accurately, Nia?

I swallow down the lump in my throat. I don't want to find out. Not until I'm certain that I can make my dream happen.

"Yep," I tell her. "These assignments are busting my ass though."

A heavy sigh escapes me when she laughs along. I miss her so much. I miss the shopping trips we used to take. Me, her and Nia, getting our nails done together, our hair... We haven't done anything like that together in a long time. Not since the last time with Nia.

"It'll all be worth it once you get into law school," she reassures, her cheerful tone evident in her words. "You'll see."

I squeeze my eyes closed at the pang of disappointment in my chest. I can hear how happy it makes her to think I'll be following in her footsteps. "Yeah," I say with little conviction. "I have to go, Mom. I'll talk to you later."

"Okay, darling. Get well soon."

A smile spreads across her face as I hang up the phone, sinking into bed. If I do what they want and go to law school, I know it will make them happy. And that's all I want. But in order for that to happen, it'll be at the cost of *my* happiness.

I take out my planner and scan my to-do list for the day, but there's not a single desire within me to complete any of it. I'm so damn tired. Fuck, I hate feeling like this.

I'm interrupted by a knock on my door, prompting me to stuff my planner back in my nightstand. "Yes?"

Gabi's head peeks through the door, and my gaze narrows, locking onto the blue surgical mask covering her face as she holds out a spray can in her hand. "Is it safe?" she asks, keeping the rest of her body outside of the door.

My eyes roll as a smile appears on my lips. "You're such a weirdo." She might be the biggest drama queen of all time, but I know that whenever she's around, I'll have a good time.

"I have dance practice to go to," she says, spraying some of the vanilla scent in my room. "I can't get sick."

"And room spray is going to prevent that?" I ask, amused.

She glances at the bottle, letting out a sigh. "Dammit, I got the wrong thing. One sec."

"I'm fine," I reply before she has a chance to leave. I might not be feeling great, but I highly doubt I'm contagious. The sneezing has subsided, and now all that's left is my body feeling like it's been through the wringer.

"Are you sure?" she asks, stepping into my room. "Lucas said you weren't feeling well."

"What?" My eyes widen at the mention of his name. "You talked to him? When?"

"This morning," she says, finally pulling off the mask. "He left some more chicken soup for you."

My heart starts to race, my mouth watering at the thought. "He did?"

She nods. "That guy can cook. It was fucking delicious."

"You ate my soup?" I narrow my eyes at her. "You're not even sick."

She laughs, lifting her shoulder in a shrug. "It smelled good, beside, there's loads. He brought over a pot full of it."

My stomach starts to rumble at the thought of having some more of the soup, but before I can get up, Gabi sits on my bed with a grin. "So… Lucas, huh?"

I let out a sigh. "We're in a fake relationship, Gabi. You know this."

She nods. "I know, but he was still here when I came home yesterday." A grin spreads across her face, and she wiggles her eyebrows. "What happened?"

"Nothing happened," I assure her with a shove on her arm.

She tilts her head, studying me. "I thought you hated him."

"I do," I say with a shrug, the words feeling funny on my lips. I'm not sure I do… anymore.

She smirks, reading me. "You don't."

I let out a sigh, leaning back against the headboard. "Fine, I don't hate him," I admit before shooting her a glare. "But it's not what you think."

She shrugs, a grin still on her lips. "If you say so."

"Nothing is going on with him," I repeat.

She lifts her brows, smiling at me. "But you want it to," she says matter of factly, like she knows every thought I've ever had about him.

I narrow my eyes at her. "I will cough on you."

Her eyes widen. "But… you just said you were fine," I smirk at her, and she narrows her eyes at me, gasping. "You're evil." When I laugh, she shakes her head. "You're not getting out of answering this question."

"You didn't even ask a question. You made an assumption."

She squints, a grin on her face. "Which is correct?"

"No. It's not. What about you?" I ask her.

Her brows tug. "What about me?"

"Dating anyone?" I ask her with a tilt of my head.

"No."

A hum builds in my throat. "I haven't seen you with anyone recently," I point out. "No guys or girls, for a while now."

145

She sighs. "I'm busy with dance and class and everything else," she says, waving a hand. "I don't have time for any of that."

"You know you can bring someone over, though, right?" I ask her. "It's your apartment as much as it's mine."

She rolls her eyes. "Yes, I know, *Mom*," she jokes, but then she lifts her shoulder in a shrug. "I'm just not interested in anyone lately," she says, but then adds quietly, "At least not around here."

My eyes narrow at that last part. I think back to what she said the night she crashed on my bed, drunk out of her mind. "You can talk to me, you know."

She narrows her eyes, crossing her arms. "I know what you're doing."

"What am I doing?" I ask her. "Trying to get my best friend to open up?" I roll my eyes. "Sue me."

"You're trying to change the subject," she amends.

"I'm not," I deny. How the hell does she always know what I'm thinking? Sure, I didn't want to keep talking about Lucas, especially because I didn't know what was going on. Yesterday, we were so close, and all I could think of was his lips on mine.

Not once have I thought about kissing Connor. I like his smile, and I find him attractive, but with Lucas? I almost did it. Almost leaned in, sick and all, and almost broke the promise I made to myself. To never, ever get myself lost in another guy again.

When her eyebrow lifts in disbelief, I blow out a breath. "Fine," I admit, sinking back into my pillows. "But you can talk to me about anything," I tell her, wanting her to know I care about what's going on in her life.

146

"I'll keep that in mind," she says, nudging her shoulder against mine before she gets up and heads toward the door. But instead of walking out, she turns around at the last minute. "So, where did we land on the whole you and Lucas thing?"

"Oh my god. Get out." I throw a cushion at her, and she chuckles. "You're such a meddler."

"You love meee," she sings as she walks out of my room.

"I don't," I call back, but I smile when I hear her laughing. I really do.

# 18

## Would You Rather

*Lucas*

Contrary to what people may think, I'm naturally an introvert.

Sure, I love to go to parties, even though the ones I attended were always about networking, but staying at home watching a movie? Sounds perfect. But when Leila invited me to a frat party, I couldn't say no.

"Dude," James yells, elbowing me in the ribs. James loves to socialize, where I prefer to stay home, so of course, he had to come with me. "This is so much better than the parties at Liberty," he says, adjusting his stance on the crutches. He's been using them more often than the wheelchair, determined to walk again.

I remember being seventeen, talking to James about college. Everyone was applying, and James had his mind set on UCLA, but with his mom being a single parent, he couldn't go. I had offered to help him out with school since I had been making a decent amount by then, but he refused, threatening to break up our friendship if I tried – of course, he was kidding – but I didn't push. So, he ended up attending a community college here.

I, on the other hand, knew it wasn't going to happen. I always wanted it and always thought about it, but I never let myself picture it or hope for it to happen because I knew that, in the end, it wouldn't.

I guess there was no need to. I was making good money, which allowed me to indulge in frequent travel and live a life that many could only imagine. But I couldn't shake off the lingering thought of what it might be like if I pursued something I truly loved.

"Are you sure you're okay?" I ask him when he adjusts the crutches again.

He rolls his eyes playfully. "I'm fine, jeez, I see why your sister complains about you now."

I narrow my eyes when he laughs, joking. "You're a bad influence on her."

He chuckles, shaking his head. "Trust me, that's all her."

I scoff. Yeah, my sister is her own force, even without James' or Leila's help.

James mumbles something, but I can barely hear him with the music blaring. My senses go into overdrive, examining the area. The place is way too crowded, and James is still learning to control his mobility.

"What?" I yell over the music.

"I said I'm going to get a drink."

My eyes widen. "James, you can't."

His smile drops as he shakes his head and leans closer to me. "Listen, I love you, you know that, but I need to have some fun, man. It's been ages since I've been to a party."

I let out a sigh. "You want me to come with you?"

He scoffs. "I've been glued to your hip. No offense, but I need some space."

My brows knit together. "Offense fucking taken. What the fuck?"

149

He laughs. "Do you really want to stand around watching me make out with some guy?" His brows raise, and I breathe out harshly.

"Fine," I concede, knowing he needs some private time. My mother, without a doubt, smothers him when he's at home, and he doesn't get out much since the accident. He needs this. "But if you need anything, and I mean fucking anything, give me a call."

"I will," he says. "Now go find your girl." He gives me a teasing smirk when I narrow my eyes at him.

"She's not my girl."

He laughs, walking away from me. "Whatever you say."

I shake my head, watching as he blends into the crowd. Reaching into my pocket, I pull out my phone and make sure the sound is loud in case James calls me. Even though he might not think so, I'm responsible for him tonight, and I'd die before I let anything happen to him.

My mind runs with all of the possibilities of everything that could go wrong. *Fuck, don't go there.* I pick up my feet and walk deeper into the house, pushing through the crowd.

"Lucas." I turn my head, seeing Leila with a smile on her face. "You came," she says, embracing me in a hug.

I don't miss her boyfriend towering behind her, eyeing me as I return the embrace. "Yeah," I say, pulling back. Aiden is still looking at me. At least he isn't scowling at me like the first time we met. We've hung out more since I moved back, and we've become good friends once he knew I wasn't trying to steal his girl.

"Hey man," I say, nodding toward Aiden. He returns the nod, pulling me in for a quick handshake, his body towering over me. Fuck, he's tall. "Damn. How tall are you?" I ask him.

He laughs. "6'6, I'm pretty average for a basketball player."

"Damn it, I was off my one inch," I mutter to myself.

Aiden scoffs. "That one inch is very important," he says before turning to face Leila. "Isn't that right, gorgeous?"

Leila playfully rolls her eyes, a smile slipping on her lips. "So, Is this your first college party?" she asks me as Aiden wraps his hands around Leila's waist, resting his chin on her head.

"Yeah, I brought James along too."

"Really?" Leila whips her head around. "Where is he? I haven't seen him in so long."

"He wanted some space from me," I admit, scanning around the place. "He went to get a drink or make out with someone. I don't know."

Leila lets out a laugh. "Sounds like him. Well, you can hang out with us in the meantime," she says, gesturing behind her.

I glance behind them, and that's when I see her.

Madeline.

She looks up and glances at me as she sips on her drink, her legs crossed. On her body is a champagne-colored top, showing a sliver of her dark brown stomach, with a matching long skirt covering her legs.

*Holy fuck.*

"Madeline," I say, seeing her eyes dropping to my outfit. I press my lips together to stop from smiling. *She's checking me out.*

"Lucas," she replies.

Silence falls between us, and I wonder if she's thinking about the last time we saw each other. We might not be the best of friends, but I had a really good time with her, even if she was coughing a lung out.

151

"I need a refill," she says, lifting herself off the couch before she walks away. My brows furrow, wondering whether she's trying to avoid me or not.

"It's nice to meet you," a girl says to my right. She smiles at me, tucking her blonde hair behind her ear. "I'm Rosalie, but everyone calls me Rosie."

"Nice to meet you, Rosie." I smile at her, sitting down on the single armchair available.

She leans back against the guy whose lap she's sitting on. "And this is Grayson," she says. "My boyfriend."

"Hey," he lifts his chin, and his tattooed hand reaches out to me, shaking my hand.

"And you already met me," Gabi says, dropping down on the couch. "You make good soup, by the way."

I let out a laugh. *Thank fuck.* It only took my mom yelling at me on the phone for hours when I begged her for the recipe for me to get it right. "I'm glad to hear it."

"Madi has told us so much about you," Rosie says, glancing down at Madeline.

I let out a laugh. "I hope it was all good things."

"Of course it was," Madeline says, holding a refreshed drink in her hand. "You're my boyfriend after all."

Don't know what the fuck just happened to my body from hearing that word in her mouth, but fuck, I want to hear it again.

She looks around, sees Gabi sitting in her seat, and lets out a sigh.

"Move over," Leila tells Gabi. "Make room for Madi."

"I would," Gabriella says with a deep sigh, stretching out on the couch. "But I'm just so tired." She grins, staring at Madi, who narrows her eyes back at her. What the hell is going on? "Maybe you can sit with your *boyfriend?*"

Madeline's head snaps to face me, and I watch the slender slope of her neck move with a gulp.

"I'm fine with that." I'm more than fucking fine with that. Holy fuck. My body warms at the idea of Madeline sitting so close to me, but I know how much she hates when I touch her. I can't push her into this. Not when she doesn't want to.

"I can get up," I offer, whispering so no one but her hears me.

A slight shake of her head has my pulse skyrocketing as she lowers herself onto my thigh, hovering on her heels. I snake a hand around her waist and pull her into me, seating her all the way down.

A sharp intake of her breath has me freezing up, my heart in my fucking throat. I can smell her *everywhere*. God, what the hell is she doing to me? "Is this okay?" I whisper, my lips close to the shell of her ear.

She shivers against me, and I beg myself to have some self-control, but none of that is present when it comes to this girl. What is it about her that makes me want to dive in head first?

Her head moves with a nod, and I breathe out, relaxing into the couch. "Question number twelve," I whisper, hyperaware of her body pressed against mine and my hand around her slender waist. "You talk about me?" A smirk forms on my face at the thought.

"No," she says, looking away from me.

"Really? Your friends say the opposite."

"They're lying. I hardly ever think of you."

I let out a scoff. She has a talent for humbling me. "How flattering."

"Yeah, well, I'm nothing if not honest."

Her friends are still around us, but they're in their own little world, and I let my eyes fall to the length of her again, perched up on my thigh. "You clean up good," I say.

Her head snaps back to face me, and her eyebrow lifts. "Are you saying I looked bad before?"

I chuckle, rubbing my chin. *Never.* "Considering you looked halfway to death the last time I saw you, I would say this is a big improvement."

"Good to know," she says, sipping on her drink.

"So, are you having fun?" I ask her.

She lifts her brows. "Best night of my life," she says dryly.

A chuckle escapes me as I lean in closer to her. The music in here is loud. That's the only reason. "Question number thirteen," I whisper. "On a scale of one to ten, how much do you hate me right now?" I squeeze her waist, making my question clear. I could have stood up and had her take my seat instead, but I didn't.

"Ten," she breathes out.

A smirk creeps onto my face. *Liar.*

I let out a laugh, unable to take my eyes off her. I always knew she was gorgeous, but... has she always been *this* beautiful?

"James." I snap my head up, seeing Leila embrace James in a side hug, helping him through the crowd. Fuck, I completely forgot about him. I should have been thinking about James, not my fake girlfriend who can't stand to be around me.

"Where've you been?" I ask him.

He smirks. "Got a drink, made out a little, came back."

My eyebrows skyrocket. "We've been here less than twenty minutes."

His grin covers his face. "I work fast." I shake my head, admiring my best friend for always going for what he wants. "Hey," he says, looking at Madeline's friends. "I'm James."

"Hey man," Aiden greets James, reaching out his hand. "I'm Aiden. It's nice to meet you."

Grayson lifts his head in acknowledgment, his girlfriend still perched on his lap. "Hey."

James smiles back at them. I like the fact that they don't outright ask him why he has crutches. I know how much James hates talking about the accident that took his mom away from him.

When I see a grin spread across his face, I don't even have to look to know who he's looking at. He hasn't stopped talking about her ever since that picture of us was all over the news. "And you must be Madeline," he says.

I widen my eyes at him. I haven't told Madeline that James and my family know the truth. And I hope he doesn't expose that right now.

"Hi," Madeline replies in a sweet voice I've never been on the receiving end of. What the hell? "Lucas has told me so much about you. I've been dying to meet you."

"Well, we can't have that." He lifts himself, moving toward her, and picks up her hand in his, bringing it to his lips.

My jaw clenches.

*He likes guys.* He. Likes. Guys. I repeat the sentence to myself until I start to forget about his hand holding hers, kissing it. "Nice to finally meet you. Lucas here doesn't shut up about you either."

*Asshole.*

She smirks, looking up at me. "Is that right?"

155

"He's drunk," I say, narrowing my eyes at him. "He doesn't know what he's saying."

He scoffs. "I had one beer. I think I'm fine." I glare at him, but the asshole just smirks back.

"Here," Gabi says, lifting herself off the couch. "Take my seat."

"Thanks," he says, dropping down onto the couch. He lets out a breath, and I wonder if he is exhausted. It's the most he's been on his feet since the accident.

"I thought you were tired?" Madeline asks her best friend.

Gabi grins, shrugging not so innocently. "Now I'm not. Actually, I'm kind of bored."

"Oh no," Madeline whispers.

"What's wrong?" I ask her, loosening my hold on her.

A heavy sigh escapes her. "Usually, when Gabi's bored, it's not good."

I let out a chuckle. "Why not?"

"How about we play a game?" Gabi asks, her eyes shining with mischief.

"That's why," Madeline offers, settling into me.

"What kind of game?" Leila asks.

"Would you rather." Gabriella's eyebrows wiggle as she holds out a beer toward me. I grab it from her.

She makes her way around the table, handing beers to the rest of the group, except for Leila and Aiden, who get given a coke. "You answer the question," she says, sitting down on the couch beside James and cracking open her beer. "If not, you drink."

"Hey, man." A guy comes up to Aiden, tapping him on the back.

"Hey," Aiden says. "You just got here?"

He nods, brushing his dirty blond hair back. "Yeah, a few minutes ago. What are you guys doing?"

"We're playing would you rather," James says, his eyes hardened. "You want to play?"

The guy blanches, swallowing harshly as he keeps his eyes on James. "No, I uh… I should go. It was nice to see you," he says to Aiden before heading toward the party.

"Who was that?" James asks, taking a sip of his beer.

"One of my teammates," Aiden says, fixing the cap on his head. "Carter Ruthers. Great guy."

"Okay." Gabi claps, facing us. "Let's play. Would you rather bite or be bitten?" Gabi asks, smiling.

"My girl scratches," Aiden says.

Leila nudges him, her cheeks turning pink. "I do not."

Aiden lets out a laugh. "I have the marks to prove it," he says, wiggling his brows at her. "Don't worry. I love it."

I watch as Madeline takes a sip, not wanting to answer.

"What about you?" Gabi asks me.

I feel their eyes on me, along with Madeline's, and I take a sip. *Whatever the hell she wants* isn't an answer I'm willing to give.

"Okay, I've got one," Aiden says. "Would you rather give up food or sex?"

"Food," Grayson says. "No fucking doubt."

"What about you?" Aiden asks Leila. "What would you prefer? Me, or your favorite candy?"

"Candy," she replies without missing a beat.

He laughs, pulling her into him. I swear, this is their foreplay. "You are my candy baby."

"Okay, that was the cheesiest thing you've ever said," Gabi says, her face screwing in disgust.

"What about you, Gabi?" Leila asks. "What would you choose?"

Gabi shakes her head. "There's no way I can pick one." She picks up her drink and takes a sip.

"Come on," Grayson says. "At least try."

Gabi sighs, her eyebrows furrowed. "I guess I need food," she mutters. "But…sex." She groans. "I don't fucking know." We all let out a laugh, and she narrows her eyes at us. "You're all evil."

"I have one," Rosie says. "Would you rather always get up at 5 am or always go to bed before midnight?"

"The second one, definitely," Grayson says.

"But I love waking up early," Rosie says. "I could even wake you up the way you like." She grins, and Grayson curses under his breath, brushing his hair back.

"The first one," he amends. "Definitely."

Aiden scoffs. "Whipped."

"Like you can talk?" Grayson says, narrowing his eyes. "Which would you choose?"

"The first," Aiden replies. "My girl gets… excited at night."

Leila glares at her boyfriend. "Do you want to tell them what position we fuck in, too?"

Aiden grins. "That's the game, gorgeous." He turns to face us with a grin. "By the way, my favorite is when she's on top." He groans, shaking his head. "Sexiest thing I've ever seen."

Leila shakes her head, her lips pulling at the corners. "You're incorrigible."

Aiden shrugs, wrapping his arms around her. "You love me anyway."

She lets out a breath and smiles at him, letting him know that she does love him. We can all see how much they love each other, even if she tries to deny it.

"Only give oral, or only receive oral?" James asks, taking a drink immediately after. "I need both."

"Give," Rosie says, her cheeks tinted pink.

"Fuck that," Grayson says, shaking his head. He leans in, whispering something to Rosie that makes her turn bright red, her lips parting.

"There's no way I can choose," Aiden says, taking a sip of his coke. "One without the other is hell."

"Good to know," Leila says, grinning before she takes a sip. Aiden groans and whispers something in her ear, but she just shakes her head, a sly grin on her lips.

Madeline takes a sip, avoiding the question.

"There's a lot of drinking going on over there," Gabi says, everyone's eyes on us. "Are you not feeling talkative?" Her grin makes Madeline flip her off.

"Gabi," Leila says, warning her.

"What?" Gabi flutters her eyelashes, lifting her shoulders in a shrug. "It's just a game."

Not to me, it's not. They might think we're dating, but I'm fucking glad Madeline isn't answering any of these questions. I'd always think whether or not she's thinking of Connor doing them to her.

Gabi grins. "Would you rather find your parent's sex tape or have your parents find yours?" She lets out a laugh when everyone else groans.

"What kind of question is that?" Grayson asks, taking a sip. "I'm not answering that." Everyone else drinks, too, me included.

159

"Well," James says, laughing. "I guess this is the silver lining when you don't have any parents." Everyone falls into silence, but James rolls his eyes. "I'm kidding. Jesus." He sighs. "Fine, here's another. No sex or no kissing?"

Gabi shakes her head. "No kissing," she says. "Most guys don't know how to anyway."

Rosie takes a sip of her drink. "I don't want to choose."

"Good thing you don't have to, angel," Grayson says, gripping her waist as he leans down to kiss her.

Madeline takes another sip, shuffling on my lap as she does. I swallow down a groan when she shifts against my cock. I try to ignore it, but when she does it again, my hands fly to her waist, halting her movements.

"Are you okay?" I ask her.

"Yeah," she says, with a hushed tone. "I'm just trying to get comfortable." She shifts again, and I let out a deep groan, unable to stop it from coming out of my mouth.

"Fuck, Madeline. I'm going to need you to stop that."

"You need to work out less," she huffs. "Your thigh is as hard as a rock."

My jaw clenches as I grip her waist tighter. "That's not my thigh."

She stops moving, slowly turning her head toward me. "You mean…"

I let out a breath. "That's what happens when you grind on my dick."

Fuck. Why the hell did I just say that? Her eyes widen, and I can tell she's embarrassed. She tries to lift herself off my lap, but I pull her back down, moving her to the side of my leg.

"What are you doing?" she whisper yells.

"If you get up right now, it's going to be *very* embarrassing for me."

She lets out a breath, careful not to move. Fuck, I need it to go down. But I know having Madeline this close to me isn't going to make that happen.

A loud cheer comes from deep in the party, causing everyone's heads to turn.

"What happened?" James asks, straining his neck, trying to see.

"I'm pretty sure they're playing beer pong," Gabi says.

"Fuck yeah, I'm amazing at beer pong. Who wants to play?" He looks around at the group. "Spoiler alert: I'm going to win."

"We'll see about that," Leila says, smiling at him.

"I'll join, too." Gabi lifts herself off the couch, helping James up until he's propped on the crutches.

Leila turns to face her boyfriend, smirking at him. "You want to play against me?" she asks him. "I'll switch the beers to soda."

Aiden grins as Leila stands between his legs, his hands dropping to her hips as he sits on the edge of the couch. "You sure you want to lose?"

"I won't lose," she says, narrowing her eyes at him.

He laughs. "You do remember I'm a pro at dunking balls, right?"

She smirks at him. "And you do know I'm good at playing with balls, right?"

He lets out a groan, pulling her toward him. I swear those two are a second away from saying fuck the game and heading into a bedroom or a bathroom. "You're playing dirty," he says.

Leila grins at him. "Only way to play. Come on. If you win, I'll do that thing you like."

His brows shoot up, intrigue swimming in his eyes. "And if you win?" he asks, his face an inch away from hers. "What do you get, hm?" His lips brush against hers. "What do you want from me?"

She's breathing hard, and I look around. Her friends are all smiling at them. This must be a regular occurrence. Gabi's eyes meet mine and she laughs at my expression. "I get a massage," Leila tells her boyfriend.

He laughs, pulling back. "You really want that massage, don't you?"

She shrugs. "I love your hands," she says. "They're so big and soft."

He grins seductively. "My hands are good for other things, too," he whispers, but not quietly enough.

"As much as I love watching live porn," James says. "I'd love to actually play before I die of old age."

They laugh, making their way over. Grayson lifts himself off the couch, Rosie's hand intertwined with his. "You guys coming?" he asks.

"Maybe later." *If my erection ever goes down.*

He nods, pulling Rosie toward the game. Music fills the area, and I'm so painfully aware of Madeline beside me.

"Are you…" She trails off, embarrassed to finish the sentence.

"Yeah," I breathe out, wanting her away from me and to never leave at the same time. I can't fucking think when she's near me. "You can get up now."

She lifts herself off my lap, and I don't even have time to think about how cold I feel without her because my attention is snagged by the asshole checking her out. *What a way to kill an erection.*

162

My jaw tightens when I see none other than Connor smiling at her as he talks to his friends. I turn my eyes to Madeline, seeing her stare back at him.

I let out a scoff, my body growing hot. "What's your obsession with that guy?" I ask her, lifting myself up to stand beside her.

"I don't know what you're talking about," she says.

"You know exactly what I'm talking about."

I see her look up at him once again, and their eyes lock. He can't stop staring at her, even while I'm here, right beside her. I can't blame him. Madeline is a fucking sight, especially with her dainty little outfit she has on today. She's probably the most gorgeous woman here.

But as far as he knows, she's mine. I've told him as much, but it's clear that he doesn't care. He walks toward us – no, toward *her* - and my jaw is so tight it hurts. This fucker has a death wish.

He grins when he approaches her, completely ignoring that I'm right here. "Madeline," he says. "Nice to see you." With a rich, dark voice like that, of course, she falls at his fucking feet.

This guy needs to know she's off limits, to him and to everyone else. I lift my arm, letting it drift down her back, the satiny material beneath my fingertips so soft. I wrap my hand around her waist and pull her swiftly into me. She gasps when she finds herself plastered to my side, but she doesn't make any move to pull away.

"Hey," I say to this asshole, giving him a smile that's so fake it makes me want to puke. "Connor, right?"

His eyes widen when he notices me. *Yeah, asshole. Forgot about me?* "Yeah. I'm sorry, I don't remember your name," he says.

I nod, running my tongue over my teeth. Sure, he doesn't. "It's Lucas. Madeline's boyfriend," I reiterate.

"Right." He nods, rubbing the back of his neck. "I'll uh... I'll see you in class," he says to Madeline before he heads off.

I seriously don't get what she sees in that guy. Sure, some might say he's handsome, and yeah, fine, he has a nice smile. But I was named Envy's top 100 hottest men, and she barely gives me the time of day when my mouth gapes in awe every time I see her.

I don't like that at all.

# 19

I could be so nice

*Madeline*

"What was that for?" I turn my head to face him. He's so close, his face right in front of mine, our bodies pressed together, the heat of his encompassing me.

His brows lift, and a slight frown appears on his lips. "Are you kidding?"

"I said no touching." I take a step back from him, his arm dropping from my waist. My skin heats from the lost contact, wanting it back. *Get it together.*

His eyes narrow. "Respectfully, *princesa*, I don't give a fuck if you like what I just did or not. It was necessary."

"Stop calling me that." I scowl at him, hating how it sounds like such an insult coming from his lips. "And how was that necessary?" I ask.

He scoffs, irritated, and shakes his head. "With the way he was flirting with you right in front of me? Very."

"He was not flirting with me."

"How can you be so blind?"

My eyes widen. "Excuse me?"

"You heard me. You are fucking blind if you can't tell he was flirting with you."

The intensity of his glare makes my cheeks flush with heat. and I want to go back to last week. When he made me soup and opened up to me, it actually felt like we were becoming something close to being friends. I turn around with a huff and walk away, heading toward the exit.

"Where the hell are you going?" he asks.

"Away from you," I say, looking behind my shoulder to see him right on my tail, his brows bunched as he follows.

"Mother—" he murmurs, aggravated. His steps get louder the closer he approaches me.

"Stop following me," I call out, not bothering to turn around as I push past the crowd, wanting to get away from him.

"Stop running away," he says. I'm aware of people looking our way, clearly noticing we're in a fight, but I'm too pissed off to care.

"I need space."

I hear his scoff as I move past the crowd, heading into a quieter area. "You don't need space. Not from me."

"I need space, especially from you." After what happened back there when I was sitting on his lap and when he pulled me into him when Connor was there, I can't think straight. I hate thinking about how the only thing I could focus on was Lucas' hands on me, his thumb brushing against the fabric of my dress. I need to figure out why I wanted more.

"Goddamn it." That's all I hear before his hand encloses around my elbow, and he spins me around. I gasp at the quick movement, and the next thing I know, he's pulling us into an empty room and closing the door.

"Let me go," I tell him, narrowing my eyes at him.

His eyes meet mine, fire burning in them. "You're making a scene," he says. "Did you forget we're supposed to be happy and in love? Or do you want our breakup to come sooner?" His eyes scan mine, making my breathing speed up. He's all I see, all I smell, all I feel. All over my body. "Do you want everyone to know we were lying? That our entire relationship is all fake? That it's nothing more than a contract you have to fulfill?" he asks, shaking his head when a scoff escapes his lips. "Maybe you want me to call your boyfriend back. Get him to flirt with you some more."

"Oh my god." I throw my hands up. "He was not flirting. He was just having a conversation with me. He's a nice guy as opposed to you."

His eyes harden. "Oh, I'm not nice?"

My mind flashes back to when he took care of me when I was sick, and he made me soup; he even folded my damn clothes. He's so much more than just nice, but after annoying me about Connor, I can't let him know that. I cross my arms and breathe out a heavy sigh instead.

His eyes narrow, and he leans in until he's right in front of me. My arms drop, and my lips part from his proximity. His eyes drop to my lips, licking his own. "Trust me, *princesa. You don't know me.*" His voice has gone deeper, huskier, and I'm struggling to remember my own name. "I could be so nice," he says, his thumb lifting my chin to make me look up at him. "So fucking nice to you."

I hear a soft noise, a whimper of some sort, and I'm horrified to find out it came from me. I know he heard it too, with the way his eyes darken. I see the lust swirling in them, the want, the battling with himself over this, and I think he's going to kiss me. My heart starts to race faster than ever before, anticipating it. *Wanting it.*

But he steps away from me and squeezes his eyes shut, cursing under his breath in what I assume is Portuguese. When his eyes open again, he looks away from me, tugging at the strands of his hair. "You should leave," he says.

"Lucas—"

"Leave, Madeline." He takes another step away from me again and snaps his head back to me. "You were trying to run away from me, weren't you? Well then, go."

I stare back at him, my chest rising and falling. Why does he make me feel things I don't want to feel? I shake my head, wanting to say something, anything, but when his eyes meet mine, I see the uncertainty swimming in them. He turns around and buries his head in his hands, and I do what he told me to.

I press my lips together and turn around, opening the door. My shoulder hits someone on the way out, but I don't stop to look, racing back to the party. It's not until I leave, that I realize we were shut in a dark closet, and I didn't freak out. I didn't cry or break down like I did in the elevator. I didn't even notice where we were.

And even now, all I can think of is, I wish he would have kissed me.

## 20

### Catching feelings

*Lucas*

I almost kissed her.

In that tiny, empty room with less than two inches between us, I couldn't help but let my mind wonder and needs take over as I thought about what it would be like to kiss her.

Her lips were slightly parted, glossy this time. That pink bottom lip begging for attention, those chocolate brown eyes so enticing, even in the dimly lit room. I almost did it.

I almost slid my hand across her cheek, almost wrapped my hand around the back of her head, and pulled her into me. Almost leaned down until our lips brushed together.

But then I remembered her no-kissing rule.

It was fucking agony, having her right there breathing hard, looking up at me like she wanted me to. Especially when the soft moan left her lips, I couldn't think, couldn't fucking breathe when she was right in front of me. But I couldn't have her.

I'm not the one she wants.

I'm not Connor.

"Great job." My head lifts, snapping out of it when I remember I'm at a job right now.

The photographer gives me a thumbs up, telling me our session is done. I rub a hand down my face when I walk off set.

I just hope it went well. I was completely in my head, only one thought running through my mind, or more accurately, one person.

James' moans make me freeze when I walk in the changing rooms, and I lift my head, seeing him devour a plate full of cheese and crackers.

Letting out a laugh, I head toward him, dropping onto the couch. "I'm starting to think you only come to these things for the food."

He nods, his mouth full of food. "You'd be right."

I shake my head, a laugh bubbling out of me, while I reach for my phone, subconsciously looking for her name on it. My hand tightens around my phone when I don't see any messages from her. Fuck. What has this girl done to me? I can't get her out of my fucking mind.

James lets out a laugh, and I turn to face him, seeing him stare down at his phone.

"Who are you talking to?" I ask him, wondering who has him laughing like that.

"Madi."

My heart stops at the sound of her name. "Madeline?" I repeat. "My Madeline?"

His head snaps to mine, a cocky smirk painted on his lips. "*Your* Madeline, huh?"

I puff out a breath. "You know what I mean. Why the hell are you talking to Madeline?"

"Technically, it's a group chat," he explains, munching on the crackers. "But your girl was just telling me about her audition."

My brows furrow. "She had an audition?" I ask, completely ignoring the 'your girl' comment. I didn't have time to think about why the hell my heart felt like it was going to beat out of my chest at the words.

"She didn't tell you?" he asks, his brows knitting together.

No, she fucking didn't.

I wonder if she's avoiding me because of what went down at the party. I didn't kiss her. I did what I promised her I would do, and I didn't fucking kiss her, no matter how much I wanted to, because we both knew that if I did, it wouldn't have been fake. There was no one around. It would have just been for us.

My fingers hover over her name. I shouldn't text her. I know that, but it doesn't stop me from doing just that.

Lucas:

> You had an audition?

Madeline:

> Yep.

I frown at her clipped tone, wanting to kick myself for making her uncomfortable. I can't believe I did that. I was so fucking stupid, blinded by jealousy, when I saw how her crush wants her. Yeah, well, so do I. But she won't even look twice at me when she's all I think about.

My attention is shaken when James laughs again, staring down at his phone. She's fucking talking to him, joking with him, but all I get is a one-word answer? Lifting myself off the couch, I head toward the exit, my thumb hovering over the green call button.

"Why are you calling me?" she says into the phone.

I let out a laugh, my pulse settling at the sound of her voice. "Is that how you always answer the phone?"

"When it's you calling, yes."

I shake my head, a smile on my lips even though she's trying to insult me. Blowing out a breath, my lips fall into a frown. "Why didn't you tell me?"

"You're going to have to be more specific," she says. "I don't read minds."

"About the audition," I clarify.

She's quiet for a while before I hear a sigh. "I didn't think you'd care."

My frown deepens. Does she really think I'm that kind of guy? "Of course I care," I say. "How did it go?"

"I got the rejection email twenty minutes ago," she says. I can hear the sadness in her voice, and it makes my chest ache.

"I'm sorry." Leaning back on the wall, I keep the phone pressed against my ear when I hear the subtle laugh coming from her.

"It's not your fault," she says.

*Isn't it?* It's probably been the first audition she's been to since this started, and she didn't get it. I blow out a breath, wanting her to forget about the rejection. "Question number fourteen," I start, smiling when I hear her grunt. "What does your dream house look like?"

She chuckles. "Why? Are you going to build it for me?"

I smirk, rubbing a thumb over my lip. *Hopefully.* "Just answer the question."

"I guess I don't want something too big," she says, surprising me. Usually, when you ask someone what their dream house is, they always say a huge, elaborate house, not Madeline, though. "I want my house to be clean and homey. I don't like the idea of having a huge empty void, especially when it'll probably just be me."

172

My frown returns. "Why do you say that?" I ask her.

Her silence kills me as it radiates through us until she sighs. "I just don't see myself sharing a life with someone else."

My heart drops to my stomach. I don't even know why, but hearing that come from her lips kills me. "Really?" I ask her, my pulse racing.

"Yeah," she admits, her voice quiet and not like I'm used to hearing from her. "You know how much of a control freak I am."

The corner of my lips lifts as I lick my lips and shake off her earlier words. I shouldn't care that she wants to spend her life alone. I shouldn't be thinking about what it would be like if she were to spend it with... me.

But I am.

It's all I'm thinking about.

So when I rub my hand over my face, unable to shake the thought of Madeline out of my mind, I say something I probably shouldn't. "Question number fifteen. What's your dream date?"

She laughs. "This again?"

"You didn't answer me before," I remind her.

"Why do you want to know so bad?"

*I want to know what makes you happy.* "You're bad at answering questions," I say instead, not wanting her to read too much into it.

"I told you I don't let myself think about it," she tells me, and I hear the sigh in her voice.

"Try, Madeline," I plead. "Just tell me what would make you happy."

"Lucas."

I tut, shaking my head at her tone. "It's my question, Mads. You answer, that was the deal."

A heavy sigh escapes her. "I know it'll probably never happen, but…" My ears perk up, wanting to know her answer. "I'd want the guy to plan it. I'd want to be surprised, admired… worshipped." My eyebrows raise at her boldness. Madeline has always been a closed-off, independent person ever since I have known her, so this… it surprises the fuck out of me.

"I'd want him to pick out a dress for me, pick out my hairstyle, my nails, and take me where he's never taken another girl before. I'd want to be the center of his attention, the only thought in his head."

I smirk, picturing how I would do every one of those things. I could be so fucking good to her if she'd let me.

The truth hits me right in my face before I can even begin to process what the hell that means.

I've caught feelings for my fake girlfriend.

How the hell did this happen? How did I let this happen? Even though I made her promise not to develop feelings for me, I ended up doing just that. When we met, she was a pain in my ass, and I had no interest in her. Even if I thought she was beautiful, and my body warmed every time I looked at her, the way she hated me was enough to tame down any other feelings. But now? She's everywhere. Thoughts her consume my mind, day after day And I don't know what to do about it.

"I was right," I say with a smile on my face.

"About?"

"You *are* a princess."

A scoff leaves her mouth, making me chuckle at the sound. I swear if I were dying, her laugh would cure me. "And now I regret answering your question."

I shake my head, unable to stop smiling. "Are you ready for the interview?" I ask her.

Ana managed to get us another interview with CelebCentral next week. Although I should be thinking about the interview, about how lucky we are that they gave us another chance after standing them up at the last minute, my only thoughts are of Madeline.

What might she wear, how will she do her makeup that day? Will she wear that cherry red lipstick again? *God, I hope so.* Will her hair be down, or will she have it up this time? She usually has it curly on Wednesdays. I don't even know if Madeline will want me to touch her after what happened last week, necessary or not.

"Of course," she says.

"Really?" I ask. "How are you feeling now? Any sickness coming on?"

I can almost picture her rolling her eyes. "I'm fine. I'll be there."

"You can't blame me for being worried."

She lets out a scoff. "You? Worried?"

I frown. "Yes, Madeline. I'm fucking worried for you. Is that so hard to believe?"

She's quiet for a while, and I wonder if she's thinking back to the party. I wonder If she really thinks I don't care about her or if she saw through the jealousy and realized I want her. "I wouldn't want to have to cancel the interview again," I say to ease any suspicions she may have.

"That won't happen," she says. "I'll make sure of it. I'm going to be there bright and early."

"To pretend to be my girlfriend," I fill in for her because that's what we're going to be doing. A whole day of smiling, touching, and pretending we're dating for the cameras.

"That's the deal." *That's the deal*. She says that as if it's such a hardship for her, and once upon a time, it was for me too, but not anymore. I'm anticipating it, anticipating being able to touch her without her flinching or being able to smile at her when that's all I ever want to do when I look at her.

"You're a good actress, right?" I ask her like I haven't seen it with my own eyes. Like I haven't re-watched her audition tapes a handful of times. Ana had a copy, and when I asked her to see it, I told her I needed to see if she was good enough, which was a lie. I knew Madeline was amazing before I even laid eyes on that tape, but afterward? I was speechless, unable to understand how she hadn't landed an audition yet.

"Why do you want to know?" she asks skeptically.

"So I know if I need to stop you from exposing us as faking a relationship."

She laughs. "You doubt my skills that much?"

I smirk, leaning back into my bed, loving how we're back to teasing each other after the whirlwind that was last week. "Hey, I've never seen you act," I lie. "You can't blame me for wondering."

"And you never will," she says.

My smirk widens. *Little does she know.* "I wouldn't be so sure about that."

"How come?"

I let out a sigh. "Because you're going to have to do a whole lot of pretending at the interview."

What I don't tell her is I doubt I'll have to do any.

# 21

Do we have a deal?

## *Madeline*

"Well, you two are just the cutest couple," Sarah, the interviewer, gushes.

Lucas smiles at her, making me glance up at him. I was scared it would be awkward between Lucas and me once we got here and had to see each other again, but as soon as I saw him, we went back to teasing each other like that almost kiss never happened.

My stomach dropped with disappointment at how easy it seemed for him to forget about it when it was all I could think of. Did he not care? Did he… not want to kiss me? Maybe I was just reading into the whole thing, and my feelings were one-sided.

"Thank you," he says.

She turns to the crowd, flicking her blonde hair behind her shoulder as she does. "Aren't they just the cutest?" she asks them. A wave of cheers comes from the audience before Sarah turns back to face us. "Seriously, I mean, you guys make a beautiful couple."

Lucas' knees knock against mine, making my eyes lift to his. There's not much room on the white plush couch we're sitting on, and every so often, he reaches out to touch me in some way.

*Necessary*, I tell myself. We're supposed to be affectionate. We're dating, after all. Or at least that's what the rest of the world thinks.

His eyes meet mine as he gives me a smile I feel all the way down to my toes. "That's all her," he says. A collective 'aww' resonates through the audience. His eyes remain on mine, and my heart swells with warmth as I feel a flutter in my stomach.

His hand reaches out and he places it on my thigh, rubbing his thumb back and forth over my leg. I'm wearing pants, but I still feel the burn of his touch through my clothes. "She's without a doubt the most beautiful girl I have ever seen."

Sarah smiles at us. "That's the sweetest thing I've ever heard," she says. "So, how did you guys meet? How did a normal college girl end up dating *the* Lucas Silva?"

I let out a laugh, trying to hide my discomfort. *How did I end up dating him? Well, the thing is… we're not. It's all fake, and you're all being lied to.* I clear my throat and paste on a smile. "We met in a blackout, actually."

"Oh?" Her eyebrows raise. "That sounds interesting. Tell me more."

I glance at Lucas for a second, and I can tell he doesn't know where I'm going with this. "Well, it was just us in the elevator when it broke down," I admit. "We were stuck in there with no lights, no form of contact, so we got to talking and..." I smile up at him, "The rest is history."

His brows bunch together as he looks at me. "I was completely hypnotized," he says, his eyes never leaving mine. "I knew I couldn't let her go without asking for her number." It's not even close to what actually happened between us, and I don't know which version of the story I prefer.

"Talk about a meet-cute," Sarah says, smiling at us. "I mean, we all see the way you look at her. I'll tell you, it's been a long time since someone has looked at me like that. And that photoshoot?" She blows out a breath, waving a hand in her face. "It was the hottest thing I've ever seen."

I think back to that photoshoot. It seems like just yesterday, but so much has happened since then. I still remember it, his breath hitting my skin, his hand on my cheek. I don't think I'll ever stop remembering it.

"Was that the first time you had done any modeling?" she asks me.

I nod. "I was terrified at first." I let out a nervous laugh. "But Lucas calmed me down and made me feel comfortable." And the thing is, I don't even have to lie. It's the truth.

"Well, you're a natural," Sarah says. "Lucas taught you well."

"I didn't need to do much teaching. The camera loves her," he says, glancing down at me with a smirk.

"You are right about that," Sarah says before turning her attention back to me. "So this is your first celebrity relationship. How does that feel?" she asks. "It must be nerve-wracking having paparazzi around you guys all the time."

"A little," I admit. "Sometimes they appear out of nowhere, and it's surprising for sure. Especially when we just want to go out like any other couple, but I guess we can't really do that." *Especially because we're not a couple at all.* I bite back the truth as Sarah nods sympathetically.

"That's got to be tough, but if it weren't for them, we wouldn't have known about you guys. And we love you so much." The crowd cheers again.

"I like that I don't have to hide her from the world anymore," Lucas says. "I want everyone to know how amazing she is."

God, he knows all of the right things to say. I'm even starting to believe him.

"So, how did you know she was the one?" she asks Lucas. "After all, we've all seen the pictures of the various different girls throughout the years."

Sarah laughs, and the crowd follows, but Lucas stiffens, his touch stopping abruptly on my leg. "Yeah," he says, laughing a little, which I can tell is fake. "I guess it did take me a while to want to settle down." He removes his hand completely from my leg, and I feel the emptiness soon after.

"So what was it about Madeline that made you change your mind?" she asks.

We didn't know what questions they were going to ask, so while we came prepared, making up a story on the spot was a little harder to do. I turn my head to find Lucas already looking at me. The look in his eyes is intense, making my stomach swirl with nerves.

He doesn't take his eyes off me as he says, "Every other girl stopped existing the minute she came into my life."

"Well done," Ana says when we walk backstage. "That went better than I expected." She hands me a cup of coffee and I gladly take it.

I drop down on the white couch they have in the room backstage and blow out a breath. It went way better than I thought, but I'm so glad that's over. I take a sip of the coffee and hum, my eyes closing at the warm, sweet flavor on my tongue.

"The comments are amazing," she says, looking down at her phone. "Everyone is loving this relationship. You guys are great." She grins, focusing her attention on me. "Especially you, Madeline. I knew you wanted to be an actress, and the audition tapes I have seen were great, but I don't think I realized how talented you are until I saw that performance out there."

My cheeks start to heat as I smile at her. "Thank you."

"I'll tell you what," she says. "I know somebody in the movie business. Monica Harrington, you know her?" My eyes widen. Do I know her? She's only one of my favorite directors ever. She must be able to tell from my expression because she laughs. "I can't promise anything, but I can try and see if I can get you an audition."

That's the best news I've heard yet.

"Really?" I ask her.

"Of course. I told you this would be beneficial to you, and I plan on keeping my word. You're getting so much recognition already. We might as well see if we can get you something out of it."

My lips part and I struggle for words. "I'm... thank you," I say, unable to think of anything else. An audition. I might actually get an audition with *Monica Harrington*.

"Don't mention it. Just enjoy it, and speaking of..." She glances down at her phone. "Next week, you guys are attending a gala together as a couple, obviously."

"What's this gala for?" Lucas asks.

"It's the Starlight's Dream charity gala. It helps underprivileged children. It will be great publicity having both of you attending for such a good cause."

"And, of course, to help the children," Lucas says.

She waves a hand. "That too, of course. It's at the Celestial Manor Hotel I've booked you guys a room, and everything is already set. Just make sure you show up and do what you guys do best."

A knock hits the door. "Ana, we have an issue over here." She sighs and walks out of the room.

When the door closes, it's just Lucas and I in the room. "Congrats," he says with a smile as he sits beside me on the couch.

"Don't jinx it," I tell him. "Nothing has happened yet."

"But it will," he says, sounding hopeful, more hopeful than even I am. It's Monica Harrington. The woman is a genius. "I see how talented you are, Mads." There he goes with that nickname again. It doesn't ease my stomach. It makes it flutter even more. *What the hell is that?* "I just know that when that Monica girl sees your audition, she won't be able to turn you away. You even fooled me back there."

I bunch my eyebrows. "I did?"

He nods, running a hand through his hair. "Yeah, I was even starting to believe you actually liked me."

I roll my eyes teasingly, afraid he'll see that it wasn't an act. "Don't flatter yourself."

He chuckles. "Too late. After all, don't you think you owe me a thank you?"

I blink at him. "For what?"

He shrugs. "This whole thing. If I didn't save your ass in that elevator that day, we wouldn't be here."

I shake my head. "In that case, you owe *me* a thank you."

"For?" he asks with furrowed brows.

I grin. "Saving your ass," I mock back to him. "If it wasn't for me, your career would have tanked, isn't that what you told me?"

He chuckles, shaking his head. "You want to see if that's true?"

"How?" I ask reluctantly.

"We'll see who people like more," he says with a shrug. "We make a little contest. Whoever can get the most likes on a post wins."

I frown. "That's not even close to being a fair deal. You're famous."

"Hardly." I glare at him, and he laughs at my expression. "Ok, yeah, so people know me. But you're getting up there. And after all, they like you, not me, right? So what are you afraid of."

"I didn't say that specifically."

"Semantics," he says, lifting a shoulder. "What do you say?"

I blow out a breath. "You have an advantage. I'm not going to take on a deal I know is rigged."

"You're afraid to lose," he says with a shake of his head. "I can't believe it."

He's teasing me, I know that, but just hearing the word *lose* makes me twitch. "I am not going to lose," I assure him.

He grins, knowing he's got me right where he wants me. "I wouldn't be so sure about that."

Leaning closer to him, I narrow my eyes. "I'll win. I'll make sure of it."

"And when I win?" he asks, tipping his body forward. "What do I get?"

"Bragging rights."

He shakes his head, letting out a tut. "That's not good enough for me."

"Then what do you want?" I ask him, my brows knitting together.

His eyes immediately drop to my lips, the air between us getting thicker the more time that goes on. My lips part on impulse, and his eyes seem to darken as he blows out a breath. "I can't ask for what I want."

My heart starts to race right out of my chest. "Why not?"

His eyes snap back to mine. "Because you won't want it."

I swallow, my throat feeling tight. "You don't know that," I tell him, my heart beating even faster now. "Besides, it's your choice. I'll have to go through with it."

I feel the heat of his gaze as our eyes connect, and then they fall again to the curve of my mouth. Only for a second before he sighs, closes his eyes, and runs a hand through his hair. "No, it's too risky."

"Then pick something else," I tell him, my voice thicker than normal.

He grins, turning back to face me. "I want a day," he says.

My brows tug in confusion. "A day?"

He nods. "One day, when you ditch that meticulously organized planner of yours, and I'm in control."

"Of me?" I ask, my eyes widening.

"That's right," he says with a grin.

"What do you have against my planner?" I ask with a huff.

He glares. "Madeline, you're attached to the hip to that thing. I bet you even brought it here with you."

I clutch my bag closer to me, knowing he's right. I did bring it with me. "Fine," I relent. "But if I win, you become my personal assistant."

He laughs, his face dropping when he sees I'm serious. "You want me to *what*?" he asks.

I smirk, crossing my legs as I turn to face him. "You want to control me for a day, then I control you."

His eyes sparkle as he grins. "You want me to wait on you hand and foot?" he asks. "Do whatever you want at any given moment?"

I don't know why that just sounded dirty as hell, but I nod, swallowing. "That's right."

He chuckles, rubbing his bottom lip with his thumb. "Fine, I accept." He grins, leaning closer to me. "I can't wait to win."

"Well, then you'll be waiting a long time because I won't lose."

He turns his body to face mine and leans closer. "Do we have a deal?" he asks.

I take hold of his extended hand and shake it. His thumb rubs over my knuckles just for a second, but the feel of his hand lingers, tingles spreading over my skin.

He leans in even closer this time. So close I can hear his breathing, hear his pulse knocking against his chest. "It's Wednesday," he whispers.

My breath halts as I stare up into his eyes. "So?"

His eyes drop to my lips for a second before they lift to my hair. "You usually wear your hair curly on Wednesdays."

My whole body freezes. How does he know that? But I don't have time to think before a flash happens. I blink, turning my head to see his phone in his other hand.

He just took a picture of us.

He grins, pulling back, and stares down at his phone screen. "Make sure you clear a day for me, *princesa*."

# 22

Not really a love letter

## *Madeline*

As soon as I walk into my apartment, the sound of Gabi's laughter fills the room.

That's not typically a weird thing; the girl is always laughing and smiling, but this time it's different. She's... giggling. Blushing even.

I freeze at the doorstep, the keys jiggling in my hands as I watch her cuddled up on the couch, controller in her hand, playing a video game.

When I shut the door behind me, her head snaps back and her eyes widen, just now realizing I'm home. "Oh hey," she says. "How was therapy?"

"Good." I lean down and take off my heels, groaning when my feet hit the floor. I've worn heels for so long; they're practically molded to the shape of my feet, but there's nothing like the feeling of taking off your heels when you get home. It's better than taking off a bra, I'd say. "Intense."

"Yeah?" she asks, taking off her headset. "Are you okay?"

I nod. This week's session was tough, bringing back all of my old memories of Daniel. It aggravates me that after all these years, he's still the topic of my discussions. He's still the reason I feel empty. Weak. Depleted.

"I'm good," I breathe out, exhausted from talking about the one person I wish I could forget.

"Oh, by the way," she says with a smirk. "I saw Lucas' post today."

"What post?"

"The one where you guys look like you're two seconds away from ripping off each other's clothes." Gabi's face lights up with a grin, and I roll my eyes, feeling my cheeks heat up.

Pulling my phone out of my bag, I quickly head to Lucas' page, where I see the post Gabi is talking about — the one he took three days ago after the interview. It's the moment that still echoes in my mind, capturing that moment when I thought he was about to kiss me, only to realize when the flash went off that it was just a move to win the stupid bet between us.

My lips feel dry as I stare down at the image on my screen, unable to break away from Lucas and the way he looks at me. I still remember what I felt at the time, wanting him to lean in and kiss me. It's a thought I haven't had in a long time, but it seems to be a constant occurrence with Lucas.

But it's not the picture that catches me off guard. It's the caption under the post that Lucas wrote.

*My favorite person in the world.*

My stomach somersaults and my heart bangs against my chest as I re-read it over and over again.

I *know* Lucas doesn't mean those words. I know he has to sell our fake relationship, and he's committed to winning the bet, but it doesn't stop my heart from drumming all the same, hoping a part of him actually believes that.

"Did you zone out?" Gabi jokes, her words bringing me back to reality.

I quickly turn off my phone, trying to maintain composure. "No, I was just... checking something," I lie, my voice slightly strained. "I'll be in my room." Ignoring her amused chuckles, I make my way to my room.

"Oh, I almost forgot," Gabi says, causing me to stop and look at her. "A package came for you today."

"From who?"

She shrugs and lets out a chuckle. "Probably your boyfriend."

A subtle smirk creeps onto my face, even as I try to narrow my eyes at her. "Funny."

"I know. Thanks."

I let out a laugh and head into my room, seeing a huge pink box with a bow on top sitting on my bed. My brows furrow as I approach it and lift the lid. An envelope sits on the top of the white tissue paper, and I pick it up, opening the letter inside.

*I never thought I'd be writing one of these, and honestly, I never had the urge to. But you once mentioned loving the idea of receiving a love letter. Technically, you said you didn't want one if you'd have to be in a relationship, so I guess this gets a pass, considering our relationship isn't real.*

*This relationship might be fake, but this letter isn't, and while I've never written one of these before, what I can do is be honest.*

*You're beautiful, Madeline. Probably – no, scratch that, definitely the most beautiful girl I have ever seen. I thought so since the day I met you. Even when I shouldn't, I always thought you were beautiful. I've always loved the way you smile when you think I'm not looking – I'm always looking. Even when I shouldn't be.*

*I love the way your eyes light up when you talk about acting and how passionate you are about your dreams. I admire the way you don't let anything stop you, to the point of agreeing to this charade. I think you're so brave for going after your dreams. You inspire me.*

*You're so incredibly talented, Mads, and I genuinely hope this arrangement works out for you. I hope you get that audition because you deserve it more than you realize. And I'm going to be so proud when I see your name in the credits at the movie theater one day.*

*So, here's your not-really-a-love-letter love letter. You can crumple it up and toss it aside, or you can keep it until this is all over. I just wanted to give you something no one else ever has.*

*I just wanted to make you happy.*

*Lucas.*

He wrote me a love letter?

My eyes blink away the wetness in my eyes as I scan his handwriting over and over again, re-reading the lines where my heart beats twice as fast.

My brows furrow as I place the letter on the bed and pull off the tissue paper, revealing a long, satin-black dress. My cheeks warm at the thought of Lucas buying this for me. I run my hands over the silky fabric, and a smile appears on my lips.

Before I can talk myself out of it, I pull the dress out of the box and slip it on, loving how it hugs my body like a glove, a slit running down my leg. It's so beautiful. I can't believe he did this.

I take my phone out of my bag and pull up his name, smiling to myself when I read our past conversations. I shake my head, typing out a text.

Madeline:

You bought me a dress?

Lucas:

No big deal. I just didn't want
you to come unprepared.

Three little dots dance on the screen, making me nervous. I
pull my bottom lip between my teeth while I wait for his
answer.

Madeline:

And the letter?

Lucas:

I meant what I said. I wanted
to make you happy.

My lips pull into a smile as I stare down at his text.

Madeline:

Thank you.

Lucas:

> Wow. A thank you? I believe
> that's some sort of record.

Madeline:

> You had to ruin it.

Lucas:

> I love to please you.

Madeline:

> More like displease.

Lucas:

> As long as I'm in your
> head, it's fine by me.

My heart does a blip at his words, and my eyes scan his text over and over again. Why do I like that so much? Lucas wanting me to think about him.

Lucas:

> I just have one request.

Madeline:

Oh god, what is it? You're not going to make me do anything embarrassing, are you?

Lucas:

Wear red lipstick.

My brows furrow at his text, and before I can say anything, a loud crash startles me. I turn around to see Gabi standing at the door, with her mouth dropped and a half-eaten sandwich in her hand.

"Holy shit," she says. I notice the controller on the ground when she leans down to pick it back up.

"Do I look okay?" I ask her.

She nods slowly, her mouth still gaped open. "That dress."

I let out a laugh at her expression. "Lucas got it for me."

She nods, a smirk on her lips. "So I was right. It was from your boyfriend."

I slip the dress off, putting it back into the box, along with the letter that I'm keeping close to me, where I can re-read it often. "He's not my boyfriend, Gabi."

Gabi snorts while I pick up a sweatshirt and pull it over my head. "Come on, Madi. The guy bought you a dress. He's taking you out on a date to the biggest event of the year."

"It's a charity gala," I say with an eye roll. Highly doubt it's the biggest event of the month, let alone the year. "And it's fake, Gabi. It's just something Ana set up."

She snorts, shaking her head. "It doesn't seem so fake anymore."

*That's what I thought, too.* "Yeah, well, it is." I drop down onto my bed with a sigh.

Her brows tug together, and she follows, sitting beside me. "What's going on?" she asks.

I squeeze my eyes closed, shaking my head. "Nothing. I just... I don't want to get my hopes up when I know it's not real."

She watches me for a while, not saying anything. It's weird. I don't like it.

"Say something," I tell her. "I don't like it when you're silent."

She laughs. "I was waiting in case you wanted to tell me something else."

"Like what?"

She smiles. "Like the fact that you have feelings for him."

"You're crazy," I say, but my heart beats at her words.

"I'm right," she corrects. "I can see it when you look at him. I haven't seen you this happy in a while." She smiles. "It's nice."

"You're getting emotional." I narrow my eyes. "Stop that. It's scaring me."

"I'm serious," she says with a laugh. "You were a mess freshman year."

"Thanks," I say dryly. "Remind me again why you're my best friend."

She shrugs. "Because I'm the best. Clearly. And I can tell when you're deflecting. Stop avoiding the subject."

Damn it. She really knows how to read me better than anyone. "I'm not avoiding it," I lie. "I just know better than to get involved with someone again, okay?"

The mood sobers, and Gabi's face drops. "Jesus." She shakes her head. "Your ex really fucked you up, didn't he?"

I close my eyes, letting out a sigh. "I don't want to talk about this, Gabi."

"It's not good to avoid it either."

I shake my head. "It's not an easy thing to talk about."

"About how that asshole treated you? Yeah, it's not. That doesn't mean I want to see you close yourself off to every guy that crosses your path. You've been so focused on class and trying to get an audition that you haven't stopped to think about anything else."

I've thought about it. I can't *stop* thinking about it. But the problem is, I can't let it happen. It can live in my mind where everything is safe and no one can hurt me ever again. "I don't need a boyfriend."

"No," she agrees. "You don't. But that doesn't mean you don't want one. I see how you look at Lucas, Madi. And the interview?" She shakes her head. "Come on. You like him."

I narrow my eyes at her. "I'm not dying my hair if that's what this is about."

She chuckles. "It's not. Although you'd look amazing in red."

"I know," I agree, with a smirk. "But it's not happening."

"I wouldn't be so sure about that," she says, glancing down at the pink box on my bed. "When he sees you in that dress on your date, I doubt he's going to be able to keep his hands off you."

"Not a date," I repeat. "It's—"

"Yeah, yeah, I know. It's fake," she says, "But the fact remains, he won't be able to stay away from you."

I swallow down, thinking about Lucas' reaction to me in this dress. What will I do if Gabi is right? I haven't been with anyone in over four years, and I thought I'd never want to again. But now…

Gabi lifts herself off my bed, heading toward the door, but before she walks out, she turns around with a smirk. "Just make sure you use protection."

## 23

Couples share a bed,

Princesa

*Lucas*

"What do you mean there's only one bed?"

"I'm sorry, Miss," the lady at the counter says, checking over her screen. "The booking clearly states it's one double room."

Madi's mouth is dropped open as she glances at me. Ana booked the room, so I didn't know that we'd have to be sharing a room, let alone a bed, but I can't say I'm distraught about it, either. "What are we going to do?" she asks me.

I shoot her a smirk. "Couples share a bed, *princesa*."

Those gorgeous brown eyes narrow at me, and I chuckle to myself. "Really?" she asks. "That's all you have to say?" She lets out a breath and turns to the lady. "I'll just book a room for myself, then."

"I'm sorry, Miss. The rooms are fully booked for tonight. With the gala happening, it books out weeks in advance."

She squeezes her eyes closed, shaking her head. "So, there's nothing we can do?"

The lady shakes her head.

Madeline turns to look at me and her eyebrows are tugged together, clearly bothered by this. "Do you want us to go to a different hotel?" I ask her, not wanting her to feel uncomfortable. She won't even let me touch her, for fucks sake, there's no way she'd want to share a bed with me. "I'm sure there's some rooms available."

"You're out of luck," the lady says again. "The Celestial Manor isn't the only hotel that's full for the gala. All surrounding hotels are fully booked."

I glance toward Madeline. "What do you want to do?" I ask her. If she wants to go look for a hotel with two available rooms, then I'll do that, even if it takes us all night.

She lets out a sigh. "It's late and I'm exhausted. Let's just stay here."

I'm good with that, too.

"Okay, then." I turn to the lady. "Guess that's decided."

"Great." She smiles, placing down two cards on the desk. "These are your key cards. Your room is on the fifteenth floor, room 202. If there's anything we can help you with, just ask."

"Thank you." I pick up the room keys and head into the elevator, but Madi freezes at the door when she sees me inside. "What's wrong?" I ask her.

She shakes her head and turns around. "I'll meet you up there. I'll just take the stairs."

Shit. The elevator. With the way she reacted last time, we got stuck in one, it doesn't surprise me that she's wary about going inside another one again.

I leave the elevator and head toward her. She turns her head behind her shoulders and furrows her brows. "What are you doing?" she asks, turning around to face me.

"Taking the stairs."

She lets out a harsh sigh. "Lucas, I'm fine. You can use the elevator."

"I'm good here."

She narrows her eyes. "We're on the fifteenth floor." Her hands are placed on her hips, and because she's so damn stubborn, she isn't moving.

I shrug. "I need the workout."

She laughs, her eyes dipping down to my legs. She sucks in a breath and shakes her head. "You do not."

I blink, my body warming from her eyes on me. "Did you just… check me out?"

"What?" Her eyes widen and she scoffs, snapping her head away from me. "I definitely did not." I press my lips together, loving the thought of her getting all flustered. She walks up the stairs, and my eyes instinctively drop to her ass.

*Come on.* This is torture. I mean, fuck. How am I supposed to survive fifteen flights of stairs while her hips sway with every step she takes? I stifle a groan as I watch her take step after step in front of me.

I rip my gaze away from her and head up, nudging my shoulder against hers when I'm right beside her. "I think you did."

She laughs again, but it's strained, and I know she's lying. "You're crazy."

*Yeah, crazy about you.*

Twenty minutes later, we're finally in front of our room.

"Fuck." I let out an exhale, breathing hard. "Those stairs kicked my ass." I work out a lot. As a model, I have to keep my body looking good, which means I work hard in the gym, but those stairs just wrecked me way more than an hour training session ever did.

Madeline leans against the wall, dropping her head back. "Is this what dying feels like?"

I laugh, my chest hurting when I do. "Not quite."

I pull out the keycard and open our room. When we walk inside, we both freeze and stare at the big white double bed in the middle of the room. It's a topic we haven't quite discussed yet.

"I can sleep on the floor?" I offer.

She shakes her head, but my eyes drop to her slender throat, moving as she swallows harshly. "No, don't be ridiculous. The bed is big enough for the both of us."

I smirk. "Good, 'cause I didn't want to sleep on the floor."

She scoffs. "What a gentleman."

I chuckle, but when I look at her, it settles. "I was only kidding, Madeline. If you really didn't want me on that bed with you, I'd gladly sleep on the floor."

She stares at me for a while, but then she blinks. "No, it's fine." She walks further into the bedroom and places her bag on the bed. "You can get dressed. I need a shower," Madeline says, heading toward the bathroom. "I smell like plane."

*She does not.* She smells fucking incredible. Like warm vanilla and caramel cookies. She's wearing that damn perfume again. The one that makes her smell good enough to eat.

I hear the shower turn on, and I busy myself with making sure to put all of my shit out of the way so that Madeline doesn't freak out over my mess. But when she walks out of the bathroom, my mouth drops, and I stop in my tracks.

A billow of steam trails behind her from the hot shower as she walks out looking like an angel from above. Her dark brown skin coated in little droplets of water, covered in a white, fluffy robe and her hair wrapped in a bun on the top of her head.

Holy fuck.

I can't look away. I don't want to. I don't think I understood the implications of sharing a bed with her tonight. I knew she'd be sleeping next to me, but I only just realized she'd be sleeping next to me, *looking like that*. Her soft curves just a few inches away, her beautiful face without a stitch of makeup on it, staring up at me.

I'm fucked.

*So fucked.*

I clear my throat and turn around, already missing being able to see her. "I can leave if you want to get changed."

"No need," I hear her say. "I just forgot my pajamas. I'll get changed in the bathroom."

The door closes once she's inside and I blow out a heavy breath. *Get it together.* I shake my head, and I don't waste any time. I peel off my clothes, tossing them aside into a neatly folded pile, and get changed.

When the bathroom door opens and Madeline walks out again, she's no longer wearing the white robe, replaced by a set of dainty pajamas that leave very little to the imagination. Pink, with tiny red hearts all over it. The top barely covers her, teasingly grazing her stomach and those shorts... I can't help but inwardly groan. They leave her long, slender legs on full display. They look so soft and silky, and... fuck. I can't seem to look away from her.

When I finally drag my eyes away from her legs, I meet her gaze to see she's blinking at me, looking somewhat taken aback. "Is that what you're going to wear?" she asks me.

I glance down at my naked chest and boxer shorts, and I can't help but smirk when I meet her gaze again. "I usually sleep naked."

Her eyes widen even further, and she quickly turns around, clearly flustered. "That's, uh, those are fine then," she says.

A chuckle escapes my lips. "Yeah," I tease. "I thought you might say that."

After she wraps her hair and we brush our teeth, we both climb into bed, tugging the covers up. I steal a glance toward my side and notice Madeline as far away as she can get, on the very edge of the mattress. "You're going to fall off." I chuckle, a hint of concern in my voice.

She shakes her head, a faint smile on her lips. "I'm good here."

I let out a sigh. "Madeline. Do you want me to sleep on the floor?" I ask her again, my tone earnest. I don't want her to feel uncomfortable with having me here. It kills me that she is.

"What? No. Of course not."

I narrow my eyes playfully. "Then why are you so far away from me?"

I watch her throat move when she swallows. "Fine," she concedes, shuffling a few inches closer to me. It's still way too far for my liking, but I know how much she doesn't like touching. I'm good with that. At least she's still next to me.

A smile spreads across my face, and I roll onto my side to look at her. It seems like I can't stop looking at her whenever she's around. My eyes take their fill, looking at her soft brown eyes, the slope of her nose, those plump lips. Fuck, every inch of her is perfection.

Her brows knit together, and she gives me an inquisitive look. "You're staring."

*Can't help it.* I smirk. "You're beautiful."

A dark shade of crimson coats her warm brown skin, and she quickly turns away to face the ceiling. It's the first time I've been so forward, but I'm done beating around the bush. Acting like I hate her and this situation we're both in. I don't anymore.

She's all I want, and I'm going to make damn sure that she knows that.

She remains silent for a moment, still gazing at the ceiling. "It's late," she finally says, her voice soft and vulnerable, before she twists her body to face away from me. "I should probably go to sleep."

She doesn't want to talk about it, that's fine by me. I'm a patient man. I can wait. For her, I can wait. I sigh softly, reaching out to switch off the lamp, but as soon as the room goes dark, she reacts with a gasp.

"No," I hear her cry out, her voice trembling.

I quickly flip the lights back on. "What's wrong?" I ask her, my voice filled with worry.

Madeline sits on the bed, curled up, shaking her head. "Don't turn off the lights. Please," she begs. Madeline has never begged me for anything, never asked for anything. My brows knit together as worry starts to take over.

"Okay," I reassure her. "I won't turn them off."

She lies back down, her gaze meeting mine. Tears well up in her eyes, a single droplet tracing a path down her cheek. My heart aches at the sight. I've only seen Madeline cry once before – in the elevator when it went dark. I didn't even know her, and even then, her tears were painful to watch. But now, it's a thousand times worse.

"What happened to you, Madeline?" I ask softly, my heart pounding against my chest.

She shakes her head again, more tears spilling down her face. "Nothing," she whispers.

"Bullshit." I inch closer to her, my hands hovering in the air for a moment, aching to comfort her, to feel her soft skin beneath my fingertips. But then I remember that she doesn't want me to touch her, so I clutch the comforter instead. "Tell me what happened."

She doesn't respond as she turns away from me again, facing the other direction. I'm left staring at the back of her head as I hear her shaky exhale. I close my eyes, feeling utterly helpless, wishing she'd let me in.

I wake up with a scream.

I bolt upright in my bed, my heart pounding in my chest when I hear Madeline thrashing against the tangled sheets, her body contorted in terror.

"What the hell?" I mutter, panicking as I fumble against the dimly lit room.

I glance toward Madeline, seeing her face twisted in anguish, her moans of terror alerting me. "Let me out," she shouts. Her cries intensify, growing more desperate with each passing second.

"Madeline?" I say, my voice quaking when I hear her crying. "Madeline, wake up. It's me, Lucas."

"Please," she cries again, her voice cracking with raw emotion. My heart aches as I watch her suffer, and I can't take it any longer. I reach for her, my hands trembling as I wrap my arm around her waist and pull her toward me.

I hold her tightly, my arms wrapped around her trembling form. Her eyes remain shut, but I can still see the torment painted across her face.

"Madeline," I say again, more urgently this time. My thumb brushes against her cheek, and I cradle the back of her neck. "Madeline, it's me. Open your eyes."

I feel the tension in her body slowly dissipating as I continue to hold her, my thumb stroking her cheek in an attempt to soothe her. "Madeline, please," I murmur softly, pressing my lips against her forehead. "You're safe. You're with me. It was just a bad dream. Open your eyes, baby. *Please*."

Her cries begin to wane as her eyes flutter. She blinks at me, confusion and fear lingering in her gaze. It takes a moment for her to fully take in her surroundings. "Lucas?" she whispers, her voice shaky and fragile.

I nod, relief washing over me like a tidal wave. "Yeah, Mads, it's me," I tell her. "You're safe now. It was just a nightmare."

Madeline's breathing steadies, and she clings to me, wrapping her arms tightly around my waist. My heart races, thudding loudly against my chest, and a warmth spreads through me.

She's so soft and warm. I can't help but revel in the way her body fits perfectly against mine like we're two missing puzzle pieces finally finding each other. Her eyes fall closed as she settles back into sleep, not daring to let go of me, and I let out a content sigh, resting my chin on her head as I fall into one of the best night's sleep I've ever had.

# 24

Those were your rules

## *Madeline*

As my eyelids flutter open, I let out a groan, adjusting to the soft morning light that filters through the curtains. My hand moves almost instinctively and brushes against something warm and soft. I look up, my brows tugged together, and there, less than two inches away from me, is Lucas. I'm sleeping right next to him, or to be more precise, I'm cuddled up against him.

My leg is draped over his, and my hand rests lightly against his chest, where I can feel the steady rhythm of his heart pulsating beneath my touch. I swallow hard, unable to take my eyes off where my hand meets his chest. We're so entangled together I don't even know where he starts and I end. How did this even happen?

And then it clicks. I was stuck in a nightmare last night, replaying that night that has haunted me for years.

*Open your eyes, baby, please.*

I can still hear the desperation in his voice and how he pulled me toward him, holding me in his arms until we fell asleep.

I haven't even attempted to move yet, and part of me knows I should. But I don't want to. His heart picks up pace beneath my palm as I tentatively explore, my fingers gliding across his bare chest, spotting a few tattoos on his arms and chest.

His breathing grows heavier, a subtle reaction to my touch, and I can't resist snuggling even closer, drawn to the comforting scent that surrounds him. He smells so good. I breathe him in again, and he moves this time. A slight twitch in his lower abdomen.

I stiffen, curled up against him. "Did you just sniff me?" Lucas's deep, husky voice shatters the moment, pulling me out of our intimate embrace. Panic courses through me as I lift my eyes to meet his, only to find a mischievous smirk playing at the corner of his lips.

Has he been awake this whole time? "What?" My eyes widen. "No."

A sultry laugh escapes his lips, and it's the hottest thing I've ever heard. It's rough and raspy and warms my body. "You little liar," he teases, closing his eyes again. His hand moves gently up and down my back, and I realize that I'm still cuddled up against him.

It's also in that moment that I feel something digging into my leg. My brows furrow for a second, but as soon as I realize, I gasp, pulling back. "Oh my god. Get up."

He groans, tightening his hold on me. "You're so soft and warm," he says. "Just a little longer."

I can't even explain what those words do to me. A warm sensation pools in the pit of my stomach, and I'm rendered speechless. I bite down on my lower lip, desperate to stifle any embarrassing sounds that might escape. "Lucas," I whisper. "You're... You... Why are you hard?"

Lucas cracks open one eye and lets out a laugh, his gaze dropping to meet mine. "It's morning," he points out.

I blink up at him, my cheeks warming. "And that's an excuse?"

He shrugs nonchalantly, a playful smile gracing his lips. *I really like his smile.* "It's not an excuse. It's just what happens in the mornings."

I can still feel it pressed up against my leg, and I instinctively shift my leg against it. He lets out a low groan that travels straight to my core, building a need inside me. "I can go take care of it right now… if you want me to," he whispers.

I look up at him, seeing his eyebrow lift in question. My teeth capture my bottom lip between them. My core throbs, and I swallow harshly, the intensity between us leaving me breathless. "Won't it just… go down?" I ask him.

He lets out a low chuckle, his tongue darting out to run over his bottom lip. His eyes remain locked onto mine. "Not if you keep looking at me like that," he says, his voice laced with seduction.

I swallow so harshly that the sound echoes through the room. My heart races, and my breaths grow heavier with the seconds ticking between us. "Now," I say, my cheeks burning up. "Please."

His laughter fills the room as we disentangle from each other. "Your wish is my command," he says as he rolls out of bed, leaving behind an emptiness without his warmth beside me.

My gaze follows his every move as he strolls around the bed, making his way toward the bathroom. Which means my eyes drop down to the tent he's pitching in his boxers, straining against the fabric. My eyes widen and a gasp escapes me, but not without him noticing before he walks inside the bathroom, closing the door behind him.

It isn't long until I hear the shower turn on, and I let myself picture it. The water cascades down his back as he steps in

208

under the hot water, butt-ass naked, and wraps a fist around his cock. His eyes closed as he groans, tipping his head back, fucking his fist until he releases all over his stomach.

I lie back on the bed, the room feeling uncomfortably warm. My body heats with an intense desire that courses through me, making me vividly aware of every inch of my skin and sending shivers down my spine. My hands skim my lower belly, running my fingertips all over my skin.

I let out a shaky breath, my fingers dipping lower and lower until they graze the top of my pajama shorts. I snap the fabric, feeling the soft silk graze against my skin with every little touch.

But then the shower cuts off, and I pull my hands up just in time for the door to open.

Lucas walks out, his body clad only in a white towel that clings low around his waist. So low that every chiseled line of his meticulously cut abs is on full display while water droplets glisten on his warm, tan skin.

"That was quick," I tell him, my cheeks warming.

He shoots me a knowing smirk. "I only had one thought in my mind." I follow his every move as he walks around the bed, reaching into his suitcase to grab some clothes. He grins, his gaze lingering on mine before disappearing back into the bathroom.

I can't help but let out an aggravated groan as I tip my head back. Why does he have to be so hot?

When he emerges from the bathroom again, my head snaps up, and my attention is immediately drawn to him. "You want breakfast?" he asks.

"Room service?" I ask him, sitting up on the bed. "That's expensive."

He grins. "I've got the money," he assures. "But no, I mean go out for breakfast. There's a place nearby I used to go to whenever I had a shoot."

"Right." I smooth the comforter over my legs, leaning back against the headboard. "You used to live here."

He nods, sitting at the edge of the bed. "For a while, yeah."

I tilt my head, noting how he seems off. "Did you like it? Living here?" I elaborate.

His lips form a tentative pout. "It's a fast-paced city, that's for sure," he begins. "And I needed to be here for work," he says with a shrug. "If I hadn't moved here, I don't think my career would be where it is now."

His eyes drop, and a sigh escapes him. "But I always missed home," he confesses. "I missed Sunday lunches with my family, I missed my best friend, and I even missed the little shithead who happens to be my sister." I chuckle at that, and he continues with a more somber expression. "She needed me," he says, his voice heavy with regret. "She was going through shit she shouldn't have to deal with, and she needed me. And I wasn't there."

"That's not your fault, Lucas. You couldn't have known."

He shakes his head, the weight of his emotions evident. "I should have been there for her." He lets out a harsh breath. "And then when James had his accident... I knew I couldn't stay away any longer."

I offer him a warm smile, my heart fluttering at the way he prioritizes his family above all else. The love he has for them is selfless and unconditional. "You're a good guy, Lucas," I tell him.

He returns my smile with a mischievous grin of his own. "Really?" he teases. "So, does that mean you don't hate me anymore?"

*No. I don't. Not even close.* I let out a laugh. "I wouldn't go that far."

He nods, chuckling along, but then the laughter fades, and his eyes lock onto mine, a hint of desire flickering in them. His eyes trace a path from my eyes down to my nose, lingering on my slightly parted lips. He continues exploring, his gaze drifting down to my body, feasting on every inch of my skin. My skin shivers with the burn of his gaze.

"Get dressed," he finally says, his voice huskier than before. His throat moves as he swallows. "I'm starving."

We didn't just go to breakfast.

Once Lucas found out I had never been to New York, he took it upon himself to become my tour guide. Dragging me from place to place, trying to show me as much as possible before the gala tonight.

And then we went to lunch, where he proceeded to tell me that New York pizza was better than Chicago pizza, which I was about to deny before I took a bite. He was right. New York pizza trumps pizza back home, any day.

And then he took me to get my nails done fresh for the gala. Lucas Silva stood by the door, holding my bag on his arm, for the two whole hours it took to get my nails done. And once I was done, he paid for it, not even letting me argue about it.

I glance down at them, a smile on my lips, reminiscing on when he asked to see them. They're dark red, matching the lipstick he requested for me to wear. He held my hand in his and brought it up, pressing his lips against the back of my hand. "Beautiful." His whisper still remains in the depths of my brain.

The gala is almost starting, and we came back to the room to get dressed a little over an hour ago. My hair was styled, so it just needed a little refreshing. And on my body is the dress he bought me, long and silky and so beautiful. I stare at my reflection in the mirror, smoothing my hands over the fabric. I wonder what he'll think when he sees me.

I can't stop thinking about this morning. Our bodies curled up against each other, his fingers tickling my back as the sound of our hearts beating filled the silence. I thought I hated people touching me, but that was before this morning. Before him. Because there was nothing about that that I hated.

"Fuck." I startle, my eyes lifting to see Lucas standing behind me in the mirror. I turn to face him and revel in how he looks at me. I love the way he looks at me like he never wants to look away. He wipes a hand over his mouth, his eyes darkening as his gaze travels down the length of my dress. The slit exposes my leg, and his eyes catch on it before they travel back to my face, zoning in on my red lips.

"Holy shit, Madeline." His voice is thick and rough, bringing warmth down my spine.

"What do you think?"

He shakes his head, taking a step closer to me. "Fuck, Mads. You look…"

I'm unable to hide the grin on my face with the way he can't take his eyes off me. "Yeah?"

He nods. "Yeah." It comes out breathy and hot as hell. "I see you honored my request," he says, smirking, his thumb slightly grazing my bottom lip.

I smile. "A deal's a deal." His eyes remain on my lips as his tongue darts out and traces his own.

I let my eyes travel down his suit, perfectly fitted to him. God, he looks so hot. Except his tie is slightly crooked. "Your tie," I say, raising my hand to fix it. I think twice, curling my hand in itself when I remember the no-touching rule. But after this morning, does it still stand? Would I stop him if he wanted to touch me? Not a chance.

His eyes darken, slightly narrowing at me. "Those were your rules, Madeline," he says. "They don't apply to me. You want to touch me? Go ahead."

My lips part as I look up at him, and I lift my hand again and tug on his bowtie, centering it. I smooth out his shirt, letting my hands linger on his chest, feeling the material of his white shirt beneath my fingertips.

His eyes lock on mine as we stare at each other, the tension between us too much to handle. I turn around and close my eyes, my heart racing right out of my chest. "Can you zip me up?" I ask.

He lets out a heavy exhale. "Yeah." It comes out thick and gravelly. He clutches the zipper in his hands and starts pulling it up. The sound of the zipper is the only noise between us, and when his knuckles graze my bare back, I glance up, seeing him stare down at me in the mirror. He pulls my hair over my shoulder to finish zipping the dress up.

We remain like that, standing still, staring at each other in the mirror, until Lucas steps back, causing me to turn around to face him. "You ready to go?" he asks.

213

I nod, my heart in my throat, as we walk out of the hotel room.

# 25

## Playing cupid

*Lucas*

"Dude, just go to her." James glares at the side of my head.

"I don't know what you're talking about?" I lie, taking a sip of my drink.

He scoffs, a little more drunk than everyone else here. When he heard it was an open bar, he took advantage of that, taking it upon himself to 'taste test' all of the drinks on the menu. He's still got five more to go.

"Don't play dumb with me," he says, nudging me on the elbow. "You've been looking at her all night."

Yeah, I have. But can you fucking blame me? She's the most beautiful girl in the room. She's the most beautiful girl in every room, for that matter. It's impossible to look away. "I knew I shouldn't have brought you."

He laughs at that, knowing I'm talking shit. James has always been my plus-one to these events. Even if Ana had hired a girl to be my date for the night, he was always with me. Even after the accident, I always managed to drag him with me to these things, and this time, it's no different.

"I'm your best friend," he says.

"I'm debating that right now."

A chuckle leaves his lips. "And I know you better than anyone."

"Again, debatable," I repeat.

He lets out a scoff. "You're not slick, Silva. You don't think I know you by now?" he asks. "You're head over heels for that girl."

I take another sip, feeling the burn of the alcohol – and his words – wrack through my body. "And?"

He smirks. I can see it from the corner of my eye. "Didn't deny it, I see."

I shrug, letting out a breath. "There's no point." He's right, he knows me better than anyone else, maybe even myself, because James saw that I was falling for Madeline way before I ever even thought about it. And now here she is, as my date, but she's not technically mine.

"So you do have feelings for her," he says, a hint of humor in his tone.

I nod, staring right at her. Her long, brown hair flowing behind her back, that tight, silky dress plastered to her body, showing off all of her curves, teasing me, tempting me in an irresistible way. And that damn red lipstick. I swear it's some sort of sorcery because even when I couldn't stand her, I was enraptured by that lipstick.

"Yeah," I admit, watching as she smiles and lets out a little laugh. God, what I wouldn't do to hear that laugh, preferably when her lips are on mine. Over two hundred people are in this room, but she's all I see. "I do."

James is quiet for a second before he smacks me on my arm. "Then what the hell are you doing here watching as some guy flirts with your girl?" he asks.

I rip my eyes off her and turn to my best friend. "Because she's not my girl," I tell him. "She's just some girl Ana hired."

He narrows his eyes at me. "You know that's not true. That is not how you feel about her."

I shrug. "She doesn't want me, James."

Twice. Twice, I almost kissed her when I knew she didn't want that. The party was a close call, but this morning, when she was cuddling me, her leg wrapped around mine? It took everything in me to pull away from her when she told me to go take care of my 'problem'. She was so pliant and soft against me, tracing my chest with those delicate fingertips, smelling me like she couldn't get enough of me. And then when I saw her in that dress? I almost dropped to my knees and begged her to give me a chance, to show her I could be what she needed, what she wanted.

"And you're fine with that?" James asks.

I shake my head, my shoulders slumping. "No," I admit. "But what can I do?"

He glares at me. "I don't know. Maybe tell her?"

If only it were that easy. "She thinks this is fake, James. She thinks this is just another business obligation."

"Then prove to her that it isn't."

"How?"

He sighs and presses his fingers to his forehead. "If I knew you brought me here to give you relationship advice, I would have charged you. I've got my own problems, you know."

"Like what?" I ask him. He hasn't told me anything.

He waves me off. "Another time," he says. "For now, you need to tell her how you feel."

"How?" I ask. "How do I make her see that I want her? Not just for tonight or while this fake relationship thing goes on, but forever."

217

He smirks. "It wasn't long ago that you were singing a different tune."

I breathe out a laugh. "Because she aggravated me." We might have started off on the wrong foot, but somehow, along the way, she's become the only thing I look forward to. These events used to be a drag, but I couldn't wait to come to this one just to be near her.

"And that's changed?" my best friend asks me.

I smirk, rubbing my thumb over my bottom lip as I look toward her again. "Nah," I tell him. "She still does. But I like it."

"I can't believe it." He shakes his head, a playful smirk on his lips. "I never thought I'd see you like this over a girl."

"Shut up." I glare at him. She might be across the room, but I don't want to take any chances.

"It's about time," he says. "I never thought I'd see the day where you stop thinking of everyone else and actually focus on yourself for once."

My brows furrow as I take in what he's telling me. "I do focus on myself."

He pulls his eyebrows together. "Lucas, you got accepted into Stanford," he says. "And you didn't go because you wanted to be here for your mom." He shakes his head, letting out a scoff. "You gave up New York and moved back here to take care of me."

"You needed me," I tell him with a frown. "Adrianna needed me. You all did."

"No, we didn't. Your mom is a grown woman, Lucas. Believe it or not, she can take care of herself. And Adrianna had me, she had your mom, she had Leila, and she had you.

You didn't need to move back because of it. And as for me, I'm fine."

"You were not fine," I say, narrowing my eyes at him. "James, you almost died." He turns his head, his jaw clenching. "I wasn't here, and you went through one of the hardest things someone could go through. Tell me how that's fine."

When he turns to look at me, his eyes are brimmed with tears, and I feel like an asshole for bringing it up when he tries to shove it out of the way, but I need him to know that I didn't move back for nothing. I moved back because I was needed.

"Look at me," he says. I turn my head to my best friend. "I'm fine," he reiterates. "I'm walking again, and I'm alive. I love you, and I appreciate everything you've done for me. You and your family." He swallows, his voice cracking with emotion. "You have been the best thing I could have asked for, but if anything had happened to me, it wouldn't have been your fault." He shoots me a smile. "And your mom... she loves you, Lucas. All she wants is for you to be happy. You don't need to give up your dream for her, for us. We don't want that."

I swallow harshly, shaking my head. "Even if I wanted to go back to school... I'm twenty-three. It's too late now."

"It's not too late," he says. "And it's not too late to start over with Madi, either."

I narrow my eyes at him. "Since when do you call her Madi?"

He grins. "Don't be jealous I'm befriending her. You're still my best friend."

I snicker, but when I look over at Madeline, she's still talking to that guy, and I hate it. Hate that I can't stake my claim because she's not mine.

"She likes some other guy," I tell him with a sigh.

219

"Who?"

I shake my head. "Some asshole from her school. And he's into her too. I can see it from a mile away."

"As much as you?" he asks.

I let out a shrug. "I don't fucking know. But I doubt it."

"Then go for it," he encourages.

I shake my head, unable to take my eyes off her. "Look at her," I tell him. "Just fucking look at her, man."

"I know."

I narrow my eyes at him. "But not too much."

He laughs, tilting his head to look at me. "You do know I'm gay, right?"

I smirk. "Yeah. Right around the time you told me you had a crush on me."

He laughs, closing his eyes and letting out a groan of discomfort. "Hey, you were the only guy I hung out with back then. Give a guy a break." He shakes his head and turns to look at Madeline. "But yeah, I know. She's beautiful."

That word doesn't even begin to describe her. "And every guy here is eating her up." Including me. She turns her head, looking around, until her eyes meet mine, and her plump, red lips turn in a smile. My chest caves in at the sight.

"There is no way in hell she isn't into you," James says. "Have you seen how she looks at you?"

*She's a good actress*, I tell myself. But today didn't feel like acting. It felt real. At least it was for me.

"Here," he says, and I look down to see him holding up a piece of gold foil, and my eyes widen.

"What the fuck?" I ask him, snatching up the condom before anyone sees.

He laughs. "With the way you're looking at each other? You're going to need it."

My eyes narrow. "Why did you have this?" I ask him.

He sips his drink, a smirk on his lips. "Because this has been a long time coming. And I'm a good wingman."

I shake my head, letting out a laugh, but when I look back at Madeline, she's no longer looking at me, and my stomach drops. I want her eyes on me again. I want those big brown eyes looking for me, at me. I want… her. I pour back the rest of my drink and place the empty glass back on the bar. "I'm going for it."

"Fuck yeah," my best friend calls out behind me as I beeline toward her, ignoring every single person who tries to come up to me and talk.

I'm so close, I can hear her laugh, and my jaw clenches when I remember it's for some other fucking guy. "Would you like to dance?" he asks her.

I don't even give her time to think. I swoop in between them and grab her hand, pulling her close to me. "Actually, this is my date," I tell whoever this guy is.

His eyes widen. "Oh shit. My bad," he says. "Nice to see you again, Lucas." He smiles at Madeline once again and then walks off.

When he's finally out of my line of sight, I turn to face the only girl in here that I want to be with right now. "Who was that?" I ask her.

Her hand is still in mine as I pull her onto the dancefloor. "He's a soccer player from Madrid. He was just telling me about how he bid on a vacation," she says, with a smirk, mischief twinkling in her eyes. "For two."

I narrow my eyes at her. "And he thinks he can steal my date?"

She smirks and it socks me in the chest. "I'm your date, huh?" she asks.

I lift an eyebrow. "Do you see me with any other girl here?"

She shakes her head, smiling even wider.

"Then you have your answer." I tug on her hand, loving the little gasp that comes out of her when our bodies are pressed together. "You want to dance?" I ask her, my eyes drifting to those dark, berry-red lips of hers.

She places her free hand on my shoulder, and I drift my hand to her lower back, absolutely relishing in how she's letting me touch her.

Necessary or not, this is, without a doubt, the happiest I've ever been.

"You know how to dance?" she asks, sounding surprised.

"I've been to quite a few of these things."

Her lips purse together. "With other girls that Ana set up?" she asks, a hint of jealousy coating her tone.

I can't keep the smile off my face. "With James," I correct her. "You're the first girl I've danced with."

Her lips curve in a smile, but she drops it and raises an eyebrow, determined to be stubborn as fuck. "Should I feel honored?"

My hand drifts lower onto the small of her back, pressing her even closer to me. How is it that we're only a breath away, and it's still not close enough? "Since I can't remember any of the other girl's names or what they even looked like when I can't seem to stop thinking about you, yes, you should."

Her eyes widen, and I wonder whether she's freaked out, or intrigued. I wish I knew what she was thinking. I hope James is right and that she's into me because I'm taking his advice. I'm going for it, and there's no holding me back anymore.

Her lips part causing my eyes to drop to them, like a moth to a flame. So supple, so juicy, the red making me feel dizzy. Fuck, I want to kiss her so bad.

"Mads," I whisper, staring into those beautiful brown eyes. My hand reaches up, brushing back her hair to clutch her face. "You look so beautiful."

"Lucas," she whispers, her eyes drifting closed at the feel of my hands on her.

It's the longest she's let me touch her, if I don't count the night we spent in each other's arms, and I fucking revel in it, exploring her face, rubbing my thumb over her cheek.

She's so damn beautiful it makes it hard to breathe.

But when she opens her eyes again, the softness I felt a minute ago dissipates as she sucks in a breath and widens her eyes. Her hand drops from mine and she takes a step back, my body growing cold from the loss of contact. What the hell?

"What's wrong?" I ask her, my heart thrashing against my chest. Did I go too far?

She shakes a head. "This was a mistake. I have to go."

My eyes stay locked on her as she suddenly spins around, rushing toward the exit. There's an urgency in her steps that makes my heart race. It's like she can't get out of here fast enough as she pushes the door open and steps out into the lobby.

I stare at the door when it closes behind her, wondering what the hell just happened.

One thing's for sure. I'm not letting her leave without an explanation. The two minutes I had her in my arms were the best of my life, and I'm not ready to let that go.

I don't think I can let go of her ever again.

Stop me, Madeline

*Madeline*

So close.

I was so close to leaning in and kissing him.

Hearing him whisper beautiful words in my ear and his hands on me was too much for me to handle. I let myself melt into him, believe him, until I realized we were at a public event set up by Ana.

I was his fake girlfriend.

We had to play a part.

That was it.

How could I have been so stupid? How did I let myself fall for him when I knew that this was all fake? None of it is real. Not the sweet words, not the warm touches, nothing.

"Madeline." I twist my head behind my shoulder, seeing Lucas behind me. "Where are you going?"

There's no way I can stay here tonight. I can't sleep in the same bed as him, an inch away, knowing I was stupid enough to fall for him when this has always just been a contractual agreement between us.

"Home." I don't know how I'm going to get there, but staying here is not an option.

"Now?" His hand clutches around my elbow, halting me, and my eyes fall closed at the feel of him. "We're in New York, Mads." *God*, there he goes with that damn nickname again. I wish he'd stop calling me that. It makes my brain all... fuzzy. "It's late. You'll never be able to catch a plane at this time," he says. "Let's just go back to our room and talk."

I shake my head, turning to face him. "There's nothing to talk about," I say, swallowing the gravel in my throat. "We just got carried away. It was a mistake."

"Mistake?" he repeats. "No, I think that was the realest thing I have ever done." My breath catches in my throat. "You know what I think?" he asks, taking a step closer until he crowds me. "I think you want me. I think you have for a while, but you've been denying it to yourself for so long that you don't want to admit it."

He stares into my eyes, and I swear it's like he looks into my soul. "You want to know how I know?" he asks me. I slowly nod, unable to say anything else. His eyes darken as he crowds me, bringing his hand to clutch my face. "Because I've been doing it too," he admits.

My heart races so fast I doubt I'm breathing. "You don't mean that."

His thumb glides over my skin. "I mean every word," he says. "Every goddamn word I'm telling you right now is more honest than I have been in a while." He leans in, his eyes locked on mine. "I want you."

My knees wobble, and I gather myself. "But... you don't like me."

He chuckles, and I feel the vibration against my skin. "Then tell me why I can't stop thinking about you," he whispers. "Tell me why you've been living in my mind since the day we fucking met."

My eyes attempt to flutter closed, and I force myself to open them. "You hated me back then."

"I hated how you came in and flipped my life upside down," he says, his eyes on mine. "I hated how fucking attracted to you I was. I hated how you didn't give me an inkling of attention when I couldn't stop staring at you." He pulls back an inch, shaking his head. "But not you," he says. "Never you."

A heavy sigh escapes him as he leans in, pressing his forehead against mine. "I've never even touched you, never even kissed you, yet you're all I crave," he whispers, his voice filled with longing. I drop my head, closing my eyes, his words repeating themselves in my head.

Gently, he lifts my chin, his eyes meeting mine, brimming with emotion. "Don't fight this," he pleads, his eyebrows furrowing. "I'm done trying to convince myself that every part of me doesn't call out for you."

I swallow roughly. "Lucas," I whisper, the overwhelming scent of spice and citrus invading my senses. "How do I know this is real?"

"Baby, it stopped being fake to me a long time ago." His hand curls over the back of my neck, and he rubs his thumb over my bottom lip. "Tell me to go," he urges, his eyes darkening, zoning in on my red lips. "If you don't want this, then tell me to go to bed and leave you alone, and I'll do it." His brows tug together as he keeps staring at me. "Stop me, Madeline," he begs. "Tell me to leave you alone and to never think of what your lips taste like."

All I can do is try to breathe as he sucks the oxygen straight out of my lungs.

227

"Stop me, Madeline."

I can't stop this. I don't want to.

"Kiss me."

That's all it takes for him to lean in and crash our lips together. The first touch of our lips together sends a jolt of electricity down my spine. Our mouths move together in perfect harmony. His lips are soft, hesitant at first, as if testing the waters. I wrap my arms around his neck and lift onto my toes while his hand cups my face and the other grips my waist, pulling me closer to him. The warmth of his body presses against mine and all I can think is *more*. *More* of this. *More* of him. Just *more*.

Then the kiss deepens, and holy shit, my legs go weak. Our kiss turns urgent as he lets out a delicious groan into my mouth, and I part my lips for him. He takes the invitation, sliding his tongue across mine.

"Fuck," he groans, pulling back to look at me, his eyes hooded, filled with lust. His hand tightens around my waist, and he drops his forehead to mine. "Tell me I can touch you," he pleads, pressing his lips against my cheek. "Please."

God. Just hearing him beg has me weak. "You already are," I tell him, my voice coming out breathy.

He pulls back. "I'm serious, Mads. That was one of your rules."

"Fuck the rules." I tug at his hair, and he groans, closing his eyes. "They don't matter anymore."

"They do to me," he says, pressing his lips against mine. "Say it," he urges. "I need to hear you say it."

The pleading in his voice brings out a soft moan from my lips, and I let myself fall. "Touch me, Lucas," I whisper. "I need you to touch me."

*Lucas*

Hearing those words spill from Madeline's mouth hits me with desire and absolute fucking joy within me. How long have I waited for this moment? To hear her admit she wants me, that she needs me.

It takes everything in me to pull away from her when the door opens, and more people start to leave, flooding the hotel lobby. My eyes flash to the empty elevator, and my brows furrow. There's no way Madeline will get on it, at least not without a distraction.

She's still staring up at me, those gorgeous red lips smudged from my kisses. I want another taste. Fuck. I grab her by her waist, and lift her up, throwing her over my shoulder. A squeal escapes her lips, but I don't give her time to think, rushing us into the elevator before the doors close.

"What—" she says before a gasp comes out of her lips. "Why are we in an elevator?"

"Because the thought of spending the next twenty minutes climbing the stairs and not being able to kiss you sounds like torture."

"Lucas." Her voice wobbles, and my heart tugs.

"Hey, it's going to be okay," I coax her, running my hands all over her back. "I promise, Madeline. Just focus on me, okay? We're almost there. Just keep listening to my voice."

Her breathing slows, and a few seconds later, the doors open, and I rush out of them, heading to our room.

When I drop Madeline to her feet, she lets out a yelp that brings a smile out of me. I can't wait to find out what other sounds she makes.

I pull the keycard out of my pocket, dying to get inside. The green light comes on, and I let out a breath, pushing open the door, and once we're inside, I'm back on her again, pinning her against the door while my lips explore every inch of this gorgeous girl that I can't stop thinking about.

I grip her waist and pull her into me, sealing my lips over hers. She opens up for me, letting our tongues move together, and the sounds that come out of her send jolts of lust straight to my cock.

"I've wanted you for so fucking long," I admit, kissing down her jaw, her neck, letting out a groan when I smell that perfume again. "That scent," I mumble against her skin. She tilts her head back, letting out a soft, breathy whimper that does nothing to ease the ache of being so fucking hard. "It's ingrained in my mind. I thought about this so many times. About you."

"You have?" she asks with a soft moan.

"Are you kidding?" I pull back to look into those eyes. Fuck, I never knew brown eyes could be so beautiful until I saw hers. "There hasn't been a day where you haven't invaded my mind." I lean in and press my lips against hers. "All of my thoughts are consumed by you."

Her eyes blaze with heat, and her hands lift to run across my chest. I'm thrown back to this morning when she thought I was asleep as she trailed her fingertips all over my skin. "God," she groans. "Who knew you were so hot?"

I chuckle, leaving soft kisses across her face until I land on her lips. "A lot of people," I hum against her skin. "You included. Do you think I didn't see all those times you were checking me out?" I ask her, my hands itching to take off this dress and see what lies beneath it. "I was looking right back at you."

My hands drop to the hem of her dress, slowly lifting the material, my palms running over her soft thighs. "Turn around, Madeline." My voice is unrecognizable, filled with lust for this girl, and she obeys, turning until she places her hands on the door. I reach for her zipper and start pulling it down, revealing her gorgeous skin that I can't wait to kiss. There won't be an inch of her body that my lips haven't been on.

I push the material off until it drops to the ground, and she's left in a matching pair of red panties. A groan builds in my throat when I see her, and she looks behind her shoulder, right at me, as she pulls her bottom lip between her teeth.

"You were wearing this the whole time?" I ask her, running my hands over the lace fabric covering her ass.

She lets out a moan as a response which makes my cock twitch. I lean down and press my lips on her shoulder. "Did you think anything was going to happen?" I ask her, pressing my hard length against her.

She lets out a harsh breath and shakes her head. "Part of me hoped so, though."

I smile, spinning her around to face me. "Me too," I admit, gripping the back of her neck and bringing her forehead to

231

mine. "It was agony watching you across the room the whole night." I shake my head against hers and pull back to look into her eyes. "Every other guy had their eyes on you in there. It took everything in me not to punch every single one."

"They're your friends," she says with a little smile that lets me know she likes when I get jealous.

I kiss her again. I can't seem to stop. "Not when they have their eyes on what's mine."

The corner of her lips tips up into a smirk. "I'm yours now?" she asks.

"I want you to be," I tell her, kissing her neck, pressing my lips all over her skin, all the way down, until I meet the top of her breasts, covered by that tempting red lace. "I sure as fuck belong to no one else but you."

She closes her eyes, a gorgeous smile on her face. "I like the sound of that," she says. A sweet moan escapes her when I kiss over the lace, pulling her hard nipple into my mouth. "I don't want to wait any longer."

"You're too impatient." I grip her waist and push her toward the bed. "I've wanted this for way too long. There's no way I'm rushing." I press my lips against hers and reluctantly pull back. "Lie back, *princesa*."

She visibly shivers, dropping down onto the bed.

I grin, staring down at her. Fuck. She is the most beautiful girl I have ever seen. "You like that nickname now, huh?" I ask her.

"No." It comes out all breathy, which has me laughing as I lean down.

I nip at her bottom lip and hum. I can't get enough of this woman. "Liar," I whisper. "You love it. I can tell from the way your heart's beating so fast right now, and those big brown eyes?" I make a point to stare at them. "They give you away every time." I grin, brushing my thumb over her cheek. "You love when I call you my princess, don't you?"

Her eyes narrow. "I hate you," she grunts out.

Some people would take that as an offense, but I know that what she really means is that I'm right.

I want to take my time. I appreciate having her here, wanting me to touch her, to kiss her, but I can't wait any longer. I don't waste any time leaning down to kiss her breasts, tugging and sucking on them.

She tips her head back, soft whimpers leaving her pretty little lips. Fuck, her noises make me so fucking hard.

"Still hate me?" I murmur, flicking my tongue over her hard nipples covered by the lace fabric.

She releases a heavy breath, arching into me. "Yes."

"Mmm." I tease her with the tip of my tongue, wanting to wrap my mouth around her. "It doesn't look like you hate me."

"I'm a good actress."

I lift my head. "Yeah, you are," I tell her, lifting her chin with my hand. "But I know you. I know that hate is the furthest thing you feel for me. I know how bad you want me right now." She whimpers, and I take pity on her, pulling her bra off until her breasts spill free.

"Fuck, Madeline." I lean down and wrap my mouth around the hard bud, letting out a groan when I suck her into my mouth. I'm ninety percent sure this isn't a dream, but if it is, please don't let me wake up from it. "God, your skin is so soft," I murmur, my hands running over her stomach. "How are you so soft?"

"Lotion."

233

I look up at her, and her lips are curved in a smirk. I tug at her nipple with my teeth, and she gasps, tipping her head back. "I didn't actually need an answer."

"It seemed – like – you were genuinely curious," she says, her words coming out between breaths when I twirl my tongue around her nipple. "Mmm," she moans. "I really like that."

"Yeah?" I let my lips fall down her body, kissing all over her stomach. "I bet you'll like this even more," I tell her, kissing all the way down until I reach her panties. I start to pull them off her, but when she sits up on the bed, I stop and look up at her.

"You don't need to do that," she says, looking embarrassed all of a sudden.

My brows tug together as I rest my hands on her thighs. "You don't like it?"

She looks to the side and lets out a sigh. "It doesn't work for me," she says.

My jaw clenches, my body going red hot at the thought of any guy who came before me, who saw her like this, and who let her believe she couldn't come from oral. "Who the hell said that?"

She shakes her head, looking back at me. "It doesn't matter," she says. "It just takes too long, and I know most guys don't like that."

Fucking pathetic. Whoever made her believe she wasn't worth the time it took to bring her pleasure was a pathetic boy. I lean down and press my lips against her open thighs. "I've been wanting to do this to you for a long time," I tell her, teasing her with just the press of my lips against her soft inner thigh. "The thought of eating your pussy makes me so fucking hard it aches. But if you really don't want me to, just say the word." I

234

lift my head to make sure she hears me. "I'll listen to you. Every time."

Her lips part, and I can tell she loves the idea of me between her thighs, but she doesn't say anything, so I press my lips against her thighs again. "Do you want me to stop?" I ask her.

She lets out another desperate whimper and shakes her head, pulling her bottom lip between her teeth.

I smile, fucking ravenous for a taste of her. "Good girl. Just hold on, baby. Pull my hair if you need to, scream down this whole hotel, but don't you dare tell me it takes too long." I pull down her panties and fling them across the room, staring at her bare pussy in front of me. My cock twitches, and I feel a spurt of pre cum in my boxers. Fuck, I'm so close to coming without her ever even touching me. "I'll stay here all night between your legs if need be." I grip her thighs and spread her wider. "I just want to make you feel good."

She lets out a breath and falls back onto the bed, her gorgeous body twitching, moaning when the first lash of my tongue hits her. I lick up the sides, teasing her, before I flick her clit with the tip of my tongue, savoring every inch of her pussy.

It isn't long until her hand reaches out and grips onto my hair. A moan rips from my throat. "That's it. Grab on while I eat this pretty little pussy."

She lets out another sweet little cry and lifts her hips. "God, that feels so good."

Takes her too long, my ass. I haven't even had my fill of her, and she's already right there. Her pussy spills with hot liquid from her arousal, coating my tongue.

I grip her thighs, spreading her out even wider, and dive in, French kissing her pussy like a man starved. "Você me enlouquece," I murmur against her. *You drive me crazy.* "Fuck, you taste so good." I lap up at her entrance, tasting how wet she's gotten. "I'd gladly survive on the taste of your pussy alone."

A moan escapes her, turning into a sharp gasp when I plunge my tongue in her tight entrance. Can't fucking wait to feel her tighten around my cock. She bumps her hips over my tongue, and I can tell she's right on the edge. "Fuck yes. Grind on my face, Madeline. Let me taste your cum."

My words throw her straight over the edge, and more hot liquid pours out of her, onto my tongue. The taste of her makes me into an animal, groaning as I lap her up. She throws her head back and lets out an anguished moan, her hand tightening on my hair as she comes all over my tongue.

She twitches and moans so fucking beautifully until her orgasm starts to ease away, and her breathing returns to normal. I pull back, in complete awe of her, unable to stop the grin forming on my face, as I wipe my mouth with the back of my hand.

"Holy fuck," I murmur, lifting off my knees to cover her body with mine. Her eyes open a fraction, and all I can see in them is pure lust. And exhaustion from the orgasm. "That was so fucking hot." I grab her face and cover my lips with hers, letting her taste how sweet her pussy is. Her hand curls around the back of my neck, and she lifts her hips, grinding on my hard cock.

I groan at the feel of her and pull back. Her eyes drift down at the bulge in my pants, and she grinds her bare pussy on me again. "I need you inside me."

I curse, closing my eyes. Her words make another bead of precum spill from the tip of my dick. "Jesus, Mads." I need her, too, so fucking badly. I lift myself up and grip her jaw, rubbing my thumb over her bottom lip. "You want it? Take off my belt."

She shivers before her scarlet-painted fingertips grasp my belt, working it off. Her eyes lift, looking up at me as she unbuttons my pants and pulls them down my legs and off. I see her throat bob with a swallow as her hands grip at my boxers, looking up at me.

"Take it off, *princesa*. Show me how much you want me."

Her lips part with a shaky exhale, and she pulls my boxers down, my dick bobbing free. Her eyes widen when she sees it, and she pulls her bottom lip between her teeth, her eyes locked on my erection.

I'm not prepared for when her soft hand wraps around my cock, and she slowly strokes me. I tilt my head back on a moan at the feel of her finally touching me. "God, please don't stop touching me."

When I feel a soft, wet tongue lapping at the tip, I almost come on the spot, my eyes snapping open. Her pretty eyes widen when she flicks my dick with the tip of her tongue, doing it again and again like I'm a fucking ice cream cone.

"Fuck," I groan, brushing her hair back so I can see her face. "Wrap those pretty red lips around my cock."

She obeys my command, taking the first inch into her mouth. I let out a deep groan, the visual of it too much to bear. Those plump red lips I love so much wrap around me, and she gives it a tentative suck, making my balls tighten.

"That's it," I coax her, loving how she feeds more of me into her soft, wet mouth. "You look so fucking pretty taking my cock in your mouth."

She closes her eyes, shivering from the praise. I love how she's getting lost in the moment, but I need her to look at me.

"Open your eyes," I urge, brushing my thumb over her cheek. "Look at me while you suck my cock, Madeline." She takes me deeper, and I let out a grunt. "Yes," I breathe out. "Take me to the back of your throat."

She shuffles closer, moving me in and out of her mouth, taking me an inch closer every time until I'm so deep she gags, tears brimming her eyes. Jolts of pleasure curl up my spine, and I have the urge to close my eyes and just feel, but I can't. I need to look at her. I need to have my eyes on her to know that it's her – Madeline – that has her mouth on my dick.

"Move your hand, baby. Up and down, just like that." She strokes, sucks, and moans around my cock, the vibrations making my balls tingle with the knowing signs of a release.

"Fuck yes. That's so good." I groan when she hums again and squeeze my eyes. Shit. Shit. Shit. I'm way too close. When my eyes open again, the sight of her almost takes me out, so I pull out of her warm, wet mouth.

She licks her lips, tasting me on them. "Was that good?" she asks.

Good? I shake my head, unable to form the words, and lean down to kiss her hard and bruising instead. "That was perfect. But as much as I love your hot mouth," I tug on her bottom lip with my teeth. "I need to be inside you." Reaching for my pants, I dig into the pocket and grab the condom James gave me earlier, dying to feel her.

She eyes me, raising an eyebrow at the condom in my hand. "Did you expect this to happen?" she asks.

I let out a laugh, ripping it open. "Honestly?" I shrug. "Didn't think it would in a million years," I admit. "But James seemed to believe otherwise." I let out a scoff. "Thank fuck for him."

With a seductive playfulness, she bites her lip and gazes at me with a mischievous spark in her eyes. "I would have let you fuck me raw."

She wipes the air clean out of my lungs. "Jesus," I grunt. "You're not serious."

She nods, her hands running over her body until her thumb swipes over her nipple. "I haven't been with anyone in a really long time," she says. "I want you. I want to feel you. Every hard inch of you." *Holy shit.* I shake my head, unable to say anything. She tilts her head. "You don't want to?" she asks.

*Of course, I want to.* "Don't ask me questions right now," I plead. "I can't think straight when you look like that." A groan escapes my lips when I wrap a hand around my cock, and give it a stroke. "What about birth control?" I ask her.

"I've been on the pill for as long as I can remember," she says, her seductive smile making me rock hard.

Fuck.

"But you can pull out," she says. "Just in case."

I shake my head. I don't think I can. Not when she's everything I've ever wanted, and I'm about to be inside of her for the first time. But fuck, I want to feel her bare pussy around my cock so bad, more than anything I've ever wanted. "You want that?" I ask her again.

She nods. "I want it. I don't want anything between us."

I shake my head, stretching over her body, and lean down to press my lips against hers. "Neither do I." I swipe my tongue over her lips, and she opens up for me, wrapping her arms around my neck.

She feels so perfect against me. This is what has been missing from my life. Her. Us. I pull back and line up against her entrance. She's soaked, dripping down her thighs from the orgasm I gave her, and I can't wait to feel her.

When I start to push inside her, she tenses, strangling my cock inside her. "Oh fuck," I moan at the feel of her tight walls. She lets out a pained whimper when I try to push in again. "I need you to relax, Mads." I press my forehead against hers. "I'm not even halfway in yet."

She moans, shivering against me, and lets out a breath, melting into my arms. She relaxes enough for me to push inside, thrusting slowly until she can take all of me. "Just breathe, *princesa*," I whisper against her lips. "Let me in, baby. You feel so good."

She tilts her head back and whimpers, bumping her hips to meet me. She wants me just as bad, but she needs to relax. I pull out and thrust back in slowly. "It's too much. You're too big," she whimpers.

Jesus. I squeeze my eyes closed, pleading with myself to have some self-control. "Breathe," I tell her. "Let me take care of you."

She lets out another shaky exhale, and I push inside the last few inches, bringing out a sweet little cry from her. Fuck. Being inside her all the way is too much for me to handle. "I'm so close," she gasps, blinding my eyes with pleasure. I swear I could come from just her voice alone. "Please, Lucas. I'm almost there. I need you." She attempts to move her hips, fucking herself on my cock with a needy moan.

I can't hold back any longer. I pull out of her and thrust back into her warm heat, her tight, wet pussy gripping me inside of her. "Fuck, Madeline," I grunt, the sounds in this room absolutely filthy. "You're taking every inch so fucking well." I push back into her, in and out, until she's a whimpering mess, throwing her head back in pleasure.

"You like how I fuck you?" I ask, nipping at her bottom lip. "Trying to push me away, making me think you hated me when all you needed was a little attention, huh, *princesa*?" I take hold of her hands and pin them up against the mattress above her head. She lets out another urgent cry. "Use your words. Tell me how much you love my cock in your tight pussy."

"Oh god," she moans, closing her eyes. "Yes," she says, breathless from my cock tunneling into her.

"Yes, what?" I urge, interlacing our fingers together. "Words, Madeline. Or did I fuck every thought out of your pretty little head?"

She presses her lips together, silencing a moan, and I narrow my eyes at her. "Let me hear you." Her eyes snap open, and her mouth forms a cute little O as I fuck into her. "I don't want you to be quiet. I want to hear every filthy moan from your lips." I lean down and kiss her. "Scream if you have to. Let everyone in this hotel know who's fucking you."

"Lucas!" she screams when I thrust harder. "Fuck yes. Right there."

Beads of sweat form on my forehead. Fuck, I'm close. And so is Madeline by the moans spilling out of her. "Squeeze yourself around me," I tell her, wanting to feel her come on my cock before I explode. She tightens her pussy over my cock, gripping me inside her. The groan I let out is urgent, needy for her. "Fuck, that's it."

"Lucas," she moans, my cock twitching inside her at the sound of my name on her lips. "I'm gonna—"

"Come, Madeline." I let go of her hands and grip her hips, thrusting deeper into her. "Let go. Just let go."

241

She squeezes her eyes closed, and her body shakes as her orgasm tumbles out of her, flooding my cock with her cum. I groan into the crook of her neck, feeling her strangle my dick inside her. Jesus, I'm going to come. I breathe hard, begging myself to have some control. *Just a little longer. I need this feeling a little longer.*

A grunt escapes me at the sight of Madeline drowning in pleasure. "Fuck, Mads, you look so good when you lose control." I thrust a few more times, squeezing my eyes closed, but when her pussy flutters around me again, I can't hold it any longer. "Shit." I pull out of her warmth and fist my cock over her stomach, painting her with my cum.

Her eyes widen at the mess I left on her skin before she swipes a finger across her stomach and sucks me off her finger.

She smirks when she swallows me down and I can't help but grin as I look down at her. "You're going to be the death of me."

# 28

What if this is a dream?

## *Madeline*

I wake up to lips pressed against my cheek, soft kisses painting a trail across my closed eyelids, my nose, my lips, and down to my neck.

My breathing quickens, but I don't dare to open my eyes. Instead, I squeeze them tighter, clinging to this sensation for as long as I can.

It becomes impossible to pretend I'm still asleep when I hear Lucas chuckle against my cheek. "I can tell you're awake," he murmurs, his raspy voice sending a shiver down my spine.

My eyes remain closed, even when he presses his lips against mine over and over again. "I don't want to wake up," I mumble.

"Why not?" he whispers against my skin.

"What if this is a dream?" My eyebrows tug together. Last night was perfect. I had been denying my feelings for Lucas for so long that there's a possibility I made the whole thing up, and I'm going to wake up this morning back in my apartment without Lucas there.

"It's real," he says, the feel of his thumb brushing against my cheek making my heart flutter. "I promise."

I want it to be so bad, but… "I don't know if I believe that."

He laughs again, the sound making my heart beat even faster. Wish I was awake to see it, but I don't want to risk leaving this dream. "Mads, open your eyes."

I let out a sigh and crack an eye open. Lucas is lying beside me with a grin on his face. He's still here. He didn't disappear. I take the plunge and open both of my eyes. "It's real, *princesa*," he whispers, kissing me. "There's nothing fake about this. Not anymore."

The nickname that once felt like an insult when we first met now feels like the sweetest compliment I could ever get.

I turn on my side to face him. He smiles, swiping a thumb against my cheek. His arm wraps around my waist and pulls me until I'm tucked up against his chest. We're still both naked from last night, and I can feel his erection against my leg. Nothing about this is sexual, though. It's just our bodies unable to part, needing to be close.

Twice, I've woken up in the same bed as Lucas, and while I prefer to have my own space, to be able to stretch out and have the bed all to myself, waking up to him is everything I never knew I wanted.

"I've never slept with anyone before," I murmur.

His brows tug together. "You mean…"

"No." I shake my head, letting out a laugh. *I wish.* But unfortunately, Daniel took that from me. "I mean actual sleep," I correct. "Like in the same bed. I thought I'd be too much of a control freak for that."

"You are," he says.

I shake my head. "I'm serious."

He chuckles. "So am I," he says, lifting an eyebrow. "You hogged the covers all night long. Wouldn't stop kicking your feet."

My cheeks heat at the thought of him sleeping peacefully and being woken up by the need to not be restrained. What is it with hotels and tucking the covers as tight as they can, anyway? "I'm sorry," I say, burying my head in his chest, his smell making me feel a little dizzy.

He laughs, cradling my face. "Don't be. It was the cutest shit I've ever seen," he says, leaning down to kiss me. "And so fucking worth it."

"You enjoyed last night?" I ask him. It was everything to me, but I've only ever been with one guy, and until Lucas, I never bothered to change that number. I didn't want another guy, and I didn't want to get attached to someone just to be hurt by them all over again.

He glares at me. "Thought that was obvious."

"Just wanted to hear you say it," I admit, smiling up at him.

He grins, pressing his lips against mine. "I loved last night. I loved every bit. And I can't wait for it to happen again." Our mouths move together, our tongues sliding against each other. A moan grumbles at the back of my throat, and he pulls back, lust brimming in his eyes. "I get what you mean," he says, swiping a thumb over my bottom lip. "This does feel like a dream." He shakes his head. "I never thought this would happen. I was so hellbent on denying my feelings for you, but I wanted you so bad."

I tug my bottom lip between my teeth, still feeling the burn of his kiss. "And now?" I ask him, my heart beating. "Do you still want me?"

His eyes darken as he pins me beneath him. "Yeah," he says, flicking his tongue over my lips. "I still very much want you."

My breathing gets heavier when I feel his hard cock pressed against my belly. "So I'm not out of your system?" I ask him.

His brows furrow in question. "I thought once we broke the tension between us, that would be it," I admit. "You'd have enough of me, and you'd be running out the door."

"No fucking way," he says with a grunt. "You're stuck with me. I'm afraid you made a mistake. I'm addicted now." He leans down and kisses me. "To your lips, to the taste of your pussy. To you. There's no getting rid of me."

I let out a shaky exhale when he trails down to my breasts, swiping the tip of his tongue over my nipples. I never knew they were so sensitive, but I swear, a few more licks and I'm going to come. "That's fine by me," I tell him, wrapping my arms around his neck. "I don't want you to go anywhere."

He pulls off me with a pop and smirks down at me. "Who are you, and what have you done with Madeline Davis?" His brows tug together. "She would never say such sweet words to me. She would tell me how much I annoy her, or call me an asshole, or say she hates—"

I shut him up with a kiss, getting lost in the taste of his lips. "I don't hate you," I tell him. "Far from it."

He lets out a sigh, kissing me back. "Me too," he whispers against my lips. "So far from it." His lips meet mine with need, and I open up for him, wrapping my legs around his waist. His cock slides through my pussy that's already so wet for him and I moan into his mouth.

"Meet my family."

My eyes snap open, and I furrow my brows at him. "Your cock is two seconds away from being inside me, and you're asking me to meet your family?"

He laughs. "I'm serious," he says. "They're obsessed with you, and they want to meet you." His lips find mine. "I want them to know you."

My hands wrap around his hair, my fingers getting intertwined in his curls. "But you said they don't care about who you date."

His cheeks turn a deep shade of pink, and his eyes narrow. "I lied," he says. "They knew it was fake."

My eyes widen. "They did?" Well, shit. At least I don't feel guilty about all of my friends knowing.

He nods. "Yeah." He kisses me. "You're not mad I broke the NDA?"

I shake my head. "No, I'm not mad. Especially since the girls all know."

His eyes narrow. "Which means their boyfriends also know."

I nod, a smirk on my lips. "Probably, yeah."

He laughs and shakes his head. "So at the party…"

I nod. "They knew," I admit. "They were convinced I had feelings for you."

He grins. "And they were right."

I tug his hair, which he lets out a grunt at. "Not exactly. You still annoyed the living shit out of me."

He laughs and leans down to press his lips to my neck. "Don't lie. Everyone could tell how obsessed with me you were."

My eyes close at the feel of his lips on me. "I take it back. I hate you," I breathe out.

"No, you don't," he murmurs against my skin. "You're obsessed with me."

"I am not." But my body betrays me by moving against his, wanting him closer.

"Yes, you are," Lucas says before pulling back and looking into my eyes. "But don't worry, the feeling's mutual." He grins. "So where did we land on meeting my family?"

*I'd love to.* "If they knew it was fake, then what would they think if you brought me to meet them?"

"They'd know it's real," he says. "They'd know that you're mine and that I want them to meet you." He tilts his head. "Are you okay with that?" he asks.

I nod, tugging my lip between my teeth. "Yeah, I am."

He grins and kisses me. "Want to repeat last night?" he asks.

I barely have a chance to nod before he smoothly slides inside me.

## Family ties

*Lucas*

"I'm nervous."

My eyebrows tug together. "Why?"

Madeline sighs. "It's just been a long time since I've met someone's parents," she says, making my body tighten at the thought of there being anyone before me. My whole past was erased the minute she entered my life. No other girls existed, past, present, or future. Only Madeline. "What if I mess it up?"

"You have nothing to worry about," I tell her. "My mom already loves you. And my sister…" I shrug, knowing Adrianna is already halfway in love with her, too. "She's easily entertained." Madeline laughs at that.

"I really hope she likes me," Madeline says. "I know how much she loves Leila."

I lean down and kiss my girlfriend's lips. "She wouldn't stop talking about you," I tell her. "I might even have to fight for your attention."

She smiles, her eyes lighting up. "That's fine by me."

"Yeah?" I chuckle. "You like having my attention?" I ask her. I shake my head, pressing my lips to her cheek. "You had it that very first day in the elevator. Even when you were being a pain in my ass, you caught it."

Her lips part and she looks up at me with those gorgeous brown eyes that I get lost in. I need some control, or I'll end up canceling on my own mother to go back to my apartment and spend the rest of the day buried inside of her. "Let's go, or we're going to be late."

Her eyes widen. "What? That's impossible. I checked the time before we left. I'm never late." She pulls out her phone and narrows her eyes when she sees we're still early. "You're an asshole."

I let out a laugh. "Is it weird that I find it hot as fuck when you call me that?"

"Might be."

I shrug. "Don't care. I love it." I lean down to kiss her.

She rolls her eyes when we pull back, but I see the smile on her lips. "Let's go before we really are late."

When we're finally at my mom's house, I reach out and knock on the door. Being here always brings back memories of my dad. He was the greatest father a kid could have. We used to watch futebol together all the time – I will never call it soccer. It's such a shame that Adrianna never got to meet him. He died when she was still a baby, and unfortunately, she's never going to know what it was like to have him as a father.

I interlock my hand with Madeline's when I hear her blow out a breath, and I lean in to brush her hair behind her ear. She's so damn beautiful. I can't wait to introduce her to my family.

"Mãe, já chegaram." *Mom, they're here.* I turn to see my little sister standing at the door with a smile on her face.

"Hey, froggy." I ruffle her hair as I walk inside the house.

She narrows her eyes. "Can you not call me that?" she says, her cheeks tinting with pink.

I laugh, pulling her in for a hug, which she fights against. She's so much like Leila I wonder if she's secretly just a clone. "Nah," I tell her. "It's my duty as a big brother." I leave a sloppy kiss on her cheek, which she wipes off dramatically when I pull back. "Where's mom?" I ask her.

"In the kitchen." She grins. "You better be hungry because she's cooked enough to last until next Christmas."

I sigh. "Great." I'm going to be eating leftovers for months.

My little sister's attention turns to Madeline and she smiles. "Hi, you're my brother's girlfriend."

Madeline laughs. "I am. You must be Adrianna. He's told me so much about you."

Froggy's eyebrows lift, glancing at me. "You have?"

"Yeah," Madi replies. "Your brother can't stop talking about you."

Adrianna's eyes narrow. "What's he been saying about me?"

"That you stink," I reply, ruffling her hair once more. I love this little girl. I'm the closest thing she has to a father figure, and honestly, she feels more like a daughter than a sibling.

"I do not stink," she says, fixing her hair. I can't believe how big she's gotten. I still remember feeding her and changing her diapers, and now here she is, a teenager. Christ. I just know my mom is going to have her hands full with her.

I let out a laugh. "Come on, let's go say hi to mom before she starts making another meal."

Madeline's hand finds mine, and I squeeze, her touch searing me from head to toe. "Does your mom always cook for ten?" Madi asks.

I turn to my girlfriend and give her a smile. "My mom loves feeding people. It's how she shows love, but this isn't a regular

251

occurrence for me, Mads. I've never brought a girl here before." I give her hand another squeeze. "You're the first."

Her face lights up, a grin sprouting on those pretty lips of hers. "I'm the first?"

I nod, pressing my lips to her cheek. "You're the *only* one," I correct. "You're going to do great. She's going to love you." *It's impossible not to.*

"Okay," she breathes out.

When I round the kitchen, my mom is holding a wooden spoon to James' mouth, and he's nodding at her with a grin on his face.

"Mãe," I call out to my mom. She turns around with a grin and drops the bowl on the counter, opening her arms.

"Ai, meu amor." She engulfs me in a hug, crushing my ribs in the process. Don't be fooled by my sweet, 5'4 Brazilian mother. She's strong as hell. She plants two kisses on my cheeks and turns to Madeline with a grin. "Nossa, ela é ainda mais bonita em pessoa." *She's even more beautiful in person.*

Yeah, mom. I know.

"Come here, give me a hug." She opens her arms out to Madeline and wraps her arms around her, squeezing her. Madeline's laughing, but I swear I see her wincing with pain.

Jesus, I need to pull my mom off her, or she'll end up killing my girlfriend. I grin at the sight of all the women I love – and James – in the same room. I like her here. I want her here forever.

A smile creeps onto my face at the realization that I'm falling for Madi, and fuck, it's nothing like I expected. I thought I'd freak out or something. I never expected to fall for *anyone*, but something in me settles knowing Madeline is the first girl I fell in love with and the last because there's no way I'm ever letting go of her.

"Hi, Madi," James says, walking slowly over to her. He's starting to use the crutches less and less, and honestly, It's a relief off my chest. "Nice to see you again."

She gives him a smile. "You too."

"Come eat," my mom says, placing five different serving dishes of food on the table. There's barely any room for the plates, but with the smile on my mom's face, there's no way I'm telling her that. "I forgot to ask Lucas if you had any dietary requirements, so there's a vegetarian dish, a vegan one, and the rest have meat."

Madeline smiles, tucking her hands on her lap. "I'll eat anything."

My mom gives her a smile back. "That's great because someone's going to have to eat all of this."

"Don't you worry, mama Silva," James says, grabbing some pão de queijo from the basket. "I'm starving."

"Me too." I dig into the feijoada, which makes my mouth water. My mom hasn't made feijoada in a long time. It was my dad's favorite, and I know how much it reminds her of him whenever she makes it. "And I can give the vegetarian one to Leila."

"This looks amazing," Madeline says, taking some of everything onto her plate. I grin. I don't even think she knows what half of it is. She just piles it on, knowing my mom wasted herself in the kitchen cooking for her. "Thank you so much."

My mom scoffs, waving a hand. "Nonsense. Lucas bringing a girl home for the first time is reason enough to celebrate." Her eyes meet mine, and she smiles. "I'm so happy he's found someone." Tears start to brim in her eyes. "Seu pai teria ficado tão feliz, filho." *Your dad would have been so happy, son.*

Madi glances at me, and I know she doesn't know what my mom just said, but she knows it is important because her hand sneaks under the table, and she places it on top of mine, intertwining our fingers together before she gives it a squeeze.

I look over at her and see her looking at me with those big brown eyes and a beautiful smile on her face. Fuck, I want to kiss her. And not the PG kiss that's appropriate for when you're having dinner with your family, but the wet, slobbery kiss that ends with me inside her until she cries out in pleasure.

I wish I could go back in time. I wish I could have gone back to that day in the elevator and told myself, this is the day. This is the day you'll meet the girl you'll want to spend the rest of your life with.

I'm sure I wouldn't have believed it, but now here I am, sitting with my sister, my mother, my brother, and the woman I love, who makes my heart beat faster whenever she looks at me.

She extends her hands when my mom starts to pray, and I open my eyes, glancing at Madeline, to see that she's already looking at me. She gives me a smile and mouths, "Thank you."

"For what?" I mouth back.

"For letting me meet your family. I love them."

Fuck. My heart aches with the love I have for her.

"They love you too."

*So do I.*

When I turn my head, I see my mom look between us and give me a knowing smile. James is grinning, and he pouts his lips, imitating a kiss. I'm tempted to throw some bread at his face, but I know how hard my mom worked on it, so I drop the bread, letting out a laugh instead.

The rest of the day is filled with laughter and jokes, just spending time with my family and finally being able to kiss the girl I'm obsessed with.

My little sister shares my obsession since she begs Madeline to paint her nails the same color she has on, dragging her away from me. Can't keep the smile off my face, though. Seeing her with my family is the best thing ever.

My mom passes the wet dishes, and I run the towel over them, storing them away when they're dry. "Nunca te vi tão feliz." *I've never seen you so happy.*

Her voice cracks and pulls at my heart. "Mãe."

She sighs. "I know I'm getting emotional," she says in Portuguese. "But I never thought I'd see the day."

I let out a scoff, drying my hands. "Thanks for the vote of confidence."

She tuts. "Don't be stupid. I didn't mean it like that. I just mean, I didn't think you'd ever allow yourself to open up to anyone. After your father died, you were just so focused on your career and taking care of us that you stopped thinking about yourself. Like James," she says. "You smother the kid."

I might be a little protective over him, but it's for good reason. "He lost everyone, mom. We're all he has."

She nods. "I know that. He might not have come out of me, but he's just as much my son as you are."

I grimace, wiping a hand down my face. "Jesus, Mom. Can you not say it like that?"

She lets out a laugh. "But he's strong, Lucas. You know that. He's stronger than all of us, and he'll be fine."

"Okay," I relent. "But what about you? You needed me. Adrianna needed me."

My mom scoffs. "Adrianna is a teenager. She'll always need you. But we don't want you to give up thinking about yourself for us." Her words mimic James' from the night of the gala.

I always thought this was the only path for me. Get a job that paid well and take care of my family, even if it stopped making me happy a while ago. Actually, I don't think it ever did. I was good at what I did, but it didn't bring me any joy or challenge me in any way, and I was tired of thinking it was all I had to offer.

"So, if I wanted to go back to school," I suggest. "How would you feel about that?" My heart starts to race, anticipating what she'll say. Honestly, it's something I've wanted for a while, and after talking to Madeline and knowing that I could be better for her, I know it's the right decision.

Her eyes widen, and a smile appears on her face. "Don't play with me," she says, pulling me in for a hug. "That would be amazing, Lucas."

I chuckle, tightening my arms around her, my shoulders dropping from relief. "It's all thanks to Madeline. She's the one that talked me into it."

My mom's smile matches mine when she pulls back. "I really like that girl," she says.

"Well, that's good since she's my girlfriend and all."

My mom grins. "I called it from the beginning."

"You just said she was pretty."

"She's beautiful," she agrees. "But that's not what I was talking about. I knew she'd be good for you." She smiles, patting my cheek. "It's nice to see you with a girlfriend instead of having those horrible headlines with all of those different girls."

My body turns hot at the memory. "That won't ever happen again." I won't let it. Madeline is the only girl that will be seen with me from now on.

"Good," my mom says. "You know you're falling for her, right?"

I let out a laugh. "Sim, Mãe. Eu sei." *Yes, Mom. I know. I already have.*

# 30

First date... kinda

## *Madeline*

"You cheated."

He laughs, shaking his head. "I did not."

His eyes are on the road as we drive. I glance outside, wondering where the hell he's taking me since there's nothing around us. He hasn't told me where we're going yet because that was part of the deal. If he got more likes on a post than me, he would have a whole day where he had control of me without me planning it in my planner.

And he won.

"I don't understand how you won."

He smirks, lifting a shoulder. "The picture I posted was of you. Sounds about right that it would get more likes."

I cross my arms, my lips lifting with a smile from his words, but I'm still pissed. "Question number sixteen. Where are we going?"

He lets out a chuckle. "That's not how this works. The deal was I'm in control. Just trust me, and relax, *princesa*."

The nickname makes me shiver, and I smile, attempting to hide it. "So you're really not telling me what we're doing?"

A smirk appears on his lips as he glances at me. "Legs up," he tells me, patting his thigh. I lift my feet and lay my legs on his lap. "You're getting the princess treatment today."

I press my lips together to stop the grin from sprouting. "I honestly thought I'd win. I was looking forward to having you do anything I say for a whole day."

He laughs, holding the steering wheel with one hand and running the other over my legs. "You don't need a bet to make that happen."

God, he just says the sweetest things. "Can you drive like this?" I ask him when he moves his hand to the gear stick.

"Baby, all you have to do is relax and let me take care of you. The rest I'll figure out." He goes back to stroking my leg, making my body break out into shivers at the feel of him.

"Question number seventeen."

"You're feeling inquisitive today," he says with a smile.

"Where did you learn how to drive stick?" I ask him, admiring how he's maneuvering the car, even with my legs in the way.

"James, actually," he says.

"Really?"

He nods. "He was always the daredevil between the two of us. He craved adrenaline and danger." Lucas lets out a laugh. "His dad actually taught him how to drive, only around the block, but James was addicted, even after his dad uh…"

I press my lips together, knowing it must pain him to talk about since he lost his dad around the same time. "It must have been hard to see him go through that."

"Yeah." He blows out a breath. "It fucking sucked. But it looks like he's getting better. I just hope everything keeps going well."

His expression dims, and I miss his smile, so I wiggle my feet in his lap and ask, "So, are you taking me on a date?"

His grin is back as he shakes his head. "You really hate not being in control, don't you?"

My cheeks heat as I stare up at him. "Not always." He catches on immediately, letting out a grunt. I love losing control in the bedroom. Letting him take over my body.

"Well, we haven't exactly had a first date yet," he says.

"Not true." He turns to look at me with furrowed brows, and I explain. "I mean, we went to the park, we had a photoshoot, and that gala, you can't forget that."

He laughs. "I'll never forget that," he says, glancing at me for a second before he turns his attention to the road. "But no, those were all things Ana set up," he says. "I want to be able to plan this one, make sure no one is around. Only you and I. So that I can kiss you whenever I want to, touch you wherever I want to, and be able to take you right there when your eyes burn with lust for me."

My lips part, and I have no doubt that if he looked at me, he'd see the lust he's explaining in my eyes right now.

He chuckles. "It might not have been a date I planned and set up, but I wanted it to be. I wanted you to see I wanted you for real, not part of a fake arrangement." The car comes to a stop, and I glance out of the window. "But I want to remedy that," he says. In my line of sight is a hot air balloon with a guy holding a bouquet of roses, and a bottle of champagne, and two flutes.

I don't even realize Lucas has left the car, when he appears at my side, opening the door and holding out his hand. I place my hand in his and step out, unable to stop my mouth from dropping. "Lucas," I gasp at the sight.

His fingers intertwine with mine as he walks us up to the private hot-air balloon ride. "Are you ready to go?" he asks.

260

I can't even nod. I'm completely speechless as he picks me up and places me inside, hopping in a second later. His hands cup my face, and he leans down to kiss me. "You're the best thing that's ever happened to me, Mads. I want to show you how grateful I am to have you in my life, in my arms." He places a kiss on my forehead before he pulls back. "In my heart."

The safety operator hands us a champagne flute, allowing us to drink while he explains the procedure. My eyes drop to the bouquet of roses inside the basket, admiring how big and beautiful the roses are. Honestly, I might have been jealous once or twice whenever Rosie received flowers from Grayson. I don't think I had ever received flowers before today, and I never thought I would.

Once we're in the sky, the view is utterly mind-blowing. It's completely picture-perfect, looking like something straight out of a painting. Golden fields, bathed in the warm sun, A river in the distance, glimmering from the approaching sunset. It's so peaceful up here with Lucas' arms wrapped around my waist and his lips pressed against my shoulder.

I turn to Lucas, my heartwarming. "It's so beautiful," I whisper with a shake of my head.

His unwavering gaze remains on me as he replies, "Yeah. It is." His smile makes my insides complete mush when he reaches out and brushes my hair behind my ear, leaning down to press his lips to mine.

I don't even pay attention to the safety operator inside the basket with us. In this moment, it's just me and Lucas. No one else. I wrap my arms around his neck and return his kiss, getting lost in the moment. But when a drop of rain hits my head, I wince, pulling back. "No."

Lucas squints, looking up as more drops of rainfall. "Fuck," he curses. "I checked the weather. Twice."

"It seems we're in for some unexpected rain," the safety operator says. "And it doesn't look like it's going to stop anytime soon."

"Is everything okay?" Lucas asks.

"We're going to have to start preparing for a landing," he replies. "Hot air balloons are safest when it's dry, but don't worry. I'm experienced in handling situations like these."

When Lucas turns to face me, I can only imagine what he sees. My hair curls up, drenched from the rain. He glances down at me, his brows knotted. "I'm so sorry, *princesa*," he says, as rain starts falling harder now. "If it's any consolation, you still look fucking perfect," he whispers with a smile on his lips. "You always do."

No one looks good in the rain, but the way he's looking at me has me believing the opposite. It isn't long until we're on the ground, and once we land, he picks me up in his arms, hops out of the basket, and runs toward the car.

He drops me to my feet and opens the door. "Holy fuck," I breathe out when we get inside. "I have never been wetter."

Lucas chuckles, his eyebrows lifting. "Are you sure about that?" he asks with a grin.

I let out a sigh. "We left the roses in the basket," I say with a frown.

"I'll buy you more. A hundred, a thousand even," he says, tugging on my arm. "Come here, baby. I'll make it up to you."

I climb on his lap, straddling his lap while he strips off my shirt. "What are you doing?" I ask, gasping when he grabs my breast with his hand and wraps his lips around my hard nipples, his warm mouth heating my body.

262

A little moan escapes him, and he glances up at me. "I'm not driving in the rain," he says, and my lips part when I realize he remembers what I told him about my sister. "So the least I can do is make up for this date."

My eyes start to tear up, and I shake my head, not knowing what to say, but the words are replaced with a gasp when he takes me in his mouth again. "There's nothing to make up for," I breathe out, my head feeling light-headed. Fuck, he's so good at that. "That was the best date I have ever been on. Hands down." The only date, technically, but I don't mention that to him.

He pulls back and wraps his hand around my neck, pulling me down until our lips meet in a soft kiss. "I'm glad to hear that," he says with a smile. "Now let me make it better by taking care of this pussy like I'm dying to, okay?"

I nod, happily taking that offer.

He gives me a grin as he reaches back and grips the back collar of his shorts, sliding it over his head in one fluid motion before throwing it into the back seat. The hard, sculpted contours of his chest and abs glisten from the rain as I run my hands over him. My mouth waters. Would it be ridiculous to run my tongue over it?

"I'm so happy I met you," Lucas says, unbuckling his jeans. I sit back on his thighs, pulling it off him until he's bare beneath me.

"Even though you couldn't stand me?" I ask, peeling down my black mini-skirt.

He groans when his fingers brush against my clit over my panties. "That just makes a good story to tell our kids."

His words make me freeze as I glance at him. "We're having kids?"

263

He smirks. "If you want them," he says. "Whatever it is you want, I want it too. I'm afraid I'm never letting you go now." He tugs my panties off and drags me back into his lap. "Aren't you glad we're in the middle of nowhere?" he asks before kissing me.

I moan into his mouth. So fucking glad.

I reach down to grab his cock in my hand and start stroking it. He lets out a groan, tipping his head back. "Question number eighteen. Did you think of me?" I ask him. "Before we got together." I wipe a thumb over his tip, making my question clear.

"Every day," he breathes out.

"Really?"

He nods, groaning when I lick my palm before stroking him again. "It was agony being around you when you didn't even like me when I thought I didn't like you," he admits, his jaw clenching. "You didn't even want me to touch you, and I love touching you," he says, brushing his thumb over my cheek. "I love feeling your skin on mine, love feeling you shiver whenever I do this." His fingers trail up my arm painfully slow making goosebumps pop on the surface. "Mmm." He smiles. "Just like that."

His hand travels down my stomach, going lower and lower until the tip of his finger brushes against my clit. I move my hips closer to him, and he lets out a deep groan. "Fuck, you're drenched." His finger keeps rubbing slow circles, making my head lull back. "Jesus," he groans. "Look at you, Madeline. You're so fucking perfect."

I bite my lip to control my noise, grinding against his hand.

"Don't," he says, making my eyes snap to him. "I want your noise. I like when you talk, love when you moan. Let me hear you, Mads." His fingers speed up, pressing a little harder, bringing out a cross between a gasp and a whimper from me. "Every dirty noise, every gasp. I want to hear how good I make you feel."

"So good," I cry out, grinding against his hand.

He pulls his hand away, making my eyes round at the loss. But then he leans back and grips his cock in his hand. "Show me, *princesa*. Ride my cock like the good girl you are."

I let out a whimper, shuffling closer to him and lifting onto my knees, positioning myself just above him.

His lips find their way to my neck, kissing and nibbling. "Put me inside you," he whispers, replacing his hand with mine on his cock. "I'm dying to feel you, baby."

His hands fly to my hips, helping me take him inside of me. He's so big, and I'm still not used to his size, so it takes a while until I'm seated all the way on his cock, hearing him whisper words of praise and cursing under his breath.

I blow out a breath, which turns into a moan when he thrusts up, fucking me from below. "You feel so good," I moan into the crook of his neck. "You're so deep this way."

He groans when I lift myself up before slamming back down. "God, Madeline. You're doing so fucking good." He thrusts deep inside me, making my head lull back. "So warm." Another thrust. "So fucking tight." He groans, cupping the back of my neck to bring my lips to his.

"Yes," I cry out. "Fuck. Lucas, please, don't stop. Please."

"You don't have to beg, baby," he says, bringing our foreheads together while he thrusts into me. "Anything you want is yours. You want my soul? My heart? Take it. It's yours. I don't want it back."

I throw my head back at his words, and he fucks into me harder, deeper. "I'm right there. I'm so close."

"Mmm," he moans. "I can feel it. Come for me, Mads. Let me feel you come all over my cock."

I get lost in the pleasure, gripping his shoulders while I fuck myself on his cock until a rush of pleasure rolls into me and pulls me over. I fall into him, and I can tell he's close by the way his breathing accelerates and his movements speed up.

It isn't long until he groans and pulls out of me, stroking his cock until he spills over his stomach. The sight is so fucking hot. I can feel my nipples tighten and my pussy flutter. "Fuck," he groans, staring up at me, his hard breaths coming out jagged.

"Can we do that again?" The rain has settled now, only a light drizzle hitting the windshield, but I don't want to end this date just yet. I want to spend as long as I can with him.

He lets out a laugh and captures my lips with his. "For as long as you'll have me," he replies, his dick hardening below me. I get lost in him, in how he makes me feel, in the person I am with him, and there's no doubt in my mind that I'm in love with Lucas.

# 31

I'm not going anywhere

## *Madeline*

I'm two seconds away from passing out from exhaustion.

I don't know how long I've been here, sitting in bed, surrounded by textbooks, but by the way my eyes are starting to glaze over, I can only imagine it's been a long time.

God, I want to sleep. But my assignments aren't anywhere close to being done yet, and the due date is in a week.

I glance back at the textbooks spread out on my bed, and my eyes narrow in exhaustion. Maybe a little nap won't hurt. I let my body drift down, falling back onto my pillow. Just thirty minutes, and then I'll wake up to do some more studying.

Just thirty minutes.

But then my phone buzzes, and my eyes snap open. "You've got to be kidding me." Who the hell is texting me at this time? Gabi's in her room, the girls are with their boyfriends, and my parents only check in a few times a month.

I let out a groan, reaching for my phone and opening the text.

Lucas:

I miss you.

My frown drops, and my lips immediately turn up in a smile at his name on my screen. A sigh escapes me. We've seen each other every day this week, and I already miss him. I quickly type back a text.

Madeline

I miss you too. So much.

I can't seem to stop smiling. I don't even want to. I can't remember the last time I was this happy.

Lucas:

Come to the door.

My brows knit together as I pull off the covers and get out of bed, opening my bedroom door. I can hear Gabi in her room, talking, so I creep toward the door, careful not to make any noise.

Reaching for the door handle, I crack it open, and my heart melts when I see Lucas breaking out into a grin when he sees me.

"What are you doing here?" I ask him. It's late, like really late, and while I'd love to have him here, I'm not ready for Gabi to find out about us yet.

He reaches forward, gripping my waist, and pulls me to him. His lips press against my forehead, and I instantly melt into his arms. I've never felt like this with someone before, so at ease, so relaxed. I was always on alert with Daniel, always scared, sad, and angry at myself.

The moment he leans in, and his lips brush mine, I'm putty in his hands, willing to do whatever he wants me to do. "You wear glasses?" he asks, pulling back to look at me, his eyes sparkling as he grins. "Fuck, that's so hot."

I let out a laugh, adjusting the black frames on my face. "I only use them to study."

He shakes his head. "Use them more," he says, leaning down to press his lips against mine, kissing me hard. "Please."

I'd bet I would do anything he wanted as long as he begged me. I loved hearing the urgency in his voice, pleading, begging. "What are you doing here?" I ask him again. "It's late."

"Came to see my girlfriend," he murmurs between kisses, his lips trailing down my jaw and neck.

A breathy moan escapes my lips, and I quickly press my lips together. He's called me that a few times, but it still shocks me every time. "Me?" I gasp when his teeth tug on my neck, soothing it with a lick of his tongue.

He chuckles, pulls back, and grabs onto my face, staring into my eyes. "I don't have any other girlfriend that I'm aware of," he says before he lets out a sigh. "I missed you so fucking much. I was lying in bed so painfully aware that the only place I wanted to be was with you."

He rests his forehead on mine, and my heart flutters. "I saw you this morning," I remind him. We've started a little routine of getting coffee together every morning. That way, we can still make sure the public knows we're dating, but my friends don't find out that it's real. I know I need to tell them soon, but… I *really* don't want to dye my hair red.

"Take pity on your boyfriend," he says. "I'm very needy." His lips land back on mine, and he moves his hand to the back of my neck, moving my head for better access. "Can I come inside?" he whispers against my lips.

I look behind my shoulder at Gabi's bedroom door. My brows knit together, and I turn to face him. "You need to be quiet," I tell him, pulling him inside before I close the door behind us, careful not to make any noise.

"Why?" he asks with a smirk. "You got a guy in here?"

I roll my eyes. "Funny. Like I haven't already got my hands full with you."

He chuckles, his eyes narrowing with lust. "Mmm. That's right. So full."

I push him into my room, and he lands on my bed with a laugh. "You're an idiot," I tell him. "I haven't told Gabi about us yet."

His eyebrows furrow. "You said she knew."

"That it was fake," I amend. "Not that we started dating for real."

"So tell her now," he says with a lift of his shoulder.

I let out a sigh, placing my hand on my hip. "Well, the thing is, we kind of made a bet."

"A bet?"

I nod. "Last year, after Leila and Aiden got together, Gabi was so adamant she'd end up as a fifth wheel, and I bet her that if I got into a relationship before her, I'd dye my hair red."

His eyebrows lift. "Wow. Bold for someone who plans what they're going to eat."

"I know," I say with a sigh, sitting on the bed beside him. He twists to look at me, and my stomach flips. He looks so good here. "I honestly thought I'd win," I tell him. "I never thought I'd be in a relationship. Ever again. I hated the thought."

He places his hands under his chin, blinking innocently. "Keep talking. These are such sweet words."

I let out a laugh. "You remember what I was like."

"A pain in my ass? Yeah."

I smirk, shaking my head. "I'm serious, Lucas. I never thought this would happen for me ever again."

His brows knit together in concern. "Any reason why?" he asks.

*Daniel.* "I just… didn't," I say with a shrug. I want to tell him so bad; I want to be able to confide in him and let him in, but it's so scary telling the guy you're in love with how weak you were.

His expression tightens, but then he lets out a breath. He knows I'm hiding something from him, but he doesn't push me to talk about it, and honestly, I'm so grateful for that.

"So you're scared to dye your hair?" he asks with a smirk.

"Obviously."

He reaches out and rubs a strand of my hair between his fingers. "I can't wait to see it," he says, knowing I'm going to have to dye it at some point. "You're going to look so hot."

"You think so?" Not that I think I'd look bad, but it's a big change, especially for me.

He shakes his head, letting out a scoff. "Are you serious? Mads, you could wear a paper bag, and I'd still think you were the most beautiful girl I have ever laid my eyes on." He wraps his arm around my waist and pulls me so I'm lying beside him on the bed. "If there were a contest, you'd win hands down."

He leans down to kiss me, his hand trailing down my body. "Lucas," I breathe out.

"Mmm," he moans. "I love those noises." He pulls back and stares into my eyes. "Last time I was here, I wanted to kiss you so bad," he admits.

"I was sick," I remind him.

He smirks, rubbing his thumb over my cheek. "I would have taken the risk."

I wanted to kiss him so bad that day, too, but I never thought he'd be thinking the same thing. I wonder what would have happened if Gabi hadn't come in. "I thought you hated me back then," I admit.

He shakes his head. "I told you I didn't hate you, Mads. We made a bad first impression on each other when we met. I was having a hard time with James, and my mom and…" he sighs. "He had fallen over that day, trying to take a shower." My eyes widen. "He was supposed to have a nurse taking care of him, but he fired her and attempted to do it himself. I was so fucking scared when I got the call, and then we got stuck together in that elevator." He squeezes his eyes closed. "It had nothing to do with you. If anything, you were what kept me sane during that time. You still do."

My body breaks out into shivers like it always does when he looks at me. "You're it for me, Madeline," he says, his thumb brushing over my bottom lip. "You're fucking it for me."

He leans down and presses his lips to mine, and I get lost in him, the world around me dissolving whenever he's near. He hums against my lips, pulling back. "As much I'd love to just make out with you, I actually came here for a reason," he says.

I raise an eyebrow, smirking at him. "Because you can't live without me?" I joke.

272

He lets out a laugh, smoothing his thumb over my cheek. "That's an understatement," he says, grinning down at me. "But no. I came over because… You got it," he says, breaking out into a grin.

My brows furrow. "Got what?"

"The audition," he clarifies, making my eyes widen, almost jumping out of my eye sockets. "You'll get an email soon, but I couldn't fucking wait to tell you."

"Oh my god." I break out into a grin, sitting up on the bed. "You're joking."

He shakes his head. "Ana called me an hour ago, and I came here as fast as I could," he says, holding my face in his hands. "I wanted to see the look on your face when you found out."

"Lucas." I wrap my arms around him, unable to say anything else. My head shakes as the words process through me, the earlier exhaustion coming right back. Fuck, it's late. I should be asleep. But all I can think of is I have an audition. With Monica Harrington. "Thank you." I pull back, pressing my lips to his over and over again.

He laughs against my lips, pushing my body to lie down on the bed. "You don't have to thank me, *princesa*," he says, kissing me. I open up for him, my eyes closing, and I let out a whimper. God, I'm so tired. Lucas pulls back, kissing my forehead. "You're amazing, Mads, and I'm glad other people are starting to realize that, even if I wish I could keep you all to myself," he murmurs against my skin.

I let out a small laugh, my eyes heavy, and the feeling of his lips on my neck and my jaw soothing. But it's not until his hand slides down my body, playing with the hem of my shirt, that I realize where this is heading, and I freeze when he lifts the material to my waist.

I swallow harshly, trying to make myself get in the mood. I love feeling his body on mine, and I'm sure it will be the same. I squeeze my eyes closed. *Just do it. Just go along with it. He's happy, don't make him upset.*

But Lucas's hand stops and he pulls back. I open my eyes to see him look at me with furrowed brows. "Are you okay?" he asks.

I nod, pressing my lips together. "Yeah, I'm fine."

"Madeline."

The hard tone of his voice makes me sigh. "I'm just a little tired," I admit, gulping when he frowns. God, why can't I just be normal and get myself in the mood? He's going to yell and leave, and he won't want to be with me anymore.

But he doesn't leave. Instead, he leans down and presses a chaste kiss to my lips. "Come on," he says, pulling me up until we're under the covers. "Let's go to sleep."

I glance up at him, my heart thudding against my chest. "You don't want to…"

He shakes his head, his eyes softening when he looks down at me. "You don't want that right now. And that's completely fine." His arms tighten around me. "You don't need to force yourself to get in the mood or just go along with it because I want to," he says. "When you're feeling it, you can let me know."

"You…" My lip wobbles. "You mean that?"

"Of course," he says, his brows knitting together. "Why wouldn't I?"

My eyes start to tear up, and I hold back a sob, pressing my lips together. Lucas, however, catches on because he frowns as he holds my face in his hands. "Hey," he says, in a voice so soothing it makes me want to cry even more. "What's wrong?"

I shake my head, blinking away the tears. I don't want to cry in front of him. Not again. Squeezing my eyes shut, I beg myself not to break down, but when his hands wipe away a tear, my eyes snap open, locking with his.

"Baby," he says, his voice so calm it makes me want to cry even more. "I didn't mean to imply I don't want you. I always want you, but I'm not going to push you into doing something if you're not feeling it."

I shake my head, my heart bursting with the love I have for him. "That's not it."

"Then what is it?" he asks. "You can tell me, *princesa*. Whatever it is."

"I... I don't want you to think I'm weak."

His lips turn into a frown. "I would never think that," he says earnestly. "I want you to be able to tell me anything, no matter what. You never have to *try* to be perfect with me. All you have to do is exist. Be messy, be loud, cry, scream if you have to. It doesn't matter. You'll always be perfect to me."

My heart trusts him so much that the words come spilling out. "I had a boyfriend," I tell him. "In high school."

His eyes darken, and his breathing starts to pick up. "What happened?" he asks.

The memory of it is painful, and the thought of Lucas seeing me as anything but strong is scary, but he saw me break down in the elevator, and he's still here. He still wants me.

"It was a few weeks after Nia died," I start. "I was a mess, completely lost without my sister. My parents hardly talked to me and I felt so lonely," I admit, relaxing into him while his hand rubs my back. "I know they were grieving too, but it felt like they were mad at me or something. I felt like after their real daughter died, they didn't want me."

275

"Mads," Lucas says. "You know that's not true."

I shrug. "Maybe it's stupid, but that's how I felt. And then I met this guy at school, and he talked to me, he liked me and gave me attention. It seemed like no one else cared about me, so I let myself get caught up in him." I breathe out a sigh. "It all happened so quick. One moment, he took my first kiss. The next he was calling me his girlfriend."

It was on my sixteenth birthday, and I still remember waking up to my parents being gone for work without so much as a happy birthday text. They had never done that before. Birthdays were always a big thing in our family, but when Nia died, so did all our other traditions.

"He was kind and gentle. At least at first," I continue. Lucas' hand stops abruptly on my back and I glance up at him, seeing his brows knitted so tight. "But not long after, he started to get very controlling. I don't even know how he did it, but he managed to make me turn against my parents." I shake my head, a tear rolling down my cheek when I let out a laugh. "I had spent my whole life trying to make them love me, and while I knew they did, he made me feel like I would never be good enough for them. He used to tell me that they would never love me like they did Nia. That he was the only one who could learn to love someone that was as overbearing as me."

"You're kidding," Lucas says.

"I believed him." I nod, more tears rolling down my chest. "I really believed no one would be able to love me. My own birth parents didn't want me, I didn't have many friends and had never had a boyfriend, and after Nia died, my own parents didn't want to be around me. Why wouldn't I believe him?"

"Because he was manipulating you."

276

"I didn't see it at the time," I tell him. "He made me think everyone hated me, everyone except for him. He got jealous if I had any friends, which were very few and told me to cut them off. He checked my phone constantly. He had this power over me that made me feel like I was no one without him. And he wanted things I wasn't ready to give."

"Mads," Lucas breathes out, tightening his hold on me. "Please don't tell me…" He trails off, his words clear.

"Whenever I would tell him I wasn't ready or that I didn't want to, he would get angry and call me a prude or childish. And it got to a point where…" I trail off, shaking my head. "He was sick of waiting, and I hated seeing him pissed whenever I turned him down, so I just… let him."

"You let him?" Lucas asks, his tone sharp.

"I didn't say no," I admit.

"But did you want to?"

I shake my head, burying my head deeper in his chest. "No," I admit, a sob catching in my throat. "I didn't want to. But I didn't want him to get angry."

"What do mean angry?" he asks with a bite.

I hear the warning in his voice, and I spill the words out, wanting to tell him everything. "He had a temper," I tell him. "Kicking chairs, punching walls, that sort of thing, but then…"

"Then?" His voice grows thick.

"He saw a text from a guy on my phone." I shake my head, still remembering that day. How scared I was. How *weak* he made me. "He was just my science partner, but he thought something was going on, and I was seeing someone behind his back, so he smashed my phone, and to teach me a lesson, he shoved me in his closet."

"What?" Lucas's eyes narrow on mine.

More tears spill down my cheeks, but I force myself to breathe. "He pushed a chair against it so I couldn't get out. I don't even know how long I was in there for. I was terrified. It was cold and dark, and I couldn't call anyone. I had no other company other than myself."

"Fuck," Lucas curses. "So, when you were in the elevator?"

I lift my head to look at Lucas, seeing his eyes wet, and it breaks me in half. I nod, forcing myself to continue. "And then, when the doors opened, he asked if I had learned my lesson. And I apologized," I continue. "I told him I was sorry for talking to someone without telling him." Lucas shakes his head, shivering in my arms as I continue. "He made me believe it was my fault."

"Fuck," Lucas curses, tightening his hold on me. "This is killing me." His voice cracks and it makes me break down, more tears spilling down my face.

"I'm sorry," I whisper.

"Fuck that," he says. "You have nothing to be sorry about." He wipes away my tears with his thumb. "That fucker is the one who's going to have to be sorry."

"He let me go home later that day," I continue. "But I must have been in there overnight because my parents were worried sick when I finally got home." I shake my head. "I lied to them," I tell him. "I told them I stayed over at a friend's house. I protected him, even after he did that to me. I still haven't told them." I blow out a breath. "The next day, he acted like nothing had happened, but I couldn't. I couldn't act like that was normal because I knew that if I had stayed with him, he would be taking his anger out on me instead of the furniture."

"So what happened?" Lucas asks.

"As soon as I saw him again, I told him I wanted to break up. He yelled and made a scene in front of everyone. He grabbed my face so hard and kissed me, promising me it wouldn't happen again. I was so embarrassed, I almost took him back just to shut him up." Lucas' breath stills. "But I didn't," I clarify. "I kept my distance, and blocked his number until he eventually moved on to someone else."

"I'm so fucking glad you left him," Lucas says, pressing his lips against my forehead.

"I regret not leaving him sooner, but… I guess we accept the love we think we deserve," I say, wiping away the tear trickling down my face. "And he made me think I deserved to be treated that way for way too long until I realized it wasn't worth it. I told myself that if that's what love was, then I didn't want it. That's why I didn't want a boyfriend. I didn't want to be that weak ever again."

Lucas lifts my chin up to look at him. "You are not weak," he says, and even though his eyes are wet from tears, they're turned to stone. "And that was not love. You are so fucking strong. Stronger than I ever thought possible, and he was a manipulative, abusive motherfucker who…" Lucas squeezes his eyes closed, and when he opens them, they're filled with anger. "What's his name?" he asks.

"What?" I raise my hand to wipe away my tears.

"His name, Madeline," he asks again. "I'm not kidding. I'm going to fucking kill him."

"He's not worth it," I tell him, knowing I've been in his position so many times before. How many times did I want to find him and throw a punch in his face? How many times have I thought about that night and the many others after that? How many times did I blame myself for what happened, for not saying no again?

"Damn right, he's not," Lucas says. "But you're dead wrong if you think I'm going to let him get away with it."

"Lucas, it's been five years."

"I don't give a fuck," he says, narrowing his eyes at me. "There's no statute of limitations. I'm going to teach *him* a fucking lesson."

"You can't."

"Why not."

"Because he's in prison," I tell him. "Turns out I wasn't the only girl that he liked to overpower." My parents never found out we dated, but they had told me freshman year of college that he had gone to prison, and while I was relieved, all I wanted to do was tell them that it happened to me, too. That I was hiding something from them. But I couldn't.

Lucas shakes his head, cradling my face in his hands. "Fuck, Mads. That isn't good enough. He deserves worse for what he did to you."

"I'm okay," I tell him. "My parents made me go to therapy after Nia's death, and I told her about him. I actually… told her about you, too."

"You did?" he asks, with a smile on his lips.

I nod. "She said she's proud of me for getting over the hurdle of never wanting to date ever again." I breathe out a sigh. "I was so stuck on what he had done to me and who he had turned me into that I was actively putting every other guy in the same box." I glance at him. "Including you."

"And now?" Lucas asks, swallowing harshly. "Do you still feel that way?"

I shake my head, my heart drumming three little words. "I feel safe with you."

He blows out a breath. "That is the best thing I have ever heard." He presses his lips to my forehead. "You will always be safe with me," he says. "You want to stop any time, even if I'm already inside you. All you have to do is say the word, and I'll listen. Got it?"

I nod, pressing my lips together to stop from crying. I love him so much.

"Do you want me to leave?" he asks.

I shake my head, pulling him into me. "No, please stay. I can't sleep without you anymore."

A chuckle leaves his lips. "Look who's needy now," he jokes.

But he doesn't even know the weight of his words. I need him so much that it should be scary how much power he has over me. But it isn't. Not with him. "So needy."

He kisses the top of my head and rubs his hands up and down my back. "Go to sleep, *meu amor*. I'm not going anywhere."

# 32

Meeting the parents

## Madeline

"I did it." As soon as Lucas opens the door, I jump into his arms, wrapping my legs around his waist when he hoists me up.

"Hell yes," he says, his hands gripping my ass to make sure I'm secure, or maybe he just really likes my ass. "How did it go?"

"So good," I tell him, grinning when I remember the audition. It went better than I ever expected. After rejection after rejection and feeling like a failure, I honestly think I'm on my way to getting a little win. Even if nothing comes from this, I'm happy with how it went.

"I'm so fucking happy for you." He breaks out into a grin, tightening his hold on my waist with one hand while the other reaches up to grab my face. "I knew it would happen for you."

It's still too early for him to be congratulating me. They could still pass on me, but I like how he sounds, full of hope. "I know it was you," I tell him.

"What do you mean?"

His expression gives nothing away, but I know better. I smirk, admiring him for trying to keep it a secret. "I know you called them yourself to get me that audition."

He furrows his brows for a second but then drops the act, breathing out a sigh. "Did Ana tell you?" he asks. "I asked her not to."

"She didn't have to," I admit, keeping my arms wrapped around his neck when he drops me to the ground. "I knew the moment you told me I got the audition."

He lets out a laugh, shaking his head. "I guess I wasn't very good at hiding how excited I was, huh?"

I smile, shaking my head in reply. I love how happy he was for me, how he went out of his way to get me something that I've been dreaming of forever. "Thank you," I whisper against his lips.

"It was all you," he says with a smile. "All I did was try to contact them, but it was once they saw your audition tapes that I sent them that they decided to give you that audition."

"You saw them?" I ask him, my heart beating faster. I don't know why the thought of Lucas seeing my audition tapes makes me nervous, but I would hate if he watched them and thought they were trash.

"A long time ago," he says, chuckling.

A breath escapes me. "I don't know how I feel about that," I admit.

He pulls me closer against him, his hands settling at my waist. "There's nothing to be nervous about. You were amazing." He leans down and presses a kiss on my cheek. "You *are* amazing," he amends.

His lips land on mine, and I breathe out a sigh, kissing him back. Our tongues brush together, pulling a moan from my throat. Just kissing him feels amazing. I never thought I could feel like this.

But when my phone rings, we both jump apart, and Lucas groans. "I swear to god, if that's Ana."

A laugh bubbles out of me as I reach into the back pocket of my jeans and pull out my phone, seeing my mom's name on the screen. "It's my mom," I tell him, my brows knitting together.

"How long has it been since you talked to her?"

I shrug. "A few weeks, I guess. They don't call often."

He nods, gesturing to his room. "You want me to go?" he asks.

I shake my head. "No, stay, please."

He wraps his arms around me and kisses my forehead. "Don't worry, I won't leave."

It mimics the time I was sick, and I wanted him there, even when I was battling my feelings for him. It's insane how far we've come and how important he's become in my life.

I take a seat on his couch and hit the green button. "Hi, Mom."

"Darling." Her sweet voice always makes me smile whenever I hear it. "When were you going to tell us?"

"Tell you what?"

"That you're dating?" My eyes widen, and I turn to Lucas who's also hearing the conversation. How did she find out? "Not to mention, he's famous and very attractive."

Lucas presses his lips together in an attempt to stifle his laughter.

"Excuse me," I hear my dad say. "Your husband is sitting right here."

"Your dad thinks so, too," my mom says. "Don't you?"

I hear my dad scoff. "I just said there's a reason why he's a model."

I turn to look at Lucas and see his cheeks have turned the slightest shade of pink.

"Why didn't you tell us?" my mom asks again.

My mood sobers, and I let out a breath. "I didn't know how," I admit. "I guess we never talked about that sort of thing before. Nia was always the one with the boyfriends."

The silence between us rings like a fire alarm. "I guess so," my mom says, her tone hushed. "So, this is your first boyfriend?" she asks me.

I pull my bottom lip between my teeth, turning to face Lucas. His hand settles on my thigh, rubbing back and forth, but I just sigh and hum in agreement. Daniel doesn't count. What I had with him is nothing compared to what I have with Lucas. "Yeah," I tell them. "We met a few months ago."

"Oh I saw the pictures," she says in an accusatory tone. "I nearly had a heart attack when I saw your face on a magazine. I went down a rabbit hole and saw all of the articles. I can't believe you didn't tell me." She sounds upset, and guilt coils around my stomach. "I know I haven't been checking in as often because I know how you like your independence, but I thought you'd tell me about this."

I always thought I liked independence as well. For the longest time, I thought I worked better alone; I was better off on my own, but that wasn't the truth, not even close to it. "I'm sorry, mom. I promise I'll tell you from now on."

"You promise?" she asks.

"Yeah." My lips curve in a smile. "I promise."

"So then tell me about Daniel."

My eyes widen and I freeze, staring down at the phone in my hand. "What about Daniel?" I ask her, my heart racing. She knows?

"Baby," she coos. "You think we didn't see how shaken up you were when you came home that day?" I turn my head to look at Lucas, and his expression is tight, listening to my parents. "Your father and I didn't buy the story that you were staying over at someone's house and just forgot. You had never done that before. You were always so good, so easy." I let my eyes drift closed. That's what I wanted, right? I wanted to be easy for them to want, to be able to love, but hearing that just solidifies that the only reason they did was because I didn't give them any trouble.

But they loved Nia, adored her, and she was always getting herself in trouble. Would they feel the same if I was like that?

"We followed you to school, and we saw you talking to him," she admits. "At first, I was upset you didn't tell me you had a boyfriend, but when I saw him talking to you, getting in your face like that…" I hear her shaky breath, and I press my lips together to stop from crying. "I knew there was more to the story."

She'd be right to think that. All this time. All this time, I thought they didn't know. I thought I had kept it to myself, dealing with everything that happened on my own, and this whole time, they knew?

"I don't know if it was because Nia has just died," she continues, "and you felt like you couldn't talk to us anymore, but it made me a little sad that we stopped having the relationship we once had."

"I… I didn't think you'd care," I tell her.

"Why wouldn't I care, darling?" she asks me. "You're my daughter, and after I heard about him going to prison for hurting his girlfriend, all I could think of was you." She breathes hard. "Did he ever…"

"He didn't hit me," I confirm, my lips wobbling while I try to keep it together. "But he hurt me in other ways."

"I knew it. I should have kicked his fucking teeth in when I had the chance." My dad doesn't swear much, so my eyes widen when I hear him speak.

"He was a minor," my mom tells him.

"Not anymore, he's not," he replies. "No one hurts my baby girl and gets away with it." A sob catches in my throat, and Lucas pulls me toward him, wrapping his arms around me.

"I wish you would have told us," my mom continues.

I let out a breath, shaking my head. "I do, too, but you guys were so upset about Nia that I didn't want to upset you even more. I…" My voice cracks, and I clear my throat. "I thought you resented me."

"Darling." My mom's sweet voice makes me cry even more. "Why would that thought ever cross your mind?"

"Because you lost your real daughter, and I was all that was left."

"Madeline," my dad speaks up. "Tell me you don't think that."

Lucas' hand lifts to wipe away my tears, and I let out a shaky breath. "I don't anymore… but at the time, it felt like you stopped caring about me."

My mom lets out a sigh. "We were distraught over what happened with Nia," she starts. "How could we not be? She was so smart and destined for great things. What happened to her was awful, and it broke my heart, but that doesn't mean we stopped caring about our other daughter, too. I'm sorry if you felt pushed aside because that's the last thing I ever wanted for you." Her voice cracks, and I blink away the tears, my heart warming at everything I thought I would never hear. "You were always ours," she says. "Doesn't matter who birthed you. You're my daughter."

"And you're my baby girl," my dad joins in.

"You have been since we laid eyes on you. We love you so much, Madeline," my mom says.

I wipe away the tears, letting out a laugh through the tears. "I love you guys too. So much."

"Darling, when can we come see you?" my mom asks. "I want to meet that boyfriend of yours."

I smile, glancing at Lucas, who sits up straight and brushes a hand through his hair. A laugh bubbles out of me when I turn my attention back to the phone on my lap. "He's actually here," I tell them.

"He is?"

"Yeah, do you want to see him?" I ask her.

"Oh my god," I hear my mother mutter. "It's happening." My brows knit together in confusion. "How do I turn the damn Facetime camera on?" she asks my dad, making me laugh.

"Calm down," he says.

"We're about to meet our daughter's boyfriend. How are you so calm?"

My dad scoffs. "Because I'm the only man in her life. This guy is just a little boy."

Lucas breathes out a laugh, wiping a hand down his face. He fixes the collar of his black shirt. The camera turns on, and my parents are on the screen. I smile down at them. I miss them so much. I haven't been home since Christmas, and I can't wait for them to come visit.

"Darling," my mom says with a smile on her face. "You look so beautiful."

"Thank you," I say, feeling my cheeks heat. I debate whether I should tell them or not, but after everything that I did tell them, what's one more thing? "I actually just came from an audition."

Her eyebrows shoot up. "You did?" she asks.

"Yeah," I admit, feeling suddenly a little nervous about what they're going to say. "I think it went well."

"And you're still studying?" my dad asks.

My heart drops slightly. I don't know what I expected their response would be, but I shouldn't be surprised that it's this.

"I am," I tell them. "But I'm also following my dreams. I want to become an actress."

Lucas' arm is pressed up against mine, and it brings me a sort of peace and confidence to be able to tell my parents that the life they wanted for me is not one I want for myself.

"You know it's unsteady work," he replies. "We want the best for you, Madi. We don't want you to struggle."

"I know," I agree with a nod. I know how hard it is, but I'm willing to put in the work. "But I'd rather be doing something that I love and I'm actually good at than spending years working toward something that I know I hate."

My mom's brows furrow, and my heart sinks. She's disappointed, but I make myself continue. "I'm not Nia. I know she was going to Harvard to follow in your footsteps, but that's not me. I don't want that life for myself."

My mom breathes out a sigh, and then a smile spreads across her face. "Then I can't wait to see you in a movie someday."

My heart soars, a warm feeling building inside me. I've wanted to tell them for so long that I always let the fear of them resenting me for doing what I want instead of what they pictured for me stop me from opening up to them.

289

I pan the camera to Lucas, who's eyes widen when he's suddenly on screen. "Mom, Dad, this is Lucas." I glance up at him and flash him a smile. "My boyfriend."

"You're even more handsome than I remember," my mom gushes, grinning at him.

My dad's face remains stiff as he looks him up and down. "He's alright."

I let out a laugh, and my mom smacks my dad on the arm. "It's nice to finally meet you, darling," she tells him.

Lucas smiles. "It's nice to finally meet you too, Mr and Mrs Davis."

"Are you taking care of my daughter?" my dad asks him.

My body grows hot from head to head, but Lucas remains calm as he nods. "Yes, sir," he tells my dad. "She's my biggest priority."

My dad tilts his head. "I looked you up."

Lucas winces, shaking his head. "Sir, it isn't what it looked like."

"I know what a PR stunt looks like when I see one," my dad interrupts, making me freeze. Does he know we started off as nothing but an act? "I can tell from the pictures that those girls you were with were nothing more than contractual agreements, but my daughter…" he trails off, narrowing his eyes at him. "I can see you're serious about her."

My shoulders drop, and I breathe out a sigh of relief. Lucas nods, tightening his hold on my thigh below the camera. If my dad knew where his hand was right now, I'm certain he wouldn't be so kind. "I am, sir," he says. "She's the best thing that's happened to me in a long time, and I can't imagine life without her anymore."

I glance at him, my heart thudding against my chest so loudly it's a wonder he can't hear it.

"Did you rehearse that?" my dad asks him.

"No sir," Lucas replies, his face remaining still.

"Hmm." My dad leans back on the couch, staring at Lucas for a few seconds before he says, "Just so you know, I can fight."

"Dad," I chastise.

"I didn't look out for you once," my dad says, his expression tight. "I'm not taking any more chances."

"I'd rather die than hurt her," Lucas tells him.

My dad nods. "I'll hold you to that."

"Stop threatening the poor boy," my mom says. "It was lovely to meet you, Lucas. We're coming to visit soon, so I'm excited to get to know you more."

"Likewise," he says. "My mother will be ecstatic to meet you."

My mom smiles. "I'll see you then. Bye, darling," she says, her eyes drifting to mine. "I love you."

"Love you guys."

The call hangs up, and I turn to Lucas, squinting at his expression. "You met my parents," I point out.

"I did." He grins. "Why do you look so shocked?"

I shrug. "I guess I'm wondering how you feel about it."

He laughs, tugging me up so I straddle him on the couch. His hands fly to my hips, and he pins me with a serious stare. "I couldn't wait to introduce you to my family," he says. "So, the thought of meeting the people who raised someone as amazing as you?" He shakes his head. "I loved it."

"Yeah?" My hands wrap around his neck and his hands start to roam over my body. A warm feeling pools at the pit of my stomach, and I rock myself over the bulge in his jeans.

He lets out a groan, pulling back to gauge my reaction. "Are you sure?" he asks.

I've never been more sure about anything. I grip his collar in my hands and lean down until our lips are stacked. "Kiss me."

# 33

Exposed

*Madeline*

"God, I want to die." Gabi lets out a groan, burying her head in her hands.

"Maybe you shouldn't drink your body weight in alcohol, then," Leila supplies.

Gabi twists her head and cracks an eye open. "I seem to remember you getting just as drunk before you decided to quit for your boyfriend."

Leila smirks. "And I don't miss it at all."

Gabi presses her hand to her mouth. "God, I'm going to be sick." Her eyes meet Leila's. "That was the cheesiest thing I've ever heard."

Leila rolls her eyes. "Funny."

Gabi attempts to laugh, groaning when a wave of nausea rolls through her. "Rosie," she calls out. "Be a babe and hold out your hands. I might actually be sick."

"Ew. No way." Rosie's face contorts, and Gabi lets out a chuckle.

"I'm only kidding," she says, turning to face me. "Madi, give me your bag."

I roll my eyes, Leila catching my eye when I see her smile down at her phone. "Is that Aiden?" I ask her, already knowing the answer.

She smirks, nodding. "Yeah, he's giving me a play-by-play of what's going down." The guys all invited Lucas over to play some video games, and James, too, since he's been hanging out with them since the party.

"And?" I ask her, taking a sip of my coffee to try and downplay my excitement. I love that he's hanging out with our group.

Leila tilts her head. "He said he sucks."

"Hey, that's Madeline's boyfriend. Don't insult him," Gabi pipes up.

I let out a laugh, pressing my lips together at how much I like hearing her say that. Even if they think it's still fake, they still call him my boyfriend.

"Is it weird for you?" Leila asks. "Him hanging out with our boyfriends?"

I shake my head. "No, I mean, I guess they're just trying to make him feel comfortable since they think we're dating." I eye the girls, and Rosie's cheeks tint immediately, turning beet red. Leila, however, presses her lips together to stop the laugh from coming out. "Right?"

I already know they told their boyfriends, but Rosie breaks, blowing out a breath. "I told Grayson," she blurts out. "I'm sorry. I just can't hide anything from him. He knows I'm lying before I even try."

I let out a laugh. "I know, Rosie. It's fine." I turn to Leila. "I know you told Aiden too."

"Yep." Leila smirks. "He won't say anything, though. The NDA is safe."

Does the NDA still stand if the relationship is no longer fake? I breathe out a sigh. I should tell them, but I like how it is between us right now, and I know as soon as I tell them, everything's going to change.

"Is it working out for you?" Rosie asks. "The whole fake dating thing?"

I smile, nodding. "Yeah, I guess. I've gained a ton of followers because of it, and I actually got an audition."

"Really?" Rosie asks, her eyes widening. "That's great. How did it go?"

I grin, feeling the bask of my friends' approval. They're always so supportive, and they're my biggest fans, and honestly, I'd be lost without them. "It went great," I tell them. "If they decide to go with me, then I'll be working with one of my favorite directors, Monica Harrington."

"What kind of movies does she make?" Leila asks. "I don't think I've heard of her."

"You wouldn't. She mostly works on smaller, indie movies," I supply with a shrug. "But I love her. Her movies are so real and raw."

Gabi snickers, lifting her head. "Just how I like it." She lets out a laugh, groaning a second later, clutching her head when the nausea hits. "This is your fault," she groans, glancing up at me.

I cock my head at her. "What did I do now?"

"You made me leave my bed."

I snicker, remembering how she didn't want to get up this morning. But she'd already been sleeping the whole morning, and I thought fresh air would help her.

But I doubt that's the case. I've never gotten drunk before. I love parties, and I've gotten a little buzzed before, but I never took it too far. I hate losing control. I like knowing I'm of sound mind at all times.

Leila lifts herself off the table, heading toward the counter, and comes back a minute later, holding out a green smoothie in Gabi's face.

Gabriella groans when she sees it. "Leila, I will kick you."

"Trust me, you drama queen. I used to get the worst hangovers, and while it might not cure it, it will help."

Gabi's face contorts. "It looks like grass."

Leila laughs, shaking her head. "It tastes good. I promise."

Gabi reluctantly accepts the green smoothie and glances at me. "If you'd come with me, we could be drunk together since this one," she points at Leila, "doesn't drink, and Rosie practically drinks sugar."

"Hey," Rosie says, frowning. "They taste good."

"As much as I'd love to share your hangover," I supply dryly, knowing she's joking, "I was studying."

Gabi's eyes drop to the drink in her hand, and then glances up at me. "All night?" she asks.

I shrug. "Classes keep me busy." Technically not a lie, but what I don't tell her is that Lucas came over and slept in my bed again. Gabi was out partying, so I knew it was safe to have him over.

Gabi plugs her nose and gulps down half the drink, letting out a groan when she swallows. "Oh fuck. You lied to me," she says to Leila.

"It's just fruit and vegetables," Leila replies.

Gabi shakes her head. "And I don't like either of those things."

My phone buzzes, and I glance at the screen, seeing Lucas's name. I smile instantly, grabbing it before the girls can see.

Lucas:

> Question number nineteen:

I smile when I see his text, watching the three little dots on the screen.

Lucas:

> How much do you miss me?

A grin spreads across my face as I text him back.

Madeline:

> Are you fishing for a compliment?

Lucas:

> Sue me for wanting to hear my girlfriend tell me how hot I am.

> So, how drunk is Gabi?

I shake my head, a smile on my lips.

Madeline:

> Did Aiden tell you?

Lucas:

> Yup. The guy won't stop staring at his phone. He's completely obsessed with Leila.

> I know how he feels.

I raise my eyebrow, a smirk playing on my lips. I glance up to see Leila force-feeding Gabi the drink like she's a child, and I let out a laugh, glancing back down at my phone.

Madeline:

> You're obsessed with Leila?

"Open," Leila says. I look up to see her holding the half-empty glass to Gabi's lips. She shakes her head, mumbling something while her mouth is closed. Leila breathes out a sigh, glancing at Rosie. "Help me."

"I prefer to watch you try," she says with a smirk.

My phone buzzes in my hand, and I quickly open it.

Lucas:

> Funny. Like you don't know, you're the only girl I see.

I sigh, reading over his text, glancing at the girls, letting out a laugh when I see Gabi trying to down the green smoothie herself.

Madeline:

I miss you too.

Lucas:

Me too. The guys are holding me hostage, but as soon as I can leave, I'm coming to you.

I smile, pocketing my phone.

Leila lifts off the chair, tugging at Gabi. "Come on, let's get you home."

Shit. I glance at the girls. "I um… I have to study."

Rosie smiles, and Leila smirks, but they don't say anything as they walk Gabi out.

"She's *so* going to fuck her fake boyfriend," Gabi whisper-yells to Leila, making a laugh bubble out of me.

Fuck it. Bring out the red hair dye. I don't care anymore.

"Stay away from my fresh towels," I yell out to Gabi.

She shakes her head, glancing back at me. "I can't promise anything."

Leila smirks at me. "Don't worry, I'll make sure your towels will stay clean."

The door opens, and they push it open, leaving the café.

My phone buzzes on the table, and I smile, wondering if Lucas is near, but when I swipe up and look down at the screen, it's not him.

Me too. The guys are holding me hostage, but as soon as I can leave, I'm coming to you.

Ana:

> What did you guys do?

I furrow my brows, clicking on the link she sent, and my heart drops.

***Exposed: Love at first sight or a sham all along?***

I scroll down the page, my heart sinking into my stomach at the sight of a picture of me and Lucas from the photoshoot. I haven't seen this picture in so long, and it still knocks the breath out of me when I remember how close we were when I hated being close to another person.

But now, this picture is being used to criticize our relationship and expose us. I keep scrolling down until I reach the article.

*Glitz and Glamour are what we associate with celebrity couples, but the seemingly genuine love story that captured the hearts of millions is, apparently, not at all as it seems.*

*Madeline Davis and Lucas Silva, one of the recent celebrity couples who were adored by the public, now find themselves in deep water when their seemingly picture-perfect romance was nothing but a lie.*

*For months, their relationship has been the subject of headlines, from swoon-worthy photoshoots to posts that screamed true love. The couple were thought to be genuine after a photo came out of Lucas Silvia holding Madeline Davis lovingly in his arms, but it seems like not all that glitters is gold.*

*Anonymous sources have recently come forward, claiming that Madeline and Lucas's relationship was, in fact, just another PR stunt orchestrated to distract from Lucas's previous bad press.*

*The exposé came to light when an anonymous insider, privy to a heated dispute between the couple, unveiled the truth about their sham relationship. The source guarded their knowledge until concrete evidence could validate their claims, prompting us to share this revelation.*

My eyes well up when I stop reading, and I shake my head.

How?

How do they know?

I rack my brain, trying to think back to when Lucas and I were arguing. I was so careful not to speak about our arrangement in front of anyone, always making sure to smile, even back then, when I wasn't the biggest fan of Lucas or this arrangement.

But now everyone knows.

They all know it wasn't real.

# 34

Secret's out

*Lucas*

"Fuck." James throws his hands up, clutching the controller. "How did you do that?"

I smirk, lifting my eyebrow at him. "I've always been better than you."

James loves video games and has ever since we were kids, but I always beat him. Every time. Why would he think that would change just because he's been hanging out with Aiden?

I let out a scoff, turning to face Aiden. "I think he's going to need a few more lessons if he wants to beat me."

Aiden laughs, fixing the cap on his head as he looks at James. "I don't think a hundred lessons would help you, buddy."

James shakes his head, eyeing me. "Again," he says. "I need to win."

Fuck. I let out a sigh. "James." His name comes out like a plea. I need to go see my girl. The withdrawals are real. I fucking miss her so much, and I slept in her bed last night. We didn't even do anything, and it was the best night of my life. We just cuddled, drifting off into sleep together.

After she opened up to me about her asshole of an ex, she's been more open with me, she's letting me in, and it's the best thing ever. And now, I want to see her. I want to kiss her and touch her and look into those big brown eyes that I love so much.

"This is your fault," I say to Aiden when James starts a new game.

He shrugs. "Hey, you can't fault me for trying to start some healthy competition."

Grayson lets out a scoff. "There's nothing healthy about it. You're competitive as fuck. You just love to watch others suffer."

Aiden laughs. "They both suck. I thought it would be fun to see them play."

"Hey." I narrow my eyes at him.

He smirks, shaking his head. "Don't worry. Grayson sucks too."

His best friend punches him in the arm, and Aiden fakes a wince, rubbing his arm. "Asshole," Grayson whispers.

I let out a laugh. I'm going to have fun hanging out with these guys when I attend Redfield next semester. Speaking of... I pull my phone out, smiling at the string of texts between me and Madeline. I can't wait to tell her I got accepted.

Lucas:

I'm so sorry, princesa. Five more minutes and I'll be there.

"Is that Madi?"

I lift my head, seeing Aiden grin. I narrow my eyes. "I know your girls told you about the contract." Which is why this whole, 'let's hang out since you're dating one of our friends' is a little weird.

Grayson shrugs. "I don't know shit."

I let out a scoff, knowing that's bullshit. "Madeline told me she told the girls about Ana hiring Madeline to be my fake girlfriend, which means they obviously told you."

Grayson turns his eyes to me. "Yeah, we know."

Aiden nudges Grayson. "We were trying not to say anything. The NDA and all," he replies

"Yeah, but it isn't fake anymore, so you don't have to lie," James tells them.

Shit. My eyes widen when the guys sit up, eyebrows knitted.

"Wait, what?" Aiden asks. "Leila didn't tell me that."

"Neither did Rosie." Grayson shakes his head, looking at Aiden. "Our girls are keeping secrets from us. This is not good."

Well, I guess now's as good a time as any. "They don't know," I tell them. "Madeline hasn't told them."

"Wait. They didn't know?" James asks, wincing. "Fuck, sorry, man."

I shake my head. "It's fine."

"You're keeping it a secret?" Aiden asks. "Let me fucking tell you, it's going to be hard as shit being around your girl without kissing her." He groans, shaking his head. "It was pure agony when I had to stay away from Leila."

Grayson laughs. "What the fuck are you talking about? You and Leila were so obvious."

"We were?" Aiden asks, brows furrowing.

"Yes," Grayson says, laughing. "Me and Rosie talked about it all the time," he says.

"You did?"

Grayson scoffs. "Dude, whenever you guys were in a room together, you'd eye fuck her like she was already naked."

Aiden grins, clasping his hands behind his head, and stretches his legs onto the coffee table in front of him. "Yeah," he muses, staring off, no doubt picturing his girlfriend naked. He shakes his head after a few seconds, blinking. "What were we talking about again?"

"Idiot," Grayson murmurs with a smirk on his lips.

I love knowing Leila is being treated well. She's been an important part of my life for so long, ever since we worked together, and she helped my sister whenever I asked. It's amazing seeing someone love her like she deserves.

I rub my jaw. "You guys don't talk about me and Mads, right?"

Grayson and Aiden glance at each other, speaking some kind of silent language, telling me everything I need to know.

"What the fuck?"

"Hey," Aiden says, holding his hands up. "My girl thinks you guys are destined for each other, and you'd end up dating for real. I thought she was insane, seeing as you guys hated each other, but then you had to go and prove me wrong." He shakes his head. "I owe her a foot rub now."

"A foot rub?" Grayson asks.

Aiden nods, a grin on his lips. "She loves my hands. What can I say?"

Grayson shakes his head, glancing at me. "Why don't the girls know?" he asks me. "Because I'm sure as shit not going to keep this a secret from Rosie."

I sigh, hoping Madeline doesn't hate me for outing our not-so-fake relationship. "She made some sort of bet with Gabi."

"Oh fuck," Aiden says, his eyes widening. "I remember that. Whoever ended up dating first had to do a forfeit." His eyes narrow. "Madi's going to have red hair?" he asks.

I smile. "She's going to look so hot."

My phone buzzes in my lap, and I grin, knowing it's probably her.

"Speaking of…" I trail off, grinning like an idiot. I'm dying to see her, to talk to her, to kiss her. Aiden was right. This is fucking agony because all I want to do is show her off to the world.

But when I glance down at the screen, it's not Madeline.

Ana's text makes my heart race out of my chest when I click on the link she sent and see the title of the article attached.

What the hell?

I scroll down, scanning the article, my heart racing uncontrollably the more I read.

What. The. Fuck.

They know.

They know it's fake.

"Fuck," I curse, squeezing my phone in my hand.

"What's wrong?" James asks a hint of humor in his voice. "Madi dumped you yet?"

"They know."

"Know what?" he asks, his focus on the game in front of him.

"They know," I repeat, glancing up at him. His head snaps to face me, and his face drops at my expression. "They know everything."

"Fuck," James says, his eyes rounding. "How?"

I shake my head. *I don't fucking know.* "An anonymous source," I explain, my brain turning to fucking mush, trying to comprehend what is happening. Who the hell could it be? "Apparently, they've known for a while. They heard me and

Madeline talk about the contract when it was still fake between us."

"Shit man, I'm so sorry," Aiden says, his face dropping.

"What about the NDA?" Grayson asks.

Fuck. I completely forgot about that.

"I need to go." I lift myself off the couch, ringing Ana as soon as I'm out of the door.

She picks up immediately. "Are you kidding me?" she yells into the phone. "After everything we did to save your career, you manage to throw it all away?"

My jaw flexes, every muscle in my body tightening. "Did you read the article?" I ask her. "It wasn't fucking us. An anonymous source has proof."

"What proof?" she asks. "How would anyone know? Did you tell anyone?"

I squeeze my eyes closed, thinking of Madi. She was so nervous about that goddamn NDA, I can't put her in this position.

"I told my family," I tell her. "But that's it. No one else."

"Unbelievable," Ana scoffs. "Did the contract mean nothing to you?" she asks.

"It did," I assure her. "But it wasn't them. They would never do this."

"Well, someone did," she replies. "And now everything we've worked so hard for has all been for nothing."

I shake my head, just wanting to come out and say it. "We're dating," I blurt out. "Me and Madeline are dating. Isn't that enough to discredit the source?" I ask her.

She lets out a laugh, strained and bitter. "Maybe if you had told me this before, we could have gotten ahead of it, but they heard you, Lucas. They heard a fight between you." She lets out a harsh sigh. "I should have known this would happen."

"I don't understand." I shake my head. "When would they have heard us? We didn't—" I trail off when realization hits. "The party."

"Party?" she asks. "What party?"

Fuck. Of course. How did I not think of that before? "We… we were arguing before we got together, and we were in public, so I took Madeline to a quieter place." I rub my jaw. "We talked about the contract," I admit, knowing this is going to kick me in the fucking ass. "Someone must have heard."

"God damn it, Lucas."

"Listen," I start, my hand clutching the phone in my fist. "We happened to be arguing and someone followed us, alright? I didn't see who it was, but they must have heard everything, and they have proof. I don't know what of, but it was enough that the media would post about it."

A heavy sigh comes from the other side. "This is a nightmare," she mumbles. "Your career will be done after this," she says, her voice hardened. "Your credibility is in shambles, Lucas. There's no way another company will want to associate with you after this."

I don't give a fuck about that anymore.

I haven't cared about modeling for a long time, and to be honest, I don't think I ever did.

As long as my family and my girl are taken care of, I don't care what happens to my career.

I hang up the call and shove my phone in my pocket.

I need to find Madeline. They're going to be ruthless, and she's the most important thing right now. I need to protect her, even if it's the last thing I do.

# 35

Question number

twenty-one

## *Madeline*

"How much did you get paid?"

"What was it like dating a celebrity?"

"Did you sleep with him?"

The questions just keep coming at me, one after another, and I can't seem to dodge them fast enough. I'm surrounded by a bunch of people, all eager for answers that I don't have.

I knew I should have stayed home today. Gabi warned me not to leave, but after I got the worst email of my life, there was no way I could just stay at home wallowing.

Just a few days ago, I was so happy. My parents, who I only talked to every few weeks, went from calling me every few days. I was so excited about the audition I had been waiting my entire life to get. I had a great day with my amazing friends, and I was about to meet up with my boyfriends.

Life was going so well, but I should have known it was too good to be true.

Because it all came tumbling down in a matter of hours.

After mine and Lucas' prior fake relationship was publicly exposed, I've been made out to be a fame whore, sleeping with Lucas for money and fame when that's the furthest thing from the truth.

My parents were distraught over the fact that I lied to them once again after trying to build the trust between us and my promising I'd tell them the truth.

The happiness I'd been feeling suddenly vanished when I saw the hurt in my parents' eyes. I let them down by breaking the promise I made to be truthful after we've been working so hard to rebuild our trust.

And on top of everything, I lost the audition

*We regret to inform you that you were not selected for the role in our production. In light of recent negative press surrounding your public image, we believe it's best for the project's image to explore other options.*

Another rejection.

A single paragraph.

After years and years of auditions that led nowhere, I finally thought I had a shot, and now it's out of my reach, and I have to start over once again.

"Is it true you hate each other?" Another question that makes my heart drop into the pit of my stomach.

"Okay, that's enough." I lift my head, seeing Connor push through the crowd as he heads toward me. His hand wraps around my wrist, and I suck in a breath when he pulls me away from the crowd. I forgot how it feels to have someone other than Lucas touch me. He drops his hand, and I rub at the skin, an unsettling feeling washing over me.

He shoots me a smile when we're away from everyone else, and it does absolutely nothing for me. It wasn't long ago that the mere idea of going out with him had me nervous, stumbling over my words. I had made a promise to myself not to get involved with another guy again, and I had kept it.

Until Lucas. That promise was crumbling piece by piece the minute the elevator doors shut. I just didn't know at the time that it would lead to all of this. He was everything I never knew I wanted, and I fell head-first in love with him when I was trying my hardest not to. But I didn't want to fight it. I just wanted him.

"Are you okay?" Connor asks, his eyes softening.

I haven't talked to Connor in a long time. He's been keeping his distance ever since Lucas claimed me as his at the frat party, and honestly, even back then, I was already losing interest in Connor. It was always Lucas. It still is.

"I'm okay," I assure him, returning his smile. "Thank you."

"People can be dicks," he says, brushing his hair back. My eyes follow the movement, and it reminds me of when Lucas does it whenever he's nervous. A pang of guilt hits my stomach, making me look to the side.

I've been avoiding him.

After I opened the article, I left and went home. Gabi knew something was wrong, but I didn't tell her, I didn't tell anyone. I just shut myself in my room, avoiding every one of his texts, every call, every knock on the door when he came over last night.

I just needed time. Time to figure this all out. Time to process that my dreams have crashed and burned.

"I'm sorry about what's happening," he says, his eyes narrowing. "But now you don't have to lie anymore." My brows furrow, and I wonder if the only reason why he's here, talking to me, is because he also thinks that the relationship is fake and thinks he has a shot.

"Connor," I start, shaking my head. He's a nice guy, but he's not at all who I want. He doesn't make me feel safe or taken

311

care of. He doesn't make my heart race whenever he looks at me. He doesn't give me goosebumps when he touches me. He's not Lucas.

"Fuck." He drops his head, letting out a sigh. "You're about to turn me down, aren't you?"

I shoot him an apologetic smile. "I'm sorry."

He shakes his head, his brows knitting together. "I don't get it. If you're not with him, then what's stopping you?" I open my mouth to tell him the opposite, but he continues. "I know you liked me, or did I misread things?"

"No, you didn't," I admit with a sigh. "I did have a crush on you, but that was before Lucas entered my life. I'm with him now."

"Come on. You don't have to lie to me."

My frown deepens. "I'm not lying."

"Madi," he says, narrowing his eyes at me. "I know you guys were never together. Everyone knows it was all a PR stunt to help save his dying career; you don't need to defend him."

My pulse starts to race at his words, and my body grows hot. "I'm not defending him," I snap. "What you read was a lie. I'm dating Lucas."

"That's bullshit." He shakes his head. "I heard him."

"You…" I shake my head. Heard him? Heard him when? My eyes widen, staring back at him. He curses under his breath, wiping a hand down his face.

"I didn't want you to find out like this," he says, sighing.

"It was you?" I ask him, even though I already know the answer. He blows out a breath in response, and I let out a bitter laugh. "How?" I ask him. "How did you find out?"

"I had my suspicions," he admits. "When he showed up at your apartment, he called you Madeline like he didn't even know you." He shakes his head. "And those pet names? It was clear he was only doing that to piss you off."

I remember that day, his arm wrapped around my chair, his body an inch away from mine, all to make sure Connor knew I was taken.

"And then, at the party, I saw you with him again," he says, his jaw clenching. "He seemed pissed to see me around you, so I thought I got it wrong, that maybe you guys were actually dating." His eyes lift to mine, and he sighs. "But then I saw you guys arguing."

My mind floods back to when Lucas and I were in the closet, arguing, and he told me to leave. I was so worked up I didn't even think about the person I bumped into. But it was him. He had heard everything.

"You ran off, so I followed you, and I heard you two talk about the contract and how your relationship was fake," he confirms. "I didn't have enough proof though, so I uh…" His hand rubs the back of his neck. "I followed you around for a bit until I heard you talking to your friends." A heavy sigh leaves him. "And I recorded you."

I shake my head, taking a step back from him. "Why would you do that?" I ask him.

"I was trying to help you," he says, stepping closer to me. "It was obvious you didn't want to be with him, and I thought you were being forced to do it."

"I signed an NDA," I cut him off, stepping back from him even more. "If anyone ever found out, I'd have to pay. A lot. The only thing you did was invade my privacy and make me broke."

"Fuck." He blanches, shaking his head. "I didn't know. I thought—"

He reaches for me, but before he can touch me, I flinch, stepping away from him. "Don't touch me," I tell him. "I can't believe this." How did I not see him? How long was he following me around?

"Madi." He steps closer again, reaching for me.

"She told you not to touch her."

I freeze at the sound of Lucas' voice, and Connor does, too, glancing behind me. He slowly steps away from me, and I turn to face Lucas.

My heart races at the sight of him, but his eyes are locked on Connor, his jaw clenched, as he steps forward. "I knew you wanted her," he tells her. "Even way back then, I could always see your eyes on her, and I knew she liked you too." He shakes his head, stalking closer toward Connor. "But I didn't give a shit. I took her for myself because I wanted her too."

He towers over Connor, pushing him backward with two fingers. "I should have known you wouldn't have stopped. I thought I made it perfectly clear that she was mine, but you didn't care."

Connor blanches, stepping backwards. "I thought—"

"I know what you thought," Lucas interrupts. "You thought that the only thing between us was that contract. She was always mine, even with the contract, but now?" He shakes his head. "You might have gotten a huge chunk of change for exposing us, but you'll never get her." He points at me, his eyes still on Connor. "Because you're dead wrong if you think what I feel for that girl has anything to do with a stupid piece of paper."

"Listen, man. I didn't—"

"Get the fuck out of here," Lucas snaps. "You've done enough damage, and you better stay the fuck away from my girl. If I hear you've been following her or talking to her, I will snap your fucking legs." His eyes narrow, and he dips his head closer to Connor. "I don't give a fuck what happens to me or my career because of it because it would be so fucking worth it."

Connor's jaw clenches, and his eyes slide to mine before he turns around and leaves. Lucas lets out a breath and turns to face me, his eyes scanning my face.

"What are you doing here?" I ask him.

"I came to talk to my girlfriend face to face since she's been avoiding my texts." His tone is accusatory, and I press my lips together, staring up at him. I should have known he wouldn't have stopped until he talked to me. "What the hell are you thinking coming here?" he asks. "I told you to stay home."

His eyes narrow, knowing I read his texts, I just didn't answer them. I cross my arms, looking to my side. "I couldn't stay at home."

"Why not?" he asks, taking a step closer to me. "Afraid I'd come see you again?" I can feel his body heat and my lips part, letting out a breath from how close he is to me. "Question number twenty." My breath hitches as he narrows his eyes on me. "Why are you avoiding me, Madeline?"

"Don't."

"Answer the question," he demands.

I shake my head, squeezing my eyes closed. "You warned me," I remind him. "You told me I would have to deal with this, with hate comments and lies being spread about me, and I didn't listen." I drop my head, a strained laugh leaving my lips. "I guess what they're saying about me is true after all."

He grunts, lifting my chin to look up at him. "I told you not to read those damn comments. Don't you dare listen to them.

315

They don't know us, and they don't know everything that happened between us."

I shake my head, my eyes brimming with tears. I drop my head, backing away from him. "I should have never signed that stupid contract." I squeeze my eyes closed, a rush of the past twenty-four hours flooding my mind. "This was a mistake," I whisper.

I feel him flinch, and I instinctively look up at him to see a frown on his lips. The silence between us is deafening as he processes my words. "Tell me you don't mean that." When I don't reply, his eyebrows tug together. "A mistake?" he repeats, hurt spread across his face. Taking a step toward me, he shakes his head. "No. A mistake was me taking for granted how happy I was, thinking something wouldn't bite us in the ass. A mistake was me assuming your little crush would just back off and let you go. But *we* were never a mistake."

"Lucas—"

He clutches my face while he wipes away the tears spilling down my eyes. "Question number twenty-one," he whispers, staring down at me with anguish. "Do you love me?"

My eyes widen as I look up at him. "What?"

"Say it. Tell me you don't love me," he challenges, his eyes locked on mine. "You've been ignoring me, and even now, you're acting like everything that happened between us meant nothing to you. So if you want to be done with me, at least tell me that." A shaky breath leaves his lips, and his eyes narrow. "Say it, and I'll leave. Just tell me you don't love me."

I shake my head. "I…" My words get caught in my throat. How can he ask that of me? How does he think I don't love him when he's the only person I allow to touch me, to kiss me?

"Lie to me," he urges, rubbing his thumb over my cheek. "Break my heart, Madeline. Come on."

I shake my head, tears streaming down my face.

"You can't, can you?" he asks. I tilt my head up, staring into his eyes. "Because you love me," he finishes, his frown deepening. I let out a breath, not daring to reply. "Just like I love you."

My breath gets caught in my lungs at his words, and I force myself to let out a heavy breath. "I'm not weak," I tell him, my brows furrowing. I step back, and my hand lifts, wiping away the rogue tears. What is it about him that makes it so easy to let go? I never used to cry. I didn't need a guy to make me happy. I had no interest in one. Until him.

"You're so strong," he agrees, nodding.

My breaths come faster, heavier. "I don't need you. I don't need a guy. I can take care of myself."

"I know," he assures, nodding. I see the hurt in his eyes, but he continues. "And I don't ever want to hold you back, but I need *you*. So much." His hand curls at the nape of my neck, and he leans forward, dropping his forehead on mine. "I want to marry you someday," he blurts out, making my heart stop. "So you need to tell me why you've been avoiding me, so we can fix whatever the issue is because I'm not letting you go." He pulls back, and his eyes lock on mine. "Tell me what I did, and I'll get on my knees and beg for your forgiveness, but I'm not walking out of your life without a fight."

My heart beats a mile a minute, and I glance up at him. "What?" I ask breathlessly.

"You heard me," he says, the corner of his lips lifting slightly as his thumb rubs over my cheek. "I told you before, you're it for me. So, hell yes, I want to marry you." He leans down, pressing his lips to my forehead. "Just let me in, baby, please," he whispers.

I melt into him, closing my eyes as tears fall down my face. I shake my head against his lips. "I lost the part in the audition."

"Fuck," he curses, pulling back and grabbing my face in his hands. "Because of what they're saying about us?"

I nod, closing my eyes again when he pulls me into him. "I really thought this was my shot."

"I'm so sorry," he whispers. "I'm so fucking sorry, Mads."

"It's not your fault," I tell him. "It's mine. It's all because of me. Your career's ruined because of me."

"Fuck my career," he says, frowning. "That's the last thing I care about right now. You know how miserable I've been thinking you were done with me?"

"I could never be done with you."

"Then why were you avoiding me?" he asks. "Why did you say we were a mistake?"

"Because I ruined everything," I admit. "If it weren't for me running off on you at the party, then Connor would have never followed us. It's because of me that Connor was in our business in the first place."

He shakes his head, pulling me into him. "You ruined nothing, Madeline. That was all him and his selfish reasons." His eyes lock with mine, and he smiles. "So you're not done with me?"

I let out a laugh, my eyes blurry through the tears. "Not even close."

"Good," he says, smiling. "Because I meant what I said before," he says, his thumb tracing my bottom lip. "I love you, *princesa*. I'm madly, irrevocably in love with you."

I let out a sigh of relief, smiling up at him. "I love you too."

His eyes widen in surprise. "Sweetest words I've ever heard," he says with a grin. He grabs my face and pulls me into him, his lips pressing against mine. His lips move over mine as his hand curls behind my neck, moving my head to where he wants me.

His other hand grips my waist, holding me flush against him. His tongue swipes over my lips, and I open for him, letting out a breath of relief when his tongue slides against mine, and I relish the feeling of him in my arms.

"I need you," I hum against his lips, wanting closer.

He pulls back with a smile on his face and smooths his thumb over my bottom lip. "You have me," he says, his eyes locked on mine. "You'll always have me."

# 36

You are my life

*Lucas*

As soon as I open the front door to my apartment, my lips find hers again. Madeline moans into my mouth, and I swallow it down, relishing how needy she is for me. Pushing the door closed, I turn us around and grab her ass in my hands before I lift her into my arms. Her legs wrap around my waist, not daring to move her lips from mine.

This girl does something to me. I don't even know what it is. I don't even care as long as I can keep her. Keep this. Us. No one has even gotten close to what we have. Other girls have tried to make it clear they were interested in me, but I never gave them the time of day. I always told myself having a girlfriend wasn't worth it and that my family came first.

But this girl right here? She's part of my family now, and she's my top priority in everything.

"Jesus, Mads." I grab the back of her neck, tilting her head back to deepen the kiss. "You're like a drug." And I'm addicted, completely caught up on her and only her. That damn perfume that drives me crazy, her plump lips that I love, especially when they're painted red, her long nails that she uses to scratch all over my back. Her long, gorgeous legs wrapped around my body.

She moans into my mouth, and the noise travels straight to my cock. I lift my hips, grinding my hard erection against her heat. Her head lulls back, pulling away from my mouth, and I trail open-mouth kisses along her jaw and her neck. Fuck. Her scent makes me dizzy, and I flatten my tongue against the sensitive skin of her neck, licking her up. She's just so damn *sweet*. It's maddening.

I spin us around and kick the door open. Heading into my room, I drop her down on the bed, earning a gasp from her as she opens her eyes. I groan at the sight of her on my bed, looking up at me. I swear she has me wanting to get on my knees and worship her for hours, days, forever if she'll have me.

"Você é perfeita," I murmur, lifting her dress up her thighs. *You're perfect.* One day. I've been away from her for one fucking day, and I almost went out of my mind. I don't give a fuck if it's unhealthy for me to be this obsessed with her. Just let me be fucking addicted. I'll take whatever pain if it means I get to be with her.

She shivers, licking her lips. "I missed you."

I raise an eyebrow, smoothing my hand over the soft skin of her luscious thighs. I want her to suffocate me with these thighs while my tongue is deep in her pussy. "It was your fault you kept away," I tell her, my chest cramping when I see her frown.

I was fucking miserable, calling, texting, running around looking for her, until I realized that she just didn't want to see me.

I was losing my goddamn mind yesterday thinking she was done with me, that she figured out the risk of being with me wasn't worth it. I couldn't let her go, though, no matter what I had to do. If she wanted me to quit modeling, I'd do it. If she wanted me to announce publicly that I love her, I'd do it. Whatever it was that she wanted, I would do it because the thought of not having Madeline in my life was pure fucking agony.

I was fucking foolish to think we could just go our own separate ways after the contract was done. Madeline is so deeply ingrained in my soul that if she left, I'd die.

"Maybe I should punish you," I muse, lifting her dress even higher. "Maybe I should leave you on this bed, wet and aching, desperate to come, and leave you unsatisfied."

"No," she whispers, her breaths coming out shaky when I press my thumb to her sweet, swollen clit. The material of her black satin panties is completely fucking drenched, and a groan escapes me when I let my finger trace the outline of her pussy.

"No?" I repeat, teasing her so fucking slowly that she starts to tremble. "You think you deserve to feel good after you shut me out?" I swallow harshly, pulling the material of her panties to the side, groaning when I see her drenched for me.

"It was less than a day," she whimpers, grinding her hips.

"And it was too fucking long." I drop her panties back in place, running my hand over her thighs instead.

She groans, frustrated, and bucks her hips. "Please, Lucas."

I grin, gripping her thighs in my hand and spreading her open for me. "I told you before you'd never have to beg," I remind her. "But fuck, if it doesn't sound so pretty."

A hushed moan comes from her, and before I know it, her hand reaches out, and she pulls her panties to the side again, rubbing slow circles over her clit.

Holy fucking shit.

I watch, entranced, as she moans, pleasuring her sweet little pussy. "Does that feel good, baby?"

She nods, whimpering. "So good."

I hum, my cock twitching in my pants. "You're so impatient. You couldn't wait for me?"

She shakes her head. "You weren't giving me what I want."

I chuckle, watching her needy and so fucking beautiful touching herself on my bed. "And what is it you want?" I ask her. A moan escapes her when she shows me exactly what she wants by sliding a long digit inside her tight pussy. I let out a groan when she pulls her finger out, coated in her sweet juices, only to push it back in a second later. "You wish it were me touching you, don't you?" My hand tightens on her thighs, wanting to be the one to pleasure her, even though she looks like a dream fucking her finger.

She lets out a whimper, but instead of agreeing with me, she shakes her head. "I told you before, I don't need a man to make me feel good."

My eyes narrow, and I zone in on her fingers working over her pussy. I'm about to prove her so fucking wrong. I slap her hand away and lean down, flicking my tongue over her clit. She moans so loud that I have no doubt the neighbors heard her. Let them fucking hear. Let everyone know I'm the only one who makes her feel like this.

"You don't need me?" I ask her, licking up her sweet pussy. "Because it looks like the opposite."

She thrashes her head from side to side, bumping her hips to meet my mouth. Sweet moans escape her lips with every lash of my tongue. "Lucas. Fuck."

"Say it," I tell her, burying my tongue inside her. "Tell me I'm the only one that makes you feel this good."

"Lucas," she whines. "Make me come."

I pull back, tutting. My hands grab her thighs, spreading her even wider for me, staring down at her. Fuck, this is agony. "That's not what I asked." She groans, burying her head in her hands when I deny her pleasure. "Tell me what I want to hear," I repeat, pressing a kiss to her inner thigh, less than an inch away from where she wants me. "Tell me how good I make you feel." I plead. "Say you're mine."

"I'm yours," she breathes out when I kiss the edge of her pussy. "You make me feel so good." She shakes her head, her eyes squeezed closed. "I need you."

Fuck. Yes.

I dive in, wrapping my mouth around her clit, tugging until her moans get louder and louder, and I know she's right there. "That's my good girl," I grunt when she drops her head back and moans, her orgasm hitting her like a tidal wave. I slowly lick her up before pressing my lips against her thighs. I look up at her, grinning at the sight in front of me. "You're so fucking beautiful when you come, *princesa*."

Hovering above her, I take her lips in mine, kissing her hard, letting her taste how sweet she is. She opens up, dropping her legs to make room for me. I settle between her legs, running my cock over her dripping wet pussy. "Fuck." I groan at the feel of my cock rubbing against her wetness. Her moans, the feel of her, the sight of her. Jesus, it's too much. I'm so fucking close, and I'm not even inside of her yet.

"Stop playing around," she says, breathlessly. "Fuck me."

I let out a chuckle at her impatience and line up at her entrance, slowly pushing inside. We both moan the second I slide inside, and she grips my arm, her long nails scratching at my skin. Fuck. Her need for me is maddening. I push deeper inside until I bottom out, thrusting to the hilt. Her breathless whimpers do nothing to stop the mind-bending pleasure curling up my spine.

"Fuck Mads," I breathe out, sliding in and out of her. "I missed you. So fucking much." Having her arms around me, her lips on mine, and her body stretching to take me inside of her is the best feeling in the world. Hands down.

"Harder," she gasps, sliding her hands down to grip my ass, pushing me into her.

Shit. I need to get her there, I need to feel her come around me, feel her drench me, squeeze around me, but fuck, I'm way too close. I drop to my elbows, leaning down to capture her lips with mine as I thrust into her. Her lips part as she moans, and I capture it, swallowing every sound she makes.

I moan into her ear, picking up pace. "God, you feel so fucking good," I groan into her neck, burying my head into her neck. One of her hands lifts, gripping my arm as the other clutches onto my ass. "Tão gostosa," I murmur, against her lips. "Você foi feita para mim." *So hot. You were made for me.*

She lets out a whimper, and even though she doesn't understand what I told her, she moans all the same, wrapped up in pleasure. I feel her pussy squeezing around me the closer she gets. "Don't stop," she gasps, writhing her hips against my cock the faster I thrust. "Don't stop. Don't stop."

Even if a fire breaks out right now, I'm not stopping until I feel her come around my cock. "A perfect. Fucking. Fit." I thrust with every word until she tips her head back and moans, her pussy fluttering as she comes around me, flooding my cock with her orgasm.

"Fuck yes," I groan, going faster, feeling my balls tighten. She squeezes herself around me, and I let out a moan, shaking my head, trying to bring out all the stops to stop myself from coming. But when she does it again, I lose it, pulling back to grip her chin in my hand. "I'm going to come if you keep that up."

"Do it," she whispers, a hint of a smirk on her lips. "I want you to paint me with your cum."

I groan, thrusting in faster until I can't take it anymore, and pull out of her warm heat, my dick throbbing, begging for release. I straddle her waist, stroking my cock while I stare into those gorgeous eyes of hers, interest peaking in them. And when her tongue drifts out, running over her lips, I fucking blow, letting out a deep groan when cum drips out of my cock, covering my hand and her chest, sputtering all over her body. "Fuuuuck," I groan, gripping my cock even tighter, slowing my strokes as I release over her.

I let out a breath, grunting when I drop beside her on the bed. I instantly wrap my arms around her and pull her into me, settling her head against my chest. We're sweaty from the mind-blowing sex, and she's all sticky from my cum, but you couldn't pay me to leave this bed.

"You're so fucking perfect," I murmur, pressing my lips against her bare shoulder. "Why did it take me so long to see you were everything I ever wanted?"

She releases a breath, her arms tightening around my waist. "We got there in the end," she says. "And I wouldn't want to change it."

I shake my head, a smile playing on my lips. "Me either."

My phone rings somewhere in my room, and I groan, squeezing my eyes closed. "I should have put my phone on silent."

"It could be Ana," she says, making me grunt.

It probably is. Shaking my head, I pull her into me and bury my lips in her neck. "I don't care," I murmur. "I just want to stay here with you for a little longer." I press my lips against her jaw. "Maybe a week." Another kiss to her cheek this time. "A year." I pull the covers over us and settle on top of her. "Forever if I could." My lips brush against hers, and I lose myself in her, not caring about what happens as long as I have her.

Her breathless moans get me so fucking hard, even after she fucked the soul out of my body. "We might need food."

"Delivery," I mumble against her lips, grinning when the ringing stops.

She lets out a laugh, pushing against my shoulder. "As much as I'd love that, we'll have to deal with this at some point."

I drop onto the bed beside her with a sigh. She's right. I know she's right. I just don't want to. "I hate when you're logical."

She chuckles, turning on her side to face me. Her expression sobers, and I watch her slim throat move as she swallows. "What's going to happen?" she asks, her brows furrowing.

I shake my head, reaching out for her. "I don't know," I tell her honestly. "But whatever happens, I'll protect you. I'll take care of this." My fingers trail across her arm, feeling her body break out into shivers. "I uh… I told Ana about us."

"You did?" she asks, her eyes widening.

I nod. "And I told her that I broke the NDA."

She lifts herself up so fast I get whiplash. "What?" she yells. "Why the hell would you do that."

I lift onto my elbows, clutching her face in my hands. "Because she asked if we told anyone," I tell her with a shrug.

"And I wasn't going to let you pay for my mistakes. I told her I did."

Her eyes are swimming with panic. "Lucas, that's a lot of money."

*Trust me, I know.* "I'd do anything for you, Madeline. You know that."

"But…" she shakes her head. "That's excessive."

I sigh, dropping my forehead onto hers. "I take care of my family," I tell her, pulling back to look into her chocolate-brown eyes. "I take care of what's mine. So don't argue with me about this, and don't you dare worry about it because money means nothing to me, Madeline." I lick my lips. "You do."

Her eyes soften as they brim with tears. "Lucas."

"I love you, Mads." I smile, staring at my favorite person in the world. "I love you so much, and I will fix this for you. Ok? I'll make a public statement, letting everyone know that we weren't a lie. I'll personally go to Monica and beg her to reconsider because you're so fucking talented, and you shouldn't lose everything because you decided to help me."

I promised her this would be good for her too, and look what the fuck happened. "I'll make sure you get what you want," I assure her. "I just want you to be happy."

"I am happy," she says with a smile. "You make me happy."

"Good." I grin, brushing her curls behind her ear. "That's good because starting next semester, I'll be *very* close to you." Her brows furrow, and my heart beats a million miles a minute. "I got into Redfield," I clarify.

Her eyes widen and I let out a laugh at her eagerness. "What?" she asks, grinning from ear to ear. "You applied?"

I nod. "Weeks ago," I tell her. "I got the acceptance letter yesterday, and I was so fucking excited to tell you, but then everything else happened and…" I let out a sigh, thinking back to how excited I was to tell her.

"Oh my god, Lucas, that's amazing." Her arms wrap around my neck as she straddles me, looking down at me with a huge grin painted on her gorgeous face.

I smile, rubbing my thumb over her cheek. "It's because of you. If you hadn't pushed me…" I shake my head, knowing if I had never met her, none of this would happen. I was a fucking mess, miserable and losing myself in a job I had no passion for, and in a few months, I met the most amazing woman who flipped my whole world upside down or right side up, I should say.

"It was all you," she says, leaning down to press her lips to mine. "You're so talented, Lucas. You have so much to offer, and I can't wait to be a part of your life."

I'm going to build her a fucking house. I will get on my knees and build every room myself to show her how deeply in love with her I am. I smile against her lips, my dick perking up when her bare pussy rubs against it. She lets out a little moan, and I grip her hips, slowly moving her over me before I slide home. "You're it, baby. You are my life."

# *Madeline*

"Tell me you didn't."

As soon as we walk into her office, Ana shoots us a glare that could melt ice.

Lucas arches an eyebrow at her. "Good morning to you, too."

Her frown deepens. "Lucas," she says, void of any amusement, "tell me you're here to change your mind."

Lucas saunters over to the coffee cart, grabbing our drinks before he hands one over to me. "I'm not," he says, taking a sip of his coffee.

Ana lets out a sigh, closing her eyes. "You can't just quit."

"I'm not quitting," he deadpans. "I'm just not modeling anymore."

"So, you're quitting," she insists, with a shake of her head.

I quietly slide into the seat beside him, remembering the first time we were here. Back then, I scooted the chair so far away from him that a small car could have parked between us. But now, even with our hands interlinked, it still isn't close enough.

"I just want to do something better with my life," he explains with a nonchalant shrug. "I want to do something for me for a change, something I love."

She shakes her head in disbelief. "And you couldn't have done that while modeling?"

I sneak a glance at Lucas. It's the same question I threw at him when he told me he wanted to stop modeling. Leila's been juggling both college and being a plus-size model for years, so I thought he could do the same. But in her case, it's her passion. Lucas, however, has made it clear that he doesn't love it, even if he does have the body, face, and hands for it.

His eyes lock onto mine as he says, "I want to focus on more important things."

My heart knocks against my chest as his lips curl into a smile. If only I knew he'd be the love of my life all those months ago when we met.

Ana shakes her head, pressing her fingers to her forehead before shifting her gaze to me. "This is your fault, isn't it?"

A smirk plays on my lips as I lift a shoulder. "It might be."

"She pushed me to follow my dreams, sure," he admits. "But the idea to quit was mine, so don't go blaming any of this on her.

Ana shifts her gaze to me. "And what about you?" she asks. "Are you still interested in acting?"

I open my mouth to reply, but before I can get a word out, Lucas tightens his grip on my hand and leans in, fixing a narrowed gaze on his agent. "Speaking of," he says, "I might not need an agent anymore." His eyes lock on mine, and he shoots a playful smirk my way. "But she will."

My eyes widen in surprise, and I turn to Ana who's smiling. "What? No, that's not happening." I shake my head.

"Of course it is," Lucas says. "I want to make your dreams come true."

"Lucas." I shoot him a pointed glare, but he just flashes a grin.

"Madeline." He arches an eyebrow. "Let me take care of you the way I want to, okay?"

I let out a sigh, knowing he won't let this go.

"Alright then," Ana chimes in. "I guess we have a lot of work to do, considering you two have been holed up all week," she adds, making my cheeks burn. Lucas, on the other hand, smirks, completely unabashed by the insinuation.

"What about the leak?" I ask.

A few days after the news hit, the media exposed the recording Connor had warned me about. It was just a little snippet, but you can clearly hear me talking about a contract. While I never said Lucas' name or mentioned the fake relationship, people still caught on.

"Well, the post helped," Ana says, glancing at Lucas. A few days ago, Lucas shared a picture of us on his social media, with a story on how we met through mutual friends and quickly started dating. It wasn't a complete lie since we're both friends with Leila, but only the people closest to us know the real story. "But we still need to keep your relationship strong, prove that it isn't fake." She looks at our joined hands and chuckles. "Which won't be as big of a problem as it was when this started."

"So, Lucas will still have to go on dates, interviews, and stuff?" I ask, furrowing my brows. He quit to get away from this, and now, with me in the public eye, he won't be.

"If he wants to," she responds. "As always, you do what you're comfortable with."

I turn to Lucas, finding a smile on his face. "It's not even a question, Mads. I'll do it."

"Are you sure?" I ask Lucas, a frown tugging at my lips. "I know you want—"

"I want you to have what you want. I want you to be happy and successful. So yeah, I'll do whatever you need to help you reach your goals." His thumb glides over mine, and I let out a content sigh. "Besides, it's not like I can be completely out of the public anyway," he says with a smirk. "People will get bored of me eventually when they realize I'm not modeling anymore."

I shoot him a look. "There's nothing boring about you."

He smiles, his eyes softening. "I love you."

"This is…" Ana gestures between us, "Beautiful, really, but we should get back to business."

The tension in Lucas' shoulders is visible when he releases a heavy breath and tightens his hold on my hand "What about Connor?" he asks. "Can we do something about him?"

Luckily, Ana didn't make Lucas pay the fine for the NDA once she found out it was Connor who exposed us. But we still see Connor since he still attends Redfield. He keeps his distance and doesn't try to approach me anymore, which is good since I don't want anything to do with him. But Lucas doesn't like that. He wants him to pay for what he did.

Ana shakes her head. "Even if we were to sue him for defamation, the voice recording he posted would be enough to discredit that."

"Even if we're dating now?" I ask.

And nods. "Unfortunately so," she says. "What Connor posted was enough for everyone to believe it's true. We'll just have to continue to prove them the opposite."

Lucas curses under his breath, running a hand roughly through his hair. "So we just have to see him every day around campus?"

"Lucas, it's ok," I say, attempting to calm him. I know how much Connor affects him, and I know a big part of it is my previous crush on him. But whatever I saw in Connor was a blip compared to my feelings for Lucas.

"No, it's not, Mads," he says, shaking his head. His beautiful brown eyes lock on mine, and he swallows. "That asshole won't stop until he gets you, I know it."

I turn my chair slightly to look at him and tighten my hold on his hand. "He won't be a problem, Lucas," I promise him. "I love *you*, not him."

His shoulders drop as he lets out a breath of relief. "I love you, *princesa*," he says, leaning in to brush his lips against mine. "So much."

Ana clears her throat, and we pull away from each other, our attention pivoting toward her. "Ok. Great. Now that we've discussed that, I think it's time to talk about your audition."

I frown. "What about it?"

A smirk plays on her lips. "We got a call from Monica herself," she says, sending a jolt to my chest. "She personally apologized for the rejection and has made it clear that the job is yours if you want it."

"She did?" I ask in disbelief.

She nods, smiling. "She said she'd love to work with someone as talented and work-driven as you."

"Holy shit," Lucas says. "That's huge."

"Yeah," I murmur, glancing to my side. I've wanted this moment for so long, and now it's here. It's within my grasp. All I need to do is reach out and grab it.

"What do you say, Mads?" he asks. "Are you going to take it?"

His question echoes in my head, making my heart pound. It's everything I've ever wanted, and yet… "No."

He furrows his brows. "No?"

"I don't want it."

"What?" Ana says, her eyes widening. "This is the opportunity of a lifetime. It's what you've been working toward."

"I know," I agree, with a nod, before I look at Lucas. "But I can't accept this role when I'd always be wondering whether the only reason I did was because of you."

"Mads," he says, his brows knitting together. "That's not—"

"You had to call them," I remind him. "You had to personally reach out to even pique their interest in my audition tapes. And when the news broke…" I shake my head. "All I got was a brief paragraph letting me know they were going in another direction. And suddenly, when you've cleared it up, the job is miraculously back on the table?"

Lucas settles into a sigh, knowing I'm right. "Are you sure?" he asks. "She's one of your favorite directors."

"I'm sure. If they genuinely wanted me for my talent, then the news about our fake relationship wouldn't have swung their decision. I want to know I earned the part because of my skill, not because of favors or connections. I refuse to start my acting career with a handout."

Ana releases a sigh, her shoulders slumping. "You guys are making my life complicated." She shakes her head. "But if that's what you want, then I'll let her know."

A smile spreads across my face, relieved by my decision. "Thank you."

She nods. "We'll be in touch."

Lucas and I stand up and head out of Ana's office, and as soon as the door closes, Lucas gently turns me around, his hands cupping my face. "How are you feeling?" he asks, his touch bringing me comfort.

I let out a breath, savoring the warmth of his hands. "Good," I assure him.

"Yeah?" he asks, studying my expression. "That would have been a huge opportunity."

"I know," I agree. "It's why I agreed to this fake dating deal in the first place. But I don't want it looming over my head," I tell him. "Years to come, when I'm a famous actress, I want to know I got there because I genuinely deserved it."

Lucas grins, his thumb gently caressing my cheek. "I'm so proud of you, *princesa*," he says. "I can't wait to see you walk down the red carpet at your premiere."

I let myself envision it, and my chest swells with hope. "You really think it'll happen?"

He scoffs. "I know it will. I wasn't lying when I said you were talented, Mads, and I can't wait for the world to see it."

His eyes burn into mine, and I smile up at him, taking a sip of my coffee before I end up crying in this hallway. A groan escapes me when the coffee hits my tongue, and I shake my head. "She deserves an award for being able to make my coffee just the way I like it." Lucas's cheeks turn pink, and I blink. "What?" I ask, curious about his expression.

He lets out a sigh. "Do you remember that first meeting we had with Ana?" I nod. "I brought two coffees that day, and I noticed you eyeing it, probably thinking one was for you. I felt like shit for not bringing you one, so before the photoshoot, I asked Leila what you liked to drink, so I could bring you a coffee."

"You did?" I ask him.

He nods, letting out a chuckle. "You hated me back then, and I just wanted to make you happy."

I shake my head, shocked by his confession. I misunderstood him for so long, thinking he couldn't stand being around me, completely oblivious to the subtle gestures he did for me. "Wow," I breathe out, a playful smirk on my lips. "So you're telling me you had a crush on me even back then?"

His eyes narrow. "That's not at all what I said."

I tut, shaking my head. "That's what I heard," I tease.

A laugh escapes him. "Fine," he says, his smile warming my body. "You win."

"I win?" I ask.

"Yeah, baby." His hand curls at the back of my neck, and he leans down until his lips hover just an inch away from mine. "You win. I liked you, I wanted you, and I wanted to kiss you so badly. Even back then, even with your rules firmly in place, even when you hated me."

My lips part, and I stare up into his eyes, my tongue darting out to lick my bottom lip. "You can kiss me now," I whisper, not caring that anyone could walk by at any minute. I need his lips on mine. I need him.

His smirk causes a jolt of lust to flash through me. "You want my lips on yours?" he asks. I nod, tilting on my tip-toes and leaning a little closer to him. He hums, brushing his thumb over my parted lips. "How much?" he asks.

"Lucas," I whine, impatient for him.

His chuckle burns deep in my stomach. "I love how needy you get for me," he says, leaning down to finally brush his lips against mine. Once, twice, so softly that my eyes flutter closed every time. "I love you."

Our lips brush together again, but this time, it's deeper, harder, everything I need. My arms wrap around his neck, and I deepen the kiss, letting myself get lost in him, just feel, taste, consume him. "I love you too," I whisper against his lips.

He smiles, pressing one more kiss to my lips before he pulls back. "Good," he says, staring into my eyes with a mischievous grin. "Because there's still something you need to do."

# 38

Cherry bombshell

## Madeline

I shouldn't be nervous.

Our friends already know we're together since Lucas told the guys, I know the girls know, too. It shouldn't be a big deal, but my body shakes all the same.

Twisting the doorknob, I push the door open and walk inside, catching the soft murmur of voices coming from the living room. Lucas gives my hand a warm squeeze, and I can't help but glance at him. His smile calms the nerves inside of me, knowing I don't have to do this alone. I don't have to do anything alone ever again.

"Are you ready?" he asks a glint of excitement in his eyes.

A heavy breath escapes me when I nod. "Yes," I assure him, a mix of nerves and anticipation bubbling in the pit of my stomach. "How do you think they're going to react?"

His lips curl into a grin as he leans in and presses them to my forehead. "Only one way to find out," he says. He gives my hand another reassuring squeeze.

"Oh hey, we were just— Oh my god." I turn around to see Rosalie's eyes so wide they almost pop out of her head. Her hand is pressed against her mouth as she takes me in. "You actually did it."

I grin, flicking my burgundy red hair behind my ear. "Do you like it?"

She takes a step closer, examining the color. "So much I'm considering dying mine."

I let out a laugh, thanking my trusted hairdresser for doing a good job. I definitely wasn't going to use the cheap hair-dye Gabi had stored. If I'm going to go all the way, then I'm going to do it right.

"Don't you dare," I tell her. "Blonde is your color."

She smiles and then shakes her head. "Gabi's going to flip out."

*I know.*

She pushes the door open, walking inside, and Lucas and I follow her in, feeling a little at ease now that someone other than Lucas has seen me.

"Give it back." The door opens wider, and I see Gabi standing over Grayson, who has a controller in his hand, holding it away from Gabi.

"Take it back," he says, his eyes narrowed.

"That you suck?" she says with a grin. "Never."

He shakes his head, moving the controller out of the way when she reaches for it again. "Then you're not getting it."

"I feel like this is my fault," Aiden says, laughing at the sight.

Grayson glares at him. "It is."

She lunges for him, grabbing the controller from his hands, before she wraps her arm around his head, but when she turns her head, she freezes, her eyes widening, locked on me. "Holy shit."

"Get the fuck off me," Grayson wheezes, tapping Gabi's hand, who has him in a chokehold.

340

She releases him, slowly walking toward me. "Holy shit."

I let out a laugh, feeling everyone's eyes on me. "You've said that."

"Fuck, she's strong," Grayson murmurs. "What the fuck does she eat?"

"It's Gabi," Aiden says dryly. "Did you really think she couldn't handle herself?"

"Plus, she's a dancer," Leila points out. "They're strong as hell."

Gabi doesn't even listen to them. She shakes her head, unable to believe her eyes, as she stalks over to me. "You dyed your hair red?"

I glance at Lucas, a grin on my lips. "A bet's a bet," I tell her, lifting my shoulder in a shrug. "I lost, so I paid up."

"Well, I wouldn't say you lost," Lucas says beside me.

I turn to look at him, a smile on my lips. "No," I agree. "I guess I won, after all."

"Ugh," Gabi groans, tipping her head back. "I knew it. I'm going to be alone forever."

"You won't," Aiden says adamantly.

She turns to face him, a frown on her lips. "How do you know that?"

He narrows his eyes at her. "Gabi."

What the hell? My brows furrow as I take in their interaction.

She shakes her head, letting out a sigh. "I need a drink." She whips her head around, pressing her lips together in a smile, looking at me. "I'm happy for you," she says. "I really am. You need to know that."

"I know," I assure her. If it wasn't for Gabi, I know I wouldn't have taken that step with Lucas. I had been telling myself I didn't need a guy in my life for so long that I was purposely keeping him at a distance, even when I knew I had feelings for him. Gabi made me realize that it was ok to fall for someone–that my ex didn't set the standard for every other guy who came after him.

"Good." She shoots me a smile, but it drops when she narrows her gaze on Lucas. "She's my best friend," she says.

"I know," he replies.

"And I can fight."

His chin dips in a slow nod, a hint of a smirk on his lips. "I can tell."

"Which means if you hurt her…"

"You'll hurt me?" he guesses.

She lifts her chin. "Smart guy." She walks past us, heading out of the living room.

I turn to Aiden, my brows furrowed in confusion. "What was all that about?" I ask him. "You know something I don't?"

His lips twitch. "I might."

"How?"

He shrugs. "We're friends," he says. I try not to think too much about it, but… She told Aiden and not me? He must see the expression on my face because he's quick to add, "She just needed to vent. You were busy with class and the public appearances with Lucas, and she just didn't want to bother you." He shoots me a sympathetic smile. "I'm sure she'll tell you when she's ready."

I nod, thinking back to when she crashed on my bed, rambling on about something. I should have asked her, and I should have let her know I'd always have time for her. I glance at Leila, who sat next to Aiden, his arm around her. "Do you know too?"

She laughs. "Are you kidding?" She gestures to her boyfriend with her thumb. "This one can't keep a secret to save his life."

He grins, leaning closer to her. "Not from you, I can't."

Leila shakes her head, smirking. "He's so obsessed with me. It's embarrassing." Her nose scrunches, but I see the hint of a smile on her lips.

His arms wrap around her waist, pulling her into his lap. "Fuck yeah, I am," he whispers against her lips. "And don't lie to your friends, gorgeous. We both know you're just as obsessed with me."

Leila furrows her brows. "I'm not."

"No?" Aiden asks with a smirk. "That's not what it sounded like last night." He grins before tipping his head back. "Aiden," he fake moans. "Aiden. Aiden."

"Shut up." Leila slaps his chest, and he laughs.

"Admit it," he says. "You looooove me."

Leila lets out a breath, crossing her arms. "I hate you right now."

Aiden groans, shaking his head with a smile. "Fuck, that makes me so hard."

"Meow." I turn my head, seeing Leila and Aiden's black and white cat jumping on Leila's lap.

"Shit," Aiden says, groaning into Leila's neck. "Can't say that in front of the kid."

Leila laughs. "He's a cat. Not a baby," she says, petting Tiger, who purrs.

He lifts his shoulder in a shrug, smirking down at her. "It's good practice for *our* kid."

Leila's lips part, and she keeps her eyes locked on his, breathing hard. A smile creeps onto my face. I love seeing those two so in love. They both deserve it.

"Hey bitches, we're ba— Oh shit." James winces when Lucas turns his head, his eyes widening at him. James hanging out here isn't weird. What is weird is that he's not alone. There's a tall, blonde guy standing next to him, and they're holding hands.

"James?" Lucas asks, looking at the guy whose face is as red as a tomato.

"Hey, bro," James replies with a grin.

"Don't you bro me." Lucas shakes his head. "What the hell?"

"Oh yeah." James laughs, gesturing to the guy who still hasn't spoken. "So, this is my boyfriend. Carter."

"Your what?" Lucas asks, confused.

James shrugs. "It's new?"

"How new?"

James shrugs again, brushing his hair back. "A few weeks?"

"What?" Lucas furrows his brows, shaking his head. "How did I not know about this?" He turns, looking at Aiden and Grayson, who don't seem surprised at all. "Did you guys know about this?" he asks them.

"Yeah," Grayson says with a shrug.

"And no one decided to tell me?"

"They were just hooking up," Aiden says. "It wasn't any of my business to tell you. Besides, Carter only just came out recently. I didn't want to out him." Aiden reaches up, fixing the cap on his head. "You don't need to worry. Carter's a great guy."

A sigh comes from behind us. "It's not awkward at all hearing people talk about you," Carter says.

Lucas turns back to face Aiden and narrows his eyes. "You vouch for him?" he asks. I know how much he loves James. He's his brother at the end of the day, blood or not, and he won't stand for someone hurting him.

Aiden nods, his face serious. "One hundred percent," he says with full conviction.

Lucas nods, turning around to face Carter, holding his hand out. Carter grasps his hand in his and shakes it. Lucas leans into him, tilting his head. "You better be good to him."

"Of course," Carter replies.

The door opens, and in walks Gabi. She stops dead in her tracks, her eyes landing on James and Carter. "Oh goodie," she says, cracking open a can of beer, her tone filled with sarcasm. "More people in love." She takes a gulp of her drink, downing it down. "Yay."

"You want to play against me?" Aiden asks, holding out a controller to her.

"As long as that cat doesn't come near me," she says, narrowing her eyes at Tiger. "I swear he hates me."

"He can sense that you're a dog person," Leila jokes.

"I'll give you a real challenge as opposed to Grayson," Aiden says with a teasing grin.

Grayson narrows his eyes, raising two hands to flip him off before he turns back to Rosie, who's laughing. "You think that's funny?" he asks her.

She raises a shoulder. "A little," she teases.

Grayson's head shakes as he breathes out a laugh, pulling her into him. "Oh, you like to tease, huh?" he asks. "Well, so do I." His hand skates around her thighs as he lifts her onto his lap to straddle him.

She gasps when he lifts himself off the couch, Rosie's legs wrapped around his waist. "Grayson." Her arms fling around his neck to support herself.

"Don't wait up for us," he tells us, slamming the living room door closed behind him.

The silence in the room brews until Aiden lets out a laugh. "Try living with them," he says.

"Is anyone else turned on?" James asks.

Gabi snorts a laugh, lifting her hand to high-five him. "Hell yeah." She grabs the controller and leans forward.

"Is this what you guys do all day?" Lucas asks, pulling me onto his lap when he sits on an armchair. "Play video games?" He snorts. "Useful college degrees, I see."

Aiden shakes his head, starting up a new game with Gabi. "You have to have fun sometimes. It's not all about work." He grins, turning to face Lucas. "Which I guess you'll see since you'll be joining us soon."

"You're coming to Redfield?" Carter asks.

Lucas nods, his arm tightening around my waist. "Yeah, I applied a few weeks back."

"What about you?" Carter asks James, his brows raised.

He shakes his head. "Nah, I can't afford this place." Lucas leans forward on his chair, but James' head snaps to him, holding out a hand. "And before you say anything, don't," he warns him. "I'm good at Liberty," James assures him with a nod. Lucas leans back, breathing out a sigh. "Besides, I'll come visit. I am dating someone from Redfield, after all." James laughs, shaking his head. "God, someone kill me."

Lucas laughs, but Carter narrows his eyes at his boyfriend. "Excuse me?"

"Nothing, babe." He leans in, kissing him. "I was just kidding."

I turn to see Lucas' eyes on James, a smile on his lips. "Is it weird?" I ask him.

He shrugs. "A little," he admits. "He's always been the hook-up kind, even after the accident." He shakes his head, lost in thought. "But I'm glad to see him settle down with somebody. He deserves to be happy." Lucas turns his gaze on me, reaching up to caress my face. "He deserves to feel what I feel whenever I'm with you."

My stomach warms, and my heart beats, but I let out a laugh. "That was so cheesy," I tell him, secretly loving it. "But I guess I'll allow it."

"Good," he says, wrapping his hand around the back of my neck. "Because now that you're mine… I should warn you I'm going to be so fucking cheesy, romantic, clingy, you name it."

"Yeah?" I think I kind of like that.

He nods. "Kissing you," he whispers, pressing his lips to my cheek. "Touching you." His hand traces a lazy path down my arm, causing my body to break out into goosebumps like it always does when I'm with him. His lips tilt up, brushing against the shell of my ear. "Whispering dirty things in your ear." A low moan escapes me, and he chuckles. "You like that?"

I open my mouth to respond, but I'm shocked by Gabi clearing her throat, making me snap up. "A little reminder that you're still in public," she says, amusement written all over her face. "Before you two fuck on that chair."

"Yeah, there's a kid in the room," Aiden says, gesturing to Tiger who's asleep on Leila's lap.

My body heats with embarrassment, and I turn to Lucas, my brows knitted together. "This is your fault."

"I'm sorry," he says, rubbing his hand up and down my back, a subtle laugh rumbling through his chest. "I'll make it up to you when we get home."

I lift my head, seeing the lust in his eyes. "Yeah?" I smirk, running my hands through his hair. "How?"

He groans, his eyes darkening. "Do you want me to get hard in a room full of your friends?"

There's a warning in his tone, but I shuffle on his lap, reminiscing the last time we were like this. "It might be fun."

His laugh radiates through me as he grips my hips, halting my movements. "You're a dirty girl." He raises an eyebrow. "What the hell have I turned you into, *princesa*?"

I stare into his eyes when I say, "Someone in love."

# EPILOGUE

*Lucas*

My girlfriend is a badass.

For years, I have felt at a loss while modeling, knowing I didn't love it. I spent my life making sure everyone around me was taken care of and that they were happy, only to realize I wasn't happy. Not even close.

It wasn't until this girl showed up in my life and made me realize I wasn't making myself a priority in my own life. She made me see that I was keeping my passion, my happiness, buried down nowhere to be found.

My lips tip up in a grin when I see the revolving doors spin, my girl walking through them with a huge smile on her face. I've never seen this girl run, she's not the running type, but Madeline is fucking racing toward me, her heels clanking on the ground with every step. Running in heels. That's some talent right there.

She lunges herself into my arms, and I catch her, lifting her off the ground as she throws her legs around my waist. "Holy shit, it went that good?" I ask her.

She tips her head back and lets out a cute little laugh, shaking her head. "It went amazing," she says. "I think this might be it."

She's been working so hard recently. Not only has she been studying hard as hell for her exams coming up, she's been going to multiple auditions a week, and she's even started attending some acting classes. I love how devoted she is and how passionate she is about acting. I really want this to work out for her. I want to see her achieve her dreams because she deserves it more than anyone I know.

"I'm so fucking proud of you," I murmur against her lips, desperate for a taste of her. I'm always desperate when it comes to her. Every kiss, every taste, every word from her lips has me hooked.

She lets out a shaky breath when I pull back and press my forehead against hers. "This time was different," she says. "I could feel it. They smiled, they laughed. They loved me."

"Who doesn't?" I ask, grasping her face in my hands. "It's impossible not to love you." I shake my head, staring into those eyes that tug at my heart. "I never stood a chance."

She rolls her eyes, a hint of a smirk on her cherry-red lips that drives me crazy. "That's because you're getting in my pants."

I scoff, dropping her back down to her feet. My hand snakes around her waist as I pull her into me, loving the soft gasp that comes out of her lips as she places her hand on my chest. "You know damn well I fell for you way before that."

Her eyes soften, and her lips part, no doubt thinking back to so many instances where we were at the verge of ripping apart every single one of those rules she had in place.

"Even before then," I admit. "Even back in that damn elevator, you were always mine." I breathe hard, thinking back to how we met. "If it hadn't been that, then it would have been something else that brought us together." I lift my hand to clutch her face, bringing her an inch away from me. "You were always destined to be mine."

Her eyes widen as she looks at me, and I swear I'm so fucking close to getting on one knee right here, right now. Fuck, she drives me crazy. I can't wait to spend the rest of my life with her. "You believe that?" she asks.

"With my whole heart." And every organ in my body. She was always meant to be my girl. "Minha princesa," I whisper against her lips. *My princess.*

She presses her lips to mine before she smiles, looking up at me. "Te amo." *I love you.*

My eyes widen, and my heart stops in my chest. Did I really just hear the love of my life tell me she loves me in my language? "Say that again," I plead gruffly. "Please."

She wraps her arms around my neck as she lifts herself onto her tip-toes. "Eu te amo," she repeats, making my chest pound.

"Fuck. Eu te amo tanto." *I love you so much.* I lean forward, capturing her lips with mine in a hot kiss. Her lips part as she lets me inside, and I taste her sweetness, completely fucking addicted to her.

The sound of a phone buzzing makes Madi groan into my mouth, attempting to pull away, but I hold on to her face, never wanting her away from me. "A little longer," I plead, brushing my lips against hers. "Please."

She chuckles against my lips. "It's probably my mom wondering how the audition went," she says between kisses. "I need to answer her."

"Fine," I sigh, pulling away from her. Madeline's been working on her relationship with her parents, and they've become so much more supportive of her acting career. I don't want to do anything to jeopardize that.

Madi has a smile on her lips as she types out a text. I love seeing how happy she gets whenever she talks to her parents. I remember how she felt like they didn't care about her after Nia died, and that couldn't be the furthest thing from the truth. I saw it with my own two eyes when they came to visit, how much they adore her.

I also had a not-so-fun conversation with Madeline's dad, particularly about how our relationship started off as publicity. I had to explain that it's the furthest thing from the truth now and that I'm deeply in love with his daughter. I think Mr. Davis is still skeptical, but I'll work on it. I'll spend every day proving how much I love Madeline if need be. After all, I am going to be his son-in-law one day.

I lean in to press my lips against Madeline's cheek, physically unable to be apart from her and look down at the screen, seeing how proud her mother is of her. That makes two of us.

"You want to celebrate with ice cream?" I ask her, pressing my lips to her jaw.

She sighs, pocketing her phone before turning to face me. "Just because it went well doesn't mean I'll get the part, Lucas."

I shake my head. "You will, Mads. You're so damn talented. You deserve to celebrate, even if it's the little wins. So what do you say?"

She lets out a laugh, but then she lifts an eyebrow at me. "That depends. Do you have better taste since then?"

*Little shit.* I lean down, tugging at her bottom lip between my teeth. "Don't judge my taste. After all, I fell in love with you."

"You're right," she agrees. "But mint chocolate chip is awful."

"Agree to disagree." Interlocking her hand with mine, we head to the small ice cream truck where we had our first 'date.' I would say something about how cherry ice cream is just as gross, but if I'm being honest, I can't wait to taste it on her.

A flash blinds me, and I snap my head to the right, seeing some paparazzi taking pictures of us. While I might not want to be a model anymore, my girl is now in the public eye, which means this will never go away. But I don't mind it, as long as *she* never goes away.

Madeline smirks when she looks at me. "Reminds me of our first date."

"You want to give them a show like we did back then?"

She nods, wrapping her arms around my neck while more flashes go off around us. "Kiss me, Lucas," she whispers. "Prove to them that it's real."

I lift her chin with my hand, our lips stacked together. "I couldn't care less about what they think, *princesa*. But I'll spend the rest of my life proving my love to you."

THE END

# Acknowledgements

After working on this book for so long, I am so excited to finally share it, and for you guy to finally fall in love with Madeline and Lucas like I have. I had an amazing time with Madi and Lucas, and I'm a little sad to let them go. I hope you guys love them as much as I do.

Now onto the acknowledgements. I'd first like to thank every single one of you guys who have supported me in the last two years of my author journey. Every like, comment, share and dm makes me so happy.

I'm so grateful for my amazing beta and sensitivity readers who helped make this story so much better, and were the first eyes on my book baby that I had been working on for months.

Thank you to my author besties for helping me out with this release and the endless questions I had.

I'd love to thank my editor Cassidy for taking me on, and making this book that much better.

Every single one of you that love my books, and support me are the reason I keep on doing this, and I'm so grateful for you guys.

If you enjoyed Would You Rather then please consider leaving a review as reviews help out indie authors a lot.

# About the Author

Stephanie Alves is an avid reader and writer of smutty, contemporary romance books. She was born in England, but was raised by her loud Portuguese parents. She can speak both languages fluently, though she tends to mix both languages when speaking. She loves to write romantic comedies with happy endings, witty banter and sizzling chemistry that will make you blush. When she's not writing, she can be found either reading, or watching rom coms with her two adorable dogs cuddled up beside her.

You can find her here:
Instagram.com/Stephanie.alves_author
Stephaniealvesauthor.com

Printed in Great Britain
by Amazon

43550168R00209